Land of Cannibals

The Metalist's Journey - Book 4
KD Lumsden

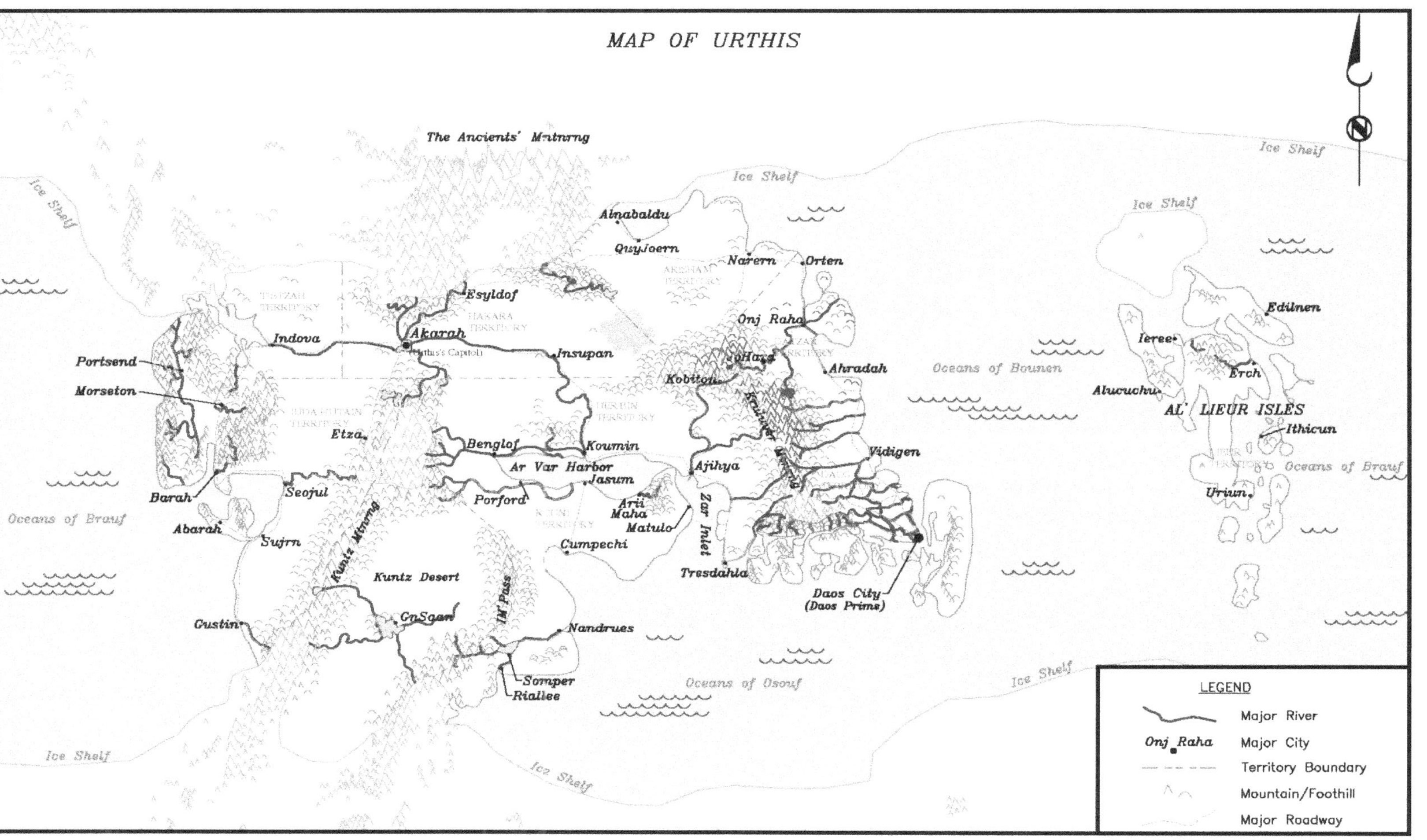

MAP OF URTHIS
N
The Ancients' Meuhrrug
Ice Shelf
Ainabaldu
Quijuoern
Narern
Orten
Esyldof
Onj Raha
Edilnen
Ieree
Indova
Akarah
Urthis's Capitoli
Insupan
Haxe
Ahradah
Erch
Oceans of Bounen
Alucuchu
Portsend
Kobitoln
AL' LIEUR ISLES
Morseton
Ithicun
Etza
Benglof
Koumin
Vidigen
Oceans of Brauf
Ar Var Harbor
Ajihya
Jasum
Uriun
Barah
Seojul
Porford
Arii Maha
Zar Inlet
Oceans of Brauf
Matulo
Abarah
Sujrn
Kuntz Meuhrrug
Cumpechi
Kuntz Desert
Tresdahla
Gustin
CroSgan
IN Pass
Nandrues
Daos City
(Daos Prime)
Somper
Riallee
Oceans of Osouf
Ice Shelf
Ice Shelf
LEGEND
Major River
Onj Raha   Major City
Territory Boundary
Mountain/Foothill
Major Roadway

THE METALIST'S JOURNEY
Book 3 ~ Sleeper Assassin
Book 4 ~ Land of Cannibals

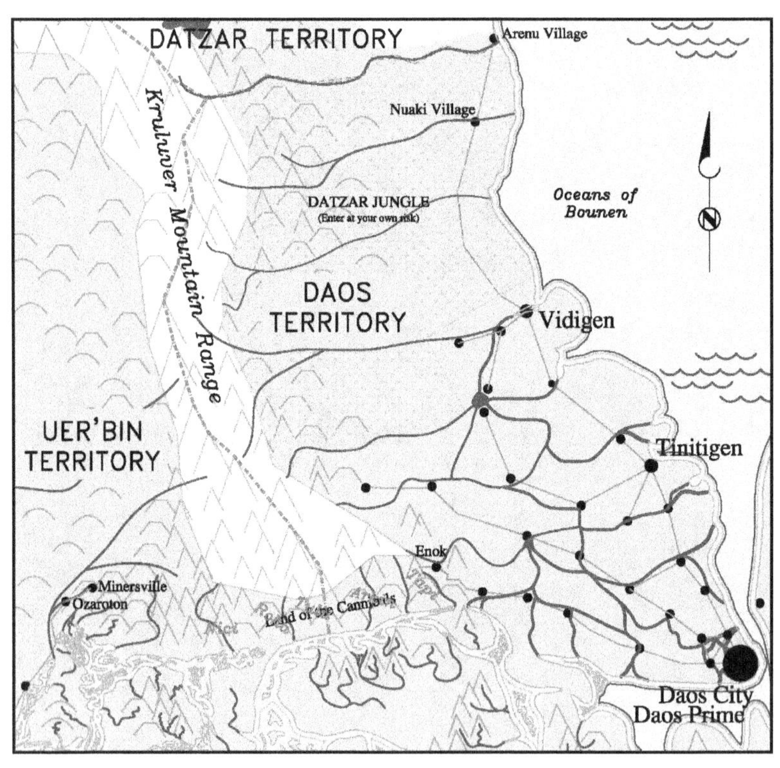

Contents

1

Their Escape

Tears splashed from Irwin and Kipp's eyes as their two giant warhorses galloped abreast. Their wagon had been left behind in Daos City, along with most of their important belongings. Everything was blurry and dark. They had finally rescued Yace. She had been kidnapped by her father, Lord and Master Dephen Ishik, and after months of a frantic and seemingly endless search, they had found her in a palace in a faraway metropolis called Daos City.

That Daosian palace was under the rule of Emperor Somer Ishik, Dephen's half-brother. By the time they had her in hand, the healthy and luminous being was now nothing but a limp and haggard woman who did not remember her dearest friends. She had seemingly been 'cleansed' of her father's essence—turning her into a personal bed companion. Many moons ago, following the first of many arduous journeys, Yace, Kipp, and Irwin narrowly succeeded in their mission to reconnect Yace with her father before he would surely die.

Yace had vanished like a cloud in a windstorm after bending over the old man's bed. Amidst confusion and determination, the two young men raced across all types of terrain to find her. What had happened to Yace? What was Dephen's purpose in kidnapping her body and mind? Did Dephen succeed in his plight to destroy his brother Somer Ishik using Yace's powers? Would Yace ever be Yace again?

Irwin and Kipp had escaped kidnappings, battles, and even entire legions of would-be captors. Now they were running for their lives once more, having narrowly escaped the Ishik palace in Daos City.

As they raced into the night, Irwin—a Metalist—could feel the heavy broadsword's metal carried by the men chasing them—the last few soldiers dedicated to the Ishik regime—few had survived Irwin's wrath in previous battles. He had killed everyone in the palace, including the emperor, his women, and children.

It was now very late, yet they persisted with their flight to the west.

They left all their luggage and pounds of food—for what was to be the long-haul home—at a psychic who had helped in their escape. She was a Telepath; she saw what was after them. Their horses had allowed them a swift getaway through the darkened streets on the edge of Daos. They rode all night with donkeys in tow, escaping the nightmare Irwin had created at the Ishik Palace. He had killed everyone in the gleaming white palace: soldiers, servants, and all the Ishik family members. Now they would escape the wrath of who might still be alive and giving orders, or they would all three die a terrible death on this unfamiliar road heading westward, heading toward a faraway home that was now a faint memory.

What will happen once the Hakran Empire and their Planetary Constable Patrol, and their PCP minions, find out what all I have done? They will probably march or sail into Daos City and take over the Territory, absorb it all. Is that a favorable result for these people? They deserve better than what they have. At least under Hakran rule, they would live better lives. Then maybe people with Talents, those with special abilities like mine, will finally be allowed to live here, to thrive. As everyone should. We all deserve the same.

The further away from the city, the less sure Kipp was that they were still being followed. Kipp's keen Clan-Duin senses were on high alert. He insisted there were sounds he could hear in the distance, but Irwin had not seen or felt anything for a while. They did not relent their pace; they could not. They had to go back to the Gypsy, to Nonbry—the only one who could bring Yace back from her catatonic state. Irwin had been told he would be able to save her; he tried everything in his power to bring her mind back to the present with no luck. For now, Yace was uncommunicative in Kipp's arms.

"Do we have to keep this up? My ass hurts." Kipp's brown eyes looked grim—black hair matted—he was disheveled, tired, yet held onto Yace who in his loving eyes was still the blond-haired beauty. Her teal nightgown and indigo robe flew behind her in the wind of their escape.

Irwin was tired of any complaints. "I can take Yace and Roper if you prefer to be in your canine form." Irwin was cleaner than Kipp; his sandy hair was trimmed, and he pushed it out of his silvery eyes. Dressed in his rich attire—lavender silk shirt tucked into well-fitting pants—his new boots shone in the moonlight.

Kipp picked up with his whining and worrying. "We left all of our stuff!! Our clothes, and hundreds of pounds of food for us and the animals!"

"It is just stuff."

"But I have no clothes. And your clothes are tight. They chafe my thighs."

"I will buy you pants."

"How? You've no more silver!"

"Really? We are having this conversation?"

"I liked my cloak."

"I will buy you another cloak."

"It was perfectly worn in. I enjoyed how it comforted me on the ground."

"Kipp!"

"And I bought Yace a new dress."

"I will buy her another dress."

"I wanted to see her in that dress. It's her favorite color, robin's egg blue. It would've made her eyes even bluer."

"It is alright Kipp."

"No, it's not! My ass hurts and I've no clothes!"

"Kipp!"

"What about all that food?"

"It was only to help us on our journey. We got away unscathed. I am thankful for that."

"How are we gonna feed the animals?"

"The old fashion way, grass on the side of the road."

"What about us?"

"You can hunt, remember?"

Kipp tossed his dark hair away from his glaring brown eyes.

"Please do not overreact, Kipp."

"But my ass hurts, and I've no clothes."

"But we have Yace."

"This isn't Yace."

Irwin didn't want to argue with Kipp. She was Yace, just not the woman they remembered. He could see that Kipp was not in a good mental space, or willing to help. For now, Irwin would ignore his best friend.

I cannot deal with this, with Kipp. I need to heal Yace, but how? How is it that my powers do not work when they have all along? How can I bring Yace back and into herself?

It is just shitty of Kipp not to acknowledge Yace. This is Yace. She is finally with us. She is finally safe. And yet he acts like this. Breathe.

Morning light crested the horizon behind them; they were on the outskirts of Daos City, well beyond the cobbled streets and the bustling city life. They had raced away from what might be called the civilized world. The sun was on their heels, but soon was in their eyes. They continued to push westward. It was late afternoon when they passed the last building and were now riding along fields filled with animals slated for slaughter.

They only stopped for Yace. Kipp made sure she was fed. Irwin allowed her time out of the saddle to rest. But neither of the young men wanted to sit around for too long. They might still be tracked by the few soldiers dedicated to the Ishik Empire.

Darkness had enfolded them when at last they stopped for a lengthy reprieve. They crept off the road and into the forest and found a glen to make camp. Kipp wandered off to find a nighttime meal (he would shapeshift to his canine self, the talented hunter); Irwin tended camp and Yace. She stayed quiet, staring forward, almost catatonic. There was nothing he could do to bring her out of this state. He had tried touching her, hugging her, but nothing broke the telepathic spell she appeared to be under. This was hard to witness. Yace had always been talkative, expressive, sometimes overly dramatic, but now she sat like a rock, staring forward.

Kipp found a rabbit for supper, and Irwin cooked it. He split the meal with Yace. Kipp had already eaten while out hunting. Being Clan-Duin meant that Kipp enjoyed fresh kills—warm flesh.

Irwin held Yace's hands. He stared at her, hoping she would reciprocate. Kipp sat fireside in silence, watching Irwin's attempts to bring Yace back. That was all the Clan-Duin wanted from his friend, to fix Yace. At this point, Irwin felt now that it was a lost cause.

Feeling like he was failing her and Kipp, after a while of holding onto Yace, he let go, left her side and walked away from the small fire muttering loud enough for Kipp to hear, "I wish Jorge was here."

"Why?"

He inhaled deeply, not wanting to admit: *So I can get a hug and feel less helpless than I do, you stubborn Clan-Duin.*

"He understood me."

"You're an asshole for thinking he understood you. Jorge was using you all along. I saw it. He wanted to get to Daos and saw you as his way out of Nuaki Village, especially after you blew the place up. He knew you'd keep him safe, could probably tell you had a soft spot for assholes like him."

"Kipp!"

"What?! You know what I'm saying is true."

"You are so callous sometimes."

"For what, speaking the truth?"

"I am glad he found his people."

"So am I." Irwin saw Kipp's lip curl in disgust.

"I know you dislike Jorge, but could you please be cordial with your words?"

Silence crept across the camp. After a while Kipp asked, "Would you have left me, left us?"

"No."

"Are you sure? I saw how much you enjoyed Jorge. Don't lie, you would have left me for him."

"Are you jealous?"

It took Kipp a long time to reply, "No."

"Then why do you care if I would have left you for him?"

"You like him more than me."

Irwin laughed. "I have always liked you more than him."

Kipp was silent for the rest of the night.

Kipp stayed next to Yace to keep her warm. He followed her around like a lost puppy most of the time. The next morning, he helped Yace with anything she might need, including climbing into the saddle. He rode with her and held her tight as Roper jogged along.

It pleased Irwin to see Kipp with his beloved. In all their time apart, over five moons, Kipp had fantasized about their reunion. But neither of them expected Yace to be like this.

The land they traveled across slowly changed from animals being restricted in small pens to large sustainable fields. A thick forest grew along the southern side of the road, buffering the roadway, offering shade from the afternoon sun.

From sunup to sundown, their unrelenting ride remained quiet, each man engaging in their private thoughts. They passed several villages with small residences and no commerce other than an open market. They did not stop to buy food, but Kipp found baggy pants left on a drying line.

Once the sky grew dark, Kipp found them a decent place to camp. They were hidden from the roadway and down the slope into the thick forest by several hundred feet. Yace dismounted and took a seat next to the campfire Irwin had made. Kipp changed into his canine form and ran off to find food.

Irwin watched Yace from the corner of his eye. She leaned against a large fir tree with far-off eyes. He moved to her and took her icy hands into his warm grasp. Slowly, her blue eyes drew to his.

"You are Yace Yellsen," he whispered. His throat tightened as he spoke, holding back his emotions. "You are Gypsy. I am Samuel Irwin Miner. Our friend who can change into animals is Kipp Hauler. You have known him for many years. I met you over half a year ago, up in the Kruluver Mountains." He could tell she was trying to understand him.

He waited for a response, but there was none. "Can you speak?"

She blinked.

"Maybe you do not know how. What do you know, Yace?"

Her blue eyes looked to be probing his, possibly telepathically. He then noticed that Yace was contemplating what to do. She stood and shed the dirty silken robe she had been wearing the last two days. A sheer teal night gown hung loose on her frail body. She pulled Irwin forward, grabbed his hands, placing them on her hips. Then she started to dance.

Slow and seductive, she pulled Irwin to his feet. He was hesitant, but she was insistent. He succumbed to her grasp, and humming, she started to grind her pelvis against his.

He pulled back. "No, Yace, no. That is not what I want."

She seemed to be crushed by his words, averting her eyes. She stopped dancing. *I did not mean to startle.*

With a deep breath, he said, "They taught you to arouse men. Oh Yace, what did they do to you? You are more than a warm body." He stared at her for a long time, his thoughts churning. "Maybe we do something that you used to do."

A metal hairbrush appeared in his hand. She stared at this magical spectacle, then picked up the brush to look it over. He spoke to Yace as though she were a child. "This is a hairbrush. A person uses it to untangle their hair. I would like to brush your hair. You used to do it every morning for yourself while watching Kipp and I spar."

She handed Irwin the brush, and he showed her how to use it by pulling the brush through his own short hair. Yace's long blonde hair was tangled, wind-blown. He whispered, "Can I brush your hair, please?"

Yace remained still and allowed Irwin to pull the brush through her tangled hair. It must have hurt. She grunted. He tried to be gentle, but Yace's hair was finer than anything he was used to brushing, especially the animals. "I am sorry. I keep pulling your head." She continued to grunt as he stroked the brush through the tangles.

2

<u>Moody Clan-Duin</u>

Kipp jumped out of the forest without warning, as though he had snuck up on them. "What are you doing?!"

Irwin pulled the brush away from Yace's hair. "I-I was just trying to—"

"She doesn't like it. It hurts her."

"Did you hear her think that?"

"The sounds she's making should say enough."

"I was just trying to help her remember the past, Kipp. She needs to remember."

"You're always saying we should look forward, not back."

"Yace needs things from the past. She needs to remember who she is."

Kipp threw two dead squirrels at Irwin and growled, "I already ate. These are for you."

"Thanks." Irwin, as a Metalist, reabsorbed the metal hairbrush, then fashioned a knife.

Kipp went to Yace, clearly wanting to be with her, to talk. Her eyes were focused on the dancing campfire. She appeared to be ignoring him, but Kipp stared at her, then huffed—more like a sob.

Irwin was only partially paying attention to his friends while removing the squirrels' skin. He fashioned a rotating spit from metal, skewered the meat and secured it over the fire to cook evenly. "Maybe tell Yace your favorite memories of her."

"Maybe you should shut up."

"Hey, Kipp! I am just trying to help. You do not need to be—"

"You don't know how to help!"

"Kipp, you are being a bit overbear—"

"Don't fukin' tell me what I am. You don't know me. You wish you did, but you don't! Only Yace knows me."

"Then tell her about you."

"Fuk you! Don't tell me what to do."

Busy cooking the squirrels, Irwin covertly watched Kipp try to interact with Yace. She stared off, while Kipp buried himself in her long hair resting on her frail shoulder.

Is this how he will be every night? He is worse off now that Yace is with us than before we rescued her. I might as well have left them in Daos. Maybe I should leave. But then what? Kipp cannot manage Yace without me.

I must remember that Kipp is just trying to process all his emotions concerning Yace. He has loved her and longed for her probably as long as he can remember. I do not think those feelings were ever returned, even if they only had sex once. For Yace, it was just that, sex. For Kipp, it was everlasting devotion. I have, I know, stuffed my feelings for Kipp down. Ignored them. No one needs to know. Jorge knew, I am fairly sure.

He snorted to himself in such a way that no one would notice, no one would question his thoughts.

There are more pressing issues. If I could just fix Yace, bring her back to herself, to her body and her life ....

My powers are either not working, or she has been cleansed beyond her own remembering. Oh, poor Yace. She does not know who we are. Does not remember what we three have gone through together. She has forgotten about her bond with Kipp, and all our deep and meaningful conversations. And instead of reminding her of those unique times, Kipp is now trying something new, maybe. I do not know. I really cannot understand his devotion to her, especially when she has made it obvious that she did not feel the same for him. It was clear as a bell when I met them, took up with them and agreed to get them safely to Dephen so she could learn about her powers. I guess that is love. I guess you will do anything for it.

He heaved a deep sigh, took in the aroma of roasting squirrel. Their juicy bodies were substantial. Cooking them would take time and patience. An owl hooted, and the rustling of pine limbs was ever present. Kipp remained nestled in Yace's bosom. Her eyes remained fixed on the dancing Erthin flames Irwin had created. Without wood, the fire burned bright and hot, like any other fire. His blossoming Erthin powers continued to amaze. It had been the Erthin Fire, along with metal spheres radiating around him, that helped him slaughter everyone in charge of the Ishik Empire.

Nonbry never said her memories were gone, only fractured. That must mean something. I think it means something is not broken; it does, but … maybe Yace's memories are not gone, just fractured. Maybe they are jumbled up, misplaced, out of order—changed somehow. I know Telepaths can manipulate to their advantage. And those Telepaths we have encountered along our journey have tricked us several times now. They manipulated us into doing what they wanted so they could have us in their clutches, under their control. Telepaths are the worst.

But maybe Telepaths cannot actually remove memories like Kipp suspects. Maybe they can only manipulate them, deny access, or change them. And in fracturing her memories, that is how they control her. She does not know what is right or wrong. She does not recall the time before being at the Ishik Palace. She only knows what she has witnessed since the cleansing of herself.

I am angry at her father even more for what he did. I am glad I killed their minions, their slaves, and their animals and family. They all deserved what they had coming.

From now on, I will be more cautious around telepathic people. I dislike how easily they use their telepathic abilities, how quickly they can change lives forever, how they rule using their amazing powers.

I must keep doing what I am doing, no matter how much it pisses Kipp off. Things are happening for Yace. The more I interact with her, the more she becomes aware. I just wish Kipp would listen to me. So sad that he does not understand why we must pull from our past. Maybe he is afraid she will remember why she does not love him. I get it. He just wants her to love him as he loves her.

Ugh. Why do I suddenly feel like I must save them both? This is all so exhausting!

He wanted to lie down and sleep, forget all this; rest his mind. But supper was at hand.

The next night Irwin did things Yace had done with him many moons prior while he was in training—while she was teaching him about his potential—he wanted to open her mind and help her locate lost memories.

Kipp had gone away from camp searching for their evening meal. Irwin had suggested he find an animal large enough to feed them for more than one meal.

He hoped the hunt would take time, enough time for him to try a different tactic with Yace.

He created two metal spheres, small and perfectly rounded. Using the tips of his fingers, he moved them across his left palm, as Yace had shown him many moons past. Yace watched with interest as his fingers navigate the spheres in a circular fashion while rubbing his palm. He did not allow them to touch. After a while, he handed the spheres to Yace, nodding his head to encourage her to try it.

"You were the one who taught me this trick." He watched her try to maneuver the two spheres. They clanked together many times, and she flinched each time metal met metal.

"It took me a while to get it. Do you remember when you first taught me you told me not to use my powers, to '… just let them roll across my hand, to use my fingers to move them, allow myself to feel how cool and smooth as the metal can be on my flesh?' I think these are your favorite objects to play with. You had rocks, perfect little rounded rocks. I coated them with my metal, and you thought that was a neat maneuver indeed."

Yace tried but sighed with frustration. After a few more tries, she passed the spheres back and shook her head while an evening breeze picked up her unusual platinum-colored long hair. In that one gesture, Irwin witnessed more independent thought in her than he had seen since her rescue. Something had happened while she tried to oblige those spheres to dance around her hand.

Irwin rendered the two metal balls into a hairbrush again. "How about you brush your hair?" He handed her the brush.

Yace took the brush, she examined the metal bristled hairbrush. The flat backside was a mirror that distorted her face. She giggled at her reflection, but then slowly—methodically—she began brushing her waist-long locks.

"You are doing it! That is wonderful!"

Again, Kipp burst into camp. "What are you doing?"

"She is brushing her hair! I did not have to show her how." Kipp had startled Yace, and she stopped. "Do not stop, Yace, your hair needs a good brushing."

Kipp spat, "Why are you doing this?"

"Because it is working, Kipp, do you not see?" He pointed., and they watched Yace return to working on the ends of her hair.

"Brushing hair is like shitting for her. Of course she can do it."

"She was not able to do it last night. And tonight, I did not have to help."

"You think brushing her hair is gonna bring her back?"

"Are you going to be depressed and angry still? We have Yace. She has been rescued. You do not need to be this way."

"This isn't Yace."

"What the shit, Kipp!" Irwin screamed, ready to face off with Kipp. He stepped into the Clan-Duin's space, Kipp's space. "This is Yace. She is lost in her own mind right now. I can see it. Nonbry saw it too. He told us her memories are fractured, that we need to find a reliable Telepath who can—"

"She has no memories of us, Irwin. None! If she did, she'd remember me."

"I believe she does." His voice yet another pitch higher. "I do not believe Telepaths can fully remove a memory. It can be pushed aside, made unimportant, maybe even lost amongst other memories, but they are not truly gone forever."

"How do you know? You're not a fukin' Telepath!"

"Ugh! You expect me to fix her, and yet when I feel like I have had a breakthrough, you dismiss it!"

"She's always been able to brush her fukin' hair."

"You are an asshole, Kipp."

"Fuk you."

"You know," Irwin didn't back down. "I think we were better off not knowing where she was."

Irwin saw the flying fist and leaned back; it flew past his face. Kipp lunged forward again, and Irwin jumped away, counteracting Kipp's assault.

Irwin chuckled, and Kipp grunted with more ferocity behind every fist-throw. Irwin turned, grabbed Kipp and threw him to the ground. Straddling the Clan-Duin, he said, "You told me never to fight when I am angry." He offered a hand, and Kipp grabbed it, tossing Irwin aside. He jumped atop Irwin and threw more punches, then tried to maneuver the Metalist into a head-lock position.

"Someone is going to get hurt here."

Kipp's arm was across his throat. "It's gonna be you, asshole!"

Irwin placed his hands flat on the uneven ground. "I do not want to hurt you." He was in a better position than Kipp realized.

Kipp elbowed Irwin's face, and that was the amount of leverage Irwin needed to flip the Clan-Duin over. They rolled down a small incline into a thick underbrush and became wedged between trees. "Give up?" Irwin asked Kipp who was back on top.

Irwin chuckled and moved his forehead up to crack it against Kipp's. Their craniums collided and Kipp fell over, stunned.

"What the fuk!" Kipp placed a hand on his bloodied face.

Irwin rolled to his side and laughed. "I told you I did not want to hurt you."

Kipp punched Irwin in the face, splitting his nose until it bled. It healed immediately, while Kipp's did not. Blood trickled down the Clan-Duin's forehead and nose. As he wiped the blood away from his right eye, Kipp cursed him again. "You fuker!"

"Man, those are some angry words." Kipp tightened his hand into a fist and threw it. Irwin caught it and growled, "Keep your hands to yourself."

Yace stopped brushing her hair. She was up-slope, the fire behind her, causing her to appear as a dark shadow watching over them. She studied them as they moved to their feet.

The two made their way out of the underbrush. Both had twigs, moss, brambles, splinters, and other pokey things all over their skin and clothes. They brushed themselves, walking back to the camp.

"Do not worry, Yace." Irwin approached her. "It was just a minor argument. I think we got it settled."

He saw her watch him walk past her.

Kipp noticed where her eyes went and stepped up to her. "Do I scare you?"

Yace recoiled.

Kipp walked over to the dead grouse he had caught. "Here's your fukin' meal." The grouse flew toward the fire. Kipp mutated back into his canine form.

"What the shit, Kipp? I do not appreciate your attitude!" Irwin shouted. "I do not want to fight with you." Kipp growled and snapped his jaw at Irwin. "Maybe you need to go for a walk."

The Clan-Duin turned on his haunches and leaped into the forest, leaving Irwin and Yace by themselves.

He watched Kipp disappear into the darkening woods. Yace moved toward him, picked up the dead grouse and handed it to him.

I do not want Kipp to be angry at me.

He held the dead bird and muttered, "I hate plucking feathers."

3

ATTITUDES AND INSULTS

Kipp had not returned to camp by the next morning. Irritated, Irwin tore it down while taking care of Yace, a two-person job. It took him a good part of the morning to get them ready to move on. When they finally emerged from the forest, returning to the roadway, it was already mid-morning.

Yace seemed a little more aware of herself, more aware of how to ride.

Maybe all this time I am spending with her is working. Somehow, I am peeling back those telepathic spells. Or maybe she is simply becoming more aware of herself since being cleansed. Whatever it is, it is working!

She was responding to his input better—watching and following directions diligently—he hated treating Yace like a child. It was a much different approach, but it was necessary.

They rode side by side, stopping frequently. By nighttime, Yace could dismount without help and walked with her horse. She could not tie a rope or unpack her animal, but it was obvious to Irwin that she wanted to help.

He settled the animals for the night, made a fire, and told Yace to stay put. He would have to find their meal. Kipp was still missing.

It was dark, and trapping a meal would be difficult. He searched the uneven terrain and returned with several tree frogs. Back in camp, he found Kipp sitting beside Yace by the crackling fire. Kipp, the Clan-Duin, had found a large rodent and was cooking it on a wooden skewer over the steady flame.

Irwin smiled and bit his tongue. He wanted to engage with Kipp, but he was unsure of the Clan-Duin's receptiveness. Instead, he held still in the background and let loose the frogs before taking a seat opposite the two of them.

"So, I was thinking about that tattoo idea," said Kipp.

"What tattoo? You mean the one we talked about moons ago?"

Yace's eyes kept creeping shut, while she struggled to stay awake to watch the fire dance. She was no doubt exhausted from all she had been through.

"Yeah, you wanted to tattoo me."

"Yes. But that was so I would know where you are and help you be less susceptible to telepathic manipulation."

"Think it'd work on Yace?"

"I am not tattooing Yace!"

"But your metal grounds out telepathic spells."

They stared at each other in the silence by the fire. "You believe that if I tattoo Yace, it will ground out whatever telepathic spell this is?"

"It'd work, right?"

"Kipp, I do not believe she is telepathically possessed. She is becoming more aware. That shroud she has been tucked behind is being pulled back. Little by little. But a tattoo? You really think a tattoo will help her?"

"Yeah. But you'd do it to me first."

Irwin cackled. "You want me to tattoo you? Last I recall, you did not want to be claimed by anyone."

"You wouldn't be claiming me unless we need to use it as a cover."

Ugh! You make my head hurt, Kipp.

Irwin pressed the sides of his nose, closed his eyes, and exhaled. "I guess I can try it on you first."

What the shit has he been thinking about these last few days?

"Good! Sooner the better."

"I am glad to see your attitude has lightened."

Yace leaned into Kipp. Her eyes were closed. She was waiting for food, trying to rest. Kipp glanced at her on his shoulder. "You still haven't fixed her. And there's nothin' I can do. Nonbry is across the world. No one can help her. Fuk!"

I do not need all this negativity. Kipp, please, try to think of what we can do for her. And please let go of your animosity over the situation. You are the stupid fuk. Ugh! I must stay positive. I hope he will snap out of this funk, and soon.

Irwin did not intervene with Kipp's supper. He wished he had. The Clan-Duin had burned their meal on one side, but it was a large rodent and there would be enough meat for a morning meal.

Kipp stayed in camp that night. The next morning, he helped Irwin prepare the animals. But the fickle Clan-Duin did not stick around long enough to help Yace and Irwin find their way back to the road.

They ascended in elevation every day, and their trek meandered farther away from the ocean's edge. Although they could no longer hear the distant roar of crashing waves, flocks of seagulls flew overhead.

The next evening, they camped along a creek crowded with fir trees. They were over a kilometer away from the last homestead they had passed. Other than an occasional nocturnal animal-call, all was quiet. They had fish Irwin had caught for supper. He carved it, cooked it, and shared it with Yace.

Kipp did not arrive back at camp until dark. He smelled wet and had a layer of dirt on his hairy canine body. He jumped into the cold, rumbling creek before coming to the fire to get warm.

Irwin asked, "Where are you going every day?"

"Wherever the fuk I want."

"I see your attitude is still with you."

"You gonna tattoo me?"

"You really think tattooing you will help, Yace?"

"If anything, you'll always know where I am."

Irwin glared back.

Kipp puffed out his chest and flared his nostrils. "You ever tattooed anyone?"

"No."

"You even know how?"

"Ink and a needle?"

Their eyes met, Kipp flexed his jaw muscles. "You know what you're gonna make?"

"You are the one who wants the tattoo. What do you want?"

"Something simple."

"If I am tattooing you, it will be a metal tattoo, not an ink one."

"What did you want to tattoo before?"

He had thought about it back then. Those ideas were several moons past, the image not fresh in his memory. "It was my initials, but slightly abstract. Something with mountains."

"Draw it."

"I am not very good at drawing."

"Ha, and you wanna tattoo me!"

"You-you are the one who wants the tattoo!"

"We don't have to do this now."

"Yes, maybe not tonight." He stared at Kipp who he had, throughout the journey, considered his friend. And truth be told, he would have liked it to be more than friends.

Maybe when your attitude adjusts. You are acting too irrational for me to even want to be around you right now. I do not want to touch you. You are being an asshole.

He tried his best to not be frustrated by Kipp's demeanor.

Yace was asleep between them. Irwin sat on one side of the fire, Kipp on the other. It seemed that neither wanted the other there.

I am done with this attitude, Kipp. This IS Yace!

He will not accept what I say. He just wants her back to her old self and blames me for not being able to help. He can be so negative sometimes. I must stay positive, for Yace's sake.

Right now, everything seemed hopeless.

Another day of riding came and went, and again, Yace appeared more helpful and aware as time went on, even if she was still mute. Her coordination was better, but she was not yet strong enough to help hoist the saddles off the horses.

While Irwin attended the animals, Yace found a comfortable seat against a tree and took up the metal spheres he had given her, practicing spinning them around on her palm without clanking them.

Once done with the animals, Irwin made a fire and waited, hoping that Kipp would bring them some food. After a while, the Clan-Duin returned with a fat dead gray rabbit. Irwin took it, skinned it, and placed it over the fire, cooking on the spit he made from what little metal he had. Camp hung in silence until the rabbit had been eaten to the bone; by then, Yace was tired. She lay down on woolen blankets Irwin had provided; and fell at once into a deep sleep.

"Alright." Kipp broke the silence. "I'm ready."

"Ready for what?"

"That tattoo."

This again? Maybe he just wants to experience a different type of pain than what he is feeling now. If only he would stay in camp and reconnect with Yace, then he too would see that she is becoming more aware.

"Are you really ready for this?"

"Just get it over with."

"I do not know why you want me to do this."

"This is for Yace, not me."

"That is a stupid reason for me to give you a tattoo."

"If it helps her, I don't care."

How torpid. Huh, now I think I know why Yace called you that so many moons ago. You are kind of apathetic, Kipp. It feels, comes across as though you haven't really considered what is going on, what you want, and how you and Yace could be hurt. Oh Kipp.

"Which arm?"

"Same as my Gypsy tattoo." Kipp lifted his left arm. "Maybe on top of it?"

"Oh, I get it. That way, it looks like only one person has owned you."

"Yeah, but it won't be you who owns me."

We've had a long journey, Kipp. I'm no longer a stranger who can't be trusted. Kipp please, lighten up.

Leaning down, Irwin used a twig to draw a symbol in the dirt. "This is what it will look like."

"I don't care. Just get it over with."

Irwin eyed the small circular tattoo on Kipp's shoulder—it was a simplistic tattoo, like all the Gypsy family had—two circular swirls made with red ink, moving in opposite directions, and connected in the center. Irwin's initials, SIM, would be turned sideways and placed across the Gypsy tattoo, making it look like googly-eyes peering between V-shaped ridges, the S and M in his name. The 'I' in his name would be a horizon line where the S and M would meet. Obscure-looking indeed.

Kipp closed his eyes, ready for whatever pain lay ahead. Irwin believed he was overreacting but was willing to humor the Clan-Duin. "You ready?"

Kipp grunted, and it almost sounded like 'No'.

With a deep inhale, Irwin stared sideways at Kipp, examined his profile.

I might piss him off by sedating him. Well, he will be punchy no matter what.

Placing his hand on Kipp's shoulder, hoping to soften his attitude, all he got from this Clan-Duin he secretly loved was a snarl.

Irwin closed his eyes, picturing the image he had just drawn. He wanted the process to be easy, quick.

Kipp growled again. "What the fuk are you doing?"

Irwin opened his eyes, exhaled, and said, "You know, we do not have to do it. Not right now."

"Yes, we do."

He pulled away. "I do not think tattooing Yace will help her."

"You're the one who told me that your metal grounds out telepathic spells, keeps Telepaths from hearing your thoughts. She needs that, Irwin."

They both turned to look at Yace who was sleeping quietly on the other side of the fire. "No, I do not see that Kipp. What I do see is that the more time I spend with her, just being patient and guiding, she blossoms. When you come into camp, she goes meek again. She is, frankly, scared of you."

"Yeah, I've smelled her fear."

"Maybe you need to be less coarse."

"Fuk you Irwin, my girl isn't my girl. You've not helped her. And ... And Nonbry can't help her. What the fuk am I supposed to do? I am just an ignorant Clan-Duin!"

"But you are *her* Clan-Duin. You have been so dang loyal to her. It is ridiculous! You go to her, sleep next to her, cuddle with her."

"She doesn't want it."

"Are you fooling .... She needs it!*" You stupid shit!*

Yace lifted her head, opened her eyes, and gazed at them as they argued about what she needed, what she wanted. She scowled and grunted, probably insisting that they cut it out.

"You see! She understands us!" Irwin said.

"She hates us."

"Ugh! You are inconsolable!"

"Fuk you."

"Why are you being like this, seriously? Yace is here, she is with us!"

"I have nothing I want."

A cave-like darkness enveloped them. Irwin looked up at the starless sky and thought about his angry father.

He was always angry.

I hate this.

Ugh. I should just make Kipp go to sleep. He needs to sleep off all this negativity, all that anger radiating from the one who was once my trusted friend, my first friend ever. No, putting him to sleep will not solve the problem. It would keep him quiet, though, until he wakes up in the morning.

Kipp grumbled, "What are you thinking?"

"You still want that tattoo?"

"With that attitude, no. I don't want you to touch me."

Irwin kept his face from showing how funny he thought Kipp was behaving.

I wish Yace was normal again. I am so sick of this shit. I know she would keep Kipp in line.

4

<u>TATTOOS</u>

When Irwin awoke at first light, Kipp was gone. Once again, no help taking down the tent, no breakfast. He could hear Yace's stomach growl while he helped her into the saddle. It was still cloudy when they exited the forest, heading west on the dirt roadway. Morning flourished into afternoon. The humidity, stifling. The sky turned dark and big, warm raindrops fell and soaked everything.

There was no one in the fields along the side of the road that day—as if the workers knew a storm was coming. Yace was drenched and probably cold by the time he got them off the road and under a forest canopy. It was as dark as dusk, even though it was only mid-afternoon; the rain never let up.

Yace huddled next to a tree, shivering. She watched while he used his Erthin powers to prepare a raging fire. He dried almost at once and let her warm up and dry off while he tended to the animals. He set up his tent's canopy next to the fire and gave Yace a woolen blanket. Her teeth chattered, and from the west came the rumbling of thunder.

Although it was warm, the landscape was soaked. There was no possibility of them freezing to death, but catching a cold was not out of the question. Irwin let the animals roam about in the forest while he took care of their camp at the edge of a meadow that sloped into a dense underbrush. Exposed to the storm, this was still a perfect place for the horses to graze in the tall, lush grass. The donkeys held close to the forest's canopy and Irwin's fire.

Kipp flew into camp after dark, a fish in his talons. He cawed at Irwin to catch it and then morphed into his two-legged form.

"Thank you for the fish, Kipp," he said, putting the fresh catch down on the ground near his feet. He allowed some water to drip from his hands in order to wash the blood and scales from the fish. "Everything got wet today." He handed Kipp the pants he had stolen from someone's clothesline.

"Fuk! You're Erthin. Why can't you dry them?"

Irwin struggled to stay calm.

I am so sick of his attitude. I want to punch you in the face every time you say 'Fuk'.

He took the pants. "You are right. I should dry them for you." He was mocking Kipp's attitude.

"What's your fukin' problem?"

Irwin exhaled.

I will not kick your ass; I will not kick your ass. But I really want to.

"I have had a long day and would like to relax."

Reaching for the pants, Kipp sneered, "Fine, I'll just sit in wet clothes." As he grasped the pants, they were hot to the touch. "Ouch! What the fuk!"

"You wanted them dry." Silver swirled in Irwin's eyes. He stared at Kipp. "Would you want your tattoo tonight too?"

"Dang. You're a bit pissy, aren't you?"

Yace held close to the fire, her teeth still chattering.

Kipp barked, "You know she's gonna catch a cold if you don't take care of her."

Irwin held his now raging temper. "How about you take care of her tonight and let me do the cooking?"

"Fuk you."

"Are you really going to be like this? She needs you. I need you. I need your help every night and every morning, and all I get is stupid shit from your mouth!"

"I brought you dinner!" Kipp took a step toward Irwin.

"And that is all you do."

Kipp looked to be ready to fight; Irwin was ready to meet the match.

Please, punch me.

"Man, you're pissy."

"Takes a pissy person to know a pissy person! If you want me to be an asshole, I will be an asshole. But Yace does not need that right now. She needs us to act like adults."

"You don't know what she needs."

Irwin cut Kipp off, throwing a hard punch.

Kipp ended up on the ground, blood oozing from his split lip. He spat. Wiping his hand across his face, Kipp snarled, "What the fuk was that for?!"

Irwin hit Kipp again, this time square in the nose. Yace squeaked as she watched him beat up the Clan-Duin. He felt his friend had finally crossed the line. He cracked Kipp twice more in the nose, and this time he stayed down.

"I hate this shit!" shouted Irwin. He stepped away from his unconscious friend.

Yace stood with her back to the fire, watching the two men fight. Her mouth hung open. She pointed at the blood oozing out of Kipps' nose. He was not moving.

"Sorry you had to see that," Irwin said, and headed toward the fish.

The young woman moved toward their downed friend. Although he seemed to scare her, Yace was obviously concerned about Kipp. She knelt at his side and studied the limp body.

There was gurgling; it was Kipp drowning from the blood pooling in his throat and lungs. "Oh, shit." Irwin grumbled, realizing what was happening. Yace was trying to shake Kipp awake. Irwin stepped in and turned the Clan-Duin on his side, allowing the blood to spill from his mouth.

She looked at him with concern. "Yes, I know. I should fix him." He put his hand on Kipp's face. "Fix his brain, that is."

Yace watched him as he used his Erthin abilities to fix Kipp's broken nose. It snapped back into place. He then summoned the blood out of his friend's mouth but did not bring him to consciousness. Instead, while Kipp was knocked out, Irwin tattooed his SIM initials over the Gypsy tattoo. Yace watched with interest as Irwin sewed his metal into Kipp's flesh. He then healed all he could around the puncture site and left Kipp to wake on his own.

It was dark, still raining, the fire small. The fish had been cooked and half eaten by the time Kipp came to.

Irwin felt Kipp move, watched him stumble to his feet, snarl, turn on his heel, and run off into the forest.

A bonus of the metal tattoo, Irwin would always be able to feel Kipp's location.

The next night, Irwin and Yace waited for Kipp to bring them a meal, but he did not. He did not come back at all that night. Irwin felt the general direction of Kipp, east of them and far away—possibly Daos City.

Once more, they rode all that day in the rain. That night, Yace, cold and wet, huddled next to the hot fire. Although the canopy was strung between trees, it did not remedy the fact that they were already soaked. But it allowed the fire to rage without going out and helped contain the heat.

"I must find us some food, Yace." He knelt at her side. "I do not think Kipp is coming back tonight." She looked genuinely saddened. Her eyes flashed back to the fire. He reached for her hand. "Come here. Let me get you warm before I leave." Heat radiated from his hands to dry her clothing. He rubbed her backside, arms, and legs, and she leaned into his chest. "I will be back soon. Please stay right here."

She nodded, and he left the warmth of the campfire. He trudged through the thick forest looking for animal trails, listening for wildlife to catch. All he could hear was rain, and all he could feel was his soaked clothing. Once again, he could only find tree frogs and brought a handful back to skewer and roast over the fire.

Yace was obviously not thrilled by the sight of this meal. She ate what was cooked, but the look on her face revealed her thoughts.

"You dislike frog. I get it. Tomorrow we can have something else."

Her blue eyes were questioning. He asked, "What is it? Are you concerned about Kipp?" She nodded. "He will be back." He felt he could hear her questions brewing. "I do not know where he went. Yes, he is angry with me. Maybe both of us. Maybe just himself." He sighed. "I cannot tell with Kipp sometimes ...."

"No, there is nothing we can do but forgive him." She moved in close and hugged him. "I love you too, Yace. We will get through this, I promise."

She buried her face in his chest, held him tight, and sobbed, "My name is Yace."

He held his breath, waiting to hear her speak again. Slowly, he pealed her off his shirt, looked into her wet blue eyes. Tears started to roll down his face. "You spoke."

Her voice squeaked, "I am Yace Yellsen."

He held her tighter than before. "Am I dreaming?"

"You ... you are Irwin."

"Yes." A smile parted his lips. His tears kept rolling down his face, soaking her hair.

"Thank you." She whispered, reciprocating his tight hug. "Thank you."

"Do you?" His lips quivered. "Do you remember us? We have been trying to save you ever since you were taken away."

"No."

"Do you remember the Gypsy, your family?"

"No."

"Do you remember anything beyond being in that palace with the other concubines?"

"No." Irwin sobbed this time. The clothing on her shoulder was getting wetter. Timidly she said, "You saved me."

"Yes." He held onto her. "Yes, we saved you."

"Why?"

He smiled and wiped away his tears and snot.

What do I tell her?

"Because you were stolen from us, from your family. A bad person took you from us. We could not let you slip away. We love you, Yace." He pulled back to look at her. "You remember nothing, do you?"

Again, she shook her head. "Only my friends. Where are they?"

"The ladies you roomed with at that palace?"

"Yes."

"They stayed behind in Daos Prime. They are familiar with that city, and I felt safe leaving them with my friend, Jorge. He will keep them safe."

"Why are they not with us?"

"Because they wanted to stay there." He heaved a deep sigh, not knowing what to admit.

Shit. Do I tell her the truth?

She whispered, "Why did we not stay?"

I cannot tell her the truth, not all of it.

"There are many reasons. You need the kind of help that Kipp and I cannot give you. We need to take you back to your family. They can help you. I know they miss you very much."

"I miss my friends," she said, referring to the concubines at the Ishik Palace.

"We could not stay." He wanted Yace to understand, "I cannot be in a city of that size for very long. I am a man of the mountains. All those people, and the metals, I become overwhelmed and anxious." He hugged her again.

"Kipp scares me."

"I know. He can be scary sometimes. Please do not take it to heart. I know he wants to talk with you, like we are now." Yace smirked. "He is your best friend, your beloved. He is the one person who knew we could save you." He lied. During most of their travels to save Yace, it had been Irwin who kept the faith in her rescue. Kipp feared the worst, but she didn't need to know that.

"Then why is he not here?"

"I do not know."

"Will he come back?"

"I hope so. I hope so."

Yace held on to Irwin's warm embrace. They sat down next to the fire, and she fell asleep nestled in his arms. He leaned into her, feeling alright with being her guardian, making sure she had what she needed. For now, Yace didn't need overly emotional caregivers. All she needed was guidance and nurturing. And until Kipp was willing to calm down, Irwin would stay calm and keep Yace safe from their brooding friend.

5

<u>THIS IS YACE!</u>

It was barely light when Kipp returned the next morning and found them sleeping intertwined. Yace's face was buried deep in Irwin's chest. He could feel the metal tattoo attached to Kipp's arm as he stood over them.

He was frothing at the mouth when Irwin opened his eyes and yawned. "Kipp."

"I can't handle this, Irwin." He pointed at Yace snuggling in Irwin's chest. "That should be me."

"You are right, Kipp; it should be you."

"Fuk you." Kipp stepped back. "I don't know what I was thinking. There's your shit!" He left the tent and jumped into the air, mutating into an owl, and flew off, leaving behind two bags of belongings.

"Kipp!" Irwin jumped to his feet.

Yace woke up.

"Kipp, wait!" He shouted as their friend flew away. Yace stood next to him, and they shouted simultaneously, "KIPP!"

Irwin yelled, "What the shit!"

Yace's voice strained. "Kipp!"

"I want to beat the shit out of him."

"Kipp!" She did not stop. "Kipp!"

Then a light went on in Irwin's eyes. "Yes, call to him." He moved around her, saw that the piled baggage was their personal bags. Somehow, Kipp retrieved Irwin's saddle bags and Yace's shoulder bag containing her throwing knives, first aid satchel, and the pretty blue dress Kipp had purchased for her.

Yace continued calling. "Kipp!"

"He went to Daos." He studied the contents of Kipp's bag.

Kipp fell from the sky and pounced on Yace. He grabbed her tight and cried, "You're back! You're back!"

She was clearly startled, but did not move under his grasp. She allowed Kipp to smother her with unbridled affection. He kissed her face and nuzzled down into her chest. He held onto his beloved for a long time before coming up for air. His eyes were red, face wet with tears. He looked at Irwin and jumped off Yace. He put his head down into Irwin's chest. "I am so sorry, Irwin. I thought you couldn't do it. I wanted you to fail. I am so sorry for not … for not believing in you."

Irwin was embarrassed by the outpouring of emotions. Yace hugged them both. Irwin put his arm around Kipp, and his friend, the Clan-Duin, sobbed. Irwin and Yace stood there holding their emotionally fragile friend.

After a long time, Kipp came up for a breath. "How are you doing, Yace?"

"I am well. How are you?"

"Oh Yace!" Irwin took a step back, and Kipp hugged her tight.

"You are hurting me." She tapped his back, and Kipp loosened his grasp.

"How did, when did, this happen?"

"Last night before supper."

"He cooked frogs." Yace stuck out her tongue in distaste.

Kipp seemed to be elated. "I should've been here."

"Yes, you should have," Irwin said, and the sun emerged behind the tree line and through the clouds.

"I'm sorry for ever doubting your powers, Irwin."

"I did not do this."

"What? But I—"

Yace confessed, "It took me time to understand how to speak."

"They took away your ability to speak?" Kipp growled. "Those asshole Telepaths should pay for what they did to you."

Irwin chuckled, "They paid already, with their lives."

"Oh, that's right." Kipp's smile grew wider, and then his eyes settled once again on Yace, the object of his devotion. "Oh, how I've missed you, Yace. Holy Hakra, I've missed everything about you. Your voice, your smile, your eyes."

"Her eyes were always there," Irwin muttered.

"The look. That look." He kissed Yace on the lips.

She gasped, not expecting that type of forwardness. "What are you doing?"

"Yace." Kipp moved back and forth as if he could see something no one else did. "Is that you, Yace?"

"Yes, I am Yace Yellsen."

He balked, "You're not Yace."

Irwin's eyes widened. "What?"

"I am Yace Yellsen." She said with confidence.

Shaking his head, rejecting the idea that this female was the real Yace, Kipp grumbled, "You are not *my* Yace."

Irwin gasped, "She *is* your Yace."

"I belong to no one," she said, hands on hips. Irwin smiled, watching the Yace he remembered beginning to emerge.

"What the fuk did you do to her, Irwin?"

"What do you keep thinking I am doing? I have been trying …. I am the seed of positivity she needs. Why are you so negative?"

"You didn't fix her."

"She is fixed, somewhat."

"No, you didn't. That's not Yace!"

"This is Yace! The same Yace we have been following since Onj Raha. The same Yace you fell in love with many years ago."

"Please do not argue over me."

"So what if she can talk? That's not my Yace." Kipp took several steps back. *Shall I break your nose again?*

"This is Yace." His tone adamant. "If you have a problem with her not acting like herself, then maybe you should stay around camp and help me out, help us out. She needs you."

Kipp looked toward the woods.

Yace pleaded, "Please. Do not leave us again!"

Kipp eyed her and huffed, "Fine, I'll stay."

"We do not have to go anywhere today." Irwin said. "You two sit here and rekindle your relationship."

"Are you fooling me?" Shaking his head, Kipp said, "I want to keep moving. We still need Nonbry, or someone like him. She's not fixed."

Not wanting to argue, Irwin said, "Fine, we ride."

Their moment of sunshine disappeared.

Morning's overcast sky never brightened; clouds blocked the sky. It would rain all day long again. They tacked up. Irwin and Yace rode on, pulling the donkeys behind. In his canine form, Kipp raced along and predictably strayed off and on into the forest that edged the roadway.

They traveled past acres of grassy fields, a few cows grazed with a herd of about thirty goats. The south side of the road was shrouded by towering trees, mostly protecting them from the onslaught of an occasional downpour.

Plodding along the muddy roadway, the horses undisturbed by nothing but Mother Nature, Irwin felt the eerie atmosphere throughout the local landscape all day long. Kipp could be seen between trees, shadowing their pace until he descended into the dark forest in search of the evening meal.

Kipp's hard attitude had eased into something more tolerable. He appeared grateful for his friends today—unlike yesterday and all the days leading up to it—a pleasant surprise. He knew to keep past regressions behind them—that everyday things would become better than previous days—and tried to remain optimistic.

Tending the frying pan that evening, Irwin cooked a fish Kipp had caught. He tried to ignore his friends while secretively watching them interact. Yace cautiously maintained her distance from Kipp, despite his duty to safeguard her. She knew, somehow, that Kipp loved her. She sat close to the fire.

Kipp rubbed his arm, his new tattoo.

She peered at the metallic emblem. "How does the tattoo feel?"

"Rough."

"Does it hurt?"

"Not right now."

"It is pretty; I want one."

"You shouldn't get a tattoo, Yace. They hurt."

"You were asleep when Irwin did that to you."

"If I remember correctly, he had hit me in the face." He glared at Irwin who averted his eyes back to the fish.

"He did. Many times." She giggled. "You made a gurgling sound. I thought you were dying, but Irwin saved you."

"Only because he knew I'd kick his ass if he didn't."

"You cannot kick my ass if you are dead."

Yace smiled, sounding like Irwin as she told the tale to Kipp. "Can I have his tattoo too? I think it is pretty."

"Please don't talk like him."

"I like how Irwin talks."

Irwin raised an eyebrow at Yace. "Are you mocking me?"

She giggled.

"I wouldn't mock him." Kipp might have been trying to scare her. "He can kill you with a flick of his wrist."

"I can only kill Erthins with a flick of my wrist," said Irwin.

"What about shooting metal out of your skin?"

"Yes, there is that."

Yace gasped, "Shooting metal out of your skin?"

"You don't want to see him do it. He's deadly."

"And accurate."

Yace pleaded, "Can I have the tattoo, please?"

"It will hurt."

"I am brave."

"Don't do it Yace." Kipp sneered. "One tattoo is better than two. Besides, you don't want to be owned by a Metalist."

"I do not own you, Kipp."

"Yeah, you do, you asshole. You imprinted me; you didn't give me a say in it."

Irwin's tongue struck the top of his mouth loudly. "Are you fooling me? You wanted me to give Yace the tattoo, but only after I practiced on you."

Does he want me to kick his ass again?

"How bad does it hurt?"

"You've had one before." Kipp pointed at her Gypsy tattoo. "You cried when you got that."

"I did?" She looked to Irwin for confirmation.

"I was not there."

"Where were you?"

"Up in the mountains."

"Will you tattoo me, please?"

"Like Kipp said, it will hurt."

"I am brave."

"You sound like a four-year-old when you talk like him."

She stuck out her tongue at Kipp. "No, maybe only three-years."

Irwin smiled, flipped the fish. "I have missed your heckling."

"Heckling?"

"I don't heckle!"

Irwin rebuked, "Yes, you do. You also taunt … jeer … and criticize…."

"You have said criticize before. What does it mean?"

Irwin wanted to stay out of their conversation, but somehow Yace kept draw-ing him back. "To criticize is to find fault with something and voice disapproval. It is the only way Kipp knows how to interact with people."

"Fuk you." Kipp frowned, and the moon suddenly appeared in a break be-tween the thick layer of clouds.

"I think you need to have your mouth washed out," said Irwin.

"Can I have the tattoo please, please, please?!"

"I don't want you to give her the tattoo, Irwin."

"And I do not think it is up to you to decide what Yace wants."

"She doesn't know what she wants."

"I know what I want. I want a tattoo."

"You're an idiot, Yace."

"Stop criticizing her. Yace is not an idiot, Kipp."

"Stop fighting over me!"

Kipp hissed, "Don't burn the fish, Irwin."

I want to punch you in the face again.

The moon disappeared. They fell silent, and only the sound of the fish sizzling in the pan pierced the darkened silence.

"Where did we get these tattoos, Kipp?" Yace asked.

"Tamera gave them to us. A talented artist, and she's really clever when it comes to her healing powers."

"Powers of healing? Like what Irwin did to you?"

"Yeah, but she's nicer than Irwin."

Irwin shook his head.

Yace said, "I think Irwin is nicer than you. So, Tamera must be really nice."

Kipp tossed a twig into the fire. "That fish smells done."

"Do you have any tattoos, Irwin?"

"No. My body heals too quickly to keep scars or tattoos." He pulled the fish from the fire. "There you go. Cooked!" Yace clapped, and Kipp groaned.

Yace licked her lips. "I'm starving."

Kipp grumbled, "I should've caught my own fish."

"You say there is a town not far from here?" Irwin looked at Kipp. "Tomorrow, Yace and I will stop at those markets; buy some dried fish and maybe some fruits too."

She smiled. "That sounds fun!"

6
<u>Revealing Conversations</u>

It would have taken twenty days to walk the same distance they had ridden in eight. Nevertheless, they continued their unrelenting drive westward as if being chased, though there was no sight or sound of anyone else on the roadway.

They entered the only town they came to that afternoon. Very few buildings were two-stories tall, and most were the dome-shaped huts they had seen their entire trip through Daos Territory. Along the river's edge, canoes breached the water. Local vendors displayed fresh and dried fish on bamboo mats, enticing customers to purchase them for their evening meal. Others were there to trade nuts, fruits and vegetables, and various household items. This market was sparse compared to so many Irwin had visited during their long journey. They stopped briefly and bought several pounds of fruit and dried fish. Then they left the small village.

On they rode, away from prying eyes, and in search of a camping spot for this night. Kipp led them to a meadow where they would take a reprieve from the long day's ride and their stop for food supplies.

Dry most of the night, they woke to a misty morning and dark clouds covering the treetops. They arose and rode on relentlessly. Day after day, it seemed. On and on. By that afternoon, it rained hard again. Once camp was made that night, everyone was glad that Irwin had replenished their supplies. No one had to hunt or cook. They stayed under the cover of the canopy near the warmth of the fire passing around bags of plentiful food.

Kipp seemed less agitated now that Yace could talk. Even though she sounded innocent when she spoke, she now wanted to know about her past—wanted to know more about these men who rescued her. Kipp's uneasy body language and reliance on Irwin's suggestions indicated his wariness in sharing anything too revealing. They had never discussed what to divulge—they did not think they would have to reintroduce Yace to her person and her powers, her entire life, it seemed.

Fear gripped Irwin's heart as he contemplated revealing the truth to Yace about her father's involvement. He had stolen her. Used her. And the whole time he had manipulated many people while trying to thwart Irwin and Kipp's rescue attempts. Both knew the evil her father possessed, and they did not want Yace to know of such deceit. All they confessed was where their journey had taken them, what they dealt with along the way. They refrained from discussing the horrific events they had endured.

"I want to know about my Talents," she said. "I know Kipp is Clan-Duin, and Irwin, you are Erthin and Metalist. But what am I?"

"You're you," Kipp replied with a nervous chuckle. His eyes settled on Irwin again.

"We must tell her," Irwin said. He did not like withholding the information Yace needed to know.

"She doesn't need to know, not yet."

"But what if something happens?"

Yace agreed, "Yes, what if something happens?"

"What do you see happening to Yace?" Kipp asked with a stern eye on Irwin. They both knew she held the power to create and destroy, like Irwin.

Yace said, "Like someone else taking me from you?"

"Nothing's gonna happen to you when you're with us," said Kipp.

"Then how did I get taken before? The truth this time."

Could she sense their lies and withholdings?

Irwin understood why Yace wanted to know more about herself. "It is time we told her of her powers. If not, she will discover them on her own."

"But maybe she won't. Maybe she needs Nonbry's help."

Irwin ran his fingers through his hair. "What was the first thing Yace learned to do, Kipp?"

"Levitate."

"Yes. Now, do you see my point?"

"What's levitate?" Yace persisted.

"But if she knows what it is, then she's more likely to do it!"

"I do not think her powers work like that, Kipp. She needs our help. We know what she is capable of. We must think of the repercussions if she does not know what she can do."

"We don't really know what she's capable of, Irwin!"

Irwin's gray eyes swirled with silver as his father's had when he was about to do someone harm. "We do know what she is capable of. She does not. It is best if we tell her now. Allow her to discover herself in a safe environment."

"Safe? Ha! Levitating most anything isn't safe!"

She sat forward, excited, "What is levitate? Come on, tell me!"

"We can't teach her about her powers." Kipp barked. "Neither of us knows how to do what she's capable of."

"We know what she can do. She just needs a safe place to learn again." Irwin turned to Yace. "You are Coterie."

"The fuk, why'd you tell her?"

"What is Coterie?"

Kipp sneered, "You're only half Coterie, half something else."

"Something else?"

"TeleCapritian, I believe is the name." Irwin glared at Kipp. "Yace, you are Coterie and TeleCapritian, which means you are powerful."

Kipp snorted, lips pressed flat.

"Kipp, do you have something to say?"

Yace was clearly hungry to know more. The campfire shined in her bright blue eyes. "Powerful. What does that mean?"

"You have many unique abilities, including levitation—the ability to make things float in the air. That was the first trick you learned. You learned to levitate jacks and marbles when you were young, but now you can levitate much more like rocks and branches, baggage, and such. You called it—"

Kipp sniggered, "And bodies."

"—telekinetic energy." Irwin eyed Kipp for speaking out of turn. "You told me harnessing that power was part mental, part metaphysical. I think it is akin to me being able to manipulate molecules, mold metals, and such. You also have telepathic abilities. That means you have the ability to hear thoughts, other peoples' inside voices. You hear their internal dialogue, their thoughts in your mind. When we first met, you called it hearing voices."

Yace's eyes darted between the two comrades. "Like I can with Kipp."

"You can hear my thoughts?" Kipp groaned.

"You and Kipp are bonded." Irwin nodded. "That is why you can hear his thoughts."

"Bonded?"

Kipp glared at the fire.

"It is a good thing." Irwin reassured.

"What else can I do?"

"Well, you once told me that Telepaths have many traits; some can see visions in dreams or while they are awake—"

Again, Kipp sneered. "Mentally manipulate the masses."

"Kipp," Irwin grimaced, "can you please practice your mindfulness?"

Kipp stared at his hands, then back at the fire.

Yace said, "He hates it when you call his name with that tone. It reminds him of his mother."

Kipp growled, "Stop reading my thoughts, Yace."

She smiled at Irwin. "Kipp wants you to finish telling me of my powers."

"Oh, he does, does he?"

"No. She's lying." Kipp snarled, "Can you fix her?"

"I can fix you."

"Yeah, you'd like that."

Irwin forced a yawn, then said, "Maybe we are done talking for tonight."

"No," said Yace. "You need to tell me what else I can do."

"Why? So you can kill us during the night?"

Irwin glared at Kipp.

"Why are you always so mean, Kipp?" Yace looked confused, maybe angry.

Irwin placed his hand on her arm. Her eyes grew large, and her voice shook. "What is happening?"

"I fixed you, per Kipp's request."

He does not appreciate having his thoughts heard, or his mind probed.

"Fix me," she said. "I just heard your thoughts!"

"When I touch someone, I can keep out telepathic influences, so to speak. This way, you do not have to listen in on Kipp's perverted mind."

"You've said that word before. Is that what perverted is?"

They both eyed Kipp, and Irwin said, "I can only guess."

He is Clan-Duin, has animalistic thoughts. We cannot fault him for that.

She recoiled from Irwin's touch.

Kipp growled, "I'm gonna sleep now," clearly upset at Irwin and Yace's closeness. He turned into his canine form and found a place to lie down.

Yace persisted with her questioning, though still seeming fearful of her two companions. "What else can I do?"

Irwin measured her reaction to him. "That is all I know you can do." There were other abilities she had, but he was unsure of disclosing that information just yet.

She frowned. "You made it sound like I was powerful like you."

"Being able to levitate anything around you, hear other people's thoughts, and see visions of future events are amazing abilities, Yace. Do not be afraid of them." Again, he made contact with her arm.

Do not let what Kipp says bother you. It is only a projection of his negative internal self.

She pulled away and screamed, "Stop doing that!"

Kipp was quick to shed his fur. "What'd you do to her, Irwin?"

"Something Yace and I did back in the day."

"Fuk, I'd hate to think you're telepathic too!"

"I am not telepathic! Not that there is anything wrong with it." He looked at Yace, trying to read her emotions. She still looked frightened of him.

Kipp pushed his arm between them. "Try your powers on me."

Irwin humored Kipp's request, grabbed his arm and thought, *I am not a Telepath. I do not want to be a Telepath. I only want to save you from the Telepaths, you torpid shit!*

"Do you hear anything?"

"No, what'cha thinking?"

Irwin broke into song, "The sun came up to play today, the sun came up to play …" It was a song he had heard while at a summit cabin in the Kruluver mountains while meeting people of Talent for the first time. At times, he would hum its catchy tune. "… the sun came up to play today, the sun came up to play." He repeated the lyrics. "You did not hear me singing that?"

"I heard nothing."

Good.

Yace stared at Irwin. Wonder in her eyes. "I did not hear Kipp's thoughts while you touched him. Why is that?"

"That aspect of my power is what made me join your journey. Back when we first met, I did not know I could ground out telepathy. I did not even know what telepathy was. I am not sure how my body does it."

"It's the metal," said Kipp, "I'm gonna sleep now." He returned to his wolf form.

"Will you tattoo me like you did with Kipp?"

"Maybe."

"Will it help me from hearing Kipp's thoughts?"

"I am not sure."

She seemed to be struggling, her face wrinkled with concern. "Could you touch me again, but this time not say anything?"

"I am sorry, Yace, for startling you before."

"It's alright. I'm just, I didn't know what all powers I have, and you have. You are amazing, Irwin."

He smiled. He had heard Yace say those exact words during the first time they met. "Thank you, Yace. You are quite amazing too. I just want you to know that we are here for you. And if you begin to feel your powers coming forth, we want to help you understand them."

Shaking her head, Yace whispered, "Kipp is afraid of my powers. He knows what I can do. He does not want you to tell me anymore."

Irwin felt stuck. She could do more than just hear voices and dreams. Her telepathy allowed Yace to see through the eyes of people she had bonded with, and influence individuals and the masses using her telepathic mind or spoken words. She also had a power comparable to Kipp's; Yace could morph into other people—only females—but all the distinct colors and shapes women could be. There were other powers Irwin could only fathom that she had at her disposal. All he could do was be supportive.

"Should I be afraid of my powers?"

"No," Irwin said, but he was slightly fearful of her abilities.

He gently placed his hand on hers. They were sitting next to the fire. Yace moved closer to him, leaned against his shoulder. Irwin stared at the dancing flames. He was trying to be mindful; meditative. But after a while of silence, a thought rippled through his mind: *I only want the best for Yace.*

Her eyes were closed, but responded in kind, *I know.*

Irwin petted her head before helping her lie down on a blanket.

Finally, he lay down too, but apart from her contact.

We need to find a tactical way to tell Yace about the rest of her powers before she accidentally does something we cannot fix.

The problem is Kipp wants to withhold information and then ruminate about her Talents. He is still moody, though nicer now. But for how long? Yace still is not Yace in his eyes. Unless she changes for him, he will never be happy.

7

<u>BLOOD! EVERYWHERE BLOOD!</u>

Kipp was calm and friendly while they ate their morning meal and prepared for another day of long-winded rides. Even the night before, his attitude was not as harsh as it had been. Yace tried to help around camp, but Irwin and Kipp took care of everything, including the animals. All Yace had to do was sit and watch the remainder of the fire dance and begin to fade.

She had convinced Irwin to tattoo his SIM emblem, and out of solidarity, he made a metal tattoo appear upon his left shoulder too—exactly like their tattoos—but no red-ink swirls.

She cried in pain, and Irwin offered to place her asleep, but she wanted to be present for all of it. Kipp watched with excitement; he had been unconscious during his tattooing. Once it was finished, Irwin removed any excessive swelling and irritability from the flesh.

By nightfall, he decided to give them time away from him. He saw how delighted Kipp was that Yace had her own tattoo. They talked about the pain and reminisced about the Gypsy. She asked him questions about their family.

Irwin went for a walk through the timbers, and he realized Kipp was more comfortable with Yace when he was not present. Kipp did not want to share Yace. After being separated from her for so long, he wanted her all to himself.

He felt safe in leaving Yace with Kipp, even though she had expressed fear of the Clan-Duin. Irwin knew Kipp would keep her safe. That was all the Clan-Duin ever wanted for her. And now that they both had tattoos, he would know exactly where they were.

He returned to camp much later, and they were asleep. Yace lay between layers of blankets near the fire. Kipp was in his wolf form under a tree—away from camp.

I hope they reconnect for Kipp's sake.

He lay down across the fire from Yace and fell asleep in a few brief minutes.

Morning arrived, the horses were tacked up, and their day began once more.

There was a constant loop of waking up, riding out, trying not to be offended by the saddening sights Daos Territory held, making camp, resting for the night, and repeating it all again. Other than the changing landscape, the occasional village or river crossing, the vegetation along the edges of the roadway, there was no change in the temperature, the people they saw, or the food they ate.

After twenty days of hard riding away from Daos City, they were gaining momentum. Irwin estimated, by the look of his map, that they would reach the last town on this journey soon. And just beyond that point, the main roadway ended on his map. He wondered if there was a secret roadway to Uer 'Bin Territory, one only known to locals. If not, this road would end in the mountains. Until then, they passed through unmarked villages and continued along the rutted dirt road without pause.

One afternoon, up in the high mountains far ahead of them on the horizon, lightning flashed across dark clouds. They watched it dance and heard an occasional rumble as they traveled westward.

"I hope that storm remains over there." Yace told Irwin when another distant clap of thunder jolted her up off the saddle.

"It should. Those clouds are moving north, not east—towards us."

They continued on until Kipp met them on the roadway later that afternoon. Blood covered his face and body, but he was smiling.

"Come see what I caught!" he shouted, eager to show off the fresh kill. He urged them to follow him into the forest to a place where they could make camp for the night—a break in the trees on a gentle slope.

Yace gasped from atop her steed at the sight of a recently killed deer.

Irwin shouted, "Well done, Kipp! He is a beauty. How heavy do you think?"

"Oh, at least two hundred pounds, but probably more. I struggled, pulling him up to here." He chuckled. "I caught him off guard and tossed him down onto a dead branch. I had speared him, and he bled out." Kipp pulled the legs up to show a puncture in the deer's lungs. "It was the easiest large kill I've ever had!"

"Good job, Kipp." Irwin jumped down from the saddle. "We should hang him to drain the rest of the blood."

"Why did you have to kill it?" Yace gasped, easing herself down from her mount.

"You wanna eat?"

"It's pretty." She approached the body. "What is it?"

Kipp looked at her as though he had seen a ghost. "A deer."

"A white-tail deer," Irwin added. "They are common in the foothills of Kruluver Mountains."

She stood alongside her horse, held the reins tight. "Is that where we are?"

"No. The foothills are where that storm we saw is." Irwin said. "We are still a few days away from there. No, this guy probably went looking for a female. They are called Doe."

"Doe?"

"Yes, and he is a Buck."

"They have names?" Yace looked down and then at Kipp. Her eyes filled with tears. "And you're going to kill it?"

"It's already been killed, Yace."

Her lips quivered, "But ...."

"You have eaten deer before, I am sure." Irwin said, trying to comfort.

"Oh yeah, she has. Venison and eggs." Kipp licked his lips. "Patrice makes the best food with venison; you love it fresh or cooked up in stews."

"Kipp, I think you are talking about yourself when you say *fresh*." Irwin chuckled, turned to retrieve a rope. "Yace, we can tie the horses over here." He motioned to her to move the horses next to a sturdy tree. She stood there holding the lines while he untied his donkeys, Nee Nee and Jenn Jenn, from the horses. She said nothing.

Irwin moved around Yace. "You have something on the back of your dress, Yace." It was a small spot, right where she had sat in the saddle. He tried to brush it off, but the blue skirt was stained. "It looks like mud. We can wash that off tonight, but you will have to change."

She tried to turn and look at the stain. "How is it I have mud on my dress?"

Irwin shrugged.

I know the saddles were clean this morning. Maybe she sat on something.

He could not see the seat of the saddle—the horse was too tall. "Let me get the ropes for Kipp to hoist and tie the deer, then I will put up the tent so you can change."

Her face turned and appeared disgusted. She flinched and winced. "Ugh. I'm not feeling good, Irwin. Something is wrong. I think I'm hurt."

"What is the matter?"

"I'm in pain, ugh!"

Shit!

Irwin sensed her oncoming panic. "Do you know how you hurt yourself?" He looked her over, not understanding why she was suddenly in pain.

"No." She slumped to her knees. "I don't know."

"Kipp!"

"Yeah, what is it?" Kipp was not paying any attention, proudly staring at his kill.

"Something is wrong with Yace."

"I'm not feeling good," she said. Kipp was at her side in one breath.

"What's the matter?"

"I hurt here," holding her abdomen.

"I do not know how she got hurt!" Irwin relived that day in his mind.

We only stopped once; she was fine then. She did not sit on anything; we were walking—stretching our legs. She had been feeling fine until after she dismounted just now. She could have hurt herself by stepping down, but how? She is always so careful.

He did not know what to do. "You take care of her, Kipp, and I will take care of the horses."

"What am I supposed to do? You're the Erthin Healer!"

"And she's your best friend. You know her better than I do. Help Yace, Kipp."

Kipp looked at Yace, "What can I do?"

"I think I want to lie down."

Kipp helped her walk away from the horses. "What the ...." Kipp sniffed around her skirt. "You're menstruating!"

"Menstruating?! What does that mean? Am I going to be alright?"

Kipp seemed delighted. "Yeah, you'll be alright. You're just menstruating!"

"What is menstruating?" Irwin wanted to know. He had never heard this word.

"It's blood."

"Blood? From where? Am I going to die?" Yace pulled at her skirt.

"You'll die at some point, but not from menstruating!" Kipp continued to chuckle. "Women bleed from between their legs every moon cycle."

"What? Why?"

"Yes, please tell us, Kipp." Irwin was as frightened as Yace seemed to be.

"This is—ha ha." Kipp was gleeful. "Holy Hakra, you've never, I mean you always wanted to …."

"Calm down Kipp; think about what you are going to say before you say it!" Irwin kept his distance.

Kipp smirked and giggled. "All the women I've ever known have menstruated; all except Yace!"

"What do you mean, all?"

"This means you can get pregnant, Yace! You can have a family, as many kids as you want!"

"I am confused," said Irwin. "How does blood make it so women can get pregnant?"

"Holy Hakra, Yace, you've always wanted this! Always wanted children, a family. This means we can have one!" Kipp cackled and spun around.

"Kipp, slow down," said Irwin. "I am confused. How can blood make it so women can get pregnant?"

"Predator animals bleed between heat cycles." Kipp said. "All canines, felines, and all humans bleed. Well, only the females."

Irwin pushed his eyebrows together.

"Why do we bleed?" Yace's lower lip quivered again.

Kipp said, "It's only for a few days, Yace. You've nothing to worry about."

"What do I do?"

Kipp shrugged, "I don't know."

"What?!" Irwin and Yace shouted at the same time.

"The women go off and do their bleeding thing together, leave the kids with the men and we have to fend for ourselves."

"What can we do for Yace?"

"I don't know." Kipp shrugged.

Yace gasped, "I don't want to have children."

"But the old you wanted children—lots of them."

"Perhaps that was you who wanted lots of children." Irwin said. "Yace never told me she wanted children."

"Did she mate with you? No! She told me when we mated, she wanted to have lots of children but couldn't."

"How sure are you of that conversation?"

"How come I couldn't have children? Why did I not bleed until now? Is there something wrong with me?"

"Those are good questions." Irwin turned to Kipp. "Why is she bleeding now, Kipp? Do you know?"

Kipp's smile fell flat. "I hope nothing's wrong with her."

They knew of her past, knew she had been raped, sodomized, and beaten—rendered unable to bear children, they had thought.

Irwin touched Yace on her shoulder. "What I know about you, Yace, is that when you were a child, you were hurt terribly. That was right about the time you met the Gypsy and Tamera, the Gypsy healer. She told you that you would not be able to have babies. When you told me your story, you did not sound displeased. But you did say you wanted a family."

She winced. "Why is there pain?"

Kipp stayed at her side. "Those are cramps. I know that those can be bad."

"Bad? How? What happens to me?"

"Really bad pain-wise." Kipp said. "My sisters and mother have bad pains."

All this new information was startling to Irwin. "Flinn menstruates?"

"She started right before I left, right after our blowout." Kipp sighed, looking to the north. "I wonder how she's doing."

"Irwin, can you help me?" Yace was pleading now.

"I do not know what to do."

Kipp stood, still chuckling. "Take away her pain. I'll take care of the horses."

Irwin said to Yace. "I want to put the fire there. Maybe sit here." He helped move her against a rock.

"Thank you, Irwin."

He whispered, "I think your blood should stay inside. There is no logical reason I can see for it to pour out of you."

"I dislike these cramps," she said, puffing.

He sat next to her and placed a hand on her belly. She felt swollen, her abdomen appeared to be growing. "Now-now I feel gross."

"What do you mean?"

"I feel stuff between my legs. I don't know." It was obviously hard for her to find words to describe what she was feeling. Instead, she closed her eyes and leaned into Irwin.

"It is okay, Yace. I will take away your pain," he said. "Are you hungry? Or do you want to sleep?"

Her voice cracked as she whispered, "Neither." There was a long pause and then she said, "I think I want to change—clean up."

"Maybe Kipp knows what to do."

"Don't leave me alone with him." Her face was still on his shoulder.

"You know Kipp would never hurt you."

She sobbed. "His thoughts. I don't want to hear his thoughts."

"Kipp." He called to the Clan-Duin who was setting the donkeys free from their baggage. "Could you bring Yace her bag, and a few of the blankets, please?"

When he was done tending to the animals, he came to them. "Is she gonna be alright?"

Irwin held close to Yace and snapped at Kipp, "You seem to think so."

"What? I'm just happy for her."

Yace whispered, "I'm not happy."

"She is in a lot of pain," Irwin said, "and does not want to sleep."

"We have a full vial of milk of the poppy," said Kipp.

"That might help. Thank you."

"You gonna make a fire?"

With a flick of Irwin's hand, a fire erupted in the center of the small, semi-flat clearing. "There you go."

Kipp said, "You gonna butcher it, or should I?"

Irwin glared. "Drain the blood first and try to remove the stick before we do too much work."

Kipp cried, "I wanna cook up the whole thing!"

"It is best if we cut a meal for us to cook now and then cure the rest in a fire pit."

"Could you cook up tonight's meal with your Erthin powers?"

"The fire will cook the meal."

"Fine, I'll wait."

Kipp continued removing the horse tack. He made piles between the trees, and then let the horses wander off. They meandered along the edge of the trees, finding sprigs of grass here and there; meanwhile, the donkeys, as always, remained close to camp.

Kipp and Irwin put up the canopy while Yace curled up on the ground with her eyes closed tight. She breathed loudly through bouts of pain and refused the milk of the poppy.

Kipp and Irwin heaved the deer's heavy body up to drain the blood. Irwin came back to Yace's side and placed a tender hand on her. Her bright blue eyes snapped open.

"You hungry?"

"Not really."

"Your cramps hurt?"

"Yes."

"Milk of the poppy will help with that. You want some?"

"Maybe. Yes."

"I want you to eat something if you take it. We have not eaten since breakfast, and your stomach might become angry."

"I'm not hungry."

"Alright, but I will not give you milk of the poppy if you do not eat at least something. Maybe if you rub your belly. Although I could warm my hand and place it on there, that might ease your cramping muscles."

Settling down next to Yace, Irwin noticed Kipp's heated eyes upon him. His hand went to Yace's abdomen once again, and he warmed her angry muscles and calmed the cramping, allowing her body to relax. Yace slept for a brief time while the blood dribbled out of the deer. The camp reeked of blood and death. Irwin carved the deer while Kipp watched.

"How can we help Yace?"

Kipp shrugged. "Let her have her space."

"What do the Gypsy women do during their menstruation time?"

"They go off together and bleed."

"What I mean is; how do they deal with it? And where do they bleed from? I am entirely confused."

"The same place we fuk them."

What little color Irwin had in his face drained. "Why would they do that?"

"I don't know. I'm not a woman."

"I figured you would know more about women than this," Irwin said. "Do they wear special garments or something? How do they cope with blood coming out of them?"

Kipp was obviously still amused by the situation. "Better than you are."

"Yace needs our help now, and you are too inept to know how to help other than laugh at the situation. She is mortified by her condition. She does not know what to do, and our inability to help her hurts her confidence in us."

Kipp shrugged. "Are you fooling me? She'll be fine."

"She is in pain!" Irwin rolled his eyes and thought.

Now I know why Yace did not want to stay mated with you.

Kipp spat, "Then she should drink some milk of the poppy!"

"I want her to eat something first, but she is not hungry."

"Then she's on her own. I don't know what the fuk to do for her." He pointed at the deer. "That hide, on the other hand ...."

"We can use that for Yace."

"What? No, I was thinking it would make a great cloak!"

"The fur can absorb her blood."

"No, ew! No! I caught that deer; that hide is mine!"

"Kipp, it would help Yace."

Kipp snapped, "No! I ... That's not ... Ugh!"

"Kipp, you will catch another one."

"But it was an easy catch."

"More reason to sacrifice. Besides, it has a hole! You do not want to sleep on a hole."

With a wide smile, Kipp replied, "I sure do."

What the shit. Does he ever think with anything other than his prick?

Irwin could only shake his head. "Do not worry; I will figure something out."

"I'm not worried. Women have been bleeding from their female parts for generations; Yace will survive."

Angered and concerned for Yace, Irwin growled at Kipp's lack of empathy. "How do you know?" Irwin's words quieted Kipp. "I want to know why she is now bleeding, especially when she never did before. Is this something that will happen every moon? Or is she hurt, broken, or is something going on inside her that I cannot feel?"

The Clan-Duin watched Yace as she rested. "Do you think something's wrong with her?"

"Why is she bleeding now when she never did before?"

"Maybe she has been healed." Kipp said, shrugging again. "Maybe Dephen was able to heal her better than Tamera could. Or maybe it happened when Dephen was pushed out of her. I don't know!"

"I hope she is alright."

"It smells of menses. I know that smell, Irwin."

"You do not think she will die?"

"Yace's too stubborn for that." They both stopped what they were doing and looked at her.

"I hope you are correct."

8

THE TOWN OF ENOK

They remained in the cozy camp for four days, a pleasant reprieve.
Kipp did not have to hunt, and they had extra linens for Yace's menstruation cycle thanks to the Clan-Duin's kill. She was embarrassed by her predicament, but the men did not care. They helped her with anything she needed, but mostly they sat around the fire, under Irwin's tent canopy, staying warm and dry and enjoying copious amounts of dried venison.

Kipp assured Irwin and Yace that what he smelled was usual for women, as was the pain and duration of her cycle. Irwin felt nothing wrong with her other than a bloated belly and could only ease her pains temporarily. They cleaned her clothes and theirs in a creek close to camp.

Once Yace recovered, they embarked on their journey again. Irwin was now more tender with her than before. He was cautious about her traveling so soon by horseback. He made her stop and take breaks more often, kept a watchful eye on her.

Ten days later, they rode into the last town on Irwin's map of Daos—the town of Enok—a mining community hidden behind a fortified wall. There was only one other entrance/exit into the isolated township, and it sat opposite the large, open gateway they rode toward. Tall guard towers clung next to those entrances. This place reminded Irwin of Kobiton, but it was much smaller. Only one man stood guard in each tower during the afternoon heat.

Once inside the tiny rectangular town, Irwin felt reminiscent of the tiny town of Goshee where, once, long ago, he had spent some of the riches he had rescued from his father's stash. There, he had outfitted himself for a long and unknown trek through the mountains. Much the same as Goshee, Enok was full of miners and their awful odors and rude habits. Enok was also about the size of Arenu Village, where they had hoped to save Yace, but her father had other plans. Arenu Village had also been set up around an open square, but here there was a maze of tents instead of a forge and open markets. He was certain that fewer people lived here than in Arenu Village too.

Yace kept her hood up. Irwin showed his face as they entered Enok. They slowed, and then halted their horses a short way beyond the bulky entry gates. Gritty-looking men walked about with shifty eyes while considering these new visitors as they breached the eastern gateway. This was the first all wooden town Irwin's crew had come across since leaving Daos City. Buildings stood no more than three-stories tall, except the four-story towers.

This place is a bit more modern than we have seen on our ride here. Nowhere else has had such tall buildings, or substantial barricades; what are they trying to keep in, or out?

Not people of Talent. No. There are seventeen Erthins in those houses by the river.

He looked beyond the tents to three buildings that stood along the river mirroring one another—separate from the rest of the buildings in Enok—and were connected by a covered walkway.

That must be where people with Talent are allowed—the only place he felt the presence of Erthins.

Enok reminded Irwin of Goshee and Arenu Village, dark and dreary and unconventional in structure. There were many Daosian miners there living their gritty, lecherous, self-righteous, egocentric lifestyles. Many sat at the portal of their tents, or just outside, their eyes and words directed to Yace. Irwin was on guard with the men and the hum of metal—bittersweet songs emanating from the metal—resonated in his ears. There was no denying it, they were back in civilization.

Covered stalls and the forge to the left, the twang of metal caught his attention. He moved in that direction, and Yace followed; both surveyed the landscape. They rode up to a hitch post and Irwin stopped Bodi and dismounted. He glanced to the sky where Kipp soared above them in his hawk form.

Once on the ground, Irwin smelled the stench of animal and human refuse. He handed Bodi's reins to Yace and said, "Stay put." She nodded, yet appeared distant.

There was a small line of donkeys, ready to be trimmed or shod, waiting just beyond the forge—tied to a hitch post. A medium-built Daosian blacksmith with dark hair and a scruffy beard stepped out of the darkened forge and strode to a rain barrel to get himself a drink. He stopped as Irwin approached.

"Ye hatan e o." Irwin said in Daosian.

The smith finished his drink, poured some water down his back, and spoke too rapidly for Irwin to understand. He also eyed Yace with a greedy expression.

"Fan de du qian?"

The smith chuckled, jested toward Yace, and said something else Irwin could not comprehend. Jorge had taught Irwin only enough of the Daosian language to find a room, or stall, or a drink. Again, Irwin asked for stalls to rent. "Fan de du qian?"

Then the smith said, "You not be from around here."

"Oh, good." He felt a sense of relief to have met someone who knew his language.

"Follow." The smith, returning to the forge, gestured at Irwin.

The place was stifling. Two younger Daosian men stood holding iron rods at the edge of an open oven, turning the rods for even heating. To the side of the oven, two teenaged Clan-Duin boys in chains worked the fire, stoking it with a large fan. They averted their eyes when Irwin looked at them.

"You from Hakerra?"

"Hakerra?" Irwin thought about it. "Oh, Hakra. No. I am from Datzar Territory. Up north."

"You speak it. You from there."

"Yes. I guess. Yes. Most of Urthis speaks it. Seems you know it too."

"We have miners from Hakerra. We learn their tongue."

"How much for one night for my animals?"

"You have their feed?"

"No," Irwin confessed, "that is something I must purchase while here."

"Ha! Thirty silver per animal per night."

"I can only afford ten per animal."

"Thirty."

"Fifteen."

"Okay, okay, I take fifteen, per animal." Irwin offered sixty Daosian silvers. The smith chuckled and took the coins. "How many nights you stay?"

"Just one."

"Only one-night stay?"

"Yes. We have far yet to travel and want to get through those mountains before winter sets in. You see, this is the journey of our marriage," said Irwin. He glanced over his shoulder at Yace and smiled at her. This was the story Irwin decided to use; he knew they needed to lie. "We have not stayed in any place for long. My beloved wants to see the sights of the world, so we are."

"Hm. Travel takes money. You have money?"

"Well, I trade knives."

"You sell knives?"

"Yes. I am a Cutlery Specialist. I have made knives, many knives. I started making them when I was young under my father's example. When I had enough to sell while on the road, we married and set off. We have been following the road, selling my wares, ever since."

"Cutlery Specialist you say? Hm. Interesting name."

"Knives, arrowheads, and darts are my specialty. I have many for sale. But you work the forge too, and have no need for any of my wares, only my money."

"How you journey through Daos? You don't know language."

"I know enough," said Irwin. The smith snickered—possibly detecting the lie. "I sold most of my items in Daos City. That allowed us to get this far. We are hoping to refill rations, pack for the colder seasons, and continue. We want to get through the pass before winter arrives."

The smith looked at his comrades and chortled. Again, he spoke Daosian, and the other two joined in his jubilation.

Irwin studied the three men. "The map I have says the road ends here perhaps, maybe up slope? I figure my map is old. Is there a road through the pass to Tresdahla? Or is Daos completely cut off from Uer Bin Territory?"

"Road ends in cave two days up. Miners go there. Iron comes here. Unless you miner, there nothin' beyond cave, only ice and death."

"No road to Tresdahla." Irwin calculated his next question. "Is there another way?"

Nonbry spoke of one. Maybe this man knows.

"Another way, yes. Up road you go, half day maybe, road turns hard right, old road goes forward through trees. Old road is wide enough for carts. There be caves down the slope, empty of iron." The blacksmith considered. "That be a warmer route."

I wonder if that is the road Nonbry spoke of; the one with cannibals.

"Thank you." Irwin said. "Should I stall my animals, or will you?"

"No." The smith then snapped at one of his two Clan-Duin workers. He turned back to Irwin. "What of your packs, saddles?"

"Yes. I hope we can leave those here, but we will take our belongings with us. There is an Inn here, correct? We would like to rent a room, maybe bathe."

"Only one Enok Inn." The smith pointed at three tall buildings across town—the ones Irwin had noticed when they were entering this dreary place. The Inn was the center building; a Saloon and Bath House mirrored the Inn.

"Do they usually have rooms, or might they be filled up?"

The smith shrugged. "Best food in town be there, stuffed quail, umm." He raised his eyebrows at the thought of a satisfying meal.

"That is good to know," Irwin said. "I know my wife would enjoy a meal that is not a ground rodent."

"Ah, they have them too! Served up in stew—mighty fine!" He pointed around the town, telling Irwin where all the best stores were located. "Mercantile has travel items, markets down at the river. They open when women come from fields. Your wife is lucky riding with you. If she is from here, she works the fields."

The shackled Clan-Duin servant hobbled out of the darkness into the light. None of his restraints were removed. His face, arms, belly, and legs were bruised. He had whip marks on his back. The shackles on his wrist and ankles cut him, and he had infected wounds along both areas. He appeared sickly and weak. His dark hair was matted, and his hazel-amber eyes kept to the ground except when the smith spoke at him.

"Thank you, master smith. I will be back later to fill my packs with foods from the mercantile and markets."

"Call me Auktun."

Yace watched as the timid Clan-Duin walked over to take Bodi's reins from her. Irwin followed, but stayed out of his way. Then he offered Yace a hand down from the saddle. "They have an Inn." He told her.

Her eyes darted to the enslaved Clan-Duin, to Auktun, then to Irwin. "We are staying the night here?"

He softened his grip but held onto her. "It is alright, Yace."

"No, it is not! Why is that man in shackles?"

Keep calm. He instructed her mentally. *There is nothing we can do about what we see. Remember, we are here to refill our ration bags and figure out where to go from here.*

Auktun lingered outside the forge, watching Irwin interact with Yace. He stared at her with greedy eyes again. "The men here like pretty flowers," said Auktun.

Yace shivered. *I dislike that man. I think he wants to take me from you.*

I will allow nothing bad to happen to you.

"The middle building is the Inn, correct?"

"Yes." Auktun pointed at the other buildings on either side of the Inn. "Bath House. Saloon."

"Does the Bath House clean clothes also?"

"Yes." He raised his eyebrows. "Beware the fiery ladies." A wicked smile crept onto Auktun's lips.

Yace stayed at Irwin's side. They followed the shackled Clan-Duin, tried to help him with the animals. He appeared intimidated by Irwin and Yace and stayed out of their way as they retrieved their personal belongings before he put the animals into stalls. They left the tack, panniers, and necessary camping items behind.

They walked, circumnavigating the town's center tent village. Many sets of eyes watched them—many of them were dirty, older, perverted miners perched outside tents leering hungrily at Yace. She kept her hood up, but a ribbon of blonde hair had trickled out, and wisps flew along the side of her indigo hood.

While they walked, Irwin took in the village of Enok. He glanced over his shoulder back at Auktun who watched them go. Unlike most of the towns and villages in Daos Territory—except Daos City—residences sat atop the local businesses. There were square towers at the entrances to Enok. A solitary Daosian man stood guard on each rampart. There were two gates, one on the west, and the other on the east. There were many shops—a tannery, mercantile, butcher, cobbler, tinman, and more. The smell of the woodworker's workshop and a bakery lingered in the air.

Down by the river, next to the Bath House, many of the local women were cleaning their own laundry. Only a few of the women raised their heads to keep watchful eyes on Irwin and Yace.

He held onto Yace, guiding her as they stepped up onto the covered walkway and ventured through the Inn's open doors. The large interior dining room appeared well-kept. There were a dozen tables. To their left, he noticed a parlor room, painted a bright blue with cushioned seating. The smell of a feast being cooked in the kitchen lingered in the air.

Two young girls were scrubbing the floor and did not look up to see the new patrons enter. A burly man who might be their father, a round Daosian man with a broad beard and squinting eyes, came from the kitchen into the dining space. He was cleaning his messy hands on his dirty apron. He walked with intent when he noticed Irwin and Yace. He stopped and shouted at the girls while pointing at the new guests. They both cowered.

Irwin held onto Yace to refrain from doing something he might regret.

The father faced Irwin and Yace. He greeted them in Daosian, "Ye hatan e o." Then he muttered something that made those girls flinch again.

Irwin could tell this man was badmouthing the girls. He asked, "Fan de du qian?"

The inn keeper's head twisted. "Where from?"

"North." He was happy that others knew the Hakran language in this tiny place.

"Why here? Search for work?"

"I am traveling the land with my lovely wife." He held her close. Yace forced a smile.

"You travel Daos with that Daosian tongue?"

"I speak enough to get by. I was told that some of the people here speak Hakran."

The Daosian man chortled. "We do. We be the only place this side of Daos City that does. You come to settle down in Enok?"

"No, we are just passing through."

The man laughed in the same way that Auktun had, as though Irwin had just told a funny joke. He looked at the women, his daughters—his faced reddened from being winded. The girls were not laughing. "Takes money to travel."

"I am a Cutlery Merchant. I trade knives for many things. Do you need a knife?"

The owner chuckled, "Cutlery Merchant. Enok is at the end of the road in Daos. Unless you stay, turn back now."

"We cannot. We are heading west to Ajihya. We do not want to backtrack."

The older man seemed jubilant. "Road ends in two days' walk, in a cave. Unless you are a miner, no reason to be there."

Irwin smirked. "Auktun told me of another way."

The Inn's Keeper's voice grew louder. "Ha-ha, yes, my friend, another way. Ha, ha." He nodded, wiped a tear from laughter off his cheek. Then his excitement toned down. "We have a few rooms; one views village or one the river."

The river view, please! Yace tugged on Irwin's arm.

"Village." He replied.

I want you to be able to see me when I leave the room.

You are going to leave me alone? Please don't Irwin!

"That is fifty silvers."

Kipp will be with you. You will be alright. What did this man just say?

Fifty silvers.

Irwin squawked, "I do not have fifty silvers!"

Not for a room in this place.

"Forty-nine!"

Irwin haggled, "Thirty." He had more than enough metal, but forty-nine was still too much. Anywhere else, a place like this would have been ten silvers.

"Forty-eight."

"Thirty-two."

"Forty-seven." The Innkeeper continued to bargain.

"Do you clean dirty linens?"

"No."

"How big is the bed?"

"Two can enjoy it," snickered the Innkeeper.

Irwin made up forty coins and handed them over. "This is all I have, unless you would like a cutlery blade."

"You could always sell your wife. She be a pretty flower; she bring you at least a pound of silver, maybe more."

"She is not for sale." He held onto Yace.

I dislike how he looks at me, Irwin.

Do not worry about this man. You are safe with me. He cannot hurt you while I am here. Trust me.

The Inn Keeper looked devious. "Follow."

I don't want to be left behind; I don't trust these people.

This is not something you should worry about. Besides, Kipp will be with you.

They followed the man into the parlor and up a set of stairs hidden behind a wall—up to the third floor, then to the end of the hallway. The bedrooms were small, and the bed was barely wide enough for one person to sleep comfortably. A small table and chair nestled near the head of the bed and a narrow chest of drawers crowded the other wall, clogging the room. The glass windows were open, dark curtains fluttered and kept out the sun's rays. The Innkeeper threw the curtains open, letting in the afternoon breeze.

"Piss pot here. When full put outside; daughters will clean and return."

"Thank you, sir."

The Innkeeper harrumphed and left their room. He had been paid, and that was all that mattered. The moment the man was gone, Irwin shut and locked the door with his metal.

"I really don't like it here, Irwin. Why must we stay?"

He pondered Yace as she placed her bag down on the sagging bed, and it sagged even more. "We need food, supplies, and time off our feet—perhaps a good meal too."

"This place scares me, Irwin."

"It scares me too, but we need—"

"Then why stay? Why stay! Kipp can catch food, and I can get better at-at something."

His hands cupped her face lovingly. "Yace, trust me." Their eyes locked. "We will not be here any longer than necessary. I do not trust one soul here to keep their hands off you."

"Then why must we—"

"Please Yace, trust me. You can stay here in the room. I can keep you safer here than out there."

"How can you do that?"

He stepped over to the window, looked for Kipp—this was the signal they had discussed earlier. "Kipp will be here to protect you. And I will retrieve all we need."

"I want to come with you."

"No. Not this time."

9

PRETTY FLOWER

Kipp landed on the saggy bed with a flourish and mutated into his two-legged self. "Dang me, Irwin, I don't like the looks of this place. There are Clan-Duin women in chains doing laundry at the river, and the Clan-Duin men in chains are out in the fields all hunched over. And-and that Clan-Duin boy at the forge who took the horses .... I thought my people weren't allowed in Daos?"

"It is obvious that this place is not like the rest of Daos," said Irwin. "But there is nothing we can do about it. This is how life is here."

"But my people—your people!"

"Kipp, we are going to see a lot of what we do not like to see here." Their eyes locked; they knew of the personal suffering, the slavery, and the human trafficking that happened every day in Daos Territory. But Yace did not know. "I need you to stay with Yace."

Yace grabbed Kipp's arm as he went through his bag, looking for clothes. "I don't want to be here."

"I don't blame you. I noticed men watching you and how they looked at you. Irwin, I wouldn't leave her alone."

"You will be with her."

"You think that's a good idea? Didn't you see what they do to people like me, like us?"

"I have laid a claim to both of you, so to speak. We have nothing to fear."

"Says the man who can't die."

Again, their eyes locked. "We need food." Irwin ignored Kipp's apparent fear. "We need our clothing cleaned. And no matter which way we go, we need more personal items—soaps and oils, brushes and sponges, clothes, linens, and such. I need to shop. You will both be safe here."

Yace sighed, "How can you be so sure?"

"Yeah, what if there's a T-E-L-L-E-A-E-P-P-A-P-A ...."

"Telepath?" Irwin laughed at Kipp's inability to spell. "Do you sense any?"

"No, but ...."

Yace's lower lip trembled as Irwin prepared to leave them. "Do not worry Yace. Kipp can break bones and rip heads off. I am not worried about you two."

"Thanks!" Kipp smiled doubtfully.

"You may not leave her side. And if she acts at all funny," Irwin summoned Yace's metal balls from her baggage, "hit one of these against your tattoo, or hers. I plan to seal the door so only I can enter and exit. If anyone comes knocking, just pretend you are not here. Your tattoos can open the door, if necessary, but you are safer in here.

"Until I return, take a nap. Please rest. If anything happens, I want you both well-rested. Later we will bathe. Alright Yace? I need it! So do you. It will make you feel better."

"You feel safe walking around by yourself?" Yace still looked worried.

"I will be fine."

"Yeah, I'm never worried about Irwin." Kipp said. "It's everyone else who should worry about him."

"Give me your dirty clothing. I will have it washed while I am out. And I will find you another dress too, and some better shoes than those slippers you insist on wearing."

"Why? I like them. And they feel good on my feet."

"Feeing good and serving the purpose of keeping your feet safe are two different things. I prefer your toes to stay on your feet and not be accidentally smashed by a horse."

"Roper moved his foot off mine the moment he felt me under him."

Kipp came to Irwin's defense, "He could've broken your toes!"

"Or rip one off. I have seen it happen."

Yace stared at Irwin. "Did it happen to you?"

"Yes, but my toe grew back. Yours will not," he said. "If I see anything at the markets you would want, what would that be?"

"Flowers. This room needs a change of air."

Kipp groaned, "Please don't talk like him."

"If I see flowers, I will bring them to you," Irwin said as he checked the contents of his laundry bag.

"Don't trust anyone here, Irwin," said Kipp.

"Do you want anything, Kipp?"

"Ale, if they got it, but I don't think they do."

"Alright, ale and flowers. Nothing else?" They watched him hold the door-knob, waiting to open it. "I will lock the door, and Kipp will be here. You will both be safe, I promise."

Kipp opened his mouth but held back—probably because he knew Irwin would chide him. Instead, he blew out air, then leaned into Yace. "You be safe too, Irwin."

Irwin locked the door and went down the stairs, laundry bags in hand. He went out onto the covered front porch and into the Bath House. Warm air blasted his face as he entered the inside foyer.

A middle-aged woman sat knitting on a stool. She looked up at Irwin and put her yarn and wooden needles down. "Ye hatan e o."

Irwin assumed this woman knew Hakran too. "I have two bags of clothing to be laundered. How much will that cost?"

"Ah, Hakerran! Yes. Yes. I saw you. Yes, I saw you with a female recently. Where is she now?"

"She is resting."

She has been watching us too. Creepy. Just like Auktun said.

"Ah! Resting." She cocked her head sideways. "Eighteen coins."

"Eighteen silvers? That is a lot for two bags of laundry. How about ten?"

"No less than eighteen."

"Fine, I will take my coins elsewhere." He turned away.

"Nowhere else does laundry."

"I can do it myself. I wanted to give you the opportunity to earn my coins."

"Alright, ten coins."

He made up the silver pieces in his pocket and handed them and the bags of laundry over to the nasty woman.

"Should be done by sunset."

"What about your bathing facilities? Are there individual rooms or tubs?"

"One large communal pool. It be gritty. Your pretty flower might not like it."

He sneered, "Thanks," then left the Bath House.

That is the third person to call Yace a pretty flower. This place is getting creepier every moment.

His feet flew down several steps, landing near the place where the locals were working on their laundry. Up the slope, there were barren booths and tables ready for the evening markets to open.

He went to retrieve a donkey and all his empty packs. He felt eyes on him, following his every move. He glanced over his shoulder and saw no one in particular staring at him. His eyes darted up to the rented room; the window coverings were closed—he felt his friends inside, stationary, resting.

His donkey, Nee Nee, was enjoying her meal and her time standing still. She put her ears back when Irwin stepped into the stall and pulled her away from a bundle of grass. He put the panniers on her back and pulled her along. He made her wait outside each store.

First, he went into the butchery and bought ten pounds of dried fish and venison. Again, the owner, a lanky butcher, spoke Hakran. The man bounced between languages while talking to his sons and Irwin. They did not haggle with Irwin and gave him—what he thought—a fair-price for the meats.

He moved on to the Tannery and picked up strings and swatches of leather for various projects. He watched the owner, a father, who was showing his two younger sons how to apply a bleaching agent to newly stretched hides. They haggled, but somehow Irwin ended up paying twice as much as he wanted.

Inside the next store, the tailor was sitting gazing lazily out the window—doing nothing. He came to life and jumped off his stool and moved toward Irwin. "Oh, hello, I've heard of you. You come from north; you have coin to spend. Come in, come in; what be your taste?"

Irwin surveyed the small room full of reams of material and clothes hung on racks. "Do you have any dresses for women?"

"No, I have dresses for men." He spoke sarcastically. "Of course, I have dresses for women. Where be yours?"

"Why do you care?"

"Why are you buying a dress for a woman? Do you know her size, her color preference? What length she prefers—long sleeve or short?"

"I know what my wife prefers."

"Come, come now. I'm just making sure you know what she wants."

He looked at the tailor, wondering if he was telepathic. He appeared to be Daosian, but ... *Could be a shapeshifter, like Yace. I hope not. He reminds me of that wagon dealer in Ahradah. That guy was a shifty Mortal, hopefully so is this one. He does not move around like a Telepath, but I will not stand near him.*

Irwin shrugged. "Please show me what you have."

They moved toward a painted chest of drawers. "We have wraparounds and pull-ons. We have all the colors." He opened a few drawers.

"Thank you. I will look through what you have."

The tailor stood behind Irwin and peered over his shoulder.

"Where is your wife now?"

Was he watching us too? This town is getting stranger.

"Napping."

"Oh! Do you know what color she likes?"

He did not appreciate having someone leering so close. "All of them." Irwin said, trying to ignore how pushy the tailor was being—trying to keep his focus on the task at hand. "Can you move, please? You are casting a shadow." He glanced at the window.

"Yes." The tailor hopped two steps to the right. "What be her measurements? If you know them, I can make something!"

"Thank you, but you do not need to bother. I am sure I will find something." He saw a dozen different shades of red, orange, yellow, and indigo, but no brilliant blues, greens, or purples—Yace's favorite colors.

He found a red and indigo skirt made from cuts of fabric and sewn together to make a checker-board design. The dark and bold colors were a great contrast, and the material looked to be perfect for colder weather.

Just in case we go up-slope, but Nonbry said down, so did Auktun.

Finding another skirt of pink and orange stripes—that wrapped around the midsection—it reminded Irwin of the meadow flowers he would see in the spring up in the mountains as a child. It looked large for Yace, but ....

She could wrap it around a few times before tying a bow with the strings.

Irwin bought those two and placed everything else back. He found a blouse that would match both skirts. Then a stack of brown work pants caught his eye. He grabbed a pair for Kipp and one for himself.

He paid a fair price for the items and was on his way out of the shop when the owner said, "Come again soon! Maybe bring your pretty flower next time."

He glanced over his shoulder after he left the shop.

Again, with the pretty flower. This guy is creepier than the last. I am not sure about this town. Keep calm, get what we need and be done.

After packing the clothing, he walked to the Mercantile. He tied Nee Nee up next to a water trough, and she took a long drink.

There were two sets of doors into the mercantile, the front counter between them. An older woman sat behind the bench sewing something while her husband and children were out on the sales floor managing supplies.

Irwin smiled at the woman, but she did not look up from her work.

Enok is something else. How these people keep talking about Yace ... even if she is a pretty flower. And the Clan-Duins in chains. At least they were not dead Clan-Duins. They allow Erthins to be here too, albeit working inside the Bath House. There seems to be more tolerance for Talented people here than anywhere else in all Daos Territory. Then why the fortress walls? Why keep Clan-Duins in shackles? I hate to think there is a Telepath in this place, but all signs point in that direction. Remain cautious. Be vigilant.

Within the large surplus store, a father and his three children—he gauged they were from seven to thirteen years old—helped move supplies around, creating a display. Irwin tried to ignore them watching him. He examined the aisles, picked up the necessary items, and looked over other things while thinking about Yace and Kipp.

He wanted to be extravagant and get something for everyone, but Irwin was not as rich as he had once been. What metal he did have he stole upon entering Enok while standing near the hot ingots. The forge had many pounds of metal, and insignificant amounts had trickled into his flesh without anyone knowing. He hoped that the mercantile owner did not excessively charge for goods, though he probably did.

There were piles of thick hemp tunics at the far corner of the store. He wanted to get Kipp a warm shirt.

Which route will we take? Nonbry said to watch out for cannibals when we last talked to him, back in Daos City. I am not sure I want to go into the land of cannibals.

He rummaged through the piles of tunics, trying to find sizes that would fit him and Kipp. He found a small pair of thick mining pants for Yace—they all needed to be prepared for whichever route they took and what it would be like along the way.

From the corner of his eye, Irwin spotted a smaller child he had not accounted for. Her dark black hair and matching eyes were a stark contrast to her yellowish skin tone. The young child's hair was in high ponytails above her ears. She stared at Irwin with studious black eyes.

"Hello," he said, and the girl jumped. "I am sorry. I did not mean to scare you." She squealed and ran toward her family.

The eldest son came around the aisle corner; he appeared angered and sternly spoke Daosian at Irwin.

"I am sorry; I did not mean to scare your sister."

The teenaged boy grunted, turned, and went back to helping his father. Irwin continued to amass all the items he was looking for.

Get what we need and get out of here.

He found bags of nuts and grabbed two. Dried fruits were not as plentiful as he was used to, so he stuffed his satchels with dried strawberries and raisins. The baggage was heavy by the time he was at the front counter.

The wife and children had vanished; only the father remained. He had a mustache, and its ends twisted into upward coils, and a short, well-kept beard. His salt-and-pepper hair was pulled back in a ponytail.

"I hear you come from Daos City?"

"You must have spoken to Auktun."

"Yeeaassseee."

Irwin paused. He studied this man who appeared to be all Daosian, like everyone else he had interacted with here.

"We talk about your pretty flower."

Those words unnerved Irwin, sent a prickle down his spine.

This has to be telepathic play. No other way to explain any of it.

He began pulling out the amenities he planned to buy. Stacking things in piles, Irwin hoped that this man would be prompt with the sale.

"She for sale?"

"My wife? No."

My patience is being tested.

The store owner looked over the piles of clothing and bags of perishable and non-perishable items. "I hear you go west. You take summit or jungle?"

"Jungle, probably."

The owner chuckled. "Maybe you sell wife, she stays here, you go west."

He stopped stacking all the items onto the counter and asked, "Would you sell your wife?"

"Depends. What be your offer?"

Irwin shook his head. "Do you sell spirits here? Alcohol?"

"The Saloon be only place to buy." He snickered, "Best potato wine!"

"Potato wine? What type of alcohol is that?"

"Clear kind." The owner chortled and looked over the things Irwin wanted to purchase. "For all this, five pounds silver."

Shocked by the offer, Irwin replied, "All this is worth maybe one and one-half pounds, not five."

"Four."

"One and one-half."

"One and a half—alright, one and a half!"

I dislike this town, these people.

He reached into his bag, made a rock of equal weight, and placed it on the counter. "I believe this is one and one-half pounds." Irwin knew it to be true; he waited for it to be weighed.

"It be all silver?"

"Yes." He replied, knowing that it was not solid silver but mixed with iron.

The rock weighed true; one and one-half pounds. "Many thanks." The greedy owner stuffed it under the counter.

"Thank you." Irwin put everything in his bags. There was more than enough food and supplies to keep them going, no matter which road they took.

Back outside, he glanced at the stables. The horses looked to be sleeping, eyes closed and dozy-eared, but Jenn Jenn was watching Nee Nee being taken from store to store.

Next stop was the cobblers' shop. It was a small L-shaped area with a display of men's shoes and boots at the door. The cobbler sat by himself, a tobacco pipe firm in his lips, his eyes reddened from smoking. He was a skinny, gray-haired Daosian man. He nodded and raised his pipe to acknowledge Irwin as he entered the shop. He slurred, "Ah, the traveler, where be your wife?"

Irwin glared at the man.

There is definitely telepathy at play here.

"Do you make boots for women?"

"Ah, I make boot for anyone who want boot. My best boot be worker boot." He pointed at the tent village. "Tough for rock. Women, eh, flat shoe?" Then he pointed at a small wall-mounted display of sandals and slippers.

"I am hoping for a boot or tough shoe, no slippers, and small enough for a female foot."

"Child boot." The cobbler pointed over his left shoulder at a small pile of children's boots. From what Irwin understood, boys as young as ten were put to work in the mines. And if they lived long enough, they were allowed to return home, old and worn out.

Not seeing anything that thrilled him, Irwin said, "I will come back with my wife. She will want to try them on, make sure they fit. Thank you for your time."

He stepped down from the cobbler's door front and looked at Nee Nee. She appeared tired; meanwhile Jenn Jenn was still tracking them. Irwin and Nee Nee passed the tall tower and western gate where there were a few more shops with residences above; they wandered around the tent village, along the raised wooden walkway which connected the Saloon, Inn, and Bath House. He glanced up at his rented room's window, the curtains still drawn closed.

I do hope that they are sleeping.

He felt their tattoos unmoving and close to one another. He went to see the markets—still closed—then went to buy some bread.

10

Locating The Telepath

Back at the Inn, he opened the door to their room. Yace and Kipp were sitting on the bed. They were talking and tears streaked down her face. When she saw Irwin, she jumped up and threw her arms around him.

"Oh, Irwin! I had a horrible nightmare about you." She said, sobbing.

Kipp grimaced, watching Yace throw herself onto Irwin.

Irwin closed the door. Yace did not let go of him. "It was scary; you took me and gave me to some hands in a tent."

"I would never do that; I will always protect you from those hands and everything else."

Yace's sky-blue eyes widened. "You spoke to me in my mind in that dream."

"Were you asleep when you said I was different from everyone else?" asked Kipp.

She gasped; her eyes glistened with fear. "I said that out loud?"

Irwin touched both of his friends' arms and said, "I think there is a Telepath in town."

"Ya think!" said Kipp, peering at Yace.

"I have not seen him or her." He shook his head at Kipp. "But several of the store owners seemingly knew about me. Some of my interactions have been alarming and made me wonder if you two were alright."

"We slept," said Kipp. "She jolted awake a few minutes before you arrived and began telling me of her dream."

Yace retold her dream to Irwin. "You and I went for a walk around the town, around the tents. I saw so many miners—gritty, stinky men—watching us. I could tell they were jealous of us. Then you said–you said ...." She looked at Kipp, apparently afraid to confess what happened next, but she did. "You said you wanted to bond with me and then the hands pulled me into a tent."

"You didn't tell me he wanted to bond with you!"

"Kipp, it is just a dream," said Irwin.

Yace's lips quivered. "It felt real."

"I am positive there is a Telepath living amongst these people. I do not know where they are." He wanted a moment alone with Kipp to tell him everything he had witnessed, but he was fearful to leave Yace alone.

I am wondering if it is the same person manipulating the whole town.

"I have not seen any telepathic types," he said, "but I am on high guard around these people."

"Maybe that's why she had the weird dream," said Kipp.

Irwin tried to nod without Yace noticing.

She stared lustfully at him. Irwin held her arm, but then let go. "I got everything on my list. I also found a few things you two did not ask for—dang it!"

Both Yace and Kipp jumped at his outburst. "What?"

"Your flowers." Irwin said as he remembered the one thing Yace had asked for. "I knew I was forgetting something."

"What about my ale?"

"I have not yet made it to the saloon, and that is the only place to purchase alcohol." He looked at Yace. "But first we must stop at the cobbler's shop. He has boots that should hopefully fit your feet."

"You found some?" she asked.

"They are in the children's pile, but hopefully one of those pairs will fit. And I found wintry weather pants in case we need them, and a few tunics. Oh, and Yace, I found these skirts." He pulled all the items out of a sack. "I know you are not fond of—"

"Oh, these are lovely, Irwin!" She smiled at him and kissed his cheek. "Thank you so much."

"I also got a blouse to go with them."

Kipp cackled. "That looks like your old shirt, Irwin."

"That is what I thought too when I saw it. And some pants, maybe for riding in, or trekking up the slope."

"Trekking up slope?" Kipp raised a curious eyebrow. "We're taking the high road?"

"You said it is cold up there. I like warm weather, Irwin." Yace stared at her protector.

"Yeah, so do I," said Kipp. "I thought you said the road ends here on the map. Does it?"

"I was told it ends two days up the slope in a cave. There is no way over the pass unless we make one." He studied their reactions. "I think we will take the way Nonbry said we should take, although he did say that there will be issues. Auktun spoke about an old road about half a day up slope. He said it heads west, deviates from the main road at a hard right turn. There was something about trees for markers. It sounds like the route that Nonbry spoke of. I am hoping you, Kipp, can do some scouting for us this evening. That way, we are prepared for tomorrow."

"Sure." Kipp then hand signaled. *Be watchful of Yace. She might be the Telepath you speak of.* He looked like he wanted to say more, but then mutated into an owl, jumped off the bed, and took flight out the window Irwin had opened for him. Since the urging from Irwin long, long ago when they were desperate and on the road to rescue Yace, Kipp had learned to change into almost any bird, dog, rat, or whatever.

"Be safe, Kipp."

After Kipp left, turned to a dot in the sky and then disappeared completely, Irwin turned to Yace. "So, you had a nightmare about me giving you to hands in a tent. Did you see any faces?"

"No."

"Did you hear any voices?"

"Only yours."

"What did I say?"

"You said something about women being treated unfairly, that you did not like it. You commented on the dress you bought me. Then you wanted to take me back to your cave. You wanted to take care of me. You wanted to bond with me; make love with me." Her blue eyes grew in intensity.

He cringed, then averted his attention to the brightly dyed skirts on the bed. They were not really Yace's colors. She had already pulled on the bright red blouse; it was a little large on her petite torso. Although the red highlighted her lips, it seemed too bright for her pale skin. "I hope you like those skirts and that blouse. I was a disappointed that they had no lighter blues, only dark indigo—nothing with greens or purple either, only red, pink, orange, and yellow—none of the colors you prefer."

"I like these a lot, Irwin." She put on the one that reminded him of the mountain flowers. "Thank you." She leaned in to kiss his cheek. "You are a rare man."

He blushed. "Thank you Yace. I do try to not be like everyone else. Men can behave badly—not care about women—it happens a lot."

"What are we going to do next?"

"Get you some boots."

She reached for his hand. Once they had contact, she spoke. *I love how kind you are to me.*

I have to be.

He realized she was attached.

Yace, I love you and want to protect you. You have been a tough mission to follow through with, and I will not give up until I see this end with a positive turn. See you reunited with your family. Understand?

Yace squeezed his hand and stared at him. *You are my family, Irwin. I see that now. I mean, not that I did not see it before. Handsome! It's just that I really want to be close to—I want to feel your body on me. Oh, you just excite me so.*

Irwin recoiled his hand. "Yace, you are my friend. That is how I see you. Almost like a sister."

"Irwin, I'm sorry, I just want ... what I mean is ... I really do appreciate everything you have done for me. I know there is no way to pay you back for all your kindness. Well, there is one I can think of. I just want you to know how much I appreciate you." She leaned in close.

He patted her hand. "It is alright, Yace. You have felt this way about me before; it will pass."

"What do you mean? I just want—"

Irwin was firm. "I am here as a friend, Yace, nothing more."

Her eyes fell to her hands. She looked ready to cry.

If only he could tell her the truth—that he liked men, that he loved Kipp. But he still had a hard time admitting it. To speak it out loud—and to Yace, as naïve as she was—he did not want to draw more attention. They had a ruse to keep. "You look beautiful in that skirt and blouse." He smiled and took her hand. "Let us find some fresh produce and get you some boots. The markets were filling with venders when I arrived back here." He knew Yace was easily distracted and used that to his advantage.

"You think they will have flowers?"

"If they do, I will buy you a bouquet."

Irwin opened the door for Yace, and they descended the stairs just as several miners were coming up. The stairwell was tight; and the grungy men tried to touch, even fondle Yace, but Irwin held her and glowered at them. He ushered her past them, down to the busy dining area. It smelled of fresh bread; baskets of small rolls were being placed on the tables by the daughters he had seen them cleaning earlier. The dining room was half full—all miners—sooty and unkempt.

Irwin and Yace hustled away from the inn and strode down the covered boardwalk between the buildings.

"It was over there that you gave me to the arms in the tent." Yace pointed.

"Let us not talk about that now." Irwin grabbed her outstretched hand. "No one needs to know about your dreams; besides, it was only a dream." They walked on. "In my mind, dreams are where we work out our personal problems." *Or try to get past agonizing parts of our lives.* "They are not real."

"I hope I did not say everything I said in my dream out loud."

"Why? What all did you say?"

They passed by the Bath House's front door. Yace blushed, "Things Kipp should not hear me say."

"Why?"

"They were meant for only you to hear. Not him."

"Look, Yace, I am not like any other man you will meet." He was nervous to talk about himself here and with her. "I do not have many friends. Beyond my Jennies, you and Kipp are my only friends. That is why I value everything you two do and represent. I know you do not appreciate some of the things Kipp does. You never did. Back when I first met you two, I know you had a fondness for me, and I see it returning."

She pressed against his side, her eyes only on him. "I value you too."

They found themselves in Enok's small market. Men stood by the produce that their women and children had picked. Dozens of thatched baskets full of produce sat out in the dwindling daylight. Fresh fish filled some of the baskets; one man worked with a modest fire and fry pan, cooking up orders while sitting on the ground.

There were several miners, and just as many locals, buying from the merchants. And just as many people were either inside the Inn or Saloon feeding their needs and desires. It was a normal evening in Enok; he imagined.

No one sold flowers in this market. He remembered seeing flower venders in Kobiton and in the larger Datzar Territory cities. All he had seen in Daos were poppy flowers; even those that grew wild across the river were poppy. He wondered if wildflowers might be rare in Daos.

She whispered, "What will you buy?"

Irwin picked up pieces of fresh produce, smelled them, and then put them back. He was eyeing the man cooking fish. A small line of people waited for a fishy meal.

"What would you like to eat tonight?"

"I don't know. I know I don't want to eat at the Inn."

"That is fine. It is a pleasant night to be outside." He noticed several locals pause to watch them.

She pulled Irwin up to a basket of pears. There were also two baskets of apples on display.

He asked in Daosian how much for a dozen apples and pears, then produced the monies. He pulled out a sack and had Yace pick the fruits. They took their bounty and continued to look over the local foods.

Yace took a large bite from one of the pears. "This is good," she said with a mouth full.

Irwin smiled lovingly at her. He wanted her to have a delightful night, wanted her to enjoy something different from the monotony of the road. "We can feed a few apples to the horses if you want."

Yace smiled lustfully at him, leaning onto his shoulder. "Yes. That would be nice." Her blue eyes still aglow, she watched his every movement.

"First, we need to stop at the cobblers before he closes."

Hungry, Irwin bought a strip of smoked salmon. He encouraged Yace to walk arm in arm. She finished her pear, and he ate the smoked salmon strip.

As they walked around the tent village in the center of Enok, he felt her shudder. "I will always keep you safe, Yace." He whispered, kissing her forehead.

Yace stayed tight against his side. From his periphery vision, Irwin watched the tents, saw men leering at her.

She licked her fingers after eating the pear. He finished the fish strip before they stepped inside the cobbler's shop. The front door was wide open, and opium smoke floated out. Seeing all the men sitting around, Yace tightened her grasp on his arm.

Irwin recognized the cobbler, the tanner, and the butcher sitting around after their hard day's work. They were enjoying the vapors. They all turned to watch Yace arrive.

The cobbler stood from his stool, spoke Daosian and gestured for Yace to follow him. The other two men continued to sit and speak amongst themselves. "I found supreme boot." He smiled greedily. "They be largest of small boy."

"Thank you." She bowed at him.

The boots had short heels and came up above her ankle. The leather was rough, unfinished, and had only four holes for laces. They did not look comfortable.

I can make modifications, make them fit you better if necessary. He told her through their contact. Then he said aloud, "Try them on, Yace."

The butcher brought his seat for Yace to use. The whole time, his greedy eyes were kept on her. She moved away from Irwin's touch to sit down.

It is like they have never seen anyone like her. How could they all be so hungered by her? Shit, maybe Kipp is right. Maybe she did something telepathic when we first arrived.

Yace has not shown any capacity for her powers yet, except with Kipp. And she could not have influenced them before we walked in. I have had contact with her the whole time. How could Yace be mentally manipulating these men? Or maybe she is emitting a scent to which I am unsusceptible?

He noticed their coveting eyes studying her.

Kipp said to watch out for her. Maybe he knows she can use her telepathy. I wish we had time to talk before I sent him off.

11

<u>Personal Desires</u>

The cobbler pulled off Yace's dainty slippers and offered her a pair of silken stockings to wear while trying on the boots. He helped place each foot into the boots. His eyes drifted up her pale legs and on up her skirt.

"Thank you," she said once the second boot was secured onto her foot. She walked around the shop to get a feel for the new footwear.

Irwin went to Yace. "How do they feel?" He took her hand.

How are you doing, Yace? Do you feel alright?

"These feel great." *You were right; these boots will protect my feet. She smiled and kissed him on his lips.*

Irwin wanted to jump out of his skin but knew to go with the moment. He saw her impulse right before her action, closed his eyes, and tried to look receptive to her affection.

She told the cobbler, "I would like to buy these please."

He opened his eyes and said, "How much?"

"Twelve silver."

"Seems reasonable." He stuffed his hand into his pocket and pulled out the exact change.

"Thank you, Irwin." Again, she kissed him and then leaned into his chest. "I love you."

He was unable to respond with anything other than, "I love you too," and kissed her back. He felt numb, held in place like a statue, sweat trickling down his back.

She knows we are pretending. She knows this is not real, right? With how she is acting, I am not so sure anymore.

He wanted to leave the cobblers that instant and go see his animals. He thanked the cobbler, took Yace's hand, and pulled her away from the shop.

"Thank you." She shouted to the shop owner as they went out the door. "Ouch." *Why are you being so rough?* "Stop." *That hurts.*

He threw away her hand. He was angered that she kissed him a second time and that he felt forced to continue the charade. But instead of being honest about his feelings, Irwin wanted to walk away and cool down. He did not want to make a scene or hurt Yace's feelings. But she had crossed his personal boundary.

"Did I do something wrong, Irwin?"

"No." But he thought, *yes, of course you did. I do not want you to kiss me, but especially in front of people!*

He had to chuckle to himself.

Here we are posing as husband and wife, but we are not that. I know I talked to her about this being a ruse, but it seems she has forgotten that conversation. I need Yace to understand that I am here to help, not to mate with. What am I going to do? Tell her the truth?

She had noticed his change in demeanor. "You say no, but how you say it, I hear yes."

Shit, can she hear my thoughts now too?

He stopped and turned to talk. "I am ..."

Should I tell her the truth? People are watching. We have to keep up the ruse.

He huffed deeply before whispering, "... I am not used to intimacy. You startled me back there, and I am just–just trying to get past the moment."

"I'm sorry Irwin; I didn't know. You never told me."

"I never thought it would come up again." He did not want to talk about his past. It was as brutal as hers. "The old you knows." He covered his face, his anguish.

I am an asshole for saying that.

"What I am trying to say is that this has nothing to do with you; you did not know. Please do not be offended."

I hope that is good enough.

"I'm sorry Irwin."

"Do not be."

Breathe, be calm, redirect the conversation.

"Let us go feed our animals some apples."

"They would love that!" She grabbed his hand.

He did not want to hold her hand, but noticed men staring at them. He refrained from thinking, and they walked over to the partially covered stalls. The sky's bright colors softened; the sun now vanished behind the western mountain range.

They heard a ruckus going on at the saloon; men were fighting and rolled through the doors and out onto the porch, tumbling down the stairs. Yace gasped, then whispered, "Do we have to go to the saloon?"

He dropped her hand and turned away from the calamity. "Potato wine does not sound tasty. I am not sure they will have ale, but Kipp wants something to drink."

"What is wrong with water?"

"It does not allow one to loosen up, so to speak. We will take a jug and see what we can buy. We will not stay long." He pulled out an apple, sliced a few wedges, and ate two.

Yace turned away from the noisy saloon. Irwin passed her an apple wedge. She handed the slice to Nee Nee. "What is potato wine, anyway?"

"I have heard of it but never tasted it. I am guessing that it might be like moonshine."

"Moonshine?"

"Moonshine is a hard alcohol, hard meaning it will get you drunk with one sip. We used it with dynamite to blow up sections of caves when I was growing up."

"Dynamite? What is—"

"Dynamite is an explosive."

"You drank explosives?"

"The moonshine occasionally, yes."

"Oh. Do you think they will have Kipp's ale?"

"I hope so." He cut more wedges. "I bought Kipp a flask of ale back in Daos City, but we had to leave much behind when we rescued you. Although he retrieved our bags, he could not bring back all our purchases. Most likely, the Psychic Attendant used the food and drink as collateral for retaining our belongings.

"Would you want to go to the saloon first, or retrieve our clean clothing and take a bath?"

She smiled up at Irwin. "I want to do whatever you want to do."

An argument erupted inside the tent village. Men were grunting in battle; others were haggling over the winner.

He stared at her.

I want to be gone from this roughened place.

"I want to take a bath, but I am not sure I want to bathe where so many have been before. Miners are a gritty lot. I would much rather bathe upstream."

"I would prefer to be somewhere else too." She leaned into him. "With no one else but you around.

"Earlier, when I looked out the window, looking for you, I saw some of those miners taking their wives home. They grabbed them by the hair or by the wrist. I saw two men pick up one woman by her arms and legs. She fought them, screaming. It was like she didn't want to go."

"They are not wives."

"What are they?"

Yace had seen an ugly side of humanity. Irwin could tell those images had shattered parts of her innocence. "Those women were ..."

How do I say this without shocking her more? Yace is an adult. She can handle this.

Can she?

"... they were given to those men for the night."

"Given for the night?"

"Well, they were paid for."

"Paid for?" Her blue eyes wanted to know. "Why would they be paid for?"

He huffed and averted his gaze. "The short story, those women are whores. I guarantee most of them don't want to be here, to be a part of this. They are rented out for the night for men to enjoy sexually."

Her blonde eyebrows came together. "What is the long story?"

"In Daos, and other parts of the world, women do not live freely like men." He looked over her shoulder at the tent village. Women were screaming, crying, and men were jubilant, incoherent, and rough.

Yace looked over his shoulder toward the animals, then glanced in the direction Irwin was staring. The screams and violent noises persisted. Irwin tried to speak over the howls. "Many men mistreat women. They treat them like they are less than equal. You and I have had many discussions about this subject in the past; back when we first met. I did not understand this inequality back then. Unfortunately, only men can break the cycle. And until that happens, there is nothing we can do."

"Why are men allowed to be like that?"

"This type of behavior has been ingrained into society. Some men do not care about the well-being of others, they only care about themselves and how they can work things to their advantage. And women are not as physically strong; that is not to say women, you, are not tough. Oh, you are very tough! But this comes down to physical strength and men have that one power over women."

"But you are not like that, Irwin. You care."

"And so does Kipp, for the most part. Those men over there, in those tents, they only care about one thing."

"One thing? What is it?"

"Personal pleasure." She held a perplexed look on her face. He explained, "These men do not know better. This is what they were taught. They are stupid in their ways, uneducated. They do not think beyond themselves, beyond their personal desires. They are not empathic like women can be. They are linear thinkers who go forward with their dicks out trying to find a target."

"You are not like that. There must be others like you."

He chuckled. "There are men like Kipp, who, although he thinks about sex a lot, he is not a cruel person. He cares about women, and he cares deeply about you."

"He thinks about sex all the time, with me and other females. There is no one like you, Irwin."

"I met a man like me. Once. Well, there have been others. But he ... he was not driven by his genitals so much. He was an asshole of a man and did not like other people. But he was an Empath, so he had it in himself to be kind, understanding. He did not want to, except a few times. Of course, he did grow up in a place not suitable for children."

"An Empath? What's an Empath?"

"Our friends, the ones from the palace who stayed in Daos Prime. Many of them were Empaths."

"I barely remember them."

He gazed off. "Jorge cared about women. He did not bed with them but understood the hardened lives they had endured. The two of us talked about equality amongst all sexes. He believes women are superior to men. I kind of do too."

The moon was up, and it shined on the two friends in the road.

Someone who had been screaming inside the tent village for a long time was finally silenced.

"I'm glad you are not like those men, Irwin. I think that is why I love you so much." She said, pressing forward to kiss him on the lips again.

He pushed her back. "Yace, please."

"But I thought you loved me!?"

"It is not that I do not love you, Yace. It is just that I like men." There. He said it again.

"Of course you like men; you are one."

"No. I like men; I prefer to kiss a man."

Yace looked ready to cry. "Am I a terrible kisser?"

"No, Yace, I did not say that. Your lips are soft, but they are not what I want to kiss."

"But you said I'm beautiful, and you have been so kind and affectionate. I do not understand why you said all those wonderful things. Why would you be so nice to me and not want to kiss me?"

He whispered his confession. "I am in love with Kipp. I have been since, maybe, the first day I saw him. Maybe it was two days after, I do not remember exactly. All I know is that Kipp is unlike any other person I have met who is my age. I feel like I have a connection with him, and that is what I have always wanted.

"But guess what? He loves you. And his love for you is unwavering. He would give his life for you. And here you are, lusting after me. I love you, Yace, but my love for you is more adoration and respect than anything else." Her eyelashes held back tears.

"You were the first woman I met—after Saryh—that allowed me into your world. I had never known women before you. I had no mother. I mean, I did, and that is how I came to be. But one did not raise me, my great grandfather did. I had not met any females until I was an adult. When my father thought I was old enough to .... Back then, I was taught that women were only for procreating with—to make children. I did not know you had minds, souls. I did not know you are these amazing Beings that you are better than men in so many ways.

"Yace, you have taught me so much about females, especially now that we have been reunited. In my mind, I could not live without you, but on a soul-fulfilling basis. Do you understand?" He paused, and she stared off at nothing. "You are someone who I have always wanted in my life, but not in a sexual way—in a more nurturing, holistic way."

A tear dripped from her eye, and she moved to hug Irwin, not to kiss him. "I love you more than I love Kipp, maybe for the same reasons you love me, maybe more." She kissed his neck and pulled away. Her eyes were wet, but a big smile lit up her face.

He felt awkward now. "Apple slice?"

She giggled, took the slice, and ate it. "I think we should go see about finding Kipp's ale."

"That is a good idea. Hey, have you been feeling alright? I asked you earlier, but you ...."

"Alright meaning?"

"Telepathy? Hearing people's thoughts?"

"Only when I'm with you."

"So only my thoughts and Kipp's?"

"Yes."

"What about sensing anyone else doing telepathy?"

Yace shrugged. "No, not that I know of."

"Good."

Then I guess all of that was just men acting lustful, not telepathically manipulated.

"We will stop off at the saloon after we retrieve our clothing. It should be done by now." He pointed at the darkening sky.

12

<u>ONE WILD SALOON</u>

The sky had been the same colors as Yace's skirt earlier that evening, but now it was completely dark. It would be a clear night—no clouds or impending storms. They walked away from the animals after one last friendly pet and retrieved two large flasks for whatever alcoholic spirit they could buy at the saloon. Irwin hoped they had ale. He also hoped there would be whiskey but would purchase the potato wine if not. And if he didn't like the taste of that spirit, he could use it as a disinfectant or cook with it. That was why Irwin preferred whiskey, because he could do all three of those things with it.

They walked past the dimmed woodworker's alcove. The bakery was also closed, but the smell of baked bread permeated the evening air. People were still screaming, fighting, and hollering from inside the tent village. Some stood quietly around campfires, roasting food, or just staying warm—most of the noises came from inside the tents.

Above the stores where there were residences, you could hear sounds of children. They had seen none running around playing in Enok, and probably would not. They heard giggling and fun making from above, but also cries and tired shouts. Mothers scolded or comforted their children while no doubt trying to make it through another tough night.

These were the same scenes he and Kipp had seen all along their way to rescue Yace. The same scenarios over and over, the same sob stories of families trying to live while being subjugated—oppressed by an uncaring empire. These people had no sparkle in their eyes; they lived in fear and desperation. They had not seen one happy face on any of the roads inside Daos Territory—it was only within the capital city of Daos (where Daos Prime was located) that they had seen one single sparkle of joy.

Irwin offered Yace his arm as they ascended the steps to the Bath House. The warm air inside was a comfort after the cool breeze outside. Their clothing was folded, packed, and ready for pick up. Even the bags had been washed; everything smelled and looked clean. It was clear that Yace was delighted to have clean clothing—not just spot rinsed as it had been in past days.

They stopped at the Inn to drop off their fresh baggage. The dining room was full of hungry miners, but the two of them did not stay to eat with the locals.

They returned to the covered walkway. Although it was dark outside, the town was lit with oil lanterns, candles, and campfires. Approaching the saloon, they could hear the loud conversations coming through the wide-open front doors. Through one of the many windows, they saw a common-looking saloon where all the patrons were miners, pale-skinned Daosians—a few faces from other places—and all were dirtied from their days' labor in the mine. Very few of the women who were dancing and writhing on a stage were pale-skinned, most looked to be half-breeds—partially Daosian, partially Talented. All were naked.

The saloon servers were Daosians, also naked, and clearly beleaguered by their labors. The menacing men were all dressed in days' old clothing—matted hair, bushy facial hair, and grungy clothing—and the barroom was a sea of dirty, smelly men. Many had missing teeth. Some were scarred by the sun; others had scars and injuries from fights.

Though the barroom was chaotic, they walked toward the main doors, ready to enter. Yace gripped Irwin's arm. She pulled him to a stop and took a deep breath.

Right then they witnessed a half-breed bar-wench squeeze her tit and beat a man upside his head with it.

Are we really going in there? Yace was pulling back.

For Kipp's ale, yes. And maybe some of that potato wine. If it is anything like moonshine.

Does he really need it?

They heard the crack of a fist fight and watched a man fly out the front doorway. He crash-landed, unmoving, onto the boardwalk. No one came to see if he was alright. The beaten, haggard miner appeared to be dead. Streaming in and out of the saloon, several men stepped around the body.

I will keep you safe. They cannot hurt me, and I will let no one hurt you.

He felt her shake. *How can you be so sure?*

The beaten miner lying on the walkway moved. He rolled toward them, spit out blood and a tooth. He rose to his knees.

Yace's mouth dropped wide-open, watching the man recover. *What the shit! I thought he was dead.*

Please take a deep breath, Yace.

Irwin instructed her while doing that himself.

These people are not as bad as they appear. But with that in mind, please be ready for anything.

Her body continued to quiver. *I'm not going in there, Irwin!*

Do not worry Yace. You are safe with me.

He repeated this a few times. He had to remain calm for Yace.

Breathe. Please breathe.

She repeated, *Irwin will keep me safe.*

Once he felt her posture soften, they moved closer to the open doorway. All his senses were on guard, and using his powers, he began assessing the room and its occupants.

There are ten Erthins in here. Three Fire, one Wind, two Spirit, four Earth. There is a Fire Erthin next to the door, right side. Three are in this room, everyone else is upstairs. Keep calm, stay focused.

The barroom was filled with ornery miners riling each other up and getting drunk. Crossing the threshold into the saloon, the bar quieted down, and some of those toothless faces turned to take in the outsiders. Many put their hands on knives and daggers, and they were ready to use them.

The bar was over in the corner. They walked toward the bar but did not see the telepathic barkeep until he turned and smiled a wily grin at them. The large wooden counter the Telepath stood behind was L-shaped, and most of its stools were already taken by locals. Daosian women stepped away from the bar with trays full of mugs of liquor, but stopped mid-stride—their eyes locked onto Irwin and Yace. More and more people fell silent, all attention now focused on the two strangers.

Yace's long platinum-blonde hair was held back by her shoulders. She glanced at Irwin. They found the Telepath—the mastermind behind all the caustic conversations that had been endured during today's shopping spree. He was middle-aged, but well-kept, as most of the Ishik family members were. He grimaced, and his blue eyes shifted to Yace and beheld her.

Irwin realized this man was attempting to gain access to her, but his Metalist powers prohibited any telepathy. His hold on her remained tight. No one in the bar seemed to notice, or care, that the barkeep was telepathic. There apparently was no cause for alarm that a blue-eyed man was controlling everyone in town. Only Irwin knew what was going on.

The saloon fell eerily still, and Irwin felt sweat on his brow and on Yace's hand that gripped his.

He knew they were close enough to the door to escape, but not far enough to outrun the men trained on them.

Remain calm. He instructed Yace, then said aloud, "Ye hatan e o. I have come to purchase ale."

"You're not welcome here, Outsider," said the Telepath. "But your pretty flower is."

The male fire wielding Erthin standing guard at the door stepped up and grabbed Yace's right arm. She screamed and jerked away from the Erthin's grasp, "Irwin!"

He did not let go, nor did he allow the fire Erthin to take her away.

Irwin felt where every piece of metal was hidden or in plain sight in that room, on every person, on every floor. He also had a secure hold on the Erthins in the room, and upstairs too. Two were stepping around some of the patrons, moving toward him; one was wind, the other was earth.

The Telepath chuckled, and automatically all the men in the room echoed the jubilation. "I know who you are, Samuel Irwin Miner," he snickered. "You don't scare me. I'll take back my cousin now and turn you to dust."

Irwin chuckled, "You do not know me." He snapped his fingers and the male Erthin next to Yace ceased to be—instantly turning to dust, his molecules floating around Yace and into Irwin's flesh.

Once free from the Erthin, Irwin spun Yace into his chest. He buried her face in his shirt. She looked up at him with horror in her eyes—scared by what she had just witnessed. "Say goodbye to your cousin," Irwin whispered.

Before Irwin released his wrath, the Telepath sent out a message to everyone in the barroom. Kill them!

"Goodbye cousin." Yace said, as Irwin pushed her head against his chest.

Take a deep breath, he instructed Yace, but she hyperventilated.

He had power over all the metal that surrounded them—the men he felt running toward them, weapons in their outstretched hands, satchels of coin fixed to their hips, jewelry on their fingers and ears—all of it was at his disposal. Irwin pulled for it to surround Yace in a protective bubble—like what he had made for Kipp when they escaped Ahradah. He had to keep her safe from the push of Erthin energy he was producing deep inside his body.

He used the recently absorbed Erthin to help charge his power. Harnessing both his Erthin and Metalist powers at the same time felt easier now than before—Irwin was becoming more fluid with his abilities, with his potential.

He summoned a bout of Erthin air, pushing all the doors shut. That air had knocked down those closest to him, although others continued to charge. With a flick of his fingers, the doors locked. No one would get out of this alive—except him and Yace.

They yelled at him, ready to kill, but those shouts changed to screams of men dying. He pulsated out a blast of fire, and those attempting to harm him were set ablaze. Those closest were turned to dust, while others across the room jumped through openings, trying to flee from the fast-moving inferno.

Outside the saloon, Irwin felt Kipp land close by. He turned his head, looked out the window, and saw his Clan-Duin friend mutate into his two-legged form. They saw each other. He put his hand up and yelled, "Stay back, Kipp!"

"What the fuk, Irwin!" Kipp could see the fire, smell the death and destruction. "What the fuk have you done?!"

"Get our belongings," he commanded.

It only took a short time before the men in the tent village came to life—instantaneously sobering up and running toward the saloon that was now ablaze.

Irwin watched Kipp mutate and fly away from the frenzy. Men from the rooms upstairs tried to come down. He saw them retreat to the second floor, possibly hoping to jump out the windows above. None of the Erthins from the upper floors came down to stop him or the fires—only the miners outside appeared ready to do something. Many of them raced to the river to retrieve buckets of water, not knowing how the fire happened, but ready to help snuff it out.

He pulled back the metal cocoon and allowed Yace a breath—to see the destruction he wrought. She took in the blazing mess. Heat radiated from every direction, except Irwin's body—he was cool to the touch. "Are you alright?" he asked, placing a chilly hand on her cheek.

She shook beneath his touch. "What did you do?" She was taking in the burning tables, chairs, charred bodies, lit window coverings, and the engulfed ceiling and walls. Around them there was no fire—they were unscathed. "Holy shit, Irwin, what did you do?"

He took her face between his hands to keep her focused on him. "We are going to leave now." He took her hand and pulled her toward the door, but Yace refused to move.

"What did you do?" She tried to pull away from his grasp.

"You are safe; that is all that matters to me."

She sobbed. "You killed everyone!"

"No. Not everyone." He snapped his fingers, and the doors opened.

They heard men shouting outside the saloon, beyond the inferno. Irwin felt people coming to see what was happening—coming toward him. Soon they would be entangled with angry locals.

"We need to leave, Yace, right now." His grasp tightened on her wrist.

"I am not going with you!"

"Yace, please do not struggle."

"You are hurting me. Don't hurt me."

He turned her arm in a way that made Yace twist away from the pressure and into his body, the back of her head against his chest. He wrapped his arm around her midsection. Holding both of her wrists now, Irwin picked Yace off her feet and walked toward the open doorway. She wiggled like a fish in his grasp. "Let me go!" She was hyperventilating now. "Let me go, Irwin, please!"

"Yace, calm down. I will not hurt you."

Men approached from every direction.

"You're a monster!" Yace shouted. She kicked backwards toward Irwin's shins and groin. She leaned against his arms, pressing for freedom.

"Yace, please do not resist."

She was frantic, as was he.

The locals were closing in. Many of the men were two steps away when Irwin threw up a metallic barrier around himself and Yace. Hundreds of metal objects, mostly jagged pieces, began orbiting them, slicing into anyone who came near.

Yace did not stop her flailing or screaming. "Where's Kipp! Kipp! Kipp, help me!" She looked to the sky. "He's going to kill me, Kipp!"

Stop freaking out, Yace! Please. There is no reason for it.

Irwin made a quick decision to put Yace to sleep.

I do not want to do this.

Her body went limp in his grasp.

He hoisted her further up in his arms and walked down the stairs, around the tent village, and straight to the stable yard. No one could stop him. He would not allow it. Kipp was circling above.

"Get our belongings!"

Irwin radiated his metallic force field, killing anyone who stepped in his way or who dared to attack. With Yace in his arms, he left a trail of bloody parts and pieces—bodies littered the covered walkway, down the stairs, across the dirt and gravelly ground, around the west side of the tent village, and straight toward the stable yard. The west side roadway was completely blood-stained.

He held Yace tight, fumbling with her body a few times, trying to keep her from falling. Her skirts were soft and hard to hold.

Finally, Kipp landed with baggage. The Clan-Duin quickly donned on clothing he could ride in and readied the animals; the horses first, then the donkeys. Irwin held sentry duty, held Yace, and kept the natives at bay.

"What happened to Yace?" asked Kipp from across a horse's back. "Why was she screaming for me?"

"She became frantic after I killed her cousin and lit the saloon on fire."

"Her cousin?"

Irwin glanced at Kipp and nodded. "I found the Telepath!"

"Her cousin." Kipp paused and then went back to tacking up the horse.

"Yes. He looked Ishik—platinum hair, pool-blue eyes. He used an Erthin to take Yace from me, and that was all I was willing to put up with."

"You killed half the town because of that?"

"That Telepath has control of the whole town; this whole place was at his disposal. That explains why everyone spoke Hakran and why they all kept calling Yace 'pretty flower'."

"Pretty flower?"

"I will tell you about it later. For now, get everyone tacked. Once you are in the saddle, I will help her up into your arms. You get her and the donkeys out of here."

"What about you?"

"Do not worry about me. I will be right behind."

All the ruckuses awoke Auktun. The large smith descended from his residence above the forge. He had three Clan-Duins—turned into canines—on the end of chains. They looked ready to defend the smith. Irwin was sure they would turn tail and run the moment he let them loose from their restraints.

A snap of Irwin's fingers, and the chains disappeared from the three canines. At first the large dogs were confused, feeling their metal restraints vanish. For only a moment, they were not sure what had happened. Suddenly all three turned on Auktun, descended on the master smith with vicious teeth, killing him instantly.

The two larger dogs then jogged off to create their own level of chaos. The third one, smaller, skinnier than the others, continued to consume Auktun's flesh and body, looking at Irwin a few times while devouring the smith.

Irwin was alright with the havoc he created. Although some of the Enok people had been kind to him, he did not appreciate what he had witnessed from this town.

Across the tent village, over at the Bath House, the fire Erthins, all women who cleaned and dried the town's clothing every day, had been brought outside to fight Irwin. Their owner had not seen the destruction already reeled. They did not yet realize he could assimilate every one of them.

An order had been sent out for those women to throw flames at Irwin, but he snuffed out their fires and those Erthins instantly. He was in no mood to deal with such disgusting people any longer.

Clouds had covered the moon, blanketing the sky in an ever-present darkness.

Slavery and racism are a plagued mindset here that needs to be eradicated. Sometimes I wish people were blind—born with no eyes—then all we could do is judge each other by our other senses. We would hear the words and feel the actions of everyone. Then people with Talents would not hide, and maybe Telepaths would be held accountable.

I am perfectly fine with this whole town burning to the ground. I have no remorse this time. Huh, just like at the palace when I killed every last Ishik.

I hope mindsets will change now that I have taken away those who created the prevailing hatred. All people should be free to just be.

He did not know how, but he knew it needed to happen.

Kipp jumped into the saddle, and Irwin helped push Yace up and into Kipp's arms. Roper and the Jennies were ready to go. Irwin would follow on Bodi.

He heard yipping from Clan-Duin dogs. But then came the sound of a man screaming and a dog viciously barking.

Jenn Jenn and Nee Nee kept in stride with Roper as Kipp kicked his steed into a swift lope away from the stables. Irwin summoned the western gates to open using his Metalistic power. It was then that the three Clan-Duin canines saw their opportunity to escape, too, and raced toward the wide opening in the towering wooden wall. Kipp and company led the way out of Enok, with Irwin and Roper on their heels. Once they were a good distance away from Enok, the Clan-Duin canines disappeared down the slope and into the trees.

Irwin stayed behind even though Bodi wanted to gallop off. He made sure his friends and those dogs escaped. By this point, less than half Enok was still alive, half as many were hurt or burned by the fires. The three-story saloon and its covered porch were ablaze. If the fires were not contained, the entire wooden complex—the Inn and Bath House included—would also burn. Unfortunately, there were no Water or Fire Erthins who could summon water and put out fires left alive. There was no way Irwin would turn a kind heart toward the menacing people of Enok. He genuinely believed that they should burn—especially the men.

Once again, there was blood on Irwin's hands, but this time he did not seem as mentally wrecked by the sight of it as he had been in the past when they were fleeing Ahradah, or the Ishik palace. Spurring Bodi into a gallop, he never looked back, never questioned the state of his soul.

13

<u>WICKED MAN</u>

After several kilometers of swift riding, they stopped. It was nearly midnight, and they needed to rest. Yace was still asleep in Kipp's arms. Irwin helped place her on the bed he had made for her on the ground. Neither man wanted her to wake before morning.

"She fears me now," said Irwin, watching over her. "Has every right to be."

"What are we gonna do about her?" Kipp stared down at the frail woman.

"I do not know." Irwin shrugged, also studying Yace asleep on the ground. "She grew up some tonight. She thought I was a caring, peaceful person. She did not expect to see me lay waste to so many people without regret."

"You don't regret it this time?"

"The women of Enok did not deserve to die. But they also did not deserve a life of servitude. They are better off dead."

"Wow! That's cruel."

"It is the truth."

"She won't be scared of you for long." Kipp spoke with resentment in his eyes. "She will get over all this and go back to wanting you."

"I do not think so, and I am fine with that. All her attention focused on me was too much." He chuckled. "I yelled at her for kissing me."

"She kissed you?"

"Yes. On the lips and in front of other people—other men."

Kipp's lips and eyebrows contorted. "What'd you do?"

"I saw it coming," said Irwin. "I had to allow it to happen. We had an act going! The men in the cobbler's store believed we were married, believed that Yace is my wife."

Kipp's jaw clenched, hands tightened into fists. He spoke through his teeth. "Is that what you told the locals?"

"With how lustfully they stared at her, I had to make sure she was safe. My first inkling was to tell them we were friends, but I know better. Like you two have said since I met you, people with Talents must have an act. I have always thought that was stupid until today." He sighed, staring at her. "Even still, I do not like to act against my own personal feelings, but she pressed."

"What do you mean?"

"She told me that she wanted to mate with me." He saw the heat in the Clan-Duin's eyes. "She thought I was in love with her because I was being so nice and thoughtful, but that is not the case."

"What'd you tell her?"

"The truth."

Kipp softened. "That you like men."

Irwin felt happy that Kipp was not put off by the truth. "Yes."

Kipp chuckled, "How'd she take it?"

"She was confused. She might have thought I was lying. I think she believes that people should only be attracted to the opposite sex. I do not think she understands that two people of the same gender can love each other. Animals do it all the time!" Irwin smiled at the sight of Kipp relaxing. "Who knows? Maybe her attention will turn back to you."

"Doubt it. Yace likes what she likes."

"I guarantee she does not like me now. I imagine she will be scared of me for a while."

"A lot of people are scared of you right now, Irwin."

"Are you scared of me?"

"No. Well, at least you didn't kill me." Kipp slapped Irwin's shoulder, chuckled, "But you busted up another good town!"

"That was not a good town, nor was Nuaki Village. I am glad that Yace was not hurt."

"Would that have happened?"

"No, but an Erthin tried to take her from me."

"How long did that Erthin live?"

"Not long."

"What about the Telepath?"

"I obliterated him right after the Erthin."

"Dang! I wish I could've seen it."

"I am glad you were not present." Irwin patted Kipp's shoulder. "I would have only been able to protect one of you." He returned his gaze to Yace. "I guarantee tomorrow will be a trying day for all of us."

"Yeah, we should probably get some sleep, huh?"

"Yes, we should."

Irwin awoke the moment Yace's tattoo began to move. She jumped to her feet. Irwin felt her looking at him and Kipp sleeping on the ground; the horses and Jennies were standing close by—also sleeping. He heard her squeal, and her booted feet pattered away up the road.

"She is up early." Irwin said, yawning.

Kipp mutated from his canine form and scratched his head. "She's trying to get away."

"Yes, but she is going the direction we want her to. Like I said last night, she will wake up angry and will most likely try to escape."

"Oh, that's why we parked the horses differently. Smart!"

"Yes. Let us get tacked up. We know which direction she is going."

"What if she back tracks, you know, cuts through the forest or something?"

"Then I will let you find her."

They were several hundred feet behind Yace, kept their distance, but could see her ahead on the roadway. At first, she did not notice them. She had been running, but tired out after about a kilometer and now walked slowly. They could hear her muttering and sobbing as she climbed up the gentle incline.

When the road turned a soft corner and she saw them, screamed, and took off running again. The horses caught up with her in no time.

"I'm not going with you!" She screamed over her shoulder.

"That is fine." Irwin replied, "We are not following you."

She turned, put her hand up, and said, "Stay back."

They stopped their horses. Kipp asked, "Or what?"

She was shaking. "What?"

"Stay back or what? What'll you do?"

"I am going home!"

Kipp asked, "'Going home', meaning?"

"Back to Daos City."

Kipp shouted, "Daos City is behind us!"

She stopped. "You can't be serious?"

"Yace, there is no going back to Daos City," Irwin said, "only forward. We are taking you back home, back to the Gypsy."

"I'm not going with you—either of you!"

"Yace," Kipp pleaded, "you're acting irrational." She had said those same words to him countless times.

"I don't trust either of you." She spoke over Kipp. "You, Irwin, you-you did the same thing to me that I've seen you do to Kipp. You put me to sleep. You're an evil man! A wicked man!" She tried to push past their horses, head back the way they had already come.

"I did what I had to do to get us out of there, Yace. You were in no state of mind to make good decisions."

"Good decisions? Good decisions!" Yace screamed. "You-you made horrific decisions last night. You killed everyone in that town! What did they ever do to you?"

"Na, he only killed about half the town."

"Kipp!" Irwin grumbled and turned to Yace. "I know I killed many people last night. Some were good people, but many were rotten people who got what they deserved."

"You don't care about anybody!"

"That is false, Yace. I do care. I care about all the women in that village, more so than the lecherous men they must live with. None deserved the lives they were living. They were only servants—the only life they knew. The world is cruel, but especially to women and people of Talent. I was trying to keep you safe from them, and your cous—"

"Safe?! You killed all those people, Irwin. You're a killer!"

Kipp's voice rose above theirs. "Do you know how many people Irwin's killed to save you?"

"Kipp please, do not—"

"What?" Kipp was inflamed. "She needs to know, Irwin! She's living in a fantasy world."

"She is not ready to—"

"You are both monsters! I was better off in Daos City. You two did not save me, you stole me! I want to go back!"

"We didn't steal you!" Kipp said. "You were beaten, raped, tortured; you were a concubine, nothing else. Do you even know what that means, Yace?" He spat.

"Kipp, we do not know what all happened to Yace inside the—"

The Clan-Duin did not back down. "You were owned, Yace, owned! Men could do with you as they wanted. They'd beat you, tie you up, fuk you while they were doing so, smack your face, and you could do nothing ..." Sitting high on his horse, Kipp spat again. "... Nothing! You couldn't defend yourself. If you did, they would tie you up, beat you more and leave you for dead. That's what happened to you when you were a child. That's how the Gypsy found you; beaten and broken and almost dead! You should be thankful."

Irwin wanted his friend to shut up. "Kipp, please—"

"You were a piece of meat when you were ten, just like you were a piece of meat at the Emperor's palace. Do you know that's how most men view women? As meat that they can buy and sell. We don't." He pointed at himself and at Irwin. "We saved you from that life. Irwin saved you. How dare you fear him!"

Irwin wanted to cry. "Kipp, please! This is not helping."

Yace sobbed, "I just want to go home."

Kipp jumped down from his horse and she ran to him and slapped him. "Leave me alone!" She moved around him—slowly edging away.

Irwin called to her. "Yace, we are taking you home, back to your mother—back to the Gypsy. That is where you need to be. Your mother, Dana, she misses you, Yace."

She edged around the donkeys and broke into a run.

"Yace, we are only trying to help you." Irwin wanted her to slow down, to think, to remember everything they had done for her.

She is not thinking, only reacting.

"Shit," he muttered, watching her run from them. He turned to Kipp. "I need to talk to her, and this time you are not allowed to speak."

Kipp placed his boot in the stirrup and swung up into the saddle. Both horses spun on their haunches and lurched forward into a lope. They caught up to Yace in a few strides. She screamed again, sped up her pace. The two men looked at one another.

Kipp asked, as they rode side-by-side, "Should I pounce on her?"

"No! Rope her."

"What, with Roper?"

"Rope her!" he said, pointing at the rope attached behind Kipp's saddle.

"I don't want to hurt Yace."

"You think pouncing would be better?"

They stayed a horse-length away. The tiny woman, with long platinum hair flying in her wake, was clearly not joking. Kipp slowed his horse enough to toss the rope around her body. She was pulled to a halt and began screaming again. "Someone save me! Anyone! Help! HELP! They're trying to take me away! They are going to rape me, beat me!"

Kipp and Irwin jumped down from their horses. Kipp kept the rope tight, pulling Yace toward him.

Her screaming turned to crying. "I want to die!" She fell to her knees.

Irwin knelt at her side and was tender with her. Kipp stood over them, gripping the rope, listening to the quiet exchange.

"Yace." Irwin wanted her to look at him. "Yace, please, I do not want to cause you more distress." He waited for her to acknowledge him. Her hands were over her face, and she was still sobbing. "I have not hurt you; we have not hurt you. We are always kind and helpful, and have been here for you the entire time, Yace. Always and forever, we are dedicated to you."

"It's all a lie—a ruse. You-you told me none of this is real." Her reddened eyes peered at him from behind her slender fingers.

"When I told you we would need to pretend to be husband and wife, I was sure you understood we were pretending; that was indeed a ruse. I have always been kind to you. That is who I am, who we are. You know Kipp and I are good people; you know that our actions have always been real. How we treat you has always been real. We are your friends, Yace, we are here for you. We have gone through so much for you. You do not remember our long journey to search for your father, but we both hope that you soon will." He ran his slender fingers through the dirt. A grasshopper with an injured leg came and rested next to his leg. Irwin scooped the little creature into the palm of his hand and cupped his fingers as though to protect him. In a flash, he healed the injured grasshopper and placed him back in the dirt where it would be obvious the injured leg had been restored.

Yace was unimpressed. "Friends don't kill."

He stared back at her, fingers still shielding her face in a gesture of defiance.

After listening to a few quiet sobs, he said, "You are right, Yace. I never wanted to kill. I know it is bad to murder innocent people. And you are also correct about me being a bad person, a monster." She peaked through her fingers. "You should know that I am from a family of monsters. But your mother, Dana, took me in—adopted me—after my monster family left me to die. My monster family was worse than I am.

"Your mother, Dana, told me that I am a good person. And you have told me that she is a good judge of character." He paused; tears dropped from his eyes to the ground. "There are some days when I wish I never left the mountains. I sometimes wish I was still with my monster family. But then ..." He shifted his weight. "... I know I am here for you. You said so when we first met. And I believe that. I am here to keep you safe because there are worse monsters than me." He held still, not looking at her. A few more tears dripped, causing wet spots in the soft, loose dirt. Slowly, Irwin stood and moved away from her.

Kipp watched his friend leave. "What are you doing, Irwin?"

"Let her go."

"What?"

"Take the rope off her."

"But-but she'll take off again."

"If she does then ...." He trailed off and shrugged. Irwin believed Yace would not leave. He knew she was smart enough to remember all the kindness showered upon her, to remember Daos City and what happened to her there.

Kipp slipped the rope off Yace. She knelt for a long time before slowly standing up. Her eyes were down, hair drawn across her face. Irwin watched her as he double checked his horse's girth—pretending to make sure it was tight. He watched her from the corner of his eye. Kipp stood still, holding the rope, wringing it in his hands while watching Yace's backside.

She took off, kicking up dirt as she fled. Kipp dropped the rope and took off after her. "No, Kipp!" Irwin shouted, but he could not control the Clan-Duin.

Kipp leaped and tackled Yace, throwing both to the ground. She screamed an earsplitting screech, punching at him. "No! Let me go, let me go!" She bloodied his lip.

Irwin ran over and pulled Kipp off Yace. "No, Kipp, this is not the way. I said no!"

"She's gonna leave us!"

Yace cringed, pulled herself into the fetal position.

He held onto his friend and whispered. "No, she will not." Kipp fought against Irwin's firm grasp. "She must process this, Kipp. She is hurting. We cannot force her to stay. She must make that decision on her own."

"But she's gonna leave!"

Irwin spoke loud enough for Yace to hear. "If she really thinks that she will be happier without us, without our help, she can leave. We have shown ourselves to be true, Kipp. But the people in Enok scared both of you, remember? That place was not a good place. Both of you knew it and were ready to leave. I made you stay because we needed supplies."

A tense silence fell around them. A deer peeked out from the woods. Hesitant, but calm. Flapping of wings announced a small flock of what looked to be songbirds from the highest branches of a beech tree not far from the doe.

Irwin spoke first. "We have seen many sad and scary people along our way here. If Yace truly believes she can do better without us, let her go. I told her I would keep her safe. And I meant it. But if she thinks we are bad people, then I cannot stop her from leaving. I want her to be happy."

"What are you doing, Irwin?" Kipp whispered. "Your words sound like something a Telepath would say."

Irwin put a finger to his lips, hoping Kipp would keep quiet. They walked back to the horses. "Mount up," he instructed Kipp. They both took to their horses and began to leave when Yace decided to move. She sat up and pulled her hair back from her eyes. Irwin turned his horse toward Kipp's and whispered, "Do not look back."

Kipp did exactly the opposite, and that was what he wanted the Clan-Duin to do—glance back at Yace. They kicked their horses to leave. Irwin made Bodi jog away, Kipp nudged Roper to keep up. The donkeys stayed in stride.

Kipp leaned toward Irwin. "Why are we leaving her?"

"Do not worry. She will follow."

Kipp glanced over his shoulder again. She looked in their direction, watched them jog away. Slowly, she followed. "How'd you know?"

"She knows she needs us to survive," said Irwin, a sly smile on his lips. He did not look back. Slowed Bodi to a walk.

14

CALLING FORTH CANNIBALS

They found the hard right turn in the roadway where the old route—now overgrown—cut through the timbers and met the new road. The grass reached the belly of the horses; the donkeys were nearly covered by the green splendor as they left the main road and civilization behind. Irwin's horse, Bodi, parted the grasses. Yace followed astride Roper, and Kipp walked behind in his two-legged human form with the donkeys. They proceeded single file through an ancient grove of apple trees—some held apples, but most were too old to bear fruit.

Kipp picked a few pieces of fresh fruit, gave one to Yace and placed the rest in the bags on Nee Nee. The old road descended into a wide valley where the grass grew even taller—shoulder deep on the horses. The donkeys were entirely hidden. All you could see were their packs parting the grass.

The flattened roadway zigzagged back and forth across the descending valley, lower and lower in elevation. There were rocky bluffs with meager trees rooted in precarious places along the ridges. Over the last hundreds of thousands of years, flowing water had cut a swath through this luscious valley. Now a small stream trickled down its center.

Far below the elongated valley, there was a jungle with a thick canopy. Only a few trees protruded above the flattened crown. As they neared that jungle, crisscrossing back and forth across this first valley, the old road led them into the next valley. They were now heading east. They continued to descend in elevation, trekking from one valley into the next. As they hiked down the slope, back and forth, they passed small inclines heading into old iron caves hidden by time and overgrowth.

"Hey, Kipp, come here." Irwin dismounted from Bodi. "Stay with Yace. I want to explore." Silver swirled through Irwin's eyes as it does when the situation feels dire.

"What's going on, Irwin?" Kipp saw the look, knew it could be something bad.

"There is iron everywhere around here."

"Be safe." Kipp put his bare foot into the stirrup, swung up into the saddle and kicked Bodi onward, leaving Irwin behind.

Late that afternoon, Kipp, Yace, and the animals stopped beneath a cover of shadows that stretched across a long and wide valley, cooler, yet still humid. They had left the valley Irwin was exploring and descended further into the next valley—not as wide as the ones before and only a few trails led to barricaded caves.

Irwin trailed behind by several hundred feet. At the crest, he stared down into the valley where his friends had stopped at a small waterfall where Kipp had instructed Yace to dismount and then to water herself and Roper.

Above the waterfall, plants grew on tiers of rocks and cascaded like curtains down stones into an elongated pool where the water fell, cutting through the stony ground, making a wide divot in the roadway before trickling further downslope. It looked like the perfect place to camp for the night. There was ample space for the horses and donkeys to forage, and the cascading water would be enough to drink from and a place to wash up.

Yace went to the pool and let Roper drink. She removed her boots and socks and placed her hot, sweaty feet into the pool.

Kipp snapped, "Don't contaminate that water with your stinky feet."

She jumped away from Kipp and her horse—across the creek—and strapped on her stockings and boots. Her face etched with fear—hyperventilating again—Yace took off and up the slope toward the next easterly ridge. She didn't look back at her friends—evidence, she wanted to get away from them.

Irwin arrived at the falls, snapped, "Could you please be nice to her?"

"Fuk it, Irwin! She's being a cunt. She needs to get over herself." Kipp pulled bags off Jenn Jenn's panniers.

"Why do you say that?" Irwin said. "Do you not remember what we talked about? We must be here for her, not push her away. You are being an asshole."

Kipp pointed at Yace ascending the hillside. "She's acting dumb. Fuk, I can't wait 'til the old Yace is back."

"Yace is Yace. She is not dumb; she is who she is. We cannot be critical of her right now. We must be compassionate. What she saw of me last night scared her. We must try to be calm, to be nice to her."

"You know she's killed people too!"

"You think pointing that out will solve our problem? What the shit, Kipp! Please be gentle with her. Go slow."

"Fuk that. We've done so much for her. She's ungrateful! Disrespectful! She's got no reason to fear us. What the fuk! We fukin' saved her life, and she wants to go back to that shit. Why the fuk did we save her then?"

"We cannot allow our emotions to rule us. We need to treat her as we have been treating her with kindness. And you need to be more thoughtful of her reactions to you and your words." Irwin unpacked Nee Nee.

"Fuk you, Irwin. We should've told her everything we've done for her."

"Kipp, you are overreacting. Yace does not need to know what all we have been through to save her. And we must let her process what happened last night. She did not know what I was capable of, but what I did was culpable.

"She has every right to be afraid of me, Kipp. I am sometimes. And the fact that I have little remorse over what I did back there last night ..." He pointed toward Enok. "... it scares me. I do not want to be like my father, but this last time I felt different in my mind and body. I acted just like him back there. But I saw all those men as vessels of evil. They had to be stopped.

"Even in Nuaki Village, I cared for other people's lives. But not last night. Last night was all about keeping Yace safe, nothing else. I acted on impulse. I did not care what happened to those people. And because of that, I scared Yace. I stopped thinking about everyone and just acted. We must think about her, and not just act on our emotions."

Kipp sneered, "Yace was never this sensitive. I miss the old Yace." He was rough about taking off Jenn Jenn's panniers. She pinned her ears at him before taking off down the long hillside after Bodi who was already eating grass.

"She is who she is, Kipp. We cannot wish to have the old Yace back. The old Yace does not exist any longer. She is changed. Everything about her life is different. She is older; the world around her has changed too.

"We both know nothing stays the same. For now, Yace's mind is childlike, but she is growing mentally every day. We have seen how she has matured. It just happened that yesterday she took a giant leap instead of a small step. We need to remember that we are the ones who need to adjust to her, not the other way around."

"Why? We've adjusted so much to her fukin' ways!"

"Think about it like this, Kipp ..." Irwin wiped sweat from his brow. "... she is just as naïve about the world as I was when we first met. You two showed me so much about Urthis, stripping away what I knew to be true, letting me explore what I was, but in a safe environment.

"The thing is, back then, I knew what I came from, what I was capable of. Neither of you did. She does not know about herself; she needs us to be as receptive as you two were to me. She is hurt, in mourning, and we need to be supportive."

"You're more reserved than she ever was." Kipp removed Roper's tack.

"We need to give her time to process everything she has gone through. I understand how hard this is. It was hard for me at first to understand that there could be people worse than my father until I met them."

"What do you want me to do?"

"Let her be for now. She will get hungry. She knows we have food. Yace will return to us."

"What if she actually leaves?" Kipp said, "What if she goes home to Daos Prime? What if she goes and finds a Telepath who controls her more than anyone else we've met?"

"You think she will get that far away before we notice? Come on Kipp, we are smarter than that. We need to be resilient for her. We know how naïve she is, we also know her capabilities. We should let her explore this world—"

Kipp finished Irwin's sentence. "But in a safe environment. Yeah, I know. I know."

Irwin glanced toward the eastern slope, toward where Yace had wandered. "Now that I think of it, this place might not be the safest environment. Remember, Nonbry said that cannibals live here."

"Cannibals? Is that a tribe name? I've heard it before." Kipp smacked Roper's rump. Roper and Nee Nee took off down the slope to find the best grass.

"No, cannibals, as in people who eat people."

"What? They eat people. And you allowed her to go off by herself?!"

"Me? Maybe *you* should shadow her."

Kipp growled, "Maybe *you* should go say you're sorry for killing all those people in front of her."

"She only witnessed me kill one person, the Erthin. But I did ask her to say goodbye to her cousin."

"Don't forget the burned bodies and the people screaming and jumping off the rooftops and out windows. Why'd you go to the saloon, anyway? Last I remember, Yace didn't want to leave the room. How'd you convince her to go?"

"Someone wanted ale."

"Now you're blaming this on me?"

He shook his head. "Although I suspected there was a Telepath in town, I did not think I would meet them in the bar."

"Yeah, Telepaths prefer owning saloons," said Kipp. "It allows them to keep an eye on visitors and patrons. In some places, it keeps the women from getting too roughed up—keeps the men honest."

Irwin scowled. "I think Yace told me that once, back when we first met."

"Yeah, they usually own inns, or taverns, or saloons; sometimes they own the bath house. What am I saying? Telepaths can own anything and everything. Dephen is an example of that." Kipp's attention drifted toward the ridge where Yace had disappeared. "I should probably go after her."

"Probably. She is just on the other side of the ridge, heading upslope, most likely hoping to find the roadway."

"What if she goes that way?"

"Hit your tattoo with a rock. Almost everything here has some trace iron in it. I will feel it resonate and come with a horse or two."

"You should be the one who goes and gets her," said Kipp. "You're the one who she's most angered at. Maybe you could have a shouting match. Call forth all those cannibals."

"You are the lesser of the two evils we pose. I am sure she will talk to you."

"Cannibals."

"Are you afraid of cannibals, Kipp?"

"You're better versed in killing people than I am."

"You know," he moved to touch Kipp on the shoulder, "it is alright to be afraid of cannibals."

"Cannibals don't scare me."

The horses and donkeys bolted down the slope, away from the jungle's edge where they had been foraging. Five hundred feet from camp—below where Irwin and Kipp stood—the jungle erupted with howls. Their horses raced past camp and up above the waterfall to an open outcropping. The Jennies went straight for Irwin and Kipp.

Wild dogs sprinted out of the gnarly undergrowth. In the evening light, it was hard to count how many angry beasts ran with the large pack, but dozens howled, snarled, barked, yipped, and were clearly prepared to rip everything and everyone to shreds.

"Go get Yace!" Irwin yelled to Kipp. The Clan-Duin jumped to the sky, shedding his clothing, shifting into his owl form. He flew east into the jungle while Irwin remained behind to defend their camp.

At one time, this section of land had been heavily mined. Irwin felt the remaining iron deposits deep underground, trace amounts along the surface. There were many small and large rocks up and down many of these valleys. Grass and wildflowers grew over all the iron rich land. Metallic harmonies resonated in his ears. Between his Metalistic abilities and his Erthin powers, Irwin was invincible in this landscape. And if the pack of wild dogs dared to attack him, they would be dead before sinking any teeth into his flesh.

Several canines were trained on him while others streamed past and on up the hillside. Irwin saw that they were not after any of the animals; they were hunting something else—something two-legged. He saw their reddish-brown coats when several slowed, flanking him, eyeing their prey. He flushed his clothing with iron. It gleamed in the diminishing sunlight.

Meanwhile, Jenn Jenn and Nee Nee tried to challenge the snappy hounds. Ears back, teeth out, the Jennies chased after the hounds—kicking and biting at them, causing a new level of panic in Irwin.

"No, no, girls! Stay out of this." He moved to defend his animals. The dogs advanced toward him.

He threw up and out a Metalistic force field, radiating pieces of metal, slicing any hound that lunged for him into a bloody mess. Irwin's Metalistic stench and actions caught the attention of more hounds, although most continued upslope, possibly going after Kipp and Yace. There was no way to tell Kipp they were chasing after him, although he probably heard the echo of vicious barks and snarls, dozens of hounds on the hunt.

He could force the landscape to move. He had done it before, recreating the roadway through Datzar Jungle on their way to Daos. Moving this landscape would be easier than moving parts of a jungle.

I do not want to kill, but these dogs want to kill me.

He saw the blood thirsty looks in their canine eyes. Surrounded, hounds moved away from the donkeys. Others encroached on Irwin. Working together, the hounds distracted the donkeys. They would get to Irwin, to this outsider.

The moment his hands rose, the surrounding lands moved, shifted. Whatever his mind could imagine, the ground molded itself into that creation. First, he summoned waves, rolling the soil like an ocean. He attempted to knock down or scare these wild dogs. Some jumped with the bucking ground. And yet so many wild dogs did not balk, racing straight at Irwin.

They are unrelenting!

Two salivating hounds crept toward his left flank, a tactical maneuver, another two advanced toward his right. They lunged. Another pair of wild dogs lunged for his face, but they were diced into pieces by Irwin's metal force field. He threw daggers at the dogs to his right; they fell dead a few feet from him. From his left, the other pack of dogs lunged. His metallic force field chopped them to pieces.

He stepped back from the bloody bits of wild dog strewn about, to one killed by a dagger. He summoned the dagger into his flesh. The dog's body was whole, but dead, and shifted out of its dog form, morphed into a young teenaged girl.

His body shook.

They are Clan-Duins!

He surveyed the now quiet landscape. It was a bloody mess of dog parts and pieces. Only a few of the whole canine bodies had transformed back into their former selves. All were Clan-Duin.

15

<u>WHO'S POSSESSED NOW?</u>

Irwin felt Kipp and Yace, their metal tattoos. They were on the move. He eyed the direction they were racing. He stood a hundred feet down the slope from camp, eyes firm to the east. They were in the next valley over, running further away from him. His heart skipped and fear tightened his throat. Jenn Jenn must have been aware of his anxiety and came to nuzzle his hand.

"I am glad those dogs were not going after you or Nee Nee or the horses." He scanned the slope again. The horses were less agitated now—were above the waterfall eating grass. "I do not want to kill again, Clan-Duins at that. Nonbry said nothing about Clan-Duins. Could they be the cannibals?"

Perhaps this explains why Enok was a contained town. It would explain why they went after me and not the animals.

He heard Yace's scream echo through the valley. He looked toward where he felt her tattoo. Though even with his elevation, she was far across the terrain. He felt Kipp, upslope from her, still in pursuit. The two were not too far apart. He whistled for the horses, and called, "Nee, Nee, come!" He patted his leg, and she trotted over and followed him up to the pool beneath the falls.

Using his Erthin powers, Irwin lifted the soil, forcing a circular sod-like fence to surround their camp. He wanted to keep the animals contained and figured a four-foot wall would be tall enough. He jumped over the fence and put his hand up to their mounts and to the donkeys and said, "Stay!" He raced away.

As he crested the ridge up the slope from camp, Yace let out another blood-curdling scream—it sounded like she was falling. He felt her body moving rapidly, felt the metal in her arm turn cold.

Shit!

He jumped over downed trees and rocks and descended into a dark jungle. He felt Kipp closing in on Yace.

Kipp's metal had turned cold too.

They must be in the water.

He tripped over roots hidden across the path as he ran. He fell. Irwin could barely see in this darkened land. He created an Erthin fire-orb to light his way. Many nocturnal animals were watching him, eyes glistening in his light. He stepped over snakes and under giant spider webs. He accidentally touched a slimy lizard and saw its glistening eyes staring down at him between a thick layer of leaves. He shivered and tried not to be fearful of all the nightlife staring at him from every direction.

Although he was honed onto Kipp and Yace's location, he was not going as fast as he wanted. They were now next to each other, and their tattoos felt warm again. Irwin wanted to pick up his pace, but proceeded with caution.

His heart fell cold at the ringing of Kipp's tattoo as it was hit by an iron laced rock. The high-pitched vibration filled Irwin's inner ear. A moment later, Yace's tattoo resonated. He sped up once more, found an animal trail to follow, and descended the vertical slope toward Kipp and Yace.

Snarling and barking dogs again interrupted the stillness of the jungle. It sounded like they were fighting each other. The noise came from the direction of Kipp and Yace. He knew he was getting closer.

Her voice echoed, "Stop it!"

"Yace." He whispered, leaving the trail he had been following. He headed straight for her.

And then they started to move again. Irwin tracked their movements—their tattoos. Their pace quickened. They descended away from him—running away from him at full speed. Now he had to backtrack.

Irwin found the roadway and followed it down. The old road was full of switchbacks, and after the fifth one, he detoured again, making his own trail through the jungle once more.

It was not so overgrown in this section of jungle. He found foot trails that merged into a larger trail. He would intercept his friends' path soon.

He jogged down the hill. His eyes had adjusted to the dark landscape. He saw branches, jumped over logs and rocks. He slipped on a mossy patch but caught himself in time.

The roar of the ocean grew louder, and the steepness of the hill increased. Kipp and Yace stopped. They were almost directly ahead of him, but Irwin could not yet see them—he was too high in elevation.

He heard Yace's voice, but her words were indistinguishable. Again, angered dogs barked at one another, but it did not sound like there was fighting, just growling noises. Irwin hurried to get to the beach.

Breaching the forest, landing on the sandy beach, he saw Yace hovering above the ground, floating. At her side, Kipp was covered with bloody bite marks. Some of the pack who stood around looked like the dozens Irwin killed earlier. Ahead of the pack, to his right, an old naked woman, save for a shawl loose on her shoulders and head, leaned on a bamboo cane that supported her frail old body. She and Yace stared at one another—possibly engaging in telepathic dialogue.

Irwin took an extra breath, seeing her levitating two feet off the ground. "Yace!?"

She turned to look at him and smiled. "You're not supposed to be here, Irwin."

"You are levitating."

"You can go now," she said with a flick of her hand.

He felt a soft breeze, but her push of power had no effect on him. She flicked her hand a few more times. Her push of air lifted his hair and cooled his face but did not vanish him from her sight. "Why isn't it working?" Yace muttered, looking at her hand.

The moon rose higher; its light reflected across the ocean waves and highlighted Yace's blonde hair and its streak of red. She was bleeding from the back of her head.

"Yace, I think you are hurt."

"Stay back, Irwin, or I will release these dogs. They will attack you."

There was a difference in her voice, in her tone, and in how she held herself. "Yace?" He held his breath. "Is this the real you?"

Ahead of Yace, on the beach between her and the older woman, a younger dog moved away from the pack of about forty. That canine stepped up and into her two-legged form. She looked back at Irwin, then began talking with clicks and pops to the older woman. Once they stopped communicating, both sets of Clan-Duin eyes were on Irwin.

"Leave now, Irwin," Yace's bold voice shook. "You're not supposed to be here."

The dogs closest to him turned and growled. "Yace, I can see you are hurt. There is blood in your hair. I think you hit your head. Let me help you."

"Stop where you are, Irwin." She attempted to use her powers on him again, to hold him back. Flicking her hand, she kept looking at it; fear etched her dirty face. "Why isn't it working?"

"Can you let Kipp be himself, please?"

Her eyes grew wide as her hand and fingers continued to flick spells at him. Spells that would not work on Irwin. "Why can't I do this?"

"Yace."

"Irwin, you're not supposed to be here. You're not a part of this sacrifice. Nor are you the one who's supposed to kill me. Not this time."

I believe she does not think this is real.

"Yace, do you know where you are?"

She looked at the jungle, out to the ocean, and back to Irwin. "Well, this is not a place I have ever been. Usually it is, but those Telepaths ...." She laughed, pointing a finger in the air. "Those Telepaths are sneaky assholes. They've been trying to break me for a long time. But I'm on to them."

"Yace, this is real." His heart fluttered, beat against his rib cage. "Everything around us is real."

"You cannot fool me." She cackled. "Kipp tried to fool me, but now look at him."

"Yace, this is real, not a dream." He wanted to move closer, but the vicious growls kept him submissive.

She dismissed him with another flick of her hand. Her attention turned to the old woman. "I am to be sacrificed." She watched the old woman and the teenager speak. "This is how it's supposed to be. This is what my dream showed me."

"Your dream? What dream was that?"

She kept staring off, listening to the Clan-Duin conversation, ignoring Irwin.

"What do you remember, Yace? Do you remember Enok?"

"Enok?" His words stirred her interest. She glanced at him. "Who or what is Enok?"

"You do not remember me decimating the saloon?"

She laughed, "You're afraid of going into saloons! Oh, you Telepaths are trying to fool me, to lure me in. I am not falling for it ever again."

"I am not a Telepath, Yace. I am Samuel Irwin Miner; I am your friend. I traveled with you and Kipp to Onj Raha to meet your father, Dephen Ishik. Do you remember?"

"Dephen Ishik?"

"Yace, I need you to look into Kipp's mind. Look and see what has happened to us." He took another step closer.

The canines closest to him, along with Kipp, lunged at Irwin, ready to devour him. "I told you to stay back," warned Yace.

He was knocked over and mauled. Irwin put up his arms to protect his face but did nothing more to save himself. His Metalistic power grounded out Yace's telepathic spells on all the hounds that touched, chewed, and tried to rip him apart. He did not defend himself, not this time. And one by one, they shed the telepathic spell Yace had placed on their minds. They stopped gnawing on him, spit out his flesh and moved away, scared to have taken a bite.

Even Kipp had sunk his teeth into Irwin's foot. The Metalist's blood dripped from his lips as he spit his friend out. "What the ... I'm sorry, Irwin. I didn't mean to bite you." Kipp offered Irwin a hand, looked up at Yace.

"What's happening?" Her voice fluttered. "This isn't how it's supposed to go. And why can't I use my powers on you?"

Irwin noticed her fear of him grow. He winced from the pain of ripped flesh and torn body parts as they mended. "Yace, it is okay. I will not hurt you."

"This isn't how it's supposed to be! I don't want to be killed by you—not again!" She drifted toward the ocean, away from him.

"Yace, I will not hurt you." He grasped a muscle ripped from his arm and pushed it back against the bone. The clan of cannibals, Yace and Kipp, watched as his body repaired itself.

"But you have. You've killed me hundreds of times." She recoiled further from Irwin. "I don't want to go through that again. Please!"

"What is she talking about, Irwin?"

"Kipp, I believe this is Yace. The real Yace. I believe she thinks this is a dream. She needs to understand that this is reality, that we are real. If she kills us, we are really dead."

His wounds healed quickly. Yace watched his body regenerate, eyes bulging, then scoured the landscape. "I—I don't want to, but I will!" Yace lifted her hands and telekinetically ripped a tree out of the ground, roots and all, and tried to hit Irwin with it.

The dogs were too short to be hit by the monstrous tree. Yace barely missed Kipp's head, but hit Irwin across his chest, tossing him onto the hard and dry sand. The wind knocked out of him. He now had several broken ribs. He struggled to his feet.

Soon, he approached her once more. "Yace, I am not here to hurt you."

Again, she tossed the tree at him like a spear this time. But Irwin moved his hands, harnessed his Erthin powers, and seized the tree from Yace's telekinetic grasp. He used the force of her toss and threw the tree behind him into the jungle.

Her blue eyes bulged. Irwin's power clearly scared her. "What the?! You've never done that before." Yace summoned five trees from the edge of the jungle, uprooting them, and hurled them on top of Irwin's body. He shrieked from surprise more than the pain.

He used his Air Erthin powers and launched those five trees into the ocean. They landed with a splash, and Irwin seized that ripple of water and propelled it across Yace, dousing her, trying to calm her, bring her back to reality.

She screeched and fell to her knees from the force of the water. Pulling her soaked hair back from her face, she rose, ready to defy him. "Oh, you're going to die for that, Irwin!"

Kipp had stood back from this confrontation long enough. "Yace, stop!" He raced toward her. Thrusting her hand toward Kipp, he lurched forward and mutated into his canine form. Barred teeth, he raced like an arrow for Irwin.

Irwin could not stand by and allow Yace to manipulate Kipp like this. With a bout of wind, he picked up Kipp and flung him into the rest of the pack.

"You need to keep Kipp out of this, Yace. I do not want him to be a casualty."
Irwin saw Kipp shake his head back and forth as if bothered by flies.

"I'll kill you where you stand!" Yace shouted. "You will not hurt me again!"

"I am not playing games, Yace." Irwin said, spittle flying from his lips. He summoned the sand around Yace into a ball, then rolled it over to where he stood. He stepped inside the sandy sphere as it came to a stop. Yace was in the center, hyperventilating and crying. She was on the ground.

He placed a cool hand on her shoulder. "Yace, you are free from the telepaths," he whispered.

Yace's eyes closed tight, her lips moving, inaudibly muttering.

He touched her face, lifted her chin, waited for her eyes to open. "Yace. You are free."

"Please, Irwin. Be quick with it."

"Yace. I would never hurt you."

"But you-you've killed me at least a dozen times. So has Kipp. I've been trying to, trying to defend myself. But your powers kill me every time." Eyes shut tight, the white-haired young woman shook, heaved as if to vomit.

On his knees, Irwin tried to pull her up. "Yace. You are safe. Those Telepaths cannot get you while I am around, remember? Look into my mind."

"I promised I'd never do that again." She crumpled, and he gathered her into his arms. She felt lighter than normal, and more vulnerable than before.

The sphere of sand fell to the surrounding ground, and a full moon shone down on them. The Clan-Duins watched with wonder.

Kipp rushed to them, tripping as he went in the sand. "Yace!"

She lingered in Irwin's arms. Not sure if she was conscious, he said, "We might need to let her have some air, some space."

"Kipp?" She turned her head to her friend. "Kipp, is that you?" Slowly her hand rose and touched Kipp's prickly face.

"Yace!" He reached his arms around Irwin and Yace, hugging them both. "Yace." Kipp sobbed. "You're back."

"Kipp! Irwin! What happened? Where are we?"

"You are safe," said Irwin.

Kipp held on to her, plainly not wanting to let go.

16

<u>The Sacrifice</u>

A frail woman stood next to a young woman and with their canine family. Yace explained, "This is Anari. She is the great grandmother to many of these Clan-Duins. She is also the leader of the Ta'Api Tribe. It sounds like you, Irwin, rescued her great granddaughter Anari Asa Kasi Asra. That is why they are allowing you to go free, and they also say you taste like Death."

"I saved her?"

She must have been the smaller Clan-Duin Auktun held captive.

"They should know that my flesh will kill them if it is ingested. I do hope they have spit me out."

"Go free," said Kipp, "What does that mean?"

"Well, it seems that Oki Okat Tark Turk defiled the hunt." Yace said.

"He claimed you!" snapped Kipp.

"He saved me." She glared at Kipp. "Had he not done what his impulses demanded, I would have been eaten in front of you."

"I wouldn't have allowed anyone to eat you."

She reached for the back of her head. "What is ..." Yace rubbed her fingers together and studied them in the dark. "Am I bleeding?"

"Yes, you are," said Irwin. "I can heal you if you wish."

"Heal me? That's not a power you hold." She shook her finger at him. "I still don't believe any of this is real. Telepaths are good at deception. Maybe this is all an elaborate dream, a new tactic to get me to let down my guard."

Irwin kept his head down, like he once did when his father came after him with murder in his heart, when he belittled his only son, and threatened to snuff him out. "What would it take for us, Yace, to prove to you that what you experience here and now is real, not a dream?"

She surveyed the tropical landscape and softly lapping ocean waves. "To believe all of this is real?"

"Yes."

Kipp grabbed her metal tattoo and tried to pull it off. "This is definitely real!"

"Ouch, what-what is this?" She looked down at her arm and then at Kipp.

"Don't look at me. You're the one who wanted that tattoo."

"You did ask for it, but only after I gave one to Kipp."

"It's a tattoo?" She turned her arm, taking in the gleaming SIM symbol. "I don't remember. I only recall … Gladis Humphreys and that house of hers. She was a talker!"

Kipp asked, "Do you remember where your father lived?"

"I kinda remember."

"Before we go too far back in our memories," Irwin said, "you said that I am allowed to go free, but what about you two?"

"I am to be eaten. But since Turk defiled the hunt, he is to be sacrificed first. Right before you arrived, Irwin, I was telling Amari that their pack could eat all three of us whenever they wanted."

"Wait, what?" Kipp squawked, "I don't want to be eaten."

"I am not allowing either of you to be eaten," said Irwin, flushing his skin and clothing in silver again.

"Wow, you're quick with that!"

"Yes, I am better with my Talents than I used to be."

"You must be. You were picking up trees and hurling them skyward! That was never one of your powers, which makes me still skeptical that this isn't a weird dream."

"Not until Onj Raha," Kipp said, rolling his eyes.

Irwin smirked, remembering the night he brought down an entire city's Public Constable Patrol, remembering his remorse. "We can talk about powers later, Yace. How can we make it so you and Kipp walk away, and I do not kill any more of these people, these Clan-Duins?"

"They call themselves Tropogagi."

"Tropogagi?"

"Yes. They're Clan-Duin, but prefer to be called Tropogagi."

"Why?"

"Because it means cannibalistic Clan-Duin."

Irwin and Kipp said nothing.

Yace talked with Anari. Irwin and Kipp sat together on the beach, watching and waiting, while Yace used her telepathy to consult with the elder. All the canines—even those on two-legs—were heavily tattooed, the elders more so than the youngsters. They looked to be clothed, though they were not. All the Clan-Duins were studiously watching the silent conversation among Yace, Anari, and her great granddaughter. After a while, Yace was granted freedom for herself, Kipp, and Turk, but they were ordered to leave the beach immediately.

Another catch to their freedom—they were told to return up the slope and to go back the way they had come, toward Enok. Irwin stepped in, insisting they could not return east. They needed to head west.

The problem was this was Tropogagi land. From here until the far side of the Kruluver Mountain range, the landscape was filled with these Clan-Duin cannibals. There were many tribes with only a few rules; anyone outside the tribe found on tribal lands could be eaten at a whim, and all animals living in the jungle were not to be hunted. That revelation troubled Irwin and Kipp who preferred consuming four-legged animals, or birds, over two-legged people.

As they arose to leave the beach, Anari instructed one of her runners to locate an emissary named KaryKaryn. She would be the only one able to take them through Tropogagi territory. But they were required to wait for her up slope.

The foursome, Irwin, Kipp, Yace, and Turk, would be followed by the pack. They departed the beach and took up following the overgrown roadway back to their camp at the waterfall.

"Why?" Kipp boiled at the interloper, Turk, who was now, apparently, part of their group.

"He saved me. And like Irwin said, he doesn't deserve to die, to be eaten alive." Yace would not budge, and both men recognized this stubborn rebuff.

"I wouldn't listen to what Irwin says." Kipp had taken on another angry stance. "He's been on a high since killing so many in Enok, and at the palace, and in—"

"You know, Kipp, I have saved more people than I have killed." Irwin took the lead as they trudged up the hill.

"You think so? You should see how quiet that palace is now that everyone who lived there is dead." Kipp snickered.

"What are you two talking about?" Yace stopped walking. Her blue eyes darted back and forth. "And where on Urthis are we? I don't think I've ever been here before. It looks to be a jungle; is this the Datzar Jungle?"

Kipp tittered, "Try west of Daos City." He kept on walking. Yace lurched forward to keep up.

"West of Daos City? We're in Daos? Our people are killed on sight here!"

"Unless you have a wealthy Mortal-appearing person to keep you safe." Kipp pointed at Irwin.

"How is this possible? We were in Onj Raha and-and-and then what happened?"

"You think this new emerging Yace can handle the truth, Irwin?"

Even in the dead of night, the jungle was filled with strange sounds that quieted when passed. She watched and walked, cushioned between these fellow travelers who looked more and more familiar at every turn. Turk kept his canine form at her side. "What happened to me?"

"The short story?" Irwin slowed his stride to match Yace's. "You were mentally taken by your father, used as a decoy to taunt us along the way, brought to Daos to destroy your family, but were somehow found out. We had been following you, chasing pieces of you for almost five moons. Thankfully, we found you before too much damage was done."

Kipp laughed, "Damage."

"Are you fooling me?" Yace stopped walking.

"No," said Irwin.

"Do I want to know the long story?"

Irwin shook his head. "I want to know what you remember."

"My memories are so disjointed." She said, "I remember everything we did before arriving in Onj Raha—you two jousting, practicing sparing techniques."

Kipp said, "Irwin's way better a fighter than me at this point."

"No, I am not."

"He kicked my ass!" Kipp told Yace, "He put me down with one punch to the face."

"That was just a good shot," Irwin said.

"You two still practice?"

"No." Irwin replied firmly.

"No, that was the night I pissed him off. He cracked me a good one. He broke my nose, then healed it."

"You had angered me multiple nights in a row, at that point, leaving me with a catatonic Yace and camp to set up and maintain." Irwin said. "You had a chip on your shoulder over Yace, not being Yace and me not living up to your expectations. So, yes, I snapped and beat you for it."

"Catatonic? Why was I catatonic, and why would you leave, Kipp?" Yace pressed for more information.

"Because you weren't you, and what Irwin was doing didn't seem to help."

"And you thought leaving me would be helpful?!"

"You weren't you. I didn't know what to do. He wasn't helping, and you were just sitting there, blank as a cloudless sky. I couldn't stand seeing you like that. There was nothing I could do!"

She looked at Irwin. "Why was I catatonic?"

"At first, I thought you were under some sort of telepathic spell that I could not shed, but then I came to realize that your memories of us had been made unimportant. You forgot about us. It took a while, but I did what I could to bring you back."

"I don't remember any of that."

"You were being held prisoner at the Ishik Palace." Irwin frowned.

Kipp butt in, "Actually, you were a concubine to the Emperor of Daos."

"I was a concubine to the Emperor of Daos. Damn, how'd that happen?"

"He was your grand uncle, Yace."

"My grand uncle?"

"Your father was Ishik, Dephen Ishik, Emperor Somer Ishik's bastard brother."

"You're not gonna go into the details with her, are you?" Kipp said, trying to catch Irwin's eyes.

"He made you into an assassin, and somehow you infiltrated the palace, but then you were found—and they took Dephen out of you." Irwin paced in front of her.

Kipp twisted toward Yace, "I hope!"

"And then turned you into a warm body to please the men in your bastard family."

"But then we rescued you!" Kipp kept along her side.

"This is all too confusing. How long ago did you rescue me?"

Kipp looked at Irwin. "Maybe half a moon."

"It has been longer than that, Kipp." Irwin counted on his fingers. "It has been thirty days. No, thirty-one, including today."

"We are thirty days removed from Daos City?"

"We are farther along than that. At this point, we are beyond the furthest town on the west side of Daos Territory."

Yace muttered, "They kill people like us in Daos all the time. I remember Dana's lectures."

"Not exactly true," said Irwin. "The rest of Daos Territory, except the town of Enok—"

"Which Irwin destroyed!"

"I did not destroy the whole town … just parts of it. Anyway, in the rest of Daos territory, people of Talent are not allowed to exist, that we saw. They put the Talented on a cross, tie us up, and leave us for the birds and elements."

Kipp hugged himself and bumped against one of his cuts, wincing. "Ouch. I still remember seeing those Clan-Duin bodies, what was left of them."

Irwin talked over Kipp. "But in Daos City, on the Prime side, the southern part of the city had all different types of people living and working there." He added, "And I do mean all different kinds of people. I did not know that many people, that many creatures existed. There were also visitors arriving by spaceship."

Kipp interrupted, "Daos is just like Akarah, Yace! Remember those space platform things, and all those weird-looking people we saw there? You called them space creatures. Daos has them too!"

Irwin piped in, "I believe that is how my people came to Urthis by spaceship. I recall Papa Edwin mentioning it once, long, long ago—now it makes sense."

Silence enveloped them. They walked on for several strides before Yace said, "I only remember my dreams. They were nightmares, really. I remember nothing of this place." She stopped. "Well, I do remember a few things, but I'm not sure if they're real. I mean, they seem real, but …." She rubbed her arm where Irwin had inscribed the tattoo. "I can't believe I wanted a tattoo!"

"It's only because I got mine that you wanted yours." Kipp smiled.

She moved in close to look at Kipp's tattoo.

Kipp hobbled and chuckled, "We're now owned by a Metalist!"

Kipp and Yace paused again along the overgrown road. Vines and snakes stretched out to touch those passing by—the air was dank, smelled of composting plant-life and pungent flowers that lured flies, and tree bark that looked like wrinkled people.

Irwin thought he saw faces in the overgrowth. "Like I said, Yace, you asked for the tattoo."

"You liked the one Irwin gave me so much, you begged him for it. You know, I think he likes it when you beg." Kipp glanced at Irwin's glower.

"It makes it easier for me to find either of you. I hoped it would bring you back to us."

Yace looked confused—a common expression lately.

"For a while, I believed you were lost in telepathic spells. Nonbry told me I could break them—that my Metalist power could shed them. And I tried, but nothing I was doing seemed to work. Kipp suggested I use my metal on your skin."

"This was Kipp's idea?"

Kipp stared at Irwin. "You think that's what brought her back to us?"

"No. I believe that whatever happened to her head is what brought her back to us." Irwin turned, ready to keep on going up the slope.

"She fell off a waterfall and hit her head on the rocks below. I barely missed them myself!"

"It feels weird." She rubbed the tattoo.

"I can remove it if you do not want it."

"No, I want to keep it." She said, "I like it. I think it's a great idea for us to have them. Especially if we're ever separated."

Kipp muttered, "Of course you would." He hobbled along, wincing and grumbling.

Yace told Irwin, "I want you to put one on Turk too."

"Why?"

"Yeah, why?" Kipp balked. "I really don't know why you want to keep him."

Yace was adamant. "He doesn't deserve to die by being eaten alive—"

"Irwin could kill him better than they would," Kipp said. "I mean, being eaten alive is a bad way to go, but Irwin can make death painless."

"You think the destruction I bring is painless?" He grumbled. "I hear people screaming as I kill them. As I have said before, I do not want to kill. Perhaps you want him dead, Kipp. Maybe you should do it!"

"You're better at it than me."

Irwin pulled his hands into fists. *I want to kick your ass right now.*

"Why do you think Irwin's so good at killing?" Yace wondered aloud. "I don't think he likes to kill, not one bit."

Irwin spoke through clenched teeth, "I do not want to kill." He walked away.

"He's done it many times." Kipp sneered. "Irwin's killed at least a thousand people by now!" He chuckled, then winced and placed a hand over an open wound on his arm.

Irwin did not reply to Kipp's verbal attacks.

"Maybe a few less," Kipp carried on. "It doesn't bother him anymore. He enjoys obliterating Erthins, tearing Telepaths to shreds, even Clan-Duins. His blood poisons us!"

"That is a lie, Kipp. I regret most of those that I killed."

"But only most."

"I do not regret what happened to Enok, nor to Yace's relatives."

She gasped. "You killed my relatives?"

"Yes."

"He killed all of them," Kipp snickered. "Including your last cousin living in Enok! Oh, ouch."

Yace reached for Irwin. "Have you killed as many people as Kipp claims?"

Irwin did not respond. After a while, he turned to Kipp. "I do not have to heal your wounds, Kipp. I could let you die from infection."

"You'd probably enjoy that!"

Irwin walked on, said nothing.

The jungle was far from quiet, but the foursome walked on in silence, bird calls and a constant rustling.

Irwin finally replied to Yace's question. "I have killed about five hundred Erthins."

She paused and stared. "You killed how many?"

"I have absorbed nearly five hundred Erthin lives." Irwin was saddened to admit to her what all he had done; how many he had killed. "Who knows how many Clan-Duin and telepathic lives I have snuffed out."

"How's that even possible? You were too scared to fight the last time I remember."

"Well, he's not scared to fight now," said Kipp, lips curled. "In fact, Irwin takes every opportunity to fight."

Irwin stayed ahead of them by at least one pace.

"I wouldn't want to be on the receiving end, but I have. Irwin's a mean ol'buggard!"

Yace snapped, "And yet you continue to provoke. You're such an ass, Kipp!"

They walked on, and then Irwin slowed to Yace's side. "Everything changed the moment you allowed your father into your body."

Her voice trembled. "I did not think to question him. Dana and Nonbry led me to believe that he was kind and willing to help. I know I allowed him in, and I know he took me and my body. But he said he had wonderful plans. I can still hear his voice saying those words to me, hypnotizing me, I suppose. That was my first mistake. My second mistake was leaving you two behind."

"Our past is behind us." Irwin placed a hand on her frail shoulder. "We do not need to—"

Yace cut him off. "I believed he could help me back then. I had no clue what would happen. He told me he would ... he said he could make me better—heal my body and cleanse my burdens. But-but then I was put behind a piece of glass and wrapped in a bubble. I couldn't get out."

17

DON'T PISS IRWIN OFF

After a while of walking quietly, Irwin confessed, "When you left us, you left me without a grounding post."

"What?" He had caught Yace off guard. "I was your grounding post?"

"I did not hear the metal all around me, not as intensely as I did once you were gone. Well, I did, but I ignored it—I guess. But then it became uncontrollable. I realized we are connected. I needed you as much as you needed me. Without you around to keep me calm, I went a little crazed in Onj Raha."

"A little crazed?" Kipp was jubilant. "You blew up an entire city block! The whole Hall of Onj Raha was decimated. What was it you said, one-hundred and seventy-two Erthins you killed?"

"It was one-hundred and seventeen, Kipp." Irwin was tired and hungry, and not wanting Kipp's provocation. "I could recite to you how many of each type if you want. And we barely escaped with our lives so we could save Yace. Forget that part, did you?"

Yace grabbed Irwin's arm. "How did you kill one-hundred and seventeen Erthins? Do you know how hard killing just one is?"

"Irwin has a really neat trick!" Kipp moved closer to Yace. "Look into my mind and see what he did to Arny."

"Arny?"

"Yeah, Arny!"

"Arny was the Erthin who brought us to the Hall in Onj Raha—one of them, that is," Irwin said.

"What was that big guy's name, the one you killed in Arenu Village?"

"Barnst." Irwin closed his eyes and pinched the bridge of his nose. *Please do not do this, Kipp.*

"Yeah, that guy! He was a brute of a Clan-Duin."

"He was also Earth Erthin, Kipp."

"But he was like ten-feet tall, a huge Clan-Duin—"

"Barnst was maybe eight-feet tall."

"And you kicked his ass! You should've seen him, Yace."

Yace moved her arm down his sleeve and took Irwin's hand. He pulled away, not wanting to have contact with her. "What happened to you, Irwin?" She waited for a response. "You've grown-up."

He hung his head, shameful of all he had done while they were apart—including the night prior. There was nothing he could say that would defend his actions. Irwin knew his cruelty should be condemned. He felt at times he should never have been born, nor should he have left the mountains. His powers were ruthless, and with anger added into the mix he became deadly. That was the reason he did not want Yace to know how much he had 'grown-up.'

Kipp could not contain himself. "He's grown bitter. But he's a better marksman than I am—a better killer!" He chortled. "Samuel Irwin Miner, the lethal assassin." He continued to laugh and provoke. "Oh, I know, Samuel Irwin Assassin. Oh, what was it the PCP and Dephen called you ... Sleeper Assassin was it? Oh, no ... yeah, Irwin the Sleeper Assassin, I like it!"

Irwin felt trapped, like living with his father and grandfather. They had badgered and tormented him with their degrading and enraging words. Kipp would make Irwin flashback. He loathed these types of interactions. He did not want to be constantly reminded of his past life, but he knew how Kipp could prod and poke to no end.

"I am glad you finally have Yace back, Kipp. That is what you have wanted ever since she left us. And Yace, you seem more than capable now than yesterday. You appear to have full control over your powers. Neither of you needs my help now. I have fulfilled my end of our bargain, the mission. Maybe this is where we part."

"Irwin, you know Kipp's just fooling," said Yace.

"Irwin's just full of himself, Yace." Kipp scoffed, "Ignore him."

"Is? You're the one who's full of himself." Yace put her hand on her hip. "You don't know when not to provoke, do you? I saw a flash of what he did last night in that town through your eyes, Kipp. I saw how he was defending us, defending me. I saw how powerful he can be. And you want to piss him off, or better yet, have him leave us? We are better off with Irwin than without him."

"Earlier you were disgusted by him."

Irwin's pace picked up.

Yace turned and growled at Kipp, "You know, I see the beauty within the ugliness of life. Irwin is no different."

He was already five strides ahead of them.

"He's going to leave us because of your arrogance, Kipp."

"No, he's not."

"It's not supposed to end like this." Yace caught up with Irwin. "Please do not mind Kipp. He's obviously had a rough time these last few—"

"Kipp has had a rough time since you left us," Irwin growled. "I have been the one dealing with him and his attitude. You can have him back, Yace." Hearing those words fly off his tongue crushed Irwin on the inside. He did not mean it, but in the heat of the moment he wanted Kipp to understand that his words hurt, even if he believed he was just being playful.

Kipp caught up. "Did Irwin mean that?"

"You're being such an asshole right now." Yace didn't talk to Kipp until they reached camp.

They had a long walk back up the steep slope. They were back at camp by dawn's first light. The clear-cut was bright as they ascended from the dark jungle. They had spent all night running after one another, defending each other, walking with comfort, if only wanting to be apart at the end of their quest.

The horses and donkeys called out as they exited the jungle's thick foliage. Yace stopped while Kipp walked up to where Irwin stood. His hands on the sod fence, Irwin pushed the raised ground down, flattening it with the rest of the land.

Yace gasped. "How'd you do that, Irwin?"

Irwin did not want to talk about himself. He was exhausted. Although he just wanted to lay down and sleep, he did not want to be around anyone who would boil up his blood. Though he was happy that Kipp was back to being smitten with Yace—the upbeat attitude meant he was feeling better. It also meant that Kipp would go back to treating Irwin as he had before Yace left them.

Irwin assessed their food rations and split up the supplies. He was determined to make it look like he would leave, even if he did not want to.

Kipp was the first to notice the absence of dialog. "What are you doing, Irwin? I thought you were gonna heal me."

"And I thought you did not trust my healing abilities?"

"Well, not for broken bones and things, but for fleshy bite marks. Yeah, I guess I can trust you to heal my skin. So, you'll heal me, right?"

Irwin did not reply.

"Yace, come talk some sense into this guy, will ya?"

She looked at Kipp as he stood over Irwin. "Why?"

"I'd like to be healed. These bites hurt."

Irwin kept his eyes on what he was doing but could tell that Yace and Kipp were probably speaking telepathically to one another. He ignored them, continued to decide what to pack.

Kipp stepped up behind him. "I don't want you to go, Irwin."

"It is not your decision to make, is it?"

"Was it me calling you assassin? Maybe I meant to call you Bearer of Admonishes."

"Same difference."

"Irwin, did you ever tell Kipp how you feel about him?"

"I know how he feels about me." Kipp's lips upturned.

Irwin knew Kipp relished their relationship. They had grown remarkably close during their journey to save Yace. They had to rely on one another and accept each other's flaws. "Then kiss and make up." Yace was becoming more and more her old self. The crack in her head from the fall must have really done it. "You two have obviously been through much without me being present. There's much more to your relationship than just babysitter and asshole. I can see it, even if you two can't."

A small smile erupted on Irwin's lips. Indeed, he had felt like a babysitter to Kipp on many occasions, but they had grown to become great friends. Still, he didn't like how provocative Kipp could be at times. It reminded him of home.

"I can leave you two half the food supplies."

"That's horseshit. You can leave us more than that." Kipp broke the spell—snapped at Irwin. "You can make money, whereas—"

"You are Clan-Duin. You can hunt."

"Do you need to go fuk your donkey or something?"

Irwin kept his eyes on the parcels.

Maybe you should go fuk Yace. Reclaim her as yours some more; calm your nasty attitude!

He arranged the food into smaller pouches and placed them into new satchels.

Kipp huffed, "Whatever." He walked away.

Yace came to Irwin. "You're not really leaving us, are you?"

"He will not say he is sorry."

Kipp must have heard Irwin. "Is that what you need?"

Yace added, "Maybe a hug too."

Irwin nodded.

"Kipp, apologize. Irwin will leave us if you don't."

"Why should I apologize? What did I do?"

"You're insensitive! You don't care or think about your words before you speak them. That's always gotten you into trouble. Be nicer!"

Irwin was having none of it. "Ha."

"Come on, Kipp," Yace coaxed, "just tell him you're sorry for being an asshole."

"You know, Irwin likes assholes."

This time Yace growled, "Kipp."

Kipp stomped his feet. "Fine. Fuk!"

"I do not want a forced or fake apology." Irwin rose from the satchels of food.

"Holy Hakra." Kipp barked. "We've gone through so much fukin' shit. The least you could do is act like a man and just shake off the stupid shit I say. You know I don't ever mean any of it."

There was a quick embrace.

"You sure sound like you do most of the time." Irwin looked down at his worn boots.

"Oh, for fuk sake."

"What did I say about using that word? I dislike that word. It makes you seem torpid."

Yace laughed and slapped her thigh.

"Fuk you both!"

Irwin clenched his fists, ready to break Kipp's nose again.

Kipp put his hands up. "I don't want to fight you. You'll kill me."

Yace growled again. "Kipp, be nice!"

Irwin took one step forward, and Kipp jumped back at least six. "That is the shit I hate hearing from your mouth." Irwin's stomach was knotted.

"I'm sorry Irwin. You're not an asshole. And I'm sorry for making you be one now."

"Takes an asshole to know one." He took another step toward Kipp—again, Kipp jumped back.

"You know I'm fooling every time, right?"

Irwin did not back down. He wanted to intimidate Kipp, to make him feel powerless. "And I could kill you at any time. How does that make you feel?"

Kipp straightened, flattened his expression, and looked at Yace. "Like I don't have any friends."

"Is this what it was like when you first met us, Irwin? To witness you two badgering each other like you are, I might have left camp too, if I was you, now that I think about it." She stared at the two men facing off.

Irwin flattened his fists, his hands dropped to his sides. "I will not kill you, Kipp. So long as you do not say fuk anymore."

"You know I will! I could say I'm sorry a hundred times and still fuk it—I mean mess it up." Kipp chuckled, his eyes held a golden hue. He moved forward, opening his arms to hug Irwin again. "I am sorry about everything. Thank you for rescuing us," he whispered, wincing from the pain of his bites. "Now you can heal me before infection sets in. The bite on the back of my leg hurts the most."

Irwin looked Kipp in the eyes and said, "Are you going to tell me what happened down there when I was separated from you two?"

"Of course! Well, you know I was chasing after Yace through the jungle, right? We came to a creek, and she jumped off it trying to get away from me, but I followed her. But when she fell, she hit her head. Bonk, unconscious. She floated down the stream to where several Tropogagi clansmen were waiting. Turk, the asshole, saw her and pulled her out of the water and claimed her before I could get to her. So then, I swim up and find Turk having his way with her. Meanwhile, the other clansmen, those dogs, are bent on killing her and him. So, we defended Yace, but got in a vicious fight—that's how I got these injuries. That's when she came to. And then she silenced all of them using her telepathy. She was there floating, and we were all staring. I didn't know she didn't think this was real, but when I saw the blood on her head, I guessed that's how she came back to us. She just needed a good hard hit. I mean, she wasn't her timid self anymore. After that, she had the pack of dogs lead us to the beach, where we met the rest of the Ta'Api clan. I didn't know she was negotiating for us not to be eaten until you arrived and saved us all. Now, will you heal me or not?"

"Thank you, Kipp. I wondered how you two got hurt. Are you sure you want me to heal you? I feel like you will complain the second I put a hand on you, scream that I do not know what I am doing?"

"You know what you're doing, right?"

They eyed each other, and Irwin said, "Mostly."

"You never answered my question about your powers, Irwin," Yace said, maybe hoping to diffuse the situation.

"Like I told you, you were a grounding post for me. I was overwhelmed in Onj Raha without you by all the metallic sounds. And after we were taken in by the PCP, I destroyed the Hall, and we ran."

"How'd you destroy an entire hall?"

He shrugged. "What I remember is that I snapped earth Erthins out of existence. I made spells that reacted to the Erthin's powers, which I did not know I could do, and I also remember seeing a wind Erthin have his breath sucked out of him. A fire Erthin erupted into flames. Water Erthins liquefied. And the metal twisters I made .... Those twisters probably did the most damage. I remember the towering gates that led into the grounds where the Hall sat. I used them to run down soldiers and anyone else standing in my way."

"Yeah," Kipp commented, "that's the one thing I still remember seeing were those enormous gates crushing all those people. The street between the saloon and hall was one big, bloodied mess."

"How'd you two get messed up with the Hall?"

Irwin cocked his head. "I suspect Dephen had a hand in bringing us into the Hall."

"Really?" said Kipp, "How so?"

"Well, if you remember, we were followed by that brigade for at least three kilometers, maybe longer. We were not stopped by any other brigade, and we passed by several."

"Most of them were on the ground, if I remember correctly."

"We have been overlooked in many places by men, by Clan-Duins, on the ground and on horseback. Raha, Radia, even in Ahradah we were not followed, and we looked out of place. But in Onj Raha, we were followed. I believe Dephen told them to look for us."

"We looked out of place in Onj Raha," said Kipp.

"Yes, we did. There were two of us on one horse, but we would not have been followed unless someone was instructed to look for us. None of the other soldiers we crossed paths with stopped or questioned us. Those Erthins had been sent after us—to bring us back. I am sure Dephen gave a description of us to the foreman at that Hall. He used Yace's knowledge of us to identify us as targets for those PCP."

Kipp lifted his shoulders. "Alio told me there are protocols within the PCP."

"And Dephen probably knew about those protocols," Irwin added. "He used the PCP to his advantage several times. I am so glad he is no longer within you, Yace." He moved to give her a hug.

"I still don't understand how you can harness Erthin powers?" She pondered aloud. "I thought you were a Metalist and a Mortal."

"I was told that I am Erthin by an Elementalist Erthin." He raised his eyebrows. "But then, I also heard I could be Coterie. Which would explain so much more about what I can do, like that flick of the wrist Erthin absorption trick. I was told that is not an Erthin power, that it comes from more powerful blood—most likely my mother's family."

"Who told you that you could be Erthin or Coterie?"

"An Elementalist from Nuaki Village said that I could be like him if properly trained. He saw that I could yield all five Erthin powers. And two others mentioned I could come from Coterie blood."

"It'd explain a lot." Kipp watched the distant treetops sway in the morning breeze.

"Coterie?" Yace was having a challenging time grasping the concept that Irwin might be as powerful as she, if not more. "Or an Elementalist Erthin? How could your father ... do you think he knew what powers your mother possessed?"

Irwin shrugged. "It is possible that my mother did not know her power. She might have been too young, not strong enough. But she is dead, so I will never know. I do know that I can use all five Erthin powers almost equally—healing others being my weakest suit, and fire being easiest for me to control."

Kipp chuckled, "That's because you've absorbed so many of them."

"Your power for self-healing came first, right?" Yace pressed.

"By the time we arrived in Ahradah, I was more aware of what I could do. At that point, I had over a moons' time to feel my Erthin powers and work with them. And we had faced several desperate situations. There was no water. Nothing but an endless stream of dirt roadways."

Kipp stepped in. "All you could do was summon fire at that point. And he wasn't that good at it either."

"I could turn lights on and off, make a spark with my finger." Irwin said, snapping his fingers—showing off his favorite trick.

"Maybe you just needed a stressful moment to ignite the rest of those powers." Yace contemplated her friend.

Irwin felt tears well in his eyes. "Believe me, we have had enough stressful moments since you were taken from us."

Yace looked to Kipp, "You'll have to show me." She placed a kiss on his lips. "I want to know what I've missed."

Kipp rubbed his neck. "I'm not sure I want you to see what all happened to us."

"We knew this time would come." Irwin looked at Kipp. "Maybe you should not have slept with all those women."

Yace addressed Irwin. "I want to know what has happened since arriving at my father's house in Onj Raha."

He held her blue eyes for a long time, placing his hand on her arm. "I will warn you that we have witnessed you doing things which are contrary to your habits. We might have even said things or thought things that could make you angry."

Her eyes were steady on him. She returned the warm gesture, placing her hand on his arm. "I will not judge as you two might have. I understand you went through much to rescue me, keep me safe. I know not to criticize the choices or mistakes you've made along the way. I think that is why you both are so close now, because of everything that happened to you two. It's absolutely beautiful, even if it was ugly—all those things you had to wade through along the way. What you two have done for me, I will remember forever."

Kipp's eyes pleaded, "I'd really like to be healed now."

18

<u>Turk The Cannibal</u>

Irwin practiced his healing power on Yace first, reducing the swollen lump on her head from where she had fallen from the waterfall. She was no longer bleeding. He took more time healing Kipp's bite marks. It was good practice for him, regenerating flesh, and breathtaking for Yace to witness. She never would have believed he could do it. Once Irwin was done fixing Kipp's injuries, Yace asked if he would mend Turk too. Irwin had almost forgotten the younger canine who did not whine or complain, unlike Kipp. Turk was clearly appreciative to have been healed. Kipp never uttered words of thanks.

While Irwin tended to Kipp's wounds, he examined Yace's memories. "Did Dephen deny you access to everything?"

Yace couldn't recall one single event from the time they arrived in Onj Raha except the Inn's owner, Gladis Humphries, and her long and drawn-out stories. Dephen had kidnapped Yace's mind. She did not remember the soldiers she had indentured, nor did she recall Dephen taking advantage of all those people and situations. There were no memories of her father setting Kipp and Irwin up, several times, to be caught by PCP, or meeting Lady Gretchen—Yace's now deceased aunt who Irwin had killed in desperation after she buried him alive. She was but one more set-up Dephen had arranged for the unsuspecting travelers.

She conceded. Yace did not remember any of the cities, the long stretches of horse or carriage time, nor did she recall Arenu Village and breaking several whore's pelvises. Nor did she remember any of her soul's metaphysical travels. She was unaware of how much time she spent outside her body, visiting Kipp, Nonbry, and Dana.

The lands she had raced through on horseback were gone from her mind. She did not know how she arrived in Daos City or what happened after that. Either her father, Dephen Ishik, or his half-brother, Emperor Somer Ishik, and other family members had buried all those memories of being taken—of being used and abused by her father.

All Yace recalled were the horrible nightmares she had to swim through, day and night. She had been living in a constant state of mental survival. She told them that many of her dreams were about being chased. A looming and dooming beast, or person full of terror, would either kill her or send her falling off a cliff, out of a window, from a roof, from a treetop—tumbling her into the next horrible nightmare.

Her dreams, before being taken by her father, had always been of tumultuous times that happened in her younger life. Dephen took those events and made them even grander—probably hoping to break her will to live in her own body.

It hadn't taken her long to learn that she was stuck in a dream-state. The realities Dephen had tossed into her dreaming mind were far worse than what she had ever experienced. That was how she had figured out a master Telepath was manipulating her.

After a while, she began voluntarily leaving each nightmare by killing herself. She forced herself off cliffs, out windows, threw herself against jagged rocks, daggers, or into spikes, knowing she would end up in another nightmare—yet hoping that at some point it would all end. She had been executed every way imaginable in these dreams—drowned, hung, sliced and diced, burned, beaten, and eaten alive by hideous beasts.

That was why being awake now was surreal for her.

Irwin and Kipp listened to her stories, horrified by the reality she had lived in. Yace had changed mentally and physically during their time apart. How she now sat, refraining from eye contact, and often pleading with Kipp to be at her side; the young woman appeared fearful, slightly dismayed, and not totally aware that this was real and not some corrupt nightmare.

But she was not defeated. Her words were shaky. Although Dephen Ishik had attempted to break her will to live, he never killed her spirit. She had sat there before them, appearing scared yet renewed.

She never left Kipp's side. He held her hand and rubbed her back, trying to be supportive, loving her as always. She smiled and leaned into him, continuing to confess what she could remember. For Yace, this was therapy. They could see how glad she was to be alive and back in reality. The days after being rescued from Daos Palace seemed to have escaped her mind too. Now, instead of falling, she could fly. She could make light with a snap of her fingers too—just like

Irwin—and use that energy to light, ignite, or even incinerate; she too could create a campfire if necessary. She could also levitate anything when she willed it—not just accidentally anymore. It appeared that her time under her father's guidance wasn't without merit. She had retained the knowledge about how to shift from persona to persona without blinking; akin to how swift Kipp was with his shapeshifting abilities.

Irwin felt warm inside, having now understood her transformation. The renewed closeness of his two dear friends was also a delight to witness. That morning, they conversed lightly while eating. Each one yawned from time to time.

Kipp did not leave Yace's side. Even when she went to relieve herself, he stayed with her. Both Irwin and Kipp sensed that she did not want to be alone—still wary of the world. Although she had let her physical guard down in front of Irwin and Kipp, her mental guard was still on alert. Her eyes darted. She pulled on strands of hair, nervously twirling them in her fingers—a new quirk. And when Kipp left her to relieve himself in private, she sat close to Irwin.

Once at his side, Yace drew her head down, as he would have for his father. She looked mangy and her hand slipped onto Irwin's. She startled him once, and he pulled away, not meaning to.

"I'm sorry, I should have asked."

He placed his hand on hers and wiped a tear from her cheek.

"I-I just need to hold on to something."

"It is alright, Yace, I understand. You have been through so much. I would probably seek contact too had I experienced everything you have."

Yace leaned into his shoulder. "I am glad your kindness has not diminished, Irwin. I think that's the one thing I love the most about you."

They both inhaled deeply, enjoying the serene, fertile landscape. The grass rattled in the morning wind; the scent of wildflowers flowed from all around; bugs buzzed around their faces. Unusual bird calls echoed back and forth across the open valley where they sat. Light, wispy clouds broke, revealing the deep-blue sky.

When Kipp returned, her attention went back to him. He yawned and nestled into her arms.

"We're not allowed to separate, ever again." Yace said, tearful. "The three of us. We're a family now. It's obvious that you two have an unbreakable bond. You've gone through so much to save me." She grasped both their hands. "I love both of you so very much. And the fact that you love each other … this is meant to be! We are meant to be a family.”

What is she talking about? Kipp does not love me. Yace must be tired.

Irwin pulled his hand from hers, stretched his arms as he yawned, and said, “I think it is time for sleep.”

“We’re family. We now sleep together,” insisted Yace. “We must reinstate our bonds. Show our eternal devotion to each other.”

Kipp blinked several times. His sleepy eyes fell upon Irwin. “I’m alright bonding with Irwin, just not with Turk.”

“I am not …. You two have the bond. Not me.”

“Don’t you want to bond with us? With Kipp? You two could deliver your eternal devotion to one other.”

Irwin stared at Yace, glanced at Kipp who was half-asleep.

Did she just …? Why would she …? Eternal devotion. She sounds like Emperor Somer. But he is dead. They are all dead.

His gaping mouth soon filled with a yawn. He was exhausted from everything endured the last two days. And yet it appeared that Yace was trying to take advantage of his weary mind.

“Look. We’re all tired. You two have yawned more combined than I have!” She pointed at Turk. “Don’t worry, he’ll be our sentry.”

Irwin’s body stiffened with skepticism. Although Yace was finally acting like her old self, there was an off-putting energy she now held. It was reminiscent of long ago, when they first met, and she wanted to have a closer relationship with Irwin, laced with the mental manipulations they had endured since their departure. She seemed to want to have some sort of control over him.

Of course, I could be misconstruing what I am seeing. I am very tired.

He glanced at the young cannibalistic canine Clan-Duin. “You trust Turk not to eat us while we sleep?”

“Yes. He’s devoted to us now. He will let me know if anything approaches. Besides, Turk’s been asleep this whole time. He can stay awake and watch the tree line while we rest.”

Kipp grew more awake as his anger rolled through again. “I just don’t understand why he has to be here. Maybe we should eat him—get it over with.”

“Kipp, like I said, Turk is under my protection. You needn’t harm him, please!”

Kipp barked at Yace. “He fuked you! He fuked you without your permiss—”

"He saved me from being eaten alive, Kipp. Please understand that! I wouldn't be here if not for Turk. You would've found seven canines devouring me had he not fuked me and stood over me, protecting his claim."

"I was right behind you!"

"If you were right behind me, then why didn't you stop him?" Kipp looked at Yace, mouth hanging open.

"There were dogs fighting over you when I arrived. I wasn't gonna get into the middle of that! Meanwhile, that little shit pulled you into the brush and began humping you. I didn't know where you were!"

She reached out and petted Turk's backside. "He told me I was too beautiful to kill. He thought he was saving me."

"By fuking you! That's not how you get water out of someone's lungs, Yace."

"I too cannot understand how you defend him for claiming you, Yace." Irwin said. "It sounds like Turk raped you while you were unconscious."

"He didn't hurt me."

Kipp spat, "You didn't feel anything because you were unconscious!"

"Would it help if I told you his prick was tiny?"

"I side with Kipp on this; Turk does not need to be here. Besides, there must be a place upslope where he can live." Irwin gestured with a sweeping hand motion. "Between the three of us, we can keep each other safe. I can be a sentry for now. I do not mind—"

"Irwin, I thought you—of all people—would understand!" Yace said. "Turk is staying. He is our sentry. And that's the end of this conversation."

Irwin stared at Yace, wanting to say more, but he could not think of anything polite to say.

I forgot how quick to command you are.

"Now, let's rest." She told Kipp, and she hinted for Irwin to come and lay down with them on the blankets.

"I am fine right here," said Irwin. He lay back on the uneven surface and used his Erthin powers to contour that spot for his body to sleep in. He began snoring before his friends were gone from sight.

Kipp and Yace slept down the slope on a few blankets. Irwin was the first to wake. They had all been exhausted. It was late afternoon, and the valley was already shady. He made hot water and a pot of rice for everyone. Turk looked intrigued watching him prepare the food. He watched intently as Irwin performed his Erthin Talents—bringing water to a boil, tossing in the rice, placing a lid on the meal, and waiting for it to steam.

Once it was cooked, he offered some to Turk. The horses and donkeys always enjoyed the cooked rice treat, but they liked it cooled. For now, the animals grazed freely and enjoyed continuous access to cool, fresh water. Turk ate what was given, then stared at Irwin with puppy-dog eyes. He wanted more. "I want to save the rest for Yace and Kipp. I have nuts, or smoked fish we can eat." He retrieved a satchel of macadamia nuts and split several handfuls with Turk.

He knew Yace and Kipp were awake by the sounds they were making. He tried to ignore them and decided to take a bath. He created two tall steps down into the pool at the base of the waterfall and made it deeper. Along the edge, he placed their satchel of soaps and then merged into the hip deep water.

Ah, this feels good.

Laying back, he made the water hot enough to relax in. It had been a long time since he had truly relaxed.

...since Daos Prime with Jorge. I wonder how he and his family are doing. I miss him.

Soon, Kipp and Yace walked into camp. Her hair was a mess, and Kipp's smile stretched from ear to ear. Irwin could smell the scent of procreation.

"You gonna start a fire?" Kipp said to Irwin who was still sitting in the hot pool.

"When I am done, yes."

Yace knelt next to his head and put her hand in the water. "Wow, that's hot!"

He sat up and opened his eyes. "Makes it easier for relaxing."

Now that they are up, I guess I am done.

He stood and pulled the heat from the water. Bar of soap in hand, he washed up under the cool waterfall.

Yace waited for Irwin to finish cleaning himself. She offered him a hand up, before taking a step into what she assumed was still a hot pool. "Yikes! How'd it get so cold?"

She hustled out of the water. Irwin snickered. "What temperature would you like it to be?" He knelt, arm in the water, turning it warm again.

She raised an eyebrow. "Are you now my bath servant?"

He coolly replied, "I am not your bath servant." He smiled and gestured toward his friend, "But Kipp is. He will be your friendly scrubber tonight."

Kipp clapped his hands. "I'd like the water medium hot servant!"

Irwin sat back from the water. "I was thinking of a boil for you!"

"Maybe for Turk. I've never had boiled dog before."

Yace slapped Kipp's butt. "Why be so mean?"

Kipp jumped into the pool. "You gonna get in, Yace?"

She stood next to Irwin, her blue eyes studious. "I cannot imagine you being so fluid with all the Erthin talents so quick. I'm truly impressed, Irwin!"

"Thanks. I do try. I would like to be better at healing people."

"I think you did a fine job on Kipp's injuries."

"I still have scars," Kipp complained. "Not the best healing job, if you ask me."

"At some point, I would like to get formal training. Maybe Tamera could teach me when we finally meet up with the Gypsy again." Irwin gazed at the clouds traveling overhead. He wondered about the weather ahead. They had a long way to go.

"That would be amazing! She was taught by a master healer. It's one of the reasons the Gypsy saved her."

Irwin remembered hearing that story from Kipp. Many years ago, long before Kipp and Yace had joined the Gypsy, the Gypsy had come into a town and set free all those with Talents after noticing the resident Telepath's hold upon the community. They had later learned that it had been Dephen who had telepathically orchestrated a whole town to give up Tamera and many other people of Talent.

I do not think Yace needs to know that much information right now.

19

<u>Don't Go Onj Raha</u>

"It's okay with me if you don't join." Kipp said as he laid back, taking up the entire pool. "Might be too crowded in here with the two of us."

Yace looked up at Irwin. "Kipp showed me more of the destruction you've wrought, and all the people you've killed."

He glared at Kipp. "It is not something I am proud of."

"He also showed me how you absorbed Barnst. Impressive! How'd you do that?"

"I am not sure if it is my Metalist power or my Erthin power that allows me to do things that require so much power and will. Maybe it is my Coterie abilities. Who knows?" He rubbed the back of his neck and avoided her eyes. "But when I take an Erthin's life, I absorb them, their power—their whole entity."

"Or it's a combination of all three. What I saw ... that's powerful magic you hold, Irwin."

"Barnst became a permanent part of me that day. Every Erthin life I take I remember. They make me more powerful. I feel what each person could do—has done with their abilities. Some, like Barnst—for example—were not that powerful; they use their looks and their suggested powers as an intimidation tactic rather than actually using powers.

"We both know that proper training is key to mastery of any Talent." Irwin kept on watching the cloud formations and remembering all the Erthins he had killed. "Many of those lives I took in Nuaki Village were amazingly talented—so powerful. I took the lives of four Elementalist and many multi-talented Erthins. They were all very well-trained. I assimilated all that power and have it now as an aid when things get heavy. But none of them were masterful healers."

"I'm impressed, Irwin. May your powers never cease." Yace looked down at the pool. "Where am I to sit, Kipp? Are you gonna move?"

Kipp jerked up, set his feet down on the bottom of the pool. He stretched his hand out for Yace. She considered his offer, then the water. "It doesn't look big enough for the two of us." She told him, shaking her head at his handout.

"I can make it bigger," said Irwin. "Kipp, you will want to get out."

He leaped out of the water.

Irwin widened the pool, making it deeper so all three of them could enjoy soaking space and not be in each other's way. He then heated the water. Yace kept watching him play with his talents. Kipp acted impatient—he had, no doubt, seen enough of Irwin's abilities and was often scared of them.

The sky finally darkened as the sun set and the stars turned bright before the moon that, without hesitation it seemed, emerged on the horizon. Kipp and Yace soaked, Irwin made a fire and ate food—once again offering a meal to Turk.

Another day came and went. They had been told to stay, to wait for the Emissary, KaryKaryn, but the foursome did not know what to do with themselves—all the free time. Kipp and Yace were reconnecting. It was odd—for Irwin who knew their past—to see them so smitten, so happy to be around each other. He had missed seeing Kipp's ecstatic puppy-dog face, but knew how their relationship worked.

How long will it take before this romantic time changes, before Yace loses interest in Kipp again?

While Kipp and Yace enjoyed one another, Irwin explored the landscape alone. He went up the slope, hiked into the previous valley they had descended two days ago. He toured the hillsides, ventured into a few of the more accessible and interesting caves—the few that had not collapsed.

It was here amongst the rugged landscape that he realized that being inside caves was his calling; Irwin missed the darkness and solace. Being underground made him happy—mostly because of the iron sounds. He had brought saddle bags with him and loaded them up.

All this iron ore might be useful. I can use it for future trades or making things.

On his return to camp, Irwin found Yace and Kipp copulating out in the open, close to where Turk lay. Their Clan-Duin protector looked at Irwin as if hoping he would help—would ask them to stop carrying on right there. Irwin shook his head.

I thought there were other ways to enjoy being close to someone besides sex.

Kipp was relentless in conquering Yace. It was a sight Irwin was not used to. He wanted to walk away, but his baggage was heavy, and he was hungry.

They finished up and met Irwin in camp. He walked straight for the food bags. Yace and Kipp stepped into their clothing and took seats near the widened pool, still smitten with each other.

Retrieving several satchels of food, Irwin turned to find Kipp groping Yace.

Sarcasm dripped from Irwin's lips. "Hungry for food? Or more sex?"

Kipp responded by reaching his dirty hand into the bag of smoked fish fillets. Irwin was thankful that Yace washed her hands before enjoying their evening meal.

Once everyone was filling their mouths and their guts, Irwin asked, "When do you think that emissary will arrive?"

Yace replied, "Anari suggested it could take many days, depending on where KaryKaryn is coming from."

"Do we know if she lives close to here? And how well does she know the terrain? We want to go west to Tresdahla and hopefully without too much difficulty."

"Turk has only met her once—that was after Asra, Anari's great granddaughter, was captured by the men of Enok. They asked KaryKaryn to rescue her."

"Well, that didn't happen," said Kipp. "Only Irwin can rescue Clan-Duins."

He rolled his eyes. "Do you think she can take us all the way to Tresdahla?"

"Turk says KaryKaryn travels all along the base of the mountains, through all the Tropogagi Territories. He also says she's someone who eats animals, as we do."

Kipp turned to Irwin. "You want to get going, don't ya?"

"This place is not that bad. But there is a lot of iron here. The songs are tolerable. But … yes."

Although Irwin enjoyed being around the metal, he wanted to be away from it. Besides, they had become used to constantly moving; it was strange to be idle for this long.

"You're that sensitive?" asked Yace.

"When I am not around it for a while, then suddenly find myself sitting in iron for days. Yes, it can be deafening. Besides, iron always sounds off when not mottled with another ore like silver or nickel."

Kipp said, "You're not gonna go all fukin' Onj Raha, are ya?"

"Only if you make me."

"Is that what you call it when you can't contain how you feel?"

"Onj Raha was the only place I was not in control of my powers. I have had complete control everywhere else."

"What about Nuaki Village?"

Yace said, "Kipp showed me what you did there. I can't believe you leveled the entire fortress! Had I not seen your powers through his eyes and in his mind, I never would've imagined the destruction you can now summon."

"He's the Bearer of Admonishes, I tell ya!"

"I will admonish you if you are not careful."

"Oh, my!" Yace slapped her knee. "You just reminded me of Hauss, Irwin. Oh, I wonder how all our family is doing." She stared off into the trees as if hunting for prey.

The last time they talked to Nonbry, Irwin was chided for the state of things in Onj Raha, Nuaki Village, and the Ishik Palace. He did not want to be reminded that people of Talent who travel the world would now be further impeded because of his horrific actions. Local plantations and PCP Halls would gain more soldiers, brothels and bathhouses would be brimming with female workers. And laws would be changed when it came to dealing with those of exceptional power, all because of Irwin.

As it was, Talented criminals now had no place to go for rehabilitation. There was no place to train powerful children either. And though the Ishik regime crumbling was a good thing, Irwin was unsure if being part of Hakra's Empire would be any better for the people of Daos. He wished he could take it all back, everything he had done, but he reminded himself that everything he had done was for Yace, as instructed by Nonbry, 'You must be willing to give your life to save her.'

"I still have the talisman." Kipp told Yace. "We can visit Nonbry."

"Really? I'd love to talk to my mama. I miss her." A tear raced down Yace's cheek. She wiped it away.

Kipp leaned into Yace. "I miss Flinn. You think they'd let you talk to her?"

"I would hope."

Irwin felt them thinking about home and their own families.

I miss no one. Well, maybe the cool crisp breeze.

"Oh! We found out something about your family that you did not know."

"We?" Kipp asked, "What are you talking about? We?"

"Nonbry is ...." Irwin tried to lead Kipp into remembering.

"Nonbry's what?" said Kipp.

"I know you dislike listening to him, but do you remember him saying that he and Dephen had the same mother?"

Yace gasped, "What?"

"Oh," Kipp brushed his knee. "That's right!"

"Are you serious?" Yace's eyes could have popped out of her skull. "I'm related to Nonbry?"

Kipp chuckled, "Yeah, it seems you are!"

"Nonbry was the youngest child," Irwin said, "whereas Dephen was the eldest. We were told that their mother used her children as footholds in her relationships. She used Dephen to undermine the Ishik Empire and to have free access to Daos ports."

Kipp gasped, "That might explain why us Talented aren't allowed in Daos."

"Nonbry is related to my father!" Yace stared blankly at Irwin. "That explains how he knew him. Nonbry is my uncle!"

"It might explain how he found you when you were a child." Kipp said.

"Nonbry is my uncle," Yace repeated. She leaned into Kipp's chest.

20

<u>Emissary KaryKaryn</u>

Three friends, and their Tropogagi guardian, remained in that valley for another two days and nights. Kipp and Yace stayed in each other's arms. Irwin kept to himself and took care of the animals, including Turk.

Occasionally, they would see movement along the jungle's edge or the reflection of eyes spying their fire at night. Irwin kept the camp bright, especially at night—a hopeful deterrent for the rest of the Tropogagi clan, and possible cannibals, downslope. The firelight was also a hopeful beacon for the emissary, KaryKaryn. Sometimes his stomach grabbed tight at the sound of a crackling branch, flapping wings flying too low in the dark.

One morning, Turk woke before sunrise. A deep growl resonated in his throat. They all sat upright from their slumber. Irwin was sitting by himself near the fire. Yace and Kipp were entwined in each other's arms downslope.

Along the crest of the valley, to the west of camp, they all saw her dark silhouette. A middle-aged woman, mostly naked, was descending into the valley. Her face and body had tattoos and scars, which made her look older—scarier—than she probably was. She wore a long-knitted hood, which she had pulled down around her shoulders, hiding her sagging breasts. The naked woman stared at the outlanders with cautious curiosity as she moved toward their camp.

About thirty feet from the fire, KaryKaryn called out, "Good day."

"Good day," Yace and Irwin echoed. Kipp went into his stealth mode, his eyes and nose trained on this new person. Yace asked, "Are you KaryKaryn?"

"I am." The emissary pulled her graying-brown hair back over her left shoulder. Her vibrant green eyes took in each youthful face, then settled on Irwin. "You be the man who destroy Enok."

He could not tell if KaryKaryn was asking or making a statement. "Yes," he confessed.

KaryKaryn smiled. "Afta and Ounin, grateful for saving them from smith. They from my tribe, Arkin. They say you save them from smith, from Auktun. They be trapped by him in Enok many moons. Arkin asked that I save them, but white man shifty. They lure women. They try to get me, but I smart. Many Tropogagi are not. White man capture and make them obey, serve white man's needs."

"They must have been the shackled Clan-Duins Auktun had at the forge. He was not a Telepath—that I could tell. The man who made them obey had blue eyes, like my friend here. He was a Telepath. He worked at the saloon—a really dangerous man."

"Yes, Telepath. They be worst." KaryKaryn smiled. "They say you kill him."

"I did. I do not appreciate people who think they can control others."

KaryKaryn looked at Yace. "Yes. Many blue-eyed people be evil."

"Hey, I'm not evil," said Yace, hands in the air.

"You wish to go west?"

"Yes, west," agreed Irwin, "past the slopes."

Yace said, "We really want to get to Tresdahla."

"Ozaroton, I take you."

"Ozaroton? Where is that?"

"Far west. Be place for people like us." She told them. "You travel ready?"

"Um, no. We have to pack." Yace gestured toward the piled baggage against the rocky façade near the waterfall. A mist from the falls had gathered on their belongings.

"It takes us no time to get the animals ready, Yace." He said, tossing a look at Kipp to help.

Kipp was on guard, eyes firm on KaryKaryn. The Clan-Duin did not see Irwin trying to get his attention.

KaryKaryn said, "Where we go be hard on animals."

Irwin assured her, "They are well versed in hard terrain."

KaryKaryn gestured, "Steep hill, no trail."

"My donkeys can cover any ground. And the horses are tall enough to climb and step over downed trees and such."

"No trail." KaryKaryn reiterated. "We pass Tropogagi territories. They will smell animals. We be quick." She pointed at the animals. "They not quick. If found, we die unless gift given."

Yace huffed, "You're not saying we should offer our animals to the tribes, are you?"

"I can make offerings," said Irwin. "Metal trinkets of any type—bracelets, necklaces, rings, cups, you name it, I can make it."

Yace asked, "KaryKaryn, how do you pass through the territories and not get eaten?"

KaryKaryn was a mix-raced Clan-Duin. Her skin was light, her eyes bright green, and her face freckled the same color as her graying-brown hair. She raised a coy eyebrow, then disappeared—invisible.

Kipp struggled for breath. "That's why she smells."

"She's a rarity, like Irwin." Yace said. KaryKaryn was three steps back from where she had been and reappeared. Everyone gasped. Yace gleamed with excitement. "You can be invisible! I've never met anyone like you. How'd you find out you have that power?"

"I am rarity."

"Invisibility is not a Talent you'll ever see in this world," said Yace, "until now, that is."

"Thank you."

"It must be a fun power to have!" Yace said, and KaryKaryn glared at them.

The emissary insisted, "Leave all horse behind. Take what need, nothing more. Food, water on way."

"I am not letting loose my animals in this place." Irwin said. "Besides, they can navigate any type of terrain. They know how to carry themselves in tight spaces with packs. And if we ascend in elevation, they will keep us warm."

"Please don't get him started," Kipp said. "He won't give up those donkeys for anything. Trust me, I've tried!"

"They have been with me since the beginning. I am not leaving them."

"Fine. They be your responsible."

"Yes. I will be responsible for them."

"How long will it take you two to get packed up?" Yace was already impatient.

Kipp turned and whistled for Roper. Once one animal began walking toward camp, the others followed. He put packs and sacks into piles.

Irwin asked loudly, "How long will this journey take?"

"Full moon two nights back. Three full moons pass between here and Ozaroton."

Irwin and Yace echoed each other, "Three moons to Ozaroton?"

Kipp wailed, "That's nearly half a year!"

"That is only a quarter of a year," chided Irwin. They watched Kipp count on his fingers. Irwin turned to Yace, "How long do you think it will take the Gypsy to get to Koumin?"

"Where were they when you last spoke to them?"

Kipp went back to work tacking the horses. Irwin answered, "Nonbry said they were sailing from Arisham to Uer 'Bin."

"Sailing?" Yace laughed. "They wouldn't sail. They can only go by wheels. Well, Captain Hari can sail, but ... no. The roadway is the best way for our carts and wagons. Besides, why would they go north to Arisham, then back to Uer Bin? I mean, we'll have to backtrack to get back home, but why would they've gone so far to the north?"

Irwin said, "Maybe it has something to do with the Cyclops."

It has everything to do with the fact that I blew up the hall in Onj Raha and changed the balance of things on Urthis forever.

He chuckled at his thoughts.

"Oh, that's right! They've their own mission."

Had Yace forgotten all about the secondary plan for the Gypsy?

"I wonder if they have found any leads on the Cyclops," she said.

"I was told of a book, a log of travelers who passed through Nuaki Village since its beginning. They kept records of everyone that stepped foot in Nuaki." Irwin said.

"Really? Did you get to see it?"

He shook his head. "I know they had information on my great grandpa Edwin and his twin brother Edger, and drawings of their likenesses. I saw those when I was confronted the first time." He reflected, "I look just like them. I had never seen such detailed facial drawings. And they knew about my family living along Kruluver Mountains too."

"That's no good."

They knew about you and Kipp too.

He was afraid to tell her that. "They wanted to know about my father. I told them he was dead. No one needs to go looking for that man; they would not survive what they find."

Yace shuddered. "That's disturbing Irwin."

"Indeed."

"You didn't tell them more about yourself, did you?"

"No. They only know what I have shown them."

"You've shown them a lot! You blew up Nuaki Village, a place they send the worst of Talented offenders. The PCP will know about that soon enough. Not to mention what you did in Onj Raha. I'm sure someone knows about all of it."

You are probably right, Yace. They know everything, including what I did to your bastard family.

He stared at her, not wanting to have this conversation.

Yace leaned into him. "Do you know if Nuaki Village had ever seen any Cyclops?"

"I blew the place up, Yace. Those records are gone."

Kipp spoke up from across Roper's back, "Maybe your boyfriend, Jorge, knows."

"I doubt it." Irwin missed the Empath, the first one he had shared intimacy, especially while seeing Kipp and Yace be so intimate.

Kipp did most of the work of packing their worldly belongings onto the four animals. Irwin stepped in to help. The two horses were tacked up and ready to go. Once he was present to aid in distributing the weights in the panniers, tacking the donkeys took only a few minutes. Soon it was done. Morning light filled the valley, and the three friends were finally moving forward again, ready to start anew.

KaryKaryn drew the knitted hood over her head and took the lead.

As they hiked, Turk and KaryKaryn led; Yace walked behind the middle-aged woman. Kipp and Irwin each had a horse in-hand, and the donkeys were free to roam, although at this time they were full of eating and ready to travel. In tandem, they hiked back through the two valleys they had already traversed down; they ended up close to where the old and new roads met. By then, it was late in the day and shadows of the larger hillsides to the west occluded the sun's descent. Everyone wanted to rest, except KaryKaryn, but she conceded.

As they enjoyed time off their feet and a small meal, Irwin wanted to know, "How often do people travel through Tropogagi lands?"

"Most come from Enok." KaryKaryn pointed in that direction. "They send stupid men out, sacrifice for Tropogagi. Usually, we see white men enter jungle," coyly adding, "but none leave.

"White men be stupid. They drink, they smoke, they be dirty in mind, they believe they strong. They be weak. Tropogagi enjoy toxins white man eat and drink. Say it changes meat, make tasty. I say it changes Tropogagi mind to eat toxic man."

Irwin offered KaryKaryn a pear, and she took it.

"Toxins change white man mind. They see sparkly rocks, they marvel over color, fight overweight. They be stupid. I watch white men hunted by Tropogagi. They easy catch. Tropogagi enjoy weakness; they enjoy disgusting white man." She spat. "I better than Tropogagi, I eat animal." KaryKaryn gestured toward Turk. "Some Tropogagi learn not to eat white man."

Kipp said, "Some just like to fuk them."

"Kipp!" Yace hit his arm with a swift right hand.

"What? You are obviously gonna defend him, so I'm gonna provoke."

Irwin sneered, "Why must you be such an asshole, Kipp?"

"You're still jealous over Turk?" Yace cackled. She must have read Kipp's mind. "After all we've done in front of him, you're still jealous."

Kipp crossed his arms and snorted at her.

KaryKaryn pointed at Turk. "He not a threat." Her finger moved toward Kipp. "You be threat."

"I'm no threat," said Kipp.

"You want to kill him," said KaryKaryn. "I see it."

Kipp rose from his seat. "We should go now." He stuffed a handful of nuts into his mouth.

Yace grabbed his hand. "We're not moving."

"Nighttime be better to hike," said KaryKaryn.

"Better to hike?" Yace exclaimed. "I can't see anything at night."

Kipp grumbled, "I can see."

"So can I," Irwin added.

"Shut up, you two!" Yace ordered. "We're going to rest now."

KaryKaryn said, "Tropogagi rest when they rest, hunt when they hunt. We want to be uphill, safer there."

Yace snarled. "I thought we were safe!"

"Turk family want you dead," KaryKaryn said. "You want to live?"

"I can defend myself," she said. "I'm not scared of Tropogagi."

KaryKaryn glared at Yace. "We travel now."

"We should listen to KaryKaryn, Yace. She knows this landscape better than we do." Irwin said.

"Fine! Lead the way." Yace jumped to her feet and gestured for KaryKaryn to start walking. A light rose from Yace's hand, lingered above her head, and followed her closely as they left camp.

KaryKaryn stopped. "No light."

"Then how am I going to see?" Yace whined. "You all have no problems, but I'm not a Clan-Duin or a miner. You can't expect me to walk without some sort of help."

Kipp came to her aid. "I'll lead you." He held her hand and pulled Roper along behind.

Irwin brought up the back of the line, the donkeys between him and Roper's backside. Turk heeled at KaryKaryn's side as she navigated the travelers into the next valley—into the dense jungle. It was steep, and indeed hard on the four-legged animals.

Irwin thought about the time, as a youngster, following his father into Kobiton for the first time. He was brought back to reality when he tripped on a tree root.

KaryKaryn had been correct about bringing the horses and donkeys, although Irwin would never admit to that. He moved the ground, rolling rocks and logs, pushing aside trees, and parting gnarly bushes to make it easier for the horses and donkeys to maneuver.

They walked until Yace complained so much they stopped to rest. She slept the longest. When it was time, everyone waited for her to be ready before journeying on. This was not the trek Yace wanted to be on, but it was the way they had to go to get to Ozaroton—to the Gypsy in Koumin.

"Why are we always going up?" Yace complained. "Can't we go downhill for a while?"

KaryKaryn told them it was necessary to keep upslope, away from those who would harm them. The first day of hiking, the two women argued about routes. KaryKaryn was headstrong, and she did not bow to Yace. She acted as if she did not care if the tribes ate them—probably didn't.

Irwin and Kipp refrained from petty squabbles for once.

I do not recall Yace arguing so much. Maybe because she was the leader last time. Now she must share that seat with KaryKaryn. I wish she would just follow without instigating.

The further they trekked into the dark, dense jungle, the more they fell into a hardened cycle of walking until Yace complained too much. Then they would rest until she was ready to depart. They were on Yace's schedule—not KaryKaryn's. Had their emissary conceded?

At the next stop, Irwin asked, "How many other travelers have you led this way?" KaryKaryn had been studying Yace, not realizing he asked her a question.

Finally she said, "Few. People like you be rare to Daos. Few travel this way. We see more white-skin, stupid men. Many years back, large pack traveled through here. Large packs be safer here sometimes. Those travelers smell horrible, like you. Their meat bad."

"There were travelers that smelled like me?" Irwin said, curious to know more.

KaryKaryn shook her head, placed a hand over her eye. "Not like you. They have dark plum skin and one eye. They smell better than you, but still rotten meat."

Yace and Kipp gasped in unison. "Cyclops."

"You've seen the Cyclops!" Yace jumped. "How long ago was that? Do you know how many? Which way did they travel from? Where did you take them?"

"They shipwrecked. Tulu find them, ask for Umpa and me. We walked Cyclops to Ozaroton." She counted her fingers to show how many of them had traveled through volatile Tropogagi territory; thirteen Cyclops had earned safe passage.

"Shipwrecked! I'm glad you were able to rescue them." Yace appeared ecstatic. "Do you know if they continued on after Ozaroton? They're from a village called Riverview."

KaryKaryn shook her head. "They live Ozaroton now."

"They live there now?"

KaryKaryn nodded.

Yace continued to boil. "Holy Hakra!" The young woman turned to Kipp, standing now, and doing a little dance. "Did you hear that? We get to meet Drah and Ede's family! Oh, they're going to be thrilled. We'll have to find a Telepath in Ozaroton to communicate this information to Dana and Nonbry. But how will we do that? I guess we will have to trust that good things will happen." Her eyes bulged. "Holy Hakra, they'll be so happy!"

"Why can't you communicate with them?" Kipp asked Yace, "I've got the talisman."

"You do!" She paused, looked at her companions. "When did you last speak to Nonbry?"

"They said they were in Arisham territory, heading to Uer'Bin, right Irwin?" Kipp said, handing over the talisman.

"No, I mean, how long ago did you talk to them?"

"It was right after we saved you," Irwin counted, "about thirty-seven days ago."

"Well, it's dark and late. So contacting them now would be a bad idea. No one would be up to talk to, anyway. And we all know how angry Nonbry can get if he's woken up. Last thing anyone needs is a Nonbry headache!"

Kipp muttered, "He's annoying."

Yace clapped her hands. "Well then, it's settled. First thing tomorrow morning we'll make contact. Hopefully, they're not on the road by then."

KaryKaryn said, "I wake you when sun comes."

"Good idea." Yace remained exuberant. "So, KaryKaryn, do you go to Ozaroton often?"

"Yes. Umpa live there. I live there, sometime. I not like smell of town."

Yace pried, "Who is Umpa?"

"Me papa." KaryKaryn said. "He unwelcome here."

"Is that how you learned to speak like us, living in Ozaroton?" Yace's questions were relentless. "Is it a friendly town? Is that why Umpa lives there? Is he the one with the power of invisibility? Are there others with that power?"

"Umpa banished from Tropogagi. Mama, she be invisible. She be dead." KaryKaryn hung her head.

"Your mother's dead?" Yace's demeanor softened. "I'm sorry. I know how hard it is to grow up with only one parent. It is just me and my mother, Dana."

"Mama died when I born," KaryKaryn went silent.

"Oh, that must have been really hard for your father. I can't imagine what it's like to have a child born, if only to lose the person you're bonded to. That must have been a ridiculously hard for Umpa."

"Yes. Ava, Umpa sister took me, taught me."

"Do you have any siblings? Brothers or sisters?"

"No, I only. Many cousin. No brother. No sister."

"How did your parents meet?"

KaryKaryn stared off and told them the story. Her father had found her mother malnourished and scared. She had escaped from Daos City, although KaryKaryn had never been told the reason why. All she knew was that her mother fled, as far and quick as she could, living off the land and trying to remain hidden. Umpa discovered her sleeping in a tree crook.

For a long time, Umpa had kept the invisible woman hidden from his tribe. When they found out Umpa had been concealing a two-legged woman, he was immediately banished from the tribe—until KaryKaryn was born. Umpa sought his siblings to help raise the motherless child.

KaryKaryn had stayed with her Tropogagi tribe, the Arkin, until her coming of age ritual and the start of her menses. She was supposed to pick a mate, but refused to bond with any man from any tribe. Consequently, she was cast out. Intermingling amongst the Tropogagi tribes was acceptable, but to outright walk away from partnering meant immediate banishment. It was the way of these Cannibalistic clansmen. The Tropogagi also detested those who partnered with the same sex, as procreation was key to their survival.

At the end of her story, she confessed, "I prefer female." She continued to tell them that inbreeding and incest were heavily promoted within the tribes, and anyone who did not follow the Tropogagi's precarious ways was banished. Of course, there was always the option to be eaten by family, a more honorable way to serve the clan, especially if one was a disgrace.

Several of the scars KaryKaryn had on her body, face, and limbs had been from her continual defiance of Tropogagi rules before she became an adult. All her other scars happened since then and usually because she continued to travel through all the Tropogagi territories without remorse. KaryKaryn was unlike other Tropogagi. In so many ways, she used her uniqueness to act impervious to Tropogagi rules. She kept in contact with all the tribes, knowing that they had a need for a person like her; in the meantime, she used her stealth to stay alive.

Yace said, "Kipp and I have traveled across this planet. We've seen so many people, different societies. And what you say about the Tropogagi is common; there seems to be a general dislike of those who don't conform to the stereotypes. I mean, Irwin is a fitting example." He was horizontal, half asleep. "He is a loner, a miner, and prefers a man in his bed. I think it's sad that so many cannot be happy, when—it seems—that it's the people who are most miserable want everyone else to be miserable like them." She paused in thought. "It makes no sense to me. Why wouldn't people want others to be happy? Just because they're miserable with their life choices doesn't mean they should make everyone else feel that way. Good on you, KaryKaryn, for being true to yourself."

KaryKaryn smiled. "I am rarity."

"Yes, you are an amazing type of rare too!" said Yace.

KaryKaryn stifled a yawn. "Sleep now. Wake soon."

They were all tired. Only Yace appeared to have the energy to stay up and talk the night away. Irwin was already lying on his side with closed eyes, using his arm as a pillow, mostly asleep. Kipp encouraged Yace to lie down with him, and after a long moment, she did. Meanwhile, KaryKaryn sat in the nook of a tree. She sat up, but with eyes closed. Turk slept away from everyone with perked ears. They all slept through the night, lightly, until the sounds of morning birds woke them.

21

<u>Talk To The Gypsy</u>

After breakfast, Yace laid down, holding the talisman in her fingers. Irwin sensed her excitement. Soon she would have a metaphysical connection with her Gypsy family. This was how they kept in touch with those who would keep them safe on their journey back home to the Gypsy Camp—where Kipp and Yace had grown up, where they learned and practiced their power, their metaphysical talents. These were referred to as Talents throughout Urthis, but some people referred to them as Volatiles, or Vols. Yace hoped Nonbry would allow enough time for her to talk, to connect with all those she wanted to see and to visit with the family who now she remembered, missed dearly.

On the other hand, Irwin and Kipp were not looking forward to their conversation with Nonbry. The last few times they had contacted their telepathic advisor they had been chided for indiscretions beyond their control, Irwin more than Kipp. Although he had destroyed many places, killed many PCP—add to the list the palace in Daos City and the town of Enok—making travel more difficult for those with Talents. Still, Irwin hoped the people of Daos would be treated as people and not as they had been for many millennia—like animals slated for slaughter.

Irwin knew that Nonbry's advice was warranted, though at times cryptic. Kipp held much criticism toward the old man and his drawn-out stories. But it had been Nonbry who urged them to save Yace at all costs. And now that she was back to acting like herself, their crisis for a swift return to the Gypsy had been averted. Still, they needed to get through the land of cannibals and back home. Irwin wanted Yace to make the telepathic connection with Nonbry—wanted Yace to reconnect with her Gypsy family.

Soon her lips smacked together, announcing his presence, but the moment her eyes turned white, KaryKaryn sat back. Concern washed across the older woman's face. Turk whimpered, watching it all unfold.

Nonbry harrumphed, as he was known to do. "Your timing is impeccable." He was angry, as always.

Kipp stiffened. "Why?"

Irwin kept his cool and was cordial, as always. "Good day, Sir."

"Why have I been summoned?"

Kipp fidgeted. "Because Yace wants to talk to the Gypsy."

"Yace? Where is she?"

Kipp stammered. "You're speaking through her."

"So, the miner actually did his job and healed her?"

Irwin cleared his throat. "Yes, Sir."

"How sure are you sure of that? That you've healed Yace? That she's not still possessed? Last we spoke, you sounded defeated by the task."

"It took me a while to pull off all the telepathic spells, Sir, but she is healed." He tried not to let his nervousness show. "She remembers some things from her past, but her memory of what happened after her father took her is gone."

"Of course it is. He cast her out and with the help of a Witchtress of a woman. And though it's been a while since Dana has sensed Yace, we're not completely sure she survived the experience. It takes a strong psyche to reconnect with one's body after being cast out. It's possible that Dephen still has possession over her."

"How would that be possible?"

"You're not a Telepath, boy. You don't know what Telepaths are capable of. And to explain it all to you .... Regardless, whoever had access to her mind last kept her how they wanted her—pliable. If it's taken you this long to make her normal again, I'd keep both eyes on her. She could still be under some Telepath's control. If so, that person now knows all about you two and your relationship with her."

"Yace is Yace," barked Kipp.

Irwin remained level-headed. "Sir, I believe Yace is Yace too."

"How sure are you, Miner? How long has Yace been acting like herself?"

"A few days. Why?"

"Only a few days? I wouldn't trust her. If she just somehow came back while in your presence, that means she's still possessed, and you're being manipulated by a masterful Telepath. It's possible that Dephen is in her still."

He hated doubting himself, but was adamant, "Sir, my powers have worked, to a certain degree. I believe her memories of us were pushed aside, made inconsequential. It took a blunt hit to her head for her to come back to us."

"And before that. Was she still catatonic? Or did she just one day become conscious?"

"She became present in mind, a while ago, about five ... six days after leaving Daos Prime." Irwin said. "She told me it took her time to understand how to talk and do things. She was very child-like at first, but then—"

"I suspect you two have been compromised." Nonbry grumbled, "I should end this link. Dana was wrong about you, Miner."

"Nonbry, Sir, if you will just listen, we know Yace is herself. She remembers us, she remembers her family, she has memories of her past, just none from the time we were apart."

"How do you know? She could be playing you both. If she's given herself to Dephen, pledged her loyalty to him, Dephen would be unstoppable. And you'd never know because she's already accessed your minds. Though Kipp's more vulnerable than you to her powers of influence."

"And if she pledged her loyalty to Dephen, how would we know?"

"Only someone who can see their enmeshing, see the woven spells keeping them together, could."

"But you cannot."

"Not while we are enmeshed. There are people in Ozaroton who could see it."

"But my powers. I have made physical contact with her on many occasions. I know my power works on her and on Kipp—on everyone I touch."

"And every time you touch her, she has access to you."

Kipp jumped into the argument. "I've bonded with her since then! And Irwin has touched me. We'd know if Yace wasn't herself."

Irwin said, "Yace is Yace, Sir. I healed her, and we are making our way your direction now."

"Kipp, you ignorant fool. If it was Yace's idea for you two to mate, then you've been under her spell the whole time!"

There was no pleasing the cocky old Telepath.

He ground his teeth. "What gets me is how she knew there would be a Gypsy gathering going on right now? I'm highly suspicious of all this."

"Sir," Irwin said. "I am sure that Yace did not know there was a gathering going on right now. It was decided before we rested for the night that we would speak to you this morning."

"As it was here for this morning's meeting, which you've interrupted." Nonbry harrumphed again. "Dana and Yace are connected. That's how she knew what's going on here. Yes, too many coincidences for me to ignore this imposition."

"Did Dana say anything about Yace to you?" Irwin pressed, "Or is this just an imposition for you, Nonbry, Sir?"

Have I hit a nerve?

"Where are you?"

Kipp was put off by Nonbry's hard attitude, as always.

Irwin worked the conversation. "In the land of the cannibals, Sir."

"You've gone that far already?"

"Yes, Sir."

"It appears you're traveling at a decent pace compared to us. Have you found the cannibals yet?"

"Yes, Sir. They found us, actually."

"Found you, but they didn't eat you. Good to know you've survived, so far."

"They found out that my flesh is poisonous. They say I taste like Death. They spared Yace and Kipp as well." He asked then, "Why are you having a gathering of Gypsy?"

"Our soldiers are convinced that there is a shortcut across the Arisham plains." Irwin did not miss the angry tone. "I, however, want to take the road to Quy Joern and continue our search for Cyclops. We were discussing directions when you interrupted."

"We found the Cyclops," said Irwin, almost as excited as Yace had been the prior night. "That was the other reason we are contacting you. They live in Ozaroton—a town on the other side of Tropogagi territory, about three moons west of Daos Territory."

"Yes, I know where Ozaroton is—stupid Miner. How is it you know where the Cyclops are?"

"Our emissary, KaryKaryn, guided the Cyclops to Ozaroton many years ago."

"Your emissary?" He turned his head in search of this person. "Where is this KaryKaryn?"

KaryKaryn's hood was up, and she stayed hidden in the shadows, just out of view, as was Turk. Irwin flung his arm in KaryKaryn's direction. "KaryKaryn, please do not be afraid of Nonbry."

She sat forward, dropped the hood, and said, "Ivara, Yedel, Dain, Treh, Ed, Tris, aah … aah …." She knew a few of the Cyclops's names, her only proof that she knew the Cyclops.

Nonbry eyed the woman. "The Cyclops are in Ozaroton?"

KaryKaryn nodded, "Yes."

"How long have they been there?"

"Six year."

"Six years."

"What should we do when we meet up with the Cyclops?" Irwin queried the old Gypsy, younger brother of Dephen, watchdog of the Gypsy.

"Have Yace contact me. Cyclops can be fickle."

Kipp whispered, "Yeah, they are."

"I suggest you find a third-party Telepath," Nonbry said. "A reliable one should live in Ozaroton. That's the only place I'd trust in all Uer 'Bin to have a competent Telepath willing to help with negotiations. Have that reliable Telepath check Yace's mind. Make sure she's actually all there and not Dephen in disguise."

You bitter old man, Yace is Yace. If you had witnessed all we have, you would see it too. There is no way that Dephen could have survived my powers.

Irwin held back the urge to speak of it.

Nonbry is the ignorant one this time.

"Are we still meeting up with the Gypsy in Koumin?"

"Once you arrive in Ozaroton, and see a Cyclops, contact me. At that point, I will know where we are in relationship to where we want to be."

KaryKaryn confessed, "Cyclops have family, have job. They not leave Ozaroton."

"That is why we must negotiate," said Nonbry. "Six years is enough time to settle down and become part of a community. Ozaroton is much like Riverview where the Cyclops are from. Only Talented people are allowed in those places—which is what makes it appealing to people like us."

KaryKaryn smiled, "It be full of Talent."

"Had Dephen not taken advantage of my kind nature, we would have gone to Ozaroton instead of Onj Raha." Nonbry's lips contorted—probably holding back the urge to speak.

Kipp chuckled. "At least you didn't have to go all the way to Quy Joern looking for Cyclops."

"We would've. There are a few towns, one north of Quy Joern and another along the border of Arisham and Hakara. They could have taken up residence in either place. But both of those towns are chilly places most of the year. If I remember, Ozaroton is much like Riverview—warm most of the year. I don't want to take the road from Insupan to Koumin again."

Kipp whispered to Irwin, "That's where we found Olei and his family."

"There are many patrols along that road."

Irwin sensed Nonbry's irritability and asked, "Have you had any more problems since Onj Raha?"

He glared at Irwin. "Of course we have! In fact, a searchlight is on us because of our communications ... all the things you've done so far." He took a deep breath. "Thankfully, the Gypsy are resourceful and know not to get caught."

"I am sorry, Sir; I did not know the implications."

"Because of you, PCP are talking about me and my troop, and they are spreading false information about the other Gypsy. And because of the terror you wrought to Onj Raha, Ahradah, Lady Gretchen's farm, Nuaki Village, and Daos City, people with Talents won't ever be allowed free. You've not deterred my plight, but you've made many places even more wary of strangers like us."

Irwin hung his head. "I am truly sorry, Sir."

"The last thing Talented people need are more restrictions because one person cannot control himself. And saying I'm sorry does nothing to help. You've caused much chaos and destruction in too many places for you to be allowed to continue beyond Ozaroton. If I were you, Miner, I'd go back to the mines. I know there are some located upslope from Ozaroton. That's probably the only good place left for you to live on all of Urthis."

His words stunned Irwin.

"I do hope Yace hasn't corrupted too many minds on my side. Don't contact me again until you've arrived in Ozaroton." Nonbry severed the connection and Yace was summoned back into her body and her eyes opened.

Kipp's knuckles were white from making tight fists throughout the exchange. "What an asshole."

Yace was glowing with happiness as she sat up. "Oh, that was so much fun. I want to do it again. Soon."

Both men groaned. Yace bubbled with emotions.

"Oh, my goodness, it was so good to see everyone. It was like they were all huddled around to see me. They told me Nonbry was having a discussion with them when I appeared. I could tell they were relieved that I summoned him away. Oh, my! It was so much fun to see everyone.

"Flinn says hi." Yace leaned into Kipp and hugged him. "That's from Flinn."

They continued to embrace, Kipp quietly asked, "How is Flinn?"

"She's grown, oh my, how she's grown." Yace could not be contained. "You might not even recognize her! Her hair is cut short, and she's much taller now."

Kipp closed his eyes, holding onto Yace. "I miss Flinn."

She continued to talk with excitement. She pulled away from Kipp's embrace to look him in the eyes. "Even Dinill asked how you are doing. I can't remember the last time she seemed concerned about you. And then Hauss. He seemed indifferent, as always ... more stiff, almost jaded. I think ... I think he misses you the most of all your siblings.

"Oh, and the cyclops," She looked at Irwin as she spoke about their fellow Gypsy. "Ede and Drah were ecstatic to hear that we know where their older siblings are. They've not seen them since they were children. Oh, this is going to be so amazing if we can reunite them. Drah says we'll need to make contact again before engaging her sisters. They will not trust us, so we'll have to come to them with proof, stories or memories that only they would know." She squealed with excitement. "It'll be so fun to travel with them back home. I can't wait!"

Kipp muttered, "Yeah, we know they're fickle."

"You told him where we were, right?"

Irwin said, "Yes."

"Oh, my goodness. They're out in the middle of nowhere." Yace gasped. "I saw it! There is no road, only open land. I think they're lost."

Kipp grumbled, "No road, but Nonbry said—"

Yace kept on. "It is so flat and there are no trees. It reminds me of the landscape around Insupan, where we picked up Leola and everyone."

Kipp said, "Yeah, Nonbry mentioned something about backtracking through there again."

"Oh, I want to get going now. The quicker we get to Ozaroton, the quicker we get home!" Yace appeared to have found the vigor needed to continue with the arduous journey. "I'm so excited! Come on."

Irwin studied Yace.

Is Nonbry right about Yace still being possessed? Would I be able to tell if she is manipulating me?

Stepping up to face her head-on, he opened his arms for a hug and smiled at her. "I am glad you got to see your family again." She leaned in to embrace him.

"So am I. Dana says that you did a good job saving me." She squeezed him with an extra tight hug before letting go. "Thank you, Irwin. Thank you for not giving up on me."

Once they let go, Irwin thought, *yes, Nonbry does not know what he is talking about.*

KaryKaryn interrupted the happy moment. "Next land we travel be Arkin land. Land of my family. We can travel around land, but if we encounter my people, they will hunt and kill. Best if we offer gift. Tulu, Roha, and Nici are same, but meaner. They chase. We must give gift."

Yace said, "I don't want to be chased."

Irwin asked, "What type of gifts?"

KaryKaryn said, "Cloth, knives, jewelry, jugs, bowls, flask. They like shiny, useful things. Bag of shells, they take that too. Most clans, cloth represents power. They like shirt, or hood—warmer than pant."

Irwin said, "I can make up anything metal. Just tell me what they might want."

"We have clothes we can give them too," said Yace.

"My people take anything. Tulu, Roha, and Nici want weapons."

"I will make them metal bowls."

KaryKaryn looked at Irwin. "You smell funny, but I like you."

"I hear that a lot." He smiled.

KaryKaryn rose to her feet first; Turk, attentive at her side. Irwin stood. Kipp hopped up and helped Yace to her feet. With panniers and saddles already cinched, the horses and donkeys were ready to depart. Irwin took up their lead lines; he too was ready to leave, as were KaryKaryn and Turk. Yace dusted off her orange and pink skirt and reached for Kipp's hand.

They continued to follow the animal trail found the prior night. KaryKaryn led. Turk was two steps behind her. Yace strode ahead of Kipp who was pulling Roper behind. Irwin brought up the rear. The donkeys trotted along between Roper and himself. Bodi followed Irwin. Jungle bird calls echoed, highlighting the sharp rustling of bushes and branches that surrounded their caravan; there was life all around.

Their reprieves were only long enough to water and feed themselves and the animals, and then KaryKaryn got them moving again. This jungle was alive no matter the time of day. They passed animals on the hunt for food—invertebrates slithered and crawled, colorful birds played amongst the foliage, and some four-legged creatures did not rush away at the sight of them.

They crossed a path amid the sparkling scent of orchids in full bloom. It was that time of year when special flora and fauna were opening and pollinating. Every once in a while, Kipp, or Yace, would have a sneezing fit. Irwin walked on, mostly unaffected, as were the two natives of the land.

They shimmied around vine plants and ivy that tried to grab them. Irwin used his Erthin powers to move larger branches and boulders out of the animal's way. But he could not make out the trail KaryKaryn was following. Was she leading them blindly into the Tropogagi hunting land?

Turk, as sentry, kept watch while the others rested. They refreshed and relaxed in small stints and then walked for a long stretch of time. It was muggy, flies and insects swarmed with deafening buzzing and clicking. It took them several days to pass through Ta'Api territory, but without incident. They were in Arkin land, KaryKaryn's tribal home. She took them into the middle of that territory and down to the ocean to meet her family. Although the tribe had rejected her lifestyle, KaryKaryn was still allowed to visit—see her father's family.

When they came to the beach, KaryKaryn instructed Irwin to make a large fire. She wanted to draw her family's attention, if they hadn't been already aroused. It wasn't long before the elders approached the fire.

She stood between the travelers and her people while she negotiated a safe passage. The elders were leery of Irwin and Yace, and their eyes glaring. Fellow tribesmen formed shadows at the edge of the jungle. It was obvious that these Tropogagi were eager to see these outlanders. The caravan would be allowed to travel through their land.

The Arkin tribe was enormous—over three-hundred tribesmen and women—all descending from two ancient people. The tribespeople watched intently while Irwin made an offering of his flint stick and grinding stone—something he would never need to use again. The ability to make fire was highly valued amongst the tribes. Fire allowed them to smoke fish—the only other meat they ate besides human flesh—and store it for colder, rainier days.

Although KaryKaryn was not welcome to live with her tribe, they were open to her visiting. She reconnected with family members, but soon they left the beach and reentered the jungle, heading up the slope once more.

They were escorted for the first few days by a few of the younger, more curious, Arkin members. But no one bothered them. They had been allowed safe passage until they reached the border between tribes. The Tulu territory was next, then they would pass through Roha and Nici before arriving at Ozaroton.

Although Irwin had purchased many pounds of food in Enok, their rations were dwindling. Frequently, they found lavish amounts of food along the way—mangos, dragon fruit, grapes, guavas, avocados, coconuts, bananas, asparagus, a variety of herbs—all growing in abundance in the humid environment. All the food they gathered appeared ripe and ready to be eaten. As they approached the invisible line between territories, KaryKaryn encouraged them to stock up on the fresh produce.

The day all the sets of curious amber eyes were gone was the day they reached the end of Arkin territory. Now they had to cross Tulu land. Not wanting any hostile confrontations, KaryKaryn took them straight toward the Tulu gathering area on the east side of their massive territory. For them to pass without being chased down and eaten, she knew they needed to show themselves. By now, the travelers were keenly aware of their surroundings. They had grown accustomed to all types of native plants and animals and knew what was poisonous. And all the smells and wild calls that echoed throughout the shadowy landscape were now familiar.

The Tulu were unlike any Clan-Duin creature ever seen before. Their sounds shook the trees and scared the birds away. They descended all at once to the ground from the thick and shady trees from which they swung. The Tulu tribesmen were large apes with markings across their flesh that discolored their fur, making patterns. Their wailing calls and taunting grunts shook the ground and Irwin's nerves.

KaryKaryn bowed in their presence; Kipp, Yace, and Irwin mimicked her gesture. She then stood tall and spoke. She motioned to Irwin to produce a goblet in exchange for safe passage through Tulu Land. Once the shiny goblet was handed over, they were granted a ten-day reprieve. After that, the unruly tribe would down hunt them. It usually took twenty days to cross their treacherous land. The weary travelers moved on after the exchange, heading upslope once more.

During their climb, Yace fretted. "How are we going to get out of Tulu territory without being eaten alive?"

"We sleep little," KaryKaryn advised. "Run much."

Irwin said, "You want us to run through the same dense vegetation we have been walking through and do it with the horses in tow?"

KaryKaryn cocked her head sideways. "I say leave them, but you did not. You be responsible, remember?"

Yace said, "We won't make it out of Tulu territory, will we?"

"We go up slope, around Tulu."

"What about the other Tropogagi clans?" asked Irwin. "Will we need to make offerings to them also?"

"If we go upslope, we make no offer. We go around Tropogagi land." KaryKaryn was adjusting her hooded shawl, staring up the steep and dark slope of land.

Irwin scratched the back of his head. "Is that wise? It is winter further up there."

"You told me it takes about twenty days to get through each territory," said Yace. "But if we go upslope, will it take longer? I would like to get to Ozaroton in a timely manner."

"We safer upslope."

"You didn't answer my question," said Yace. "I don't want to take half a year to get to Ozaroton."

KaryKaryn's eyebrows pierced each other. "You want fast route?"

"Yes."

22

<u>Could Yace be Pregnant?</u>

Their journey became tougher now. This was what the Tulu Tropogagi wanted. They enjoyed chasing and intimidating two-legged creatures. It was rare for the Tulu to have more than one or two mortals venture into their territory. They usually had to cross over into Arkin territory to hunt—to find tasty two-legged morsels. Many clansmen and women did not heed the ten-day reprieve and followed—pursued—the travelers instead of making havoc with their Tropogagi neighbors.

Although Yace insisted they take the fastest route, there was none. And with flesh-hungry Tulu in pursuit, KaryKaryn and her guests needed to travel along the edges of the Tropogagi territory. She wanted to keep them safe and take them above the jungle, but it was a long and arduous climb. They needed to be to the north on the exposed plateaus that shadowed the canopy during the afternoon hours.

Beyond the weathered plateaus loomed jagged foothills and sky-piercing mountains—snow covered and often dressed by clouds. It would take several days to get out of the jungle and find a path that led up to the safety of the wide-open plateaus.

One evening, after settling down for a brief rest in a small ravine, they enjoyed a bushel of bananas KaryKaryn had plucked earlier that day. The horses and donkeys were free to walk around the open space along a creek's edge and uphill from where they were resting. There was no grass, so the animals ate ferns and tree leaves. They enjoyed some fruit along the way.

It was quiet, almost serene, until Yace stopped eating mid-bite. "Ugh, there is something wrong with this banana." She rushed toward a tree where she leaned and vomited.

Everyone stopped eating. Kipp threw down his mostly eaten banana and rushed to help Yace. He grasped her hair, held it out of the way, while she threw up what little food was in her stomach. "You gonna be alright?" he asked, kneeling at her side.

Yace was on her knees, trying to catch her breath.

"I don't know," she said.

KaryKaryn came over and offered a flask.

"Thank you," Yace said after taking a guzzle. Her tired eyes settled on Kipp. "Did the banana smell bad to you?"

"No. You gonna be alright? You look a little green."

KaryKaryn sniffed at the mostly eaten banana. "My banana smell good."

"Irwin, what about your banana?" asked Kipp.

He had already finished his fruit. "It tasted fine to me."

Though it is no leg of lamb. I am so hungry for a chunk of meat.

"Do we have anything else to eat? I'm still hungry. Maybe some grapes?"

Kipp helped Yace back to the circle.

"We ate the last of those this morning," Irwin said as he watched Yace sit next to Kipp and lean on him.

She closed her eyes and said, "Maybe a piece of wood then."

"Pregnant Tropogagi ask for wood," said KaryKaryn.

Yace's eyes popped opened, "I wish! But I can't have babies. My body ... I was horribly hurt when I was younger. I was told I'd never be able to have children. Maybe I should lie down for a while and sleep it off."

Kipp went rigid at her side.

"What's the matter, Kipp?" Yace gasped. "Are you fuking fooling me? You think I might be pregnant? What the fuk!" She stared at him. "I had my menses!? When the fuk were you going to tell me?"

KaryKaryn said, "Your smell has changed."

Yace struck Kipp and then began crying. Irwin watched with confusion. He couldn't tell if Yace was scared or happy to find out she was possibly pregnant. He knew she wanted a family but had come to accept she physically could not. This was a startling revelation for her indeed.

KaryKaryn withdrew from the emotional conversation and ate another banana. Irwin sat forward.

"You're a fukin' asshole, Kipp! I hate you!" Yace shouted at him, slapping him again in the face. She turned her attention to Irwin. "Did you know about this too?" He moistened his lips to speak. "You're as much to blame as Kipp."

"What?! What did I do?"

"You didn't tell me I had my menses!"

"Now you are blaming me. How am I supposed to know about women's cycles? You never bled before, and you never told me women bled, so how am I supposed to know what is going on? Do not blame me, Yace. Besides, you two are the ones who have been going at it like rabbits."

Yace's nostrils flared. Her blue eyes twitched with anger, and her lips twisted. "Do you happen to know how many days it's been since I bled?"

Irwin counted on his fingers. "Fifty-eight, give or take a day."

Yace glared at Kipp. "Fifty-eight days. Are you fuking fooling me? I'm over a moon pregnant! What the fuk, Kipp!" She slugged his shoulder.

It was obvious to Irwin that Kipp was embarrassed, ashamed of what he had not confessed to Yace. He rubbed the nape of his neck and looked at the Metalist, hoping—maybe—for some verbal help.

"Congratulations?!" said Irwin. Yace and Kipp glowered at him.

It did not matter that Yace was pregnant. They pressed on, in a northwest direction, found a trail up to the plateaus and followed the edge of the jungle's canopy.

One day, KaryKaryn told them that they were out of Tulu Territory and now walked above Roha's lands. They were safe for now. But the plateaus were cut up by deep chasms full of churning water and jagged rocks. Soon they had to descend into the jungle once more, to go around another deep breach in land. At times, the trail they took was straight up and down, with very few options for an easy descent. Everyone's body ached. All this traveling up and down the steep cliffs was harrowing for the animals and the people alike.

KaryKaryn assured them often that she knew where to go.

Beyond the rough terrain, they had to contend with Yace's livid attitude. She was still furious about Kipp's aloofness. She refused to speak to him and mumbled angry obscenities while walking along the trail. "How fuking aloof can one animal be?"

Irwin heard her ranting.

If only you knew how thoughtful Kipp is, you torpid Telepath.

He snickered.

Right now, in fact, your boyfriend is retrieving herbs for your stomach. Why are you being so ungrateful of the things he does for you?

He tried not to be angered by Yace's reaction, but nonetheless he was. "He might be aloof sometimes, but Kipp can be helpful too. I think it has been a while since you have seen that side of him."

"Stop defending him, Irwin. Kipp fuked up. You and I both know he's an idiot when it comes to women. He says he knows all about us, but he's an idiot!"

"If anyone is an idiot about women, it is me, not Kipp. Trust me."

"You're not an idiot, Irwin! You're just naïve and socially awkward around women. I trust your sense of judgement better than Kipp's. He thinks with his manhood, not his mind." She glanced around him, perhaps trying to see beyond Irwin and the animals behind him. "Where's that worthless dog, anyway?"

"He's bringing up the back of the pack," said Irwin. "He wanted me to lead the horses, so you two could have some space apart from each other."

Yace continued to stew. "Earlier he was thinking about me being pregnant and could not figure out who the father would be. Although he's sure it's not yours, he did think about it for a long time and-and you being a father to my child didn't really anger him. But the idea of Turk being the father. He did conquer me. It could be his. That realization boiled Kipp's blood.

"Now he wants to rip Turk's head off, so I must keep making him think of other things. And then you mention us procreating like rabbits back then." She snarled, "What the fuk, Irwin?!" She stopped walking and turned to him "Kipp knows how babies are made. He knows that women act different, smell different, when we are prime for baby making. He knows smells! How could he not know I was ovulating? It's part of his instinct to know!"

Irwin stammered, "I-I do not know what you want me to say, Yace."

"I don't understand why he didn't tell me I could become pregnant. He should've told me when we first reconnected!" She stomped her feet. "Why is he so fukin' selfish?"

"Kipp is aloof. He is not selfish. And you know he cares. He cares deeply about you, Yace."

"Only sometimes." She huffed. "It's probably good that he's at the back of the pack!"

"Kipp cares about you all the time, Yace, and has for as long as I've been on this journey with him. I do not understand how you can be so mad at him for forgetting one little thing in all the things that we've endured."

"It's the most important thing, Irwin! Kipp should know better." She pointed at Irwin, her finger touching his bare chest. "He should have told me about my menses. I mean, come on, Irwin, what do you think would've happened if one day I started bleeding?"

"He would have told you."

"But not before I bled! He would wait until I was, and then be like, 'Oops, sorry I didn't tell you.' Oh, I'm so angry right now."

"You did say that you wanted a family at some point."

"I do! I've always wanted a family of my own. I helped raise all the Gypsy babies believing I'd never have my own child." She paused and drew a deep breath. "Kipp knows how I feel about having a family, yet he forgot to tell me that I can actually make a family."

"Look, Yace, I understand why you are bitter. But why are you not happy about being pregnant? If you have always wanted a family, and are indeed pregnant with most likely Kipp's child, I would expect you to be happy."

"Think about it like this, Irwin. I just found out I can have a child after being told my whole life I'd never be able to. How's it even possible that this happened? I mean, come on, how was I healed when Tamera couldn't even ...? Was it my father? But how could he have? I don't have the power to heal myself, not like you—someone had to have a hand in this miracle. But did they know what they were doing? Did they heal me fully? Can I carry a child all the way until the end? Will I have a miscarriage? Will it be stillborn? Will I die during childbirth? I mean, there's a lot of questions going through my mind right now, like was me menstruating a fluke, or for real? Do you even know? I mean, how positive is everyone that I'm pregnant? Maybe something else is going on in my body? Maybe I have a disease. Maybe I'm dying?"

Maybe you are overreacting.

"KaryKaryn did say you smelled different."

"Different from what? Does she even know what a pregnant woman smells like? I don't think she's ever been pregnant, so how would she know?"

He stared at Yace with an urge to yell, *KaryKaryn is Clan-Duin, and a woman!*

Her nostrils flared. "I just want to know if this is real or not. That I'm genuinely pregnant. Smells are just that ... behaviors are another." She paused again, waiting for Irwin to respond. "I mean, I'm curious to know exactly how I was miraculously healed. When did it happen? And was it by someone who knew what they were doing? This may be something worse! Maybe something is terribly wrong with me. Maybe I *am* dying!"

Holy Hakra!

He noticed Yace looking around the animals, probably waiting for Kipp to appear. "I do not think you are dying, Yace. It may be that, indeed, you are pregnant." He shrugged. "I say, just be happy with what you have and what you can do in the here and now."

"I'm fukin' scared Irwin. This is too surreal for me." Her voice softened, and she began to sob. "I'm not sure I want to be pregnant."

KaryKaryn came back up the trail. "Quiet you. We be at edge of Roha land. See rock." She pointed. "That be Roha rock. Many Roha live there. They use rock to see over trees."

A lone spire of jagged rock jutted up from the dense canopy above where they hiked. They were along the edge of a forested plateau, about ten kilometers away from the Roha vantage point.

Yace whispered, "Can they see us?"

"Possible," KaryKaryn replied as she walked away.

Yace retched again. Irwin kept close to her, offered her the comforts Kipp would have if he had been there. He could feel their Clan-Duin friend, far off—now several days away by foot—gathering precious items for Yace. He hoped Kipp would return soon. They traveled up in elevation and were not on the same path they had been following when Kipp left the congregation.

It was during their first stop for water, food, and rest that Yace realized her beloved was no longer with them. Immediately she tore into Irwin, "Where is Kipp?"

"I do not know."

"Yes, you do. When did he leave us?"

He shrugged.

"I know you know where he is. You're covering for him! Of course you would—you two have that secret love thing going on. Fuk me, I should've known!"

"Yace, you are overreacting. Kipp has no love for me."

"That's horseshit, and you know it. He loves you a lot. Probably loves you more than me at this point." She growled and poked his chest. "What the fuk! Why Irwin? I thought you were one of the good ones?"

"What?! I do not understand what you are complaining about. Kipp left to get you ginger root, burdock root, mint, chamomile, and something else I cannot remember." He paused to scratch his ankle until it almost bled. "I hope he brings back something meaty too."

Yace softened, nearly crumpling. "He went to get me herbs for my stomach?" She sobbed now, "I'm the idiot!" Her lips trembled and tears dribbled down her cheeks. "But, yeah, I'd like a pork pie too. Are you okay? Something bite you, Irwin?"

Ignoring her, he said, "Let us not talk about pork right now. Although it sounds good, I am not too trusting of any pork product from Daos. Maybe somewhere to the west, like Ozaroton, they would have trustworthy pork."

"I'm so sorry I yelled at you, Irwin." Her hair draped across her face, making her look mangy. She leaned into him for a hug. "I haven't been feeling myself lately."

"I had not noticed," he said with a sarcastic flair.

"What's that supposed to mean?"

KaryKaryn growled at them. "Please rest!"

After a quick nap, they began moving again. There was no chatter this time. Soon they came to a wide creek that led down to a high waterfall. It was there that they stopped for a meal and refreshments. Yace did not complain. Her energy levels seemed to come and go, but for now, she looked tired. Irwin could see it in her eyes as she scanned the foliage for any signs of Kipp. After her earlier rant, Yace kept mute and appeared ready to have Kipp back at her side.

They continued hiking throughout the night into the early morning until, at last, they stopped for a long stint of rest. Kipp had not returned, and Yace looked worried. She got sick again after eating more fruit pieces. Now she looked too pale to continue.

Irwin patted her hand. "Are you going to be alright, Yace?"

"Bring Kipp back, Irwin, please."

"I can tell he is coming back to us right now." He felt Kipp off in the distance.

"I can't hear his thoughts or see through his eyes like I can when he's close. He's too far off." She held onto Irwin. "I want him back."

"If you cannot hear his thoughts, it is entirely possible that my tattoo is working."

"You believe your tattoo is blocking my link to him?"

"It could be part of the reason you cannot hear or see through his eyes."

"How will he find us then?"

"My smell. And I will pull on his tattoo, tug him in our direction."

"You can do that?"

He pointed at her tattoo. "That is my metal. It has my signature, my power mottled into it. I can feel you from many kilometers away if I concentrate."

"Your powers are amazing, Irwin. You know I don't mind being claimed by you. Just don't tell Kipp I said that."

You and Kipp are very much alike.

He smiled, "I am glad you still like me."

"Who wouldn't like you, Irwin?"

"Nonbry. He has told me what he thinks of me many times. I know how Kipp feels about me too."

"Nonbry's an ass, Irwin. You, of all people, should know that by now. And Kipp has a great appreciation of you and your abilities. He's quite fond of you, Irwin. Honor that."

He ignored her suggestion that Kipp had any feelings for him. "Kipp and I have talked about Nonbry at great lengths. But I still do not understand why Kipp does not respect his elders, no matter how crazy their ideas might be."

"To be honest, Irwin, Kipp never liked how Nonbry treated me. But finding out he's my uncle explains why he's kept a watchful eye on me ever since I joined the Gypsy. You know, without Nonbry's help, Kipp's whole family would've ended up servants to Hakra and the PCP. I think he's forgotten that." Yace confided. "It all makes me furious, though, but especially when Kipp outright ignores everything Nonbry says, which—"

"Which is what gets him into trouble! Yes, I agree. Oh, trust me, Yace, I wish Kipp was more thoughtful about his elders too."

"I always thought it was just women who were thoughtful, cognizant of others, until you came along, that is. I've always loved that side of you, Irwin." Yace placed her hand on his face. "You've grown up so much since we first met. Who would've thought you'd become so amazing?" Her blue eyes never left his. "I'm very proud of you, Irwin."

A smile crossed his usually solemn face. "I am too. Without you and Kipp, I would never have realized my true potential."

They had moved far along in their trek and were currently above the jungle, following the edge of a plateau once more. KaryKaryn had located a shallow cave to rest in; it was a place she had used as refuge many times before, especially when the weather became foul. It was also home to bats, which were out searching for bugs when they arrived. The backend of the cave smelled of guano, and there were sooty marks from campfires and left over bones. It was barely tall enough for the horses to stand, and just long enough for everyone to have a space to sleep. It was a decent place to rest and wait for Kipp's return.

They had just settled down to nap. Kipp arrived carrying his bundle of presents for Yace. The bellowing of the donkeys announced his presence right before he placed the enormous bounty at her feet. Inside an animal hide there was a woven blanket, and inside that were feather-stuffed pillows, soft clothing made for a girthed woman, goat's cheese and jerky, dried fish, a satchel of various dried fruit pieces, bundles of dried herbs, a sack of roots, and a bowl of flat-bread crackers. All of this he had stolen from towns, inside residences, and off laundry lines.

Kipp fell out of his eagle form and landed gracefully on his feet before Yace. He knelt; his dark locks hid his sorrow filled eyes. "I'm sorry I was gone for so long, my love. I bring you gifts. If you will have them ... and me."

Irwin watched, slightly entranced by Kipp. Yace smiled, placed her hand upon his forehead; he looked up at her. "I love you Kipp. Let us never fight like this again."

Their eyes locked. Kipp said, "You're right. I should've told you."

Her hand moved to his cheek, stroked his prickly facial hair. Tears welled up in her eyes. "It wasn't something you would've thought about. I understand that now."

"Oh, Yace." Kipp leaned into her, and they kissed with passion.

"Kipp," Yace pulled him atop her. They continued kissing and fondling and then began fornicating.

Is this what pregnant women do to their men? She is so emotionally charged. Is this what we get to deal with, and for how many moons?

Irwin moved away from his friends. Though he was tired, he did not want to listen to Kipp and Yace frolic again. They were loud—obnoxious—with the sounds they made.

KaryKaryn and Turk were also quick to leave. Irwin followed them out of the cave. They drifted away from the cavern entrance. Each found a place to rest.

Turk stayed closest to the entrance—a good lookout point.

23

ULTIMATE LOYALTY

It was raining the next day when they left the cave. Yace held a smitten look all day long. Kipp did too, but dropped it when not at her side. He stepped in stride with Irwin after relieving himself away from the worn path. Yace kept on leading Roper, humming a tune.

"Hey! Thank you for watching after Yace, tending to her anxieties and what-not—you know, putting up with her." Kipp swatted at some bugs and kept his eyes on Irwin.

"Of course. I am glad you were able to find her clothing and those herbs."

"I noticed you didn't eat any of the meat. You know I got it for all of us, right?"

"It smelled good, but she probably needs it more than I do."

Several strides later, Kipp said, "You always put everyone before yourself. Why do you do that?" Irwin shrugged, and Kipp pulled him to a stop. "I need you to know that I really ... I think of you more than just a friend, you know."

"Like a brother?"

"Ha! You're nicer than Hauss has ever been." Kipp rubbed his arm and looked down the muddy trail they were following. Roper's butt was still in sight. "I just ... I, ah, I appreciate you. A lot. Thank you for-for everything." He leaned in to tap Irwin's forehead with his own, but then pulled the Metalist into an embrace. "Thank you." Both men were already sweaty from the precipitation and didn't hold on for long.

"Of course, Kipp. You know I appreciate you too."

Kipp blushed, and that dopey look he would wear from time to time spread his lips. He then picked up his pace and caught up with Yace.

Yace has him spun. I hope it lasts.

KaryKaryn kept them to the outskirts of Roha territory. The landscape above the jungle was easier to traverse. But when the plateaus ended at wide chasms cut by busy waters, they were forced to descend into the jungle. Crossing paths with many amazing species, they met angry boars, slow-moving sloths, deadly snakes, and giant spiders lurking from massive webs. The insects were unrelenting; everyone furiously scratched at their bites, including Irwin.

For several days, they walked along a well-worn animal trail above the jungle. Up that high, the air was cool at night and there were no insects, but the echoing sounds of wildlife kept them on high alert. This was a trail KaryKaryn said she had taken many times and was much easier for the horses to navigate. But like any other trail along the plateaus, this one ended without warning and sent them back down the slope into the dark canopy. Although this would be an opportunity to refill food bags, they were susceptible here to detection by the Roha Tropogagi. Once again, they found themselves in the midst of an inhospitable land.

Birds called back and forth, seemingly agitated. The echoes of animals screeching and hooting was deafening. A small pack of monkeys watched them navigate through the jungle. These native animals were on high alert. Strangers with strange smells had invaded their territory. This deep into the jungle, the horses were spooked, and the donkeys' ears were keenly upright. They would bellow out but were immediately scolded by Irwin who carried a whip in his hand. This was not a place to have an attention-grabbing beacon.

They stopped briefly to stock up on fruit again. KaryKaryn whispered to Kipp, "You done?"

He stood atop Roper's rump, partially hidden by a loquat tree's foliage. He was filling a sack with mangoes, guava, and something that resembled papaya. "Almost."

Yace tied a filled bag to the back of Roper's saddle.

Irwin held the horse in place and slapped Nee Nee who bellowed out again. She was highly agitated. Both donkey's ears twitched toward every direction. Did they know what was coming?

KaryKaryn shouted, "We leave, now!"

Roper shuffled his feet sideways, knocking Kipp off balance. He slid off the enormous horse's butt and landed on his feet, facing the oncoming threat.

To the east and to the south, surrounding foliage came to life. Giant apes, black and hairy and showing large teeth, hands, and feet, swarmed around the troupe.

The apes hollered, screaming, beating their chests, tree branches, and trunks, their power on display.

Irwin muttered, "Shit."

Kipp echoed, "This can't be good."

KaryKaryn shouted, "RUN!"

Yace dropped her sack of loquats. She and Turk—in his canine form—took off as fast as they could go. She was at his side, not looking back, levitating, flying instead of running. KaryKaryn, too, jumped into her canine self, now invisible, racing away from hordes of angry apes while Irwin and Kipp stood defiant, ready to fight.

But once Kipp saw the mass of forty-plus apes, he shouted, "Don't be stupid, Irwin!" Kipp took off after the horses who had chosen their own path of escape. Nee Nee and Jenn Jenn stayed close to Irwin's side.

Without hesitation, Irwin made use of his Erthin powers and began upheaving the land, throwing trees, rocks, brush, and anything at hand to delay the aggressive animals and give his friends time to flee. He was outnumbered. He tried to beat back the mass of dark angry beasts, but then five … ten … twenty … streamed around him and the barrier he was attempting to create.

There is no end to them. Shit, I need to find everyone.

Irwin had already killed as many as two dozen Roha. Their bodies began transforming back into their two-legged selves, but dead. Panic settled in his throat. He jumped onto Jenn Jenn's back. "Run!" He told her and noticed Nee Nee bucking and kicking at a few apes. Now she ran after Irwin and her sister. He held tight to the pannier frame and bags empty of food, and kicked Jenn Jenn to go faster. They raced, and Nee Nee took the lead as they ran for their lives out of the growing chaos.

There must have been a hundred apes shadowing them and the rest of the party, but Irwin only had ten close behind. He used his Metalistic powers to get rid of them, tossing out jagged metal pieces and daggers to slice anyone in his way.

Kipp took one path, Yace another. Irwin felt them moving farther apart from each other. He wanted to stop the mass of Roha tribesmen and women, but he could not, nor could he save his scattered friends.

He spotted the black horses jumping over gnarly trees, branches, and bushes. Kipp had led them away from the wild animals in pursuit. The donkeys also saw the horses and followed their friends. Up another ridge, the horses jumped over rocky outcroppings and disappeared into the darkened and desolate jungle.

He flattened the ground and moved rocks for his donkeys. As they cleared the ridge, Irwin saw a horde of apes trained on Kipp's descent. The donkeys maneuvered down into the next dark valley—around boulders that Irwin was not quick enough to move out of their way. He was summoning trees out of the ground, slapping apes away from Kipp and the horses. But he could not stop all of them. Two dozen apes still followed right behind Kipp. The stream of black angry beasts was about to descend on his best friend.

There was nothing Irwin could have done to keep the angry beasts from Kipp and not hurt his friend in the process. Kipp howled from the pain. He was at the mercy of as many as twenty apes, helpless as they hammered him into the ground. Irwin was too far away to do anything without hurting Kipp.

The Roha were killing Kipp.

Irwin had to do something.

He was trying to kick Jenn Jenn toward the pack of angry Roha, but the donkey was not having it. She wanted to follow her sister and the other horse who dashed off. He was panicking and his donkey felt it. The apes were pounding his friend, and he was expecting too much from his frightened Jenny. Jenn Jenn bellowed for Nee Nee and then bucked Irwin off, tossing him high enough to catch a branch before it snapped and toppled on him. When he landed with a hard thud onto his back, Jenn Jenn was gone from sight.

Irwin jumped to his feet, slightly winded, and watched the apes scatter, leaving Kipp lifeless on the ground. They had taken to the trees again. Now a black stream was heading straight for Irwin. He was ready for the horde and did not hold back with his Metalistic powers. Small fragments of metal shot out of his hands—while he raced to Kipp—directly into the mass of vengeful apes. At once, the beasts fell from their branches or in mid-swing. Few made sounds before they died.

He was at Kipp's bloody body in a beat. "Oh, shit! NO!" The Clan-Duin, Kipp, did not look like himself. He looked smashed—broken bones, punctures in his skin, blood oozing out of his flesh. He could be dead.

Irwin leaned forth to feel for breath and listen for a heartbeat. He felt neither. He placed his dirty hands on the broken and bloodied body.

So many broken bones. So much blood.

"Kipp, stay with me." He held back a sob.

Do not die, my friend. Focus. I need to focus. Fix the rib cage first. Get his heart pumping, blood flowing to his brain. But his neck .... He is dead. They killed him. No. No. Dammit, he will live. Stay focused, do not panic.

Several apes returned for Irwin. He heard them coming and erected his Metalistic barrier. It floated protectively around his body and Kipp's, keeping all predators away. The beasts tried to get past the barrier but perished instead. He did not focus on anything beyond the barrier; he knew it would keep him safe. All Irwin worried about right now was Kipp—healing his beloved friend. He began by taking care of all major injuries—skull, ribcage, and vertebra.

He did not know how long he sat there, but he had lost feeling in his legs while churning his Erthin healing abilities. He changed position several times, moving around Kipp, trying to fix as much as he could. It felt like hours had passed when KaryKaryn returned.

She was excited to have found him. "Irwin, you live!" He did not hear her. She watched him for some time. "Kipp be dead."

He did not acknowledge her—busy mending parts of Kipp.

"I see bone," she said. "Much blood outside body."

Irwin's eyes swirled, his heart raced. "We can make more blood."

"You know how make blood?"

He did not know how to make blood; he had taken much of what spilled out and put it back in his friend.

"You leave him," KaryKaryn insisted. "We go."

"Kipp is not dead!" Irwin was crying, tears streaking his dirty face. He wiped them away, smearing the dirt sideways. "I am not leaving him."

KaryKaryn stood there but looked around at the unusually quiet jungle. "We leave now."

"If you are fearful of them ..." He let his force field fall, allowing KaryKaryn passage into the protective barrier. "... they cannot get us in here." He never looked at her, his eyes on Kipp.

"Yace and Turk be running to plateau." She knelt next to Kipp's other side. "They have one horse, two donkey. Roper broke leg, he dead now."

"Go, stay with them; protect them. I will stay with Kipp. I must save him."

"He be dead."

"KIPP IS NOT DEAD!" He did not care right now if he drew unwanted attention. He would not leave his best friend behind, even if he was dead.

Seeing how steadfast Irwin was, KaryKaryn conceded. "I know of healer. He live upslope, two-day walk from here. We put Kipp on carrier, take him to healer."

"I can heal him."

"You a learned healer? I see you fix flesh and bone, but he not awake, not alive. He be dead without real healer."

Hearing those words defeated Irwin's confidence. He knew he had successfully fixed Kipp's ribcage, spine, and skull, but there was still much work to do before Kipp would be ready for transport.

"Go. Keep Yace and Turk safe. I will heal Kipp, and we will catch up."

"He be dead, Irwin. You come with me."

He ignored her.

"He be dead," she pulled on his arm.

"Kipp is not dead!" He saw KaryKaryn was cut up and bloodied. Reality hit him and rippled up his spine. "Where is Yace?" He felt for her tattoo. "Oh, she is coming this way."

"What? No, no!" KaryKaryn looked in the direction from which she had come. "I told her no!"

"Welcome to my world. Yace does not listen to anyone except herself."

"No!" KaryKaryn was angry. "She bring Roha to us. She said she lead them away. But she bring them to us. We will die!"

"If she brings them to us, then I will kill them all. I do not bow to bullies."

KaryKaryn looked at Irwin in the way a mother would stare at her child for saying something that was full of nonsense. "I told you to run."

"And I tried to give you all a head start," Irwin declared. "I tried to kill as many as I could."

"Roha are many. They *will* kill us."

Indeed, every bone in Kipp's body was broken. He had lost more than half his blood before Irwin was able to heal all the major breaks in the skin. Kipp's numerous internal injuries were harder to heal. Irwin had little knowledge of the inner workings of the body; his healed on its own. He knew about bones, had felt them pop back in place and had seen his flesh reseal—flawlessly every time. But healing all of Kipp would take days.

Yace, Turk, the donkeys, and Bodi found Irwin and KaryKaryn hovering over Kipp's body. It was pitch dark by this time. Yace led the pack with a magical ball of light overhead.

Her presence disturbed the local creatures, and again they began ranting—calling all Roha's attention. Irwin's focus was singularly on healing Kipp. His metallic force field continued to radiate—he had not noticed Yace's approach or heard the animals become agitated.

"Irwin!" She sobbed.

The moment he heard his name, Irwin dropped his metallic barrier and allowed Yace and Turk into the safe space. Yace raced to his side, blubbering incomprehensible words. "I wish I … I'm sorry I-I shouldn't have left you two. I said we were family, that we stick together. Oh, Irwin." She threw herself on his shoulders, crying harder. "I don't hear his thoughts."

"I am sorry Yace. I could not get to him fast enough." Breaking his focus, he turned to hold Yace. "There were too many of them. I am so sorry." Hot tears covered his face, mixing with muddy jungle grime.

Yace's snot and tears wet his shoulder, neck, and ear. She continued to blubber. "You tried. I know you tried. You tried all you could."

He had done everything in his power, depleting his personal energy, hoping to revive Kipp. "KaryKaryn says there is a healer two days' upslope from here. We need to take Kipp there. Now!"

"We can't move him!" Yace gasped. "He might have some injury we don't know about."

He pulled back from her and looked lovingly at Kipp. "He looks better than he did when I first got to him. When I found him, Yace, Kipp was one breath from death. All of him was broken. What you see here is a mostly healed man. He needs more blood, and there are probably internal injuries; injuries I know nothing about, nothing about healing them. But he is here with us now."

Yace quivered. "What if … what if he dies before we get there?"

"I will not let him die." Irwin ground his fists into his thighs. "If I have to, I will give him pieces of my soul to keep him alive."

I already have.

"Don't do that Irwin. I don't want you to die too!"

"That is how he is living right now."

"Is that why you look so tired? You're not supposed to do that. Tamera told me that it takes her almost a full day to recover after healing these kinds of injuries. Just recently, Bay broke his arm after jumping from a tree. He's only five, and she said it was broken in four spots. She also worried about these growth plate thingies. It took her all afternoon to recover from healing him." Yace continued to fret. "When Tamera healed me, she told me that she gave pieces of her soul to keep me alive." She looked up at Irwin.

Tears in his eyes, he said, "It is what family does." Irwin kissed Yace's forehead and hugged her.

24

<u>SHAMAN</u>

Irwin and Yace fashioned a stretcher from the animal hide Kipp had brought, branches, rope, and long ivy. After placing Kipp's unconscious body into it, they fastened the stretcher to the backside of Bodi. KaryKaryn and Turk stood sentry.

Maybe after witnessing Irwin's wickedness, the hostile Roha had ceased their pursuit. But he wouldn't bet on it. For now, all they had to contend with was a hard uphill climb.

KaryKaryn assured them they were on the most direct route to the healer's home. The trees opened and so did the thick canopy, allowing more light to guide the way. But there were many rocks and boulders hampering their trek. Waterfalls were plentiful—as were wide pools, deep creeks, and boggy areas they were forced to cross.

They had to get Kipp to the healer, but there was much terrain to cover. At times, the journey was arduous—either the horse could not climb over something, or the stretcher needed to be detached and levitated across watery or rocky areas. Irwin was able to move the land most of the time, but still they were challenged by animals or nature itself.

He felt Yace run the gambit of emotions. She blubbered about her unborn child being fatherless and how hard her life would be without Kipp. She sobbed on and on about how good of a parent Kipp would have been. She spoke in past tense, making their situation sound more dire than it was. Kipp was alive, but she was not acknowledging that.

Should I have healed Kipp? Or should I have helped him die back there? I did all I could. I do not want him to die. I must believe that the healer can help him. But in the meantime, I should do more.

I have given Kipp ten souls so far; how many more will it take to keep him alive?

He walked behind the stretcher, his sad eyes on Kipp.

This is no way to live, tied to a stretcher with a piss pot between your legs. I do not think Kipp will ever be the same.

Then there is Yace. I cannot stand her right now. She is behaving just like Kipp did when she was catatonic and ruminating over worst-case scenarios.

What we are experiencing is indeed a worst-case scenario!

Every time they stopped, every time he made contact with Kipp, Irwin pushed forth all his healing energy—helping Kipp's body maintain itself, pump blood and breathe without issue—help him stave off Death. That was all he could do. The donkeys and Bodi showed their impatience for the lack of breaks—breaks not long enough to feed or hydrate. But no one wanted to stop for long; their pressing need to get help for Kipp was too important to be wasted on frivolous things like rest.

Just as KaryKaryn predicted, it took them two long days navigating through the hostile landscape—across exposed ridges, through dense valleys, and up a narrow path that hugged the edge of a plateau—to arrive at the Healer's abode.

Now that they were there, they found the cavernous residence empty.

"Shaman should be here any time." She assured them. Everyone was on edge, scared, and ready for some kind of resolution. "He live alone. I visit often. He be kind, share tea, meat. Maybe I go look for him." She left everyone behind in the cave.

His abode was a long hollow nestled on a ledge of a harrowing cliff. The base of the plateau fifty feet above the entrance, far below the jungle canopy stretched out like a dark-green ocean. All around the entrance different types of spices and herbs grew in lush patches. Several looked to be non-native, yet they all grew heartily in the humid conditions. Some obscured the view of the cave's entrance. A few climbed the rocky walls, while others cascaded down. A cacophony of aromatic scents, some were too pungent to bear as their aroma wafted throughout the cave and along the wide ledge outside. The place felt almost like a touch of magic.

Several trails led to the large, flattened outcropping and the entrance to Shaman's cave. A small creek trickled near the doorstep of the healer, cascading down the cliff's side, flowing from a narrow chasm. There was a path that paralleled the creek heading up the slope to the plateau above. There were cut steps intersecting that trail, which led to an alcove that housed a stone oven and drying racks. Other trails could be seen etched into the cliff wall—one being the trail that had led them there.

All the trails were wide enough for a single person, but not wide enough for the horse with the stretcher, or donkeys with panniers. Parts of the cliff-side path slivered off as the animals marched between their people. Irwin tried to forget, watching large gravels and rocks tumbling hundreds of feet to the jungle floor below. There had been a collective sigh of relief once they found the large, flattened area, but they would not be able to go back the way they came.

They waited for the Healer's return. Yace dealt with the piss pot, watered Kipp, and then snapped at Irwin. "He needs that iced head wrap on his head again."

"Shaman never gone long." KaryKaryn told them after returning from her brief search for him. She looked around his cave at his belongings. "He be back soon. I know this."

Yace sat next to Kipp who was now laying on the solid stone ground.

Irwin decided to take care of the animals, a distraction for at least a few minutes. He looked back at his best friends and sighed.

I hope this Shaman can heal Kipp. I hope we did not bring him here to die.

He watched Yace lean forward and sob, holding Kipp's hand.

I wish I could help Yace too. This is too hard on her and her unborn child.

It was obvious that KaryKaryn was antsy. She walked around the cave several times, looking at all his possessions, and then said, "I go find Shaman down cliff."

"No, send Turk," said Yace. "That way you're here when your friend Shaman shows up. We wouldn't want to startle an Erthin!"

KaryKaryn nodded and turned to engage Turk with their Clan-Duin speech. No words were exchanged, and then he darted out of the cave.

Yace loomed over Kipp. Irwin placed a sympathetic hand on her shoulder. "How are you doing, Yace?"

She did not look at him and replied in a hard tone, "Fine."

"In a good way or bad way."

Yace was obviously frazzled. Her eyes were puffy from crying. She had not brushed her hair in days; it was matted, and she kept pushing it out of her eyes. Her pretty orange and pink skirt was torn, and she had bruises on her arms. "I can't hear him, Irwin." She sobbed more and more loudly this time. "He has no thoughts, no dreams, no nothing. I don't want to lose him. I want him to live."

He could see she was ready to erupt. He whispered, "Everything will be fine once Shaman gets here. Kipp will be fixed, and we will be on our way."

"What if," she trembled, "what if he's not? What if Shaman can't fix Kipp? What if he says Kipp's unfixable? I don't know what I'll do, Irwin. I can't have this baby without him."

"We must take this one step at a time, Yace. No matter what happens, I will be here for you. I will keep you safe. We are a family. This is what family does."

At least I think this is what family does; mine never cared.

He held her tight and petted her head gently.

"I love Kipp so much. I don't want to lose him. But he's not here."

"You do not know that for sure, Yace." Irwin pulled back and wiped her tears away from her cheeks. "I believe Kipp is here. He is like you were not too long ago. Kipp is in a place where he is hoping to break free. And with Shaman's help, he will."

"Kipp isn't under some telepathic spell, Irwin. If that were the case, I would've set him free by now." Yace snapped, feistier than ever. "You told me all his bones were broken. You said he was one breath away from dying when you found him. Maybe he's already dead, Irwin. The body can survive without the brain. But the brain cannot survive without the body."

"That makes no sense, Yace."

"It makes perfect sense, Irwin. The heart pumps blood regardless of how smart or stupid someone is. The lungs breathe in air and keep you alive; it is up to the brain to follow through with everything else—like when to eat and poop and such. Most of the body can go on without the brain being there, but the brain cannot go on without a body."

He did not want to argue with her. "When was the last time you ate, Yace?"

"What does that have anything to do with anything?"

"I am hungry! I am only guessing, Miss Pregnant Woman, that you are hungry too." He shuffled through ration bags and retrieved a sack of over-ripened and slightly squished mangos. He opened the bag and handed some fruit to Yace. "I know this is not cooked rabbit, but it is something to eat."

"Cooked rabbit, oh, yum." Yace closed her eyes and licked her lips. "With potato cubes cooked in garlic and butter, umm. Dang me." Opening her eyes, Yace looked around the cave. "I'm hungry for a giant slab of meat right now."

Irwin smiled. "Meat would be nice."

They sat in quiet until Turk reappeared. Right behind him, the man named Shaman stepped into view. He appeared to be older than KaryKaryn—more wrinkles on his face—but his body was in better condition, probably because he was an Erthin Healer. He had thick orangish-red and white facial hair, trimmed short, but the hair atop his head was a multitude of colors from red to yellowish-white and looked like dozens of pieces of rope pulled back into one large braid. He wore a utility belt attached to the loincloth, loose on his hips. On his sweaty, hairy back, was a dead wild boar hung from a thick wooden stick secured by hooves. "Kary!" He said exuberantly, but his excitement fell flat seeing Kipp tied to a stretcher.

KaryKaryn stood. "Shaman, these be my guest."

He nodded. "Shall I guess what happened?" He strode into his abode, looking at all faces staring at him—waiting for him to work his magic.

"Roha attack."

"Hm." Shaman looked at Kipp in passing. "He looks good for being on the receiving end of Roha aggression. Better than you did, Kary, that one time."

Irwin spoke up. "I am the one who healed him."

Shaman asked, "If you healed him, then why are you here?"

"He not healed." KaryKaryn stated flatly and glared at Irwin. "He a child. He only pretend to know. You heal this one. She be with his child. She not want him dead."

"Well, that's quite a predicament," said Shaman, then pointed. "What's that on his head?"

"I made an icy bandage wrap for places that are swollen," Irwin replied. "That was Yace's idea. Well, actually it was Tamera's idea."

Shaman looked around the room. "And where is this, Tamera?"

Irwin glanced at Yace. She was not acknowledging Shaman; her focus was on Kipp. He spoke for Yace. "Tamera is not here. She is an Erthin Healer that my friend, Yace, learned from while living with the Gypsy."

"You're Gypsy? Which band are you with?"

"They are Gypsy. I am just a miner. They were a part of Nonbry's band. Do you know him?"

"Nonbry, huh? I think I've heard of him."

"Are you a Telepath?"

Shaman chuckled at the question but did not answer. Sparks of light flashed, brightening the back of the cave. Shaman was Erthin, his red dreadlocks and green eyes gave away his abilities. He set the hog down. Irwin sensed that Shaman was an Elementalist—could yield all five Erthin powers equally. He said nothing but felt humbled to be in a true healers' presence—he wanted to learn all he could from this Talented individual.

They watched the healer wash his hands in a ceramic basin and towel off before standing over Kipp's unconscious body. Yace remained vigilant at Kipp's side, consumed with grief.

"Move aside, young lady."

"I'm not leaving Kipp."

"If you want me to look him over, you need to move. Do you understand?"

She appeared ready to attack Shaman, but Irwin placed a hand on her shoulder. "Yace. It is alright. I trust this man."

25

How To Heal

I rwin pulled Yace away from Kipp, from his crumpled body. Shaman wove his hand over Kipp. The slab of stone the Clan-Duin had been placed on rose up to the healer's hands. Shaman looked over the tight bindings holding Kipp's body still. He pulled out a knife from a thin sheath on his belt and cut all the vines and ropes used to keep Kipp's body attached to the stretcher.

KaryKaryn stood close by. "He look dead when I first saw him."

Shaman was gruff with Irwin. "How is it that you healed this man?"

"I used my Erthin power." Shaman raised an eyebrow, and Irwin licked his lips. "I started with the torso first. That is where the vital organs are. I knew I needed to minimize the external damage as fast as I could." Trying to remain calm, Irwin's emotions swelled until his heart felt as though it could explode.

"Huh. I don't feel a lick of Erthin energy emanating from you, young man."

"I am. I am Coterie too. I have been told that is what masks my abilities." He noticed Yace glance at him.

Shaman's hand stayed on Kipp. His eyes, however, were firm on Irwin. "I'm impressed you were able to heal anything. You don't even feel like you could resurrect a mouse, but you can heal bones. What I sense so far, impressive. How badly broken was he before you came along?"

Yace called out, "His whole body!"

Please, Yace, stay calm.

"Every bone was broken, including his head. I fixed the ribs and spine first, then moved to the skull, arms and legs last."

"Do you know there are nerves which run along the spine? Thousands of them, each with a purpose to make your body move, to make it work. Fixing a spine takes years of lessons—if you do anything wrong, you can sever those nerves causing irreversible damage to the body. I cannot believe that you thought you could heal this man. He was probably better off dead. Even you know better, Kary!"

"Yes. I tell him to leave. But he not listen. He say he can heal. He cannot heal! You can heal, Shaman. You heal me every time."

Yace cried.

Irwin felt her weakening, her legs buckle. His chest was soaked from her snot and tears. He felt her thoughts. *What am I going to do? I can't be pregnant without a mate. Who will help me? This isn't how it's supposed to be. Not my Kipp. Not dead.*

Over her mental ramble, he thought to himself; *Wait a moment, Shaman just praised me for how well I fixed Kipp's bones, then scolded me for not knowing what to do. I do not know what to do. I know I can heal myself and have tried to heal Kipp on a few occasions. I did what I thought was best. I hope I did not cause permanent damage to Kipp. Maybe he was better off dead.*

Yace came to his defense. *What are you saying, Irwin? You did what you could; you tried your best. I know you tried!*

Trying is sometimes failing.

That sounds like shit to me. That sounds like something your father would say. She looked into his eyes.

Defeated on all counts, he leaned on her more. *I probably permanently damaged Kipp. I will be honest, Yace, I do not know what I am doing most of the time. I should not have done it. I should have helped Kipp pass on.*

Don't say that. You tried your best. He's breathing on his own. That means he's alive, Irwin. Alive because of you.

The two were so entwined in each other's thoughts, they barely overheard Shaman brag. "Yeah, I've saved you a time or two or three, huh, Kary? You've probably come to me two dozen times to be healed over the years. I'm glad I went boar hunting today. If we need any parts or pieces, he's full of them. And he's young too, so all those borrowed parts and pieces will last awhile." He looked at Irwin. "You should know, young man, that boars—domestic hogs even—are a perfect match for Clan-Duin parts and pieces. And the younger the boar—as long as it's mature—will be better for parts than the older slower ones.

"Of course, if we had a Clan-Duin willing to give his life, or willing to surrender a few extra parts—like a kidney or intestine—take it. Clan-Duin parts already know how to modify themselves when it comes to their metamorphosis powers. Hog parts are a close compromise. And once they infuse with Clan-Duin blood, they acclimate to the metamorphic ability … like learning to walk. Everything in this life takes time."

KaryKaryn pointed to her left leg. "Boar tissue here."

"Is that the one you tore off?" Shaman chuckled. "I left you half a day to go find a young boar. You were sweating so hard when I got back, we ended up transfusing your blood that day too." He stepped away from Kipp and headed toward the kitchen area.

Irwin followed Shaman. "If it is alright with you, Shaman, Sir, I would like to offer my help, with anything you need, while you heal our friend. I can part the boar—cut it up for meals. Cook it."

I wish I could do more.

"We need to keep that hog intact. I still need to do an in-depth assessment of this man's internal damage. Figure out what parts and pieces we need to save." Shaman grabbed a smoothing stone and a well-used knife and shoved both items at Irwin's chest. "What you could do for me, while I look him over, is sharpen this knife. We will need it for opening him up, exchanging parts."

Irwin touched the tip of the knife and, in an instant, sharpened the blade and rebalanced the weight. Meanwhile, Shaman waited for Irwin to take the knife and sharpening stone.

"Here you go!" Shaman said, pushing the blade and stone into Irwin's hands. "Do your job."

"I did," he said. "I balanced it too."

Shaman grabbed Irwin's hands, stuffed the knife and stone in them. "You don't listen very well, do you? Here's the stone; sharpen the knife."

"I have already sharpened your knife, Sir." He remained cool.

"I don't need a smarmy attitude, young man. Kary, could you please talk to your guest? He's not cooperating." He turned his back to Irwin and stepped over to Kipp.

"Irwin be talented like me, Shaman," said KaryKaryn.

"What do you mean?"

Irwin finally admitted, "I can also harness metal. I can make anything with it." Irwin demonstrated by pulling metal up through his flesh, around his hand like a glove, then pushed it to make a sphere and rolled it around between his fingers.

"Ah, you know, I guess that means you can help me."

Irwin took a step forward. "What do you need?"

"Do you know what a needle is?"

Immediately, three distinct types of sewing needles materialized on Irwin's palm. There was a long one, a short one, and a fat one too—all with eyelets for thread-pulling.

Shaman was clearly impressed, but not pleased. "We need to blood-let your friend. What I mean is, we need to purge his infected blood, get rid of the fluid retention in his limbs, and release the swelling in his brain." He removed the cold cap from Kipp's head. "In this area here. If I had leaches, we'd do it the old fashion way, but you've a Talent I've never seen before, so we'll use your natural abilities. For now, I need you to make a different type of needle to relieve the pressure here and switch out his blood."

Yace chewed her fingernails. "We didn't cause Kipp brain damage, did we?"

Shaman was blunt. "If anything, the Roha caused his brain damage. It was a smart idea to ice up a cloth and cold pack those swollen areas, likely that helped."

Irwin asked, "Why do we have to blood let him?"

"You did a decent job of healing the fascia," said Shaman, "but his blood came in contact with a pathogen—common in warm, humid places like the jungle. That pathogen is hindering his ability to heal further.

"But besides that, his body has been in shock for a while. If we don't get to fixing him soon, his remaining intact organs will shut down. I'm glad you found me today. And I'm glad I have a hog to part and piece. He may be near death with all his internal injuries, but I can save him."

Irwin asked in a thin whisper, "What all is wrong with him?"

"Everything," said Shaman. "And we have little time to waste. Now, what we need to heal your friend is …." Shaman instructed Irwin what type of needle to make, and the Metalist created several of them.

He studied over Shaman's shoulder, watching the older man puncture Kipp's brain. A yellowish-pink fluid gushed out, but soon turned clear. Yace could not stand around to witness and she raced out of the cave and Irwin heard her dry heaving.

Shaman continued to relieve pressure and readied Kipp for his blood transfusion and operation. The well-versed healer asked Irwin to cut every person's finger so that he could taste their blood—find the perfect blood-match for Kipp. "Very few Erthins have this Talent. Now, if no one has his blood type, I'll reanimate the hog—he's only been dead for a brief time. His blood will match if no one else does." It turned out that Turk and Yace were matches.

If Kipp finds out he has Turk's blood in him, well, I will not tell him, but Yace probably will. Oh, he will be so angry.

Turk was the first one to volunteer. He laid on a second stone slab erected next to Kipp's. When Turk transformed into his two-legged self, he became a rugged-looking fifteen-year-old with a broad nose, dark Clan-Duin features, and brilliant copper eyes. His body was half tattooed; they had seen brindle markings on his reddish-brown fur, but as a person, Turk's markings were warrior tattoos. He had a chest piece made of triangles with protective shoulder scarring—all raised bumps. His hips and outer thighs had a similar design to that of his chest, created with indigo ink. The tattoos across his feet and ankles were in X-patterns—the most impressive. He was given an animal hide to lie on for comfort and waited patiently for the entire process to happen.

Yace was hesitant when it came to giving her blood. "I'm with child; should I be doing this? I want to help. He's the child's father. I probably should, but ...." She volunteered in the end.

Irwin knew his blood could kill Clan-Duins, and Shaman reiterated that sentiment after spitting it out. Instead of giving his blood, Irwin learned all about veins, arteries, how to extract blood with a needle, and how to conduct a transfusion using one of the boar's arteries. This was all fascinating and a bit overwhelming—this was his best friend Irwin was helping to heal; there was no margin for error.

Yace watched Turk lay there giving his blood so freely. She kept muttering, "I hope this works. Please let it work." She paced around, then huddled close to Irwin.

Shaman's hands emitted a soft light as he worked his magic—extracting parts from the boar and inserting them into Kipp. He had Irwin help hold intestines, or organs, meanwhile teaching him how to use a direct tap to the ether to reanimate each part and piece.

Irwin saw firsthand how to use his newly learned gifts. He understood that tapping into the ether was not something all Erthins could do, yet he had been doing it all his life. And now he could focus that power, just like Shaman was doing, pulling the energy through his head, pushing the powers out of his hands, and grounding out all the negative energy through his feet. Only Irwin could see what was happening, and he was certain it was because of his Metalistic power, not his Coterie or Erthin abilities.

The delicate surgery went on most of the night. Once Shaman got started, he took no breaks. He seemed to find pleasure in fixing broken people. It was obvious that he understood the physical body, in all its forms, and was a master with his healing powers. He went about his job, meticulously fixing all of Kipps' broken parts. KaryKaryn too was allowed a hand in the healing process. She stitched up the large incision, allowing Shaman to walk away and take time to regenerate his powers.

While Shaman rested, Irwin practiced his healing power on the Elementalist. He wanted to give back and help the man upon whom they had intruded.

26

<u>A Trip With Death</u>

The next morning, Yace laid on the stone slab next to Kipp. She stared at Kipp, her hand grasped his. She still looked exhausted, looked to be napping.

Meanwhile, KaryKaryn walked with Shaman upslope where the healer's stone-made oven stood above the cave's entrance, barely visible. Irwin sat at the cave's entrance with Turk at his side watching the sun rise across the dark land below. Although he was enjoying being alone for a while, he overheard the conversation KaryKaryn and Shaman were having.

"I sorry Shaman." KaryKaryn groveled. "Roha will come. They want revenge against the man who smells of death."

"I'm not worried, Kary. The Roha knows to leave me alone."

"I should speak sooner."

"Don't worry, Kary. The Roha knows not to mess with me. All the tribes know not to mess with me!"

"But Roha want travelers dead. They want me dead. Death-smelling man kill many Roha and families seek revenge. If they know you help us—"

"You know better than to step foot onto Roha turf. Why'd you go?"

"Pregnant one need food and herb for stomach."

"Kary, you know better," Shaman barked. "You should take travelers like these far upslope. Follow the snowline."

"Pregnant one wants fast trail to Ozaroton. What I do, I do."

"The Roha enjoy a good pursuit. You know this. And they know that if they come anywhere near here, they'll perish. The stories of my power still echo throughout this land! They shouldn't mess with an Elementalist, if you know what I mean." He chuckled and then she did too.

Irwin smirked.

I know not to mess with them now that I am one.

He had seen them take several thick slabs of hogs' meat up to the stone oven. It sizzled when it was placed on the hot slab.

"No cook all. I want some."

"You know my gut is more sensitive to bacteria than yours is. If you want a steak or three, take what you want now. If I cook up enough, then your guests will have some to take. You know a pregnant woman needs lots of proteins and fatty foods, and if you can find milk, coconut milk is best, but any milk will do in a pinch except poppy. Don't give her that. The other milk will help her baby grow strong bones and hard teeth."

"I must find coconut now?" She sounded pained.

"Yes, that would be a good idea for the pregnant one—also those other herbs we discussed earlier."

"And poppy seeds."

"Yes, as many as you can gather. The Clan-Duin will need milk of the poppy if he is going to sleep through this process. I can show them how to make it. He will need enough for half a moon's time, maybe more, depending." Shaman paused, then added, "Have the one that plays with metal help you."

"He smell like Death."

"Then take Death for a walk."

They both chuckled and then sighed. Nothing else said, but KaryKaryn and Shaman were together a little longer before she descended the trail and found Irwin sitting with Turk. "Come with me. We get herbs." She signaled for Irwin to follow.

Can I trust Shaman with Yace? She is fragile right now, but she does have Turk. Should I trust KaryKaryn? I am not sure she likes me—that jab about Death. What if she takes me into Roha territory to find a fight? I will win. And I know I can find my way back here if anything happens to KaryKaryn.

It was dark inside the cave; he could barely make out Yace on the stone next to Kipp. "I should tell Yace I am leaving."

KaryKaryn shook her head. "Let her sleep. We be gone a half day, maybe."

"Should I bring a donkey?"

"No." It was obvious to Irwin that KaryKaryn didn't want to be responsible for anyone other than herself. "Grab sack." She instructed as she moved to do the same. At the entrance to the cave, there was a woven basket filled with assorted sizes and types of cloth pouches. KaryKaryn tied several onto a string and secured them around her waist.

Hesitant to leave, Irwin asked, "Is there anything else I should bring?"

"No. We be back soon." KaryKaryn turned and marched off.

They took the route Shaman had come from the previous day; a path Irwin had not seen when they arrived. It started with tall steps that then descended off the western side of the cave's entrance. They climbed down the cliff's side.

Neither spoke. Once at the base of the escarpment, she guided him along the jungle's edge. They followed the rocky cliff wall for a while before turning further inland.

The foliage was not as dense here as it had been in other parts of the jungle, but they had to climb over fallen trees and giant rocks, jump over shallow creeks, and swim across a large river. Then the underbrush and the overhang became denser. Birds squawked as if following them. Irwin noticed how quiet KaryKaryn was, stepping over anything that would make too much noise. He tried to be as stealthy as she, but KaryKaryn summoned her Clan-Duin instincts well. He could be nimble and silent, but he was not as good as his female companion.

They traveled for a good portion of the day in silence—using hand signals to communicate. Jungle beasts hooted and hollered as the two tiptoed through the brush.

KaryKaryn caught a large black snake dangling from a tree branch and tore into it with her fierce teeth. Irwin recognized the poisonous snake; it was like the one that had bitten him in the Datzar Jungle. These snakes were long and large and a tasty meal if cooked. She had been hungry, Irwin guessed, as she filled her belly before passing the remaining three feet of snake to him. That was their midday meal, and they kept on walking as they ate. Irwin used his Erthin powers to cook the meat to his liking. He ate his fill, packing the rest away for later. They did not pause for a break until they came to a small waterfall. KaryKaryn stopped for a drink and then told Irwin what they needed to find here—mushrooms, seeds, and roots.

The next place they stopped, they rummaged for flowers, two types of bark, onion shoots, and a flowering herb she didn't know the name of but described in detail. Everything they harvested was stuffed into satchels made from distinct types of woven material—grass, hemp, and bamboo. KaryKaryn stuffed her bags full. It was obvious that she didn't want to search for any of these later. She was done foraging.

They continued westward, and afternoon turned to evening. They stopped for coconuts and filled the largest sack Irwin had brought. He carried that heavy bag on his back. He was intrigued by KaryKaryn—how she seemed to know exactly where all the good foods and herbs were located in this volatile landscape. She had been the same in Arkin land, but in that place, Irwin assumed it was because she grew up there and knew every rise and fall of the terrain.

As the sun fell behind the mountains, the pair embarked on a steep uphill climb. No path, they scaled the cliff side with baggage slung across their shoulders and dangling from their hips. They climbed by hand and foot nearly five hundred feet. It was harrowing but especially when the winds picked up and the sun descended from sight.

Irwin was glad he had brought none of his animals; it was a treacherous climb indeed. The bag of coconuts swung around, threatening to pull him off his footholds. If he had not grown up in a rocky landscape and known how to properly climb with baggage offsetting his weight, he would have fallen to his death. As it was, he had a tough time keeping up with the nimble woman. Once they reached solid ground on a plateau shelf, they finally paused for breath before heading off again.

They walked into the shadows of the cold mountains. The temperature dropped, and the starry sky was lit with a blanket of blinking lights. The chilly air was a reprieve from the humidity, but not something Irwin was prepared for. They found a small rocky outcropping that offered protection from the winds. He made a hot fire. The winds howled and blew around the stones that hid them from the storm.

Irwin wondered aloud, "I thought we would have been back by now."

"We need one more thing. We find after sunrise."

He wanted to get back to Yace and Kipp. He did not want to be gone this long. He made small talk to calm his nerves. "I know you said you like females, but I overheard you and Shaman talking this morning and it sounded to me that you have a fondness for him. Or am I wrong?"

She sighed, pulled the hood down further across her shoulders, and gazed at the starry sky. "I loyal to him. He heal me every time. I find him good food. I visit him many times every year, many years. We friend until Death takes us home."

"Here I am, Death in physical form."

"You not Death," She snickered. "You smell like Death, but you not Death."

"I get that a lot."

"I like Death."

"Death is a funny conversation to have with someone who has as many scars as you."

"Shaman heal me many times. This be boar flesh too." She pointed at a triangular spot along her shoulder. "Roha attack me."

"Do you like to fight the Roha?"

"Roha attack me, Nici attack me, Tulu, Ta'Api ...." She pointed at many scars.

"What were you doing when they attacked? Scavenging for food?"

"I help Shaman and others. Some live up mountain, up high. There be no good food. I bring fruit, onion, mushroom, and herb."

"That is kind of you."

"Roha be worst. They enjoy hunt." She pointed at a long suture along her right thigh, past her hip. "They find me, tear me. I have many Roha scar."

"Kipp has a few scars from fights. One on his leg, another on his back." Irwin remembered how soft Kipp's skin had been before the Roha attack. "He is a good fighter. He taught me how to fight. I am amazed he allowed himself to get beaten up."

"Roha love fight. They vicious. Shaman heal my jaw, my eye, my everything." There was a tear in her eye. "He save me many time. He my best-friend."

"That is how I feel about Kipp. I think it is good to have that type of relationship with someone." He reflected on all the time spent with Kipp, all the terrors and all the magnificent times.

This has been the best year of my life.

Tears swelled at the corners of his eyes too.

"Shaman will heal Kipp. He be well soon."

His voice cracked. "I hope so."

That was the most in-depth conversation they had had their whole time apart from Shaman, Yace, and Turk. Irwin was not sure if it was him, or KaryKaryn, but neither of them wanted to engage the other more than to say what was necessary, a relief to Irwin.

They had papaya for supper, and Irwin ate the rest of the cooked snake. When morning arrived, they had nothing for breakfast. KaryKaryn assured Irwin they would find something while they walked along the bluff looking for flowers.

Irwin tried not to be angry, but his empty stomach hurt.

Had there been more forethought to this trip, I would have brought extra food, a flask for water, and a wool blanket.

She said we would be gone half a day. I hope Kipp and Yace are doing well. At least we have wild boar to eat when we do return. I am so hungry.

He could not stop his nagging yearning for something more substantial than fruits and snake meat. For now, his stomach maintained control.

27

KILLING THE ROHA

Instead of locating something to eat that morning, they walked until finding the last ingredient: poppies. KaryKaryn did not tell Irwin what it was they were looking for until they walked into a meadow of bright yellow poppies. She commenced picking only the ones that had gone to seed, although she did pluck a flower to put behind an ear.

"Are you fooling me?" He was soured after all this trekking with no food. "KaryKaryn, we have two vials of poppy milk in our medicine bag."

"How much in vial?"

"Enough to sedate Kipp for half a moon."

"Oh." KaryKaryn stood up with the beautiful golden bounty in hand. "Shaman show you how to make."

He did not want to admit it, but his heart became heavy thinking about the man he secretly loved. "If Kipp needs more than a moon's supply ...." His heart ached, and his stomach felt like a knot.

KaryKaryn rested her full gaze on Irwin. "I see how you feel for Kipp. You love Kipp like Yace love Kipp."

He exhaled, his face awash with emotion. "Yes. Yes, I do."

"He know you feel that?"

"Yes. Yes, he does. And he makes fun of it on occasion."

"Because he loves you," she said. "I see it."

"He loves Yace."

Kipp does not love me like I love him.

This was not something Irwin wanted to discuss with KaryKaryn. "I think that should be enough poppies to show me how to make the liquid."

She persisted. "Clan-Duin be loyal to those they love. You be loyal to Clan-Duin you love."

He did not want to think about his relationship with Kipp. "Let us leave here."

"Let me grab more poppy." KaryKaryn bent down and plucked more bulbs.

Irwin stood back, angry—frustrated. He did agree with KaryKaryn. He was loyal to Kipp, almost to a fault, but it was unfathomable to believe that Kipp would be just as committed to him. All he ever saw from Kipp was his undying dedication to Yace. He knew Kipp and Yace deserved one another, believed that Kipp's Clan-Duin insistence sealed his and Yace's destiny to be together forever.

After Kipp is healed, and Yace and he are in Ozaroton, maybe I should heed Nonbry's words. Maybe I should return to the mountains. Find a cave. Do the one thing I know to do. I need to be in a place where I do not have to worry about hurting others. A place where I can just be the monster I am.

Besides, Yace and Kipp's child does not need to be raised around me. I know nothing about bringing up a baby. I cannot be of help to them. What if I accidentally do something wrong, say something wrong? I grew up in a horrible place. I cannot be trusted with innocent beings like children. I know nothing about them—they scare me.

She interrupted his reverie. "We go now."

The hike back took little time compared to the day before. The poppy meadow was only a few kilometers from Shaman's abode. But the trail they took was a reminder of why he had left the high mountains. They were forced to walk along the edge of a single-track path, across the cliff-face, for over a kilometer.

I hate single wide paths.

The winds tugged and pulled him all over the place. KaryKaryn was in her canine form, closer to the ground and able to hunker down. Meanwhile, Irwin had to use his Erthin powers to keep his hold on the rocky wall. When the winds came along and pulled at the bag of coconuts strung across his shoulder, he feared he might be thrown off the ledge. He was never one for steep, straight up and down heights. Even the cliff climb they did the previous day had been harrowing, but he had seen the end of that trail. This one appeared to keep going on and on.

When they finally arrived on the outcropping where Shaman's abode sat high above all else, a sense of deep relief settled in his chest.

It was mid-morning, and Yace rushed to embrace him. "Irwin!"

She shook in his arms, and he held her tight. "Is everything alright?"

She sobbed; her tears soaked his chest. "I missed you."

"How is Kipp?"

Her voice was shaky at first. "The blood transfusion worked well so far. Turk gave him more this morning. And I'm due to give him more this evening before supper." She jumped with excitement. "Oh Irwin, you missed supper last night. You missed the best …" She licked her lips. "… the best pork-ribs I've ever eaten. Shaman made a mango marinade. Oh! They were perfectly roasted; the meat just fell off. It was the best meal I've had in a long time!"

"Please do not tell me about it." The scent of the meal still lingered in the air. "I am famished."

"Good to hear you're hungry!" Shaman spoke from the darkness inside his home. "This afternoon we'll have stuffed pork loins."

Yace was giddy. "Stuffed pork!" She continued licking her lips.

Shaman summoned KaryKaryn. She took the baggage Irwin had been carrying and set all the satchels onto the counter across the room. "Excellent."

KaryKaryn pulled out the bags he would need first. "Mushrooms, rice, fennel."

"Thank you." He took what she handed off and smiled at her and the herbs. "My plan is to make a superb meal for you and your guests, and then I expect you to leave."

"What?" Yace's voice rattled, "What about Kipp? We can't leave this soon. He's not fully healed!"

"Kipp will be fine. His healing process will be slow, but I'm sure he will fully recover in the next moon or two."

"I thought you were healing him?"

"A healer can only do so much for a body so broken," said Shaman. "I've done everything in my power to keep him alive. The rest is up to Kipp and you two. At this point, he'll need dedicated caretakers. Possibly forever. And with the extent of his injuries, Kipp will need help to relearn how to use much of his body. He's damaged. He'll probably have a gimp, and his mind won't work as well as it did. I know you fixed many of his bones, but the extent of his injuries—"

Yace spoke through clenched teeth. "You're a healer; you should be able to heal him fully! You should be able to make him rise without issue! I know what healers can do."

"I don't force the body to instantly heal. I allow it to heal naturally. There are many healers out there who fix all your ailments and send you on your way. Doing that doesn't allow your body to learn to fix itself. I prefer the method of healing where I fix all the serious issues, and then the body does most of the work."

"Are you fooling me? I'm pregnant! I need Kipp to be healthy. Now!"

KaryKaryn stepped into the argument. "Shaman, that not true. My bones are Clan-Duin bone, they move, they grow, they shrink. They heal quick."

Shaman said, "Your bones grow and shrink because of your blood. And they heal at the same rate as any other bone on any other person except for Erthin healers. But just like any bone, they need to create calluses to be whole again. It takes a lot of time."

"My bone heal quick. Kipp heal quick."

Yace fretted, twisted her skirt. "What does that mean for Kipp? Will he heal quicker than the average person? Will he be healthy soon? I need him to be healed!"

"He was near death when you brought him to me. I'm impressed that he's staved off death as long as he has. The Roha should've killed him."

Yace cried again.

"If watching him, helping him recuperate, is too hard for you, I can take him there again, wash away all I've done."

Yace shrieked, "No!"

"Then be happy that he is alive."

Irwin asked, "Is there anything I can do to help heal him?"

"No," Shaman replied. "Though I suggest you get some formal training. What I showed you is only a small portion of what there is to know about healing. If you're truly inquisitive to know everything about healing, I suggest you attend a senior seminary or visit a Healers Hall. They'll teach you all about treating wounds."

"Senior seminary? Is that where you learned? Is that why you're being like this, you religious freak!" Yace sneered at Shaman.

"Look, little girl," he stepped toward her, his long finger pointed at her. "You brought a man who should be dead into my home. You should be thankful I did anything for you, you ungrateful Telepath."

Irwin stepped between them. "Be nice."

"And you're foolish for believing you could save a mostly dead person." Shaman pointed over at Kipp. "A true Healer would have helped him go with Death."

Yace could not let this go. "How could you say that?"

"Most Healers, after seeing his body in the condition it was, would've helped the poor soul along to his final destination. Being mangled as he was, and you two not knowing how to repair ... living with a pisspot between your legs is a dismal existence."

Irwin said, "I am sorry we intruded upon you."

"Kary, take them far upslope. Don't worry about getting the things the pregnant one needs. As long as she has a meaty diet, her baby will be fine. But keep them out of Tropogagi territories. That's the only way to ensure survival on your journey to Ozaroton."

"It be longer that way," KaryKaryn bore a look of dismay Irwin had not seen before.

"You will not be challenged to fight if you go that way."

She glared at Shaman.

"You know, Kary, I'm beginning to think you want to meet Death at the hands of a cannibal. All the accidental injuries you bring me to heal are probably purposeful." The two began a staring match. "Oh! So it's true. You do want to die at Tropogagi hands."

"Shaman!"

"If you make it here again because your wing is broken, you better hope I'm home."

Yace huffed, and Shaman turned to her. "Hey, little Telepath, I've not enjoyed your attitude or your manipulative words. Had you not been pregnant, I would've sent you with Kary and your friend. And if I hadn't invited you all for supper, I'd tell you to leave now."

Irwin's face reddened with embarrassment and his fists clenched with disgust. "Thank you for healing our friend. We never meant to impose. We will leave now."

"We stay for food," said KaryKaryn.

"It is obvious that Shaman does not want us here," Irwin was adamant. "We will leave."

"Your friend isn't ready for departure," said Shaman. "And I'm cooking up more pork, so you might as well wait."

"No," Irwin folded his arms, tapped his toe. "We have impositioned you. We will leave now."

Yace gasped, "Irwin."

"Get your stuff, Yace."

"Shaman. Irwin. I not leave, not now, not when sun up." KaryKaryn looked around the room at all the angry faces.

"Why not?" asked Irwin.

Shaman growled, "You're not taking them down slope again, are you?"

"No. Food. Pregnant one needs food."

"What did I just get done saying, Kary? Hunt meat. There are beasts to eat further up the mountain. Don't worry about fruit. Have this one help you hunt." Shaman pointed at Turk, who everyone seemed to have forgotten was still there.

"Shaman?"

"I think you're looking for a fight, Kary."

Irwin turned to KaryKaryn. "If you want to go fight the Roha, let us go back down the cliffs. Just you and me. Let us find the Roha, and we will destroy them once and for all."

Yace placed a hand on his arm, looked at him with concern. "Irwin, are you alright?"

"The entire tribe will be gone; I will make sure of it. Then you will not have to worry about the Roha coming to kill Shaman. And you would not have to worry about traipsing through their land to find the foods you enjoy." His stomach growled and his hands ached from the clenched fists.

Yace kept her hand on his arm. "You want to kill an entire clan?"

"It would not be the first time I intentionally killed people, Yace. Come on, KaryKaryn, let us go fight."

Shaman spoke. "You think you could kill the entire Roha family? First off, they live in smaller groups and never come together unless—"

"Unless it is revenge they seek." Irwin interrupted Shaman. "Most people pact together around a common good, or a common enemy. Right now, I am an enemy of the Roha, a good reason for them to pull together and come after me. And if I were to venture into the middle of their land, smelling the way I do, that would call their attention."

"Sounds like you intend to create an uprising, young man."

"If I must, I will, but I would prefer to do it after eating."

Yace tightened her grip. *Why are you being like this, Irwin? You've never wanted to kill, not intentionally. You've always been peaceful. You don't need to be like this!*

Silver swirled around his iris. *I would be doing it for Kipp.*

Revenge? You would kill a whole family for revenge? That's a stupid reason to attack a whole people! She snorted; her blue eyes were firm on him. *Maybe you need to trust that KaryKaryn will keep us safe.*

He studied their emissary. *She has not so far. I am not sure we can trust her.*

She didn't intentionally get us in that fight with the Roha. She was trying to help me, trying to help us. We needed more food.

She took us intentionally into Roha land, Yace, when we knew we should be above it. We should have been upslope in the snow, like I planned.

But KaryKaryn said there isn't food upslope.

Anger churned in his empty gut. *Yace, you are forgetting that I lived in the mountains my whole life. I know what type of animals live high up. You can find all types of food up there. It is scarce, but Kipp would still be with us and not on a stretcher had we gone along the snowline.*

Shaman said, "Well then, I'll get to preparing the meal." He took a few of the satchels and went outside to the hearth.

KaryKaryn turned to them, "We stay for meal. Then go up slope. We leave Roha behind us. We hunt meat in hills. No reason for uprising."

28

<u>Keeping Secrets</u>

It was late afternoon when they embarked on the chasm trail up to the plateau and then continued walking into the oncoming night. The moon was nearly full and already lighting the horizon. Bodi, now their only horse, went along at a moderate pace. Kipp was affixed to the stretcher behind the giant warhorse and Yace rode. From time to time, she looked back at Kipp. Turk guided the horse, walking alongside in his two-legged form. That night, Irwin gave the teenager some clothing for warmth. KaryKaryn led the group, and Irwin brought up the rear. The donkeys walked between the stretcher and Irwin. Untethered, they were free to roam, but they did not.

That night, they ascended in elevation, passing through various poppy fields. They decided to make camp above the jungle on the exposed plateau, steadily moving closer to the foothills and snowline. From where they stopped, they could see anything coming their way.

The wind was chilly at night. Yace wore the cold-weather clothing Irwin bought her in Enok. He offered KaryKaryn a donkey hide to wear across her shoulder and wrapped himself in one too. The moon and the stars shone brightly all night long. They stopped around midnight, and Irwin built a fire to keep them warm.

Yace was beginning to look pregnant—her abdomen bulging enough to show, and she walked with a noticeable waddle; her hips were expanding. She was still nauseous most of the time, but getting better at keeping food down. Turk became Yace's personal attendant, making sure all her needs were met. She sought Irwin's comfort also, but as time went on, the only solace Yace found with Irwin was ruminating over Kipp's condition—neither saw improvement. Irwin was bothered by the change in their relationship and became cold toward her and her annoying habits.

Although he did not want to listen to Yace ramble on about the same things, he was surprised to see the level of dedication she gave to Kipp. Her loyalty was much the same as Irwin had been toward her when she was catatonic. She took care of Kipp's physical needs, watered him, made his medicines, and administered them. Her devotion to him was unwavering, a surprise for Irwin—yet greatly appreciated.

It is not that I doubted her abilities, but I know how she has felt about Kipp in the past—before going to see her father. Yace was never this dedicated to Kipp; she had acted as if she could barely tolerate him. Maybe she does love him as much as he loves her!

He refrained from crying in front of everyone. He was worried about Kipp's future.

I hope this is not all for naught. I hope we are not watching him die, inch by inch, day by day.

They made camp early one afternoon, many days after leaving Shaman's home. They had consumed all the boar's meat Shaman bequeathed them. It was time to hunt for their meals again. KaryKaryn and Turk went out to track and kill. Irwin set up his tent; Yace attended to Kipp.

"Let me help this time," said Irwin. Yace looked tired and had dark circles under her eyes. At her side, she buried her face in his dirty shirt. "He will heal. I will let nothing bad happen to Kipp, or you. But you do not look good, maybe take a nap."

"But I need to—"

"I know what you do with him. Do not worry, Yace. I will take care of Kipp. You go lay down in the tent. KaryKaryn and Turk will be gone until nightfall. You need to nap. Your baby needs it too."

After pulling apart from their hug, her attention returned to her beloved. "Just as long as you don't heal him. Shaman said you shouldn't, that he needs to—"

"I know what Shaman said—what he did for Kipp. But I know I can help more than Shaman did. He healed Kipp up to a point; but I think there is more we can do to help him. I do not want all of this to be for naught, Yace."

"Shaman said Kipp will heal on his own."

Just go to bed, Yace.

"I just don't want you to fuk Kipp up."

He felt he could hear her say, "More than I already have."

"I didn't say that, Irwin."

"Not out loud, but you thought it. I saw it. I get it, Yace. Trust me, I feel terrible for not knowing what to do several days ago. But now, after watching Shaman work his magic, after the lessons, I know more about healing. I understand that aspect of my power now."

She never left Kipp's side, never took a nap.

The afternoon air was cooling as the sun slipped behind mountain peaks. Irwin went to retrieve a brush and clean the donkeys who had rolled in the dirt. He had to find something to do, to keep busy—to put his anxiety to rest.

Right now, I wish I had never left the mountains. Yace does not want me around for anything other than the help I offer. But that is how it has been since the beginning of our time together. I feel used. Kipp never would have been like this. And she has not said thank you in a long time. No appreciation. This is how father treated me. At what point do I leave them?

He brushed Nee Nee, maybe a little too vigorously, and she bit at his clothes. He slapped her away, continued to ruminate while brushing too hard.

I cannot leave until Kipp is better. I owe him that much. But what if that does not happen? What if, after all of this, he dies? I will not let Kipp die. I cannot. I will have to heal him while no one is watching, while they are all asleep. But what if I am caught? I will just put whomever back to sleep.

It was past dark when KaryKaryn and Turk returned to camp with several bags of fruits, nuts, and a few snakes—still alive, but ready to be made into a meal. There was enough food to keep them fed for the next four to five days.

They slept the sleep of the dead that night and woke the next day ready to go. Irwin had everything situated on the donkeys and Bodi. The stretcher was the last thing he would attach. Once again, they followed a path KaryKaryn knew, but no one could see. He was not sure she had ever come this way. Were they lost? She looked up the slope and down, trying to get bearings and possibly eyeballing the jungle because she felt safer there.

The farther upslope they meandered, the colder it became. By late afternoon, it was raining. The gentle sloping landscape was muddy, the grass sparse. A migrating herd of elk had passed through that area recently, eating the greenery that grew along the path. This place, where the Kruluver Mountain Range met Oceans of Osouf, was another strange world with its rolling open landscape compared to the overgrown jungle further south.

That night, cloudy formations enclosed around them, and rain poured in from every direction. Camp was soggy, and everyone was ready to sleep. Irwin gave Yace his tent, wanting her to feel cozy and allow her privacy with Kipp. He made a fire for everyone to enjoy. KaryKaryn and Turk kept to their Clan-Duin forms and slept near the fire. Irwin slept soundly, huddled under blankets near the side of the tent.

It did not stop raining until they opened their eyes the next morning. They were getting closer to the cold zone, traversing northwest—far, far away from Tropogagi lands. They were surrounded mostly by evergreens; further up the slope the trees were dappled with snow. The following night, they felt how cold it could, and would be, after the sun left the horizon.

Grass grew thick all along the great plateaus, and herds of elk and bison mingled as they grazed. They were only a day behind a large herd of buckskin-colored beasts. Broken antlers full sized and in pieces riddled the land; torn grass and scat scents lingered in the air around the trekkers as they made their way carefully across the ever-changing plateaus.

On and on they went, day in and day out, pausing only to care for and to rest Kipp during the daylight hours. Irwin was thankful that they didn't have to navigate across the cloaked jungle where the aggressive cannibals enjoyed a good chase. But this high up, there were waterways and giant gulches in the land—slowing them and their enemies—making it harder to traverse. Everyone knew how to swim except Kipp. Yace had to float him across rough waters with her telekinetic powers.

When they stopped at the rivers along the way, Irwin made sure to catch and smoke as much fish as he could. He found wild onions and cattails growing, harvesting all he could. Once they moved on, and resources were already eaten. KaryKaryn and Turk would be the ones to hunt for food. KaryKaryn always brought back meaty treats. Turk sought out fruits and nuts downslope. Their journey was taking much longer than expected, but now it was now a safer trek. They could stop and camp for multiple days without fear of being attacked. They all appreciated time off their feet, but Irwin felt anxious about getting them to Ozaroton sooner than later.

I am ready to be idle, have a hot bath, and sleep on an actual bed!

This great expanse of land they were crossing had once been a victim of a vicious volcanic episode, leveling much of the surrounding landscape, leaving volcanic boulders strewn along the way. Lava had flowed down the mountainside in places like fingers clawing at the jungle's expanse. Large and small chunks of lava were strewn along the plateaus where Irwin took the lead and broke through the dried lava beds, making a route for them and their animals. The herds of antelope, bison and deer raced south around the breaks in flat land, but these travelers did not have time to skirt so close to Tropogagi territory. None of them wanted to fear being chased—fear being killed.

There was not much to talk about, and, according to KaryKaryn, they were still two moons away from Ozaroton. No one wanted to upset Yace. Her moods swung this way and that, and her focus was so sturdy on Kipp that she wasn't eating or sleeping very well. Irwin begged her to take better care of herself, but she ignored him.

They were almost out of opium, of poppy milk. The second vial had only a few drops left. Irwin was restless about his want to heal Kipp. The more she worried about Kipp, the worse Yace looked. Unlike her normal exuberant self, she looked haggard and worn—dark circles beneath the blue eyes—her almost white locks were matted and hung in snarls down her frail back. Her gait was now an exaggerated limp, and she rarely smiled.

I cannot sit around any longer and watch Yace wither away alongside Kipp. I must do something. I must heal him. If I heal him, in theory, I heal her too.

One night, he decided to tempt fate. He did it again the next night, and then the following night after that. He made sure to not get caught. No one saw him wake in the middle of the night. No one could feel him summoning the universal flow, a direct tap into the ether. Irwin didn't work his magic for too long, but was diligent about consistency.

Yet one night, after plowing through a large and long lava field, Irwin forced himself to wake. It was extremely late. He struggled to stay awake. Now more than ever it was critical he heal Kipp. Unfortunately, Irwin did not realize that there was a point at which he could over give Kipp his power. His exhaustion only amplified the disaster waiting to happen.

When he awoke, everyone was gone. His tent, his donkeys, and his friends.

Shit! I messed up.

He stood up and looked around at the empty grassy expanse. The bright sun loomed straight above him.

Shit. Where are they? They left. I messed up. I fell asleep while working with Kipp and Yace woke up and found me. Shit! She must be so angry at me.

He began moving, knowing he could follow their trail, but Kipp's metal tattoo was far off—only a faint pang.

I wonder how long I have been asleep. How far behind am I? I knew better. I knew better, and yet I did it anyway. But I would do it again. Yace is going to kill me.

His sides ached. He was hungry and thirsty. Irwin jogged, then sprinted, racing with the wind in his eyes. He did not know how far ahead they were until night descended and he did not see a fire on the horizon. He was starved, tired, and sore from running. He ignored his own physical pains. He had let Yace down.

He stopped late into the night, hungry and thirsty. He gave in to sleep until morning light warmed his face. Although his body yearned for nourishment, Irwin returned to his feet, mentally dazed from the lack of food and water. Hoping they were just beyond viewing, he walked on and on most of that day, but never caught up. When he found their camp from two nights prior, his anger boiled again.

I should have known better than to heal Kipp while I was tired. Yace will nag me about this until the end of time.

Maybe I should leave. Forget all I have done; all we have done ... all we have been through. I can do that. I have almost forgotten about father and Saryh.

Thoughts of Saryh's bloody body before the hands of his father kidnapped his mind; thoughts of that unnecessary slaying of the innocent and kind women seared his memory and once again broke his heart. A gust of wind from the south cleared the memories, bringing him to the here and now with all its pain and predicaments.

His body hurt from lack of food and water; he was not thinking clearly and continued to search for his friends, the people he thought of as family. Why had they abandoned him for so long? Did they take him for dead?

The fading sun sparkled on a creek as he crossed. Irwin watered himself and saw tiny purple carrots growing along the waterway's edge. He ate three and took one more for a snack later. He never stopped walking as darkness descended. He followed the stretcher's markings on the ground.

He was approached by Turk during that night.

Turk loped up to Irwin in his canine form and morphed to stand upright. The young Clan-Duin frowned, "Yace mad."

"Yes, I know." Irwin nodded. "How far away is camp?"

Turk pointed in the direction of their camp.

I bet she is here, watching through his eyes, listening through his ears.

He said nothing more and followed Turk. They raced through the night.

Morning light was still a few hours away when they arrived at camp. The tent was pitched, and a fire smoldered. KaryKaryn had been sleeping, but heard their approach. The donkeys bellowed at Irwin and came trotting.

KaryKaryn kept her tone low. "Yace be mad."

"Yes, I know." He gave the Jennies ear scratches.

"We not want to leave you, Yace do. We argue much."

"Thank you KaryKaryn. I know you did what you could."

"You should not heal Kipp."

"Yes, I know that now."

"Shaman heal Kipp."

"Yes, I know. I just ..." His shoulders sagged. "... Yace has been so depressed. I cannot watch her wither away. She is not taking good care of herself, and ...."

"You a good person, Irwin." KaryKaryn patted his shoulder. "Yace has baby brain. She not think good."

"Yes, baby brain."

"She not know what she does. She scared."

"Yes. I know she is."

KaryKaryn leaned in, whispered, "You fix Kipp some. He is better. You be strong healer."

"What?"

"Kipp move. His eyes open, he make sound. He say your name, but not speak much."

What I did worked! I wish I had been here. Ugh!

29

<u>Baby Brain</u>

"What the fuk Irwin!" Yace rushed out of the tent. "What the fuk did you think you were doing?"

Remain humble.

"Yace. I ... ah—"

She came up to his face, spit flying off her lips, her blue eyes wide—wild. "I told you not to. What the fuk were you thinking? Even Shaman, a trained healer, said not to. What the fuk, Irwin! Why'd you do it?" She slapped his face. He stood stoically. Her fists hit his chest. "I know why, 'cause you're a selfish asshole! That's why. You've always wanted him. So, you decided it was a clever idea to try and heal him using powers you know nothing about. And now, he's fuked up worse than before. He won't acknowledge me. Refuses every effort I make to bring him back. The spells you placed on him have corrupted him worse than ...." Her spit continued to spew. "You don't know what you're doing and yet you keep on doing it. Just stop it! Stop using powers you know nothing about!"

What is she talking about, spells placed? Corrupted him? How could I? She is the one trying to corrupt! I did this for her, for Kipp. No one else.

"I want you packed up and out of here ... out of my life! You've not been helpful. In fact, you're helpless!" She turned, her hair flew around her body, and she retreated to the tent.

Coult this be Baby brain? Telepathic tendencies? Or both?

It does not matter; she just wants to be right!

KaryKaryn stepped up to his side. "She need you. Don't leave."

He whispered, "I am not sure I want to be here."

"I not want be here."

"I am sorry KaryKaryn, for all of this. You came to take us across the land, not deal with ... with this!"

"Kipp need Ozaroton. You need Ozaroton." She pointed at the tent. "She need Ozaroton!"

"You do not need to deal with an emotional pregnant woman, a man who is still learning his powers, and a Clan-Duin, Kipp, injured beyond healing. I am sorry for all this drama."

"Shaman heal Kipp." She had great faith in the Elementalist healer. Irwin did not. "You heal him. You good person. You help. She help, sometime."

"Maybe ...." He looked over at the tent.

Perhaps I should leave. Take my stuff and go. And then what? Yace would have nothing if I did that.

He huffed. "Maybe we should rest. Deal with this later, after a meal." His stomach growled loudly.

Shoulders slumped, he walked past the tent and snapped his fingers, summoning light and warmth to the meager campsite. He found a flask and drained it. KaryKaryn picked up a partially eaten rodent and offered it to him. He waved off the gesture and found a sack of nuts. There were only a few handfuls left; he ate every morsel. Irwin had not realized how angry, hungry, tired, and ready for some sort of resolution to Kipp's predicament he was until he crumbled down at the fireside.

KaryKaryn went back to her sleeping spot; Turk laid down close by the fire. Irwin stared hypnotically at the leaping flames, waved his hand over the flask's mouth, refilling the water, only to drink it down again. He heard Yace sobbing in the tent. Part of Irwin wanted to go to her and offer solace—give her a hug. Instead, he took two blankets and curled up and silently cried himself to sleep.

Irwin woke when Turk rose and shook off the morning dew from his fur. KaryKaryn was slow to stand. She stretched and shook before morphing into her two-legged self. The fire was small, but as Irwin began his day, flames leaped despite the morning dew, and it came back to life.

Yace emerged from her tent, pisspot in hand, and walked away from camp and threw it into the brush. She stormed past Irwin, back into the tent. The flap did not have time to lie flat before she rushed out again. She said nothing, but angry air followed her—whipping her hair.

He went to the panniers and looked at all the packaged belongings. He called his Jennies. They came to him, eating a few bites of grass along the way. They nuzzled his hand and leaned into him, wanting to be brushed—it had been a few days since anyone had cared for them.

Yace stormed past Irwin again and grabbed Bodi's mane, haltered the large warhorse, and pulled him away from a clump of grass.

I should say something. Maybe not. I hate this. Reminds me of home and how father was with me those last few moons. He was trying to get rid of me, like she is. I want to say something, but Yace is beyond reproach right now.

Could Nonbry be correct about Yace still being possessed?

He closed his eyes and said, "Yace."

"What? What do you want?"

"What do you want to keep?"

"What do you mean?"

"It is obvious you do not want me here. I will leave."

He saw her flinch.

Did I just call your bluff?

"Why?"

"Because ...."

I do not want to deal with your attitude anymore. I cannot. I just want us all to be how we were. I do not want to leave, but you give me no other option. I am terribly sorry for everything, for assuming you would not find out I was secretly healing Kipp.

His voice stopped working, but his mind was rampant.

You two mean the world to me. I do not want to lose either of you, but I cannot handle this anymore. If indeed you are possessed by Dephen, I want to help you get rid of him. I want you to become yourself once more.

She snarled, "Wild cat got your tongue?"

"You do not want me here." He hung his head.

I feel so defeated right now.

He turned away and cinched the panniers to Jenn Jenn. He did not stop to brush her or to love on Nee Nee either. He wanted to be far away from this situation.

"You're right. I don't want you here, but you're not going to leave us. You love Kipp too much to do that to him."

I do love Kipp, but I do not want to be around you. Not when you are like this.

"But your audacity! I can't believe you thought you could heal Kipp. You're not a trained healer! You can't heal anyone but yourself." She hissed. "And now we get to watch him slowly die because of your inability to think of other people. You know Kipp doesn't want you to heal him, and yet you went and …. He was doing just fine before you … you …. And now he's worse. This is all your fault, Irwin! All your fault!"

His back was to her. He leaned on Jenn Jenn, heaved a sob, and then wiped the tears from his eyes. "I am sorry Yace."

"Sorry won't cut it with me, Irwin. You should've thought this through! Your actions will resonate forever."

He found something to chuckle about.

You sound like Nonbry. I just want to resolve this.

"You know, I actually thought you were smarter than this. I can't believe that you'd be so-so-so despicable!"

Although Irwin had battled against cunning Telepaths, incinerated volatile Erthins, slaughtered carnivorous cannibals, he couldn't stand up to her. Yace (but maybe Dephen) terrified him. His voice cracked when he said, "I did it for Kipp."

"Horseshit! I know you healed him for yourself. The spell he's under speaks volumes about the lengths you'll go through to get what you want. You're a selfish, arrogant asshole!"

Her attitude was beginning to spark him, anger him. "I do not know what you are talking about, Yace. But selfish?! I am not." He turned to her. "I healed him for you."

"You didn't heal him, Irwin. You trapped him. Cut him off from everything. He's worse off than he was because of you. You should stop attempting things you know nothing about, on people who've asked you not to heal them!"

"What do you mean, I trapped him?"

"He's doomed because of you."

"But what do you mean? Trapped? I did nothing."

"Horseshit! You shouldn't harness your powers any further until you've been properly trained. You don't know what in Hakra you're doing. So stop!"

I want to throw you off a cliff right now, Yace. Keep calm.

"I did not doom Kipp."

"You're an idiot, Irwin."

"Why do you say that?"

"He heal Kipp." KaryKaryn came to Irwin's defense. "He move. He speak. He drink. He open eye. Kipp better than before."

"No. He's not, Kary. Kipp's worse off than before, not better!"

"He move. He see you. He speak. He better."

"You're wrong, Kary. He's worse because of Irwin. I can't hear him. Won't even acknowledge me. He's worse!"

"Maybe Irwin heal Kipp more, fix more."

"NO! I'm not letting that liar anywhere near my Kipp."

"KaryKaryn, it is alright. I am resolved to not be a burden to Yace or anyone else. I have only wanted to help. That is all I have ever wanted to do."

"No! All you ever wanted was warmer weather and flatter land. I think you've found it! Maybe you should just go. Yeah, go, Irwin. Take your donkeys and go back to that mountain of yours. Stop being a burden to us. We don't need you. You're not family. Never have been. You don't even know what it means to have a family."

His jaw dropped.

KaryKaryn growled, "You be nice to Irwin! You pregnant. You baby brain, remember? You need sleep."

"Shut up Kary! You don't know what I need. You've never been pregnant."

KaryKaryn put her hands on her hips; her emerald-eyes narrowed. "You hormonal! You not know me, what happened to me, what I do to survive. I know more than you. I know pregnancy, I know what happens to us. Baby brain real."

Yace raised a curious eyebrow. "You have a child, Kary?"

"You have baby brain. You need more sleep. Go sleep now!"

KaryKaryn stepped over to Irwin and whispered while Yace stomped her feet. "You stay. I handle baby brain woman; you handle animal." She patted his shoulder and walked off.

He chose not to leave that day. All Irwin could do was pack everything, take down the tent, and stay out of Yace's way.

This is not Yace. Nonbry was correct. There must be someone else inside her. Dephen? Somer? But how could that be? How could my powers not have worked? I thought Dephen was banished from her. Was he? Nonbry said they might be enmeshed. If that is the case, how do they get separated? Can they be separated? Or are they so together they have created this new person?

All I know is Yace would never say such venomous things—reminding me of my father. Only someone who enjoyed manipulating, who has access to those horrors, would use those to manipulate me. Dephen would. I know Yace is not like that, not that I remember. Quick to order, perhaps, but not vicious. Not like this. This is all Dephen.

Unless .... It could be hormones .... She is under a lot of stress.

Or maybe she is scared that I hurt Kipp worse than he was. Maybe she is correct about me. Maybe I should not have tried to heal him.

I just wish there was something I could say or do to fix this. All we can do is get past it.

Yace continued with her animosity for many days. She reminded him of his grandfather Jebadia—who often looked to have bitten something sour. Every time she looked at him, when they paused to water the horses, or had to take care of Kipp, her blue eyes glowered. She never asked for his assistance; instead, she had Turk help her. He was there to take Irwin's position: to turn Kipp over, remove the pisspot, retrieve herbs, a flask, a pillow, a blanket—anything.

Every day they journeyed further into uncharted wilderness. KaryKaryn finally admitted that she had never traveled this high nor this far into the shadows of the mountains. On a cloudless day, they could see all the way to the ocean. Islands covered in thick greenery hugged the coastline. Thousands of migratory birds gathered down there and flew as high up into the sky as could be seen. Usually, the party was hidden behind clouds and rainstorms. Sometimes the storms would flush up from the ocean with warm rain and winds, but lately, icy cold winds drew down the mountainside. Thankfully, they were never long lasting.

Irwin remained kind, but Yace wanted nothing to do with him. She continued to either ignore him, criticize, or harshly order him around. Her behavior was not anything he wanted to deal with.

The farther removed they were from Shaman's abode, the more Irwin ruminated over Kipp.

I do not think Kipp will recover. But Yace believes he will come back. What if ... what if Kipp never comes back? I cannot live with myself if that happens. I love Kipp enough to know that if we have to let go, we should do it sooner than later.

But what about Yace? I must talk to her. We must talk about the inevitable. Maybe she knows more than me. Maybe she can hear his thoughts, know his dreams.

He shuddered.

Kipp cannot exist like this. He is just withering away. A slow death. That is worse than a quick one. This is not fair to Kipp, or anyone who loves him. She will be devastated. But I cannot allow Yace to just pretend Kipp will magically come back. We must talk about the big 'what if?'

"I am worried about Kipp," he said, one quiet evening—startling her.

They had not acknowledged each other in days. "Why?"

"We are at least a moon's time removed from Shaman's home."

"It's been over a moon's time. We ran out of poppy milk days ago." She spit. "Of course you wouldn't remember. You were asleep for two of those days."

She does not let things go.

He did not want to be sidetracked because of her anger toward him. This was not about him; it was about Kipp. "I am worried about Kipp. His mind and body."

"I've done everything Shaman told me to do. You're the one who disobeyed orders. He said Kipp will heal himself. I must believe that will happen; that Kipp will return to his old self."

"Shaman also said that Kipp might not be the man he once was. We must prepare for that inevitability." She glared at him as he said, "I think Kipp is slowly dying."

Her blue eyes stared through him; her nostrils flared.

"Days ago, he had more reaction to what you were doing for him than he does now. KaryKaryn said that he looked at you, seemed more aware of his surroundings—"

I know what I did worked.

"—But now he is like he was before I ..." *decided to heal him.* "... I thought by now we would see more improvement, but ...."

"Shaman said it would take time for Kipp to heal fully. I know he'll come back to me."

Irwin ran his hand through his gritty, dirty hair. He repeated Shaman's words. "Shaman also said Kipp would not be the same person he once was. Yace," His brow creased. "Do you hear his thoughts? Have you looked in on his dreams? Do you know if he is mentally aware of anything?"

Her eyes moistened, and she turned away from Irwin. "No." She sniffled and placed a hand on Kipp.

"No, meaning you have not tried, or no meaning ...?"

"No, meaning there is nothing. He's been silent ever since you went and ...." Yace admitted, "I keep telling myself that he's in a deep sleep. That he'll wake up soon and ...."

"It is not like he is catatonic, like you were, Yace." He tried to erase the stress from his face. "What are we going to do? If he is not .... Are we going to keep this up? He is barely alive as is."

"What are you saying, Irwin?"

He raised his voice, "Look at Kipp, Yace, look at him. He is physically wasting away. It does not matter how much water you moisten his lips with, or how much tincture you think he needs. Kipp will die this way. Do you want him to die slowly or quickly? We need to be forthcoming with this decision."

He watched panic wash across her face. She wiped away some tears. "Well ... Well, I can try ... I can transfer his consciousness into Turk."

"What? No! That is what your father did to you. Kipp deserves better than that."

"Are you saying you want to kill him?"

"He does not deserve to go with Death slowly. Not like this."

"I can transfer his consciousness into Turk. Then I can—"

"Is that what Telepaths do?! Is that your solution for defeating Death, transfer souls into other people's bodies? What about Turk?"

"He's Clan-Duin, Irwin. He's Tropogagi. He's banished from this land. He doesn't—"

"What does any of that have to do with anything? Turk is his own person. You cannot just .... What you are suggesting is transferring Kipp's conscious into Turk's body! What about Turk? Do you even care about him as a person?"

"Turk's Clan-Duin, a very timid one at that. It would be an easy transfer, and Turk can then—in theory—turn into Kipp. Most Clan-Duins look alike; they can look alike with a few telepathic tweaks."

"You are going to turn Turk into Kipp? Yace! That is so messed up." He stared at her. "I will not let you do that to Turk. Or Kipp!"

"Turk is mine to do with as I please. Besides, he won't mind."

His tongue hit the roof of his mouth. "'He won't mind', are you mad? I mind! You do not own Turk. I do not care if he claimed you; you have no right to change him."

"I do too," Yace straightened. "And as such, I can do with him as I want."

"That is such a telepathic thing to say."

"You are being an asshole right now."

"You know, I think I am okay with being an asshole. At least I am not a Telepath bent on changing people."

"Fuk you, Irwin."

Pregnancy is not good for women, but especially for you, Yace.

"When we get to Ozaroton, we need to find a qualified Telepath to make sure you are not possessed, because I am beginning to suspect that you are not Yace."

Yace snarled. "When we get to Ozaroton, you don't have to burden me and Kipp any longer."

"Me, a burden?" He wanted to shout at Yace, but all he could do was laugh.

I have been grateful for every moment I get with Kipp. I have been appreciative, helpful, and forthcoming. I know you cannot say that in truth, Yace. Baby brain woman! Oh, I want to kick your ass right now, Yace.

He licked his lips. "That is fine. Once we arrive in Ozaroton, we will part from each other's paths."

"Good."

I hate you right now.

He forced himself to breathe.

Could this all be hormonal? She did not flinch when I accused her of being possessed. It could be hormones. Will it pass once she has given birth?

Breathe. She is just trying to provoke. Do not take her words like stones to the head. She cannot help being annoying right now. All her thoughts and hormones and body are out of whack. I must be patient.

He turned away, left Yace with Kipp.

Yace called to him, "I need that ice cap again."

"I thought you did not want my help."

"You want Kipp to suffer more brain damage?"

Is that how you are going to spin this?

"The brain damage already occurred, Yace. There is nothing we can do to better it, short of me summoning healing energy into that area." He pointed at Kipp's head. "But you will not allow me to help him in that way anymore, so why do you need that ice hat?"

"Just do as I ask."

How did this get so out of hand? I do not want Yace mad at me, nor do I want to be angered with her. She seems scared. Emotional. Hormonal. Maybe it is a combination? Or indeed, it could be someone else. Nonbry said that she might not be who she is.

But how is it that she could still be possessed?

Do my powers not work? Does she already have my mind? How would I ... could I tell if she was?

When we arrive in Ozaroton, I must request a meeting with a Telepath. Have them look her over. I hope they will be able to answer my questions, clear up my confusion about telepathic possessions and such.

For now, I am at a loss.

I am so glad I am not a woman.

30

<u>The Big What-If?</u>

They were west of Tropogagi Territory. The weather and temperature were finally not as erratic as it had been during the last two moons—since leaving Shaman's homestead. And the sun's descent was no longer occluded by lofty peaks, keeping the ground warmer into the night. They followed the rolling landscape down the slope, back toward a thinner jungle. On this side of the mountains, there were more rolling hills instead of the jagged peaks and isolated outcroppings.

They stopped for a day. Yace was busy dealing with Kipp; Turk helped. Irwin unpacked the animals and set up camp. KaryKaryn went off in search of a meaty morsel. The last few days, they had eaten ground-rodents, but now craved something else—something more substantial. Their huntress, in her canine form, guaranteed them something large, leaving the party to wonder when she would return.

It was quiet in camp, and Irwin missed the benign conversations they used to have. Turk was getting better at speaking Hakran. Yace had been teaching him. Irwin watched them interact, wanting to be included, but refrained—feeling like an outsider amongst friends. KaryKaryn was the only one who engaged him now. Yace continued to hold resentment for Irwin, and poor Turk followed her lead—whether telepathically commanded or just out of fear of her outbursts, Irwin was unsure.

Although she said Irwin could not leave, she acted like he wasn't there.

She is using me to get what she wants: a tent over her head, a warm fire, a horse to ride and to pull her injured beloved along, and donkeys to haul her extra belongings. I hate being manipulated like this. But I do not want to cause more strife between us. I just want to get to Ozaroton and have her psyche checked—see if Nonbry's hunch is true. I am starting to believe he might be right. She might be possessed, still. But how?

I do not know. I wish I knew more about telepathy. All I know is everything I have been witnessing is all contrived just like before, back in Onj Raha.

He tried to be cordial while hoping this would all pass once they arrived in Ozaroton.

That night KaryKaryn returned with a dead medium-sized chestnut brown animal Irwin had never seen before. He looked it over, studying the large snout, stubby legs, and fat belly. He skinned it, made a metal spit, and began cooking their meal rotisserie-style. For him, it did not matter what they ate, though his stomach preferred meat over fruit, KaryKaryn sometimes brought back juicy fruits for him to enjoy.

Yace groaned, "When's that going to be done?"

"Soon," he quietly replied. "I have not seen you sick for many days now. You must be feeling better?"

She watered Kipp's lips with a rag. "It has been a while."

"Must be all the meat you are eating."

Yace leaned in close to Kipp and petted his face. She whispered something into Kipp's ear and kissed his forehead.

"I agree. You look fat," said KaryKaryn. "Fat be good, baby eat good."

Yace's face had indeed begun to fatten, retaining water; her breasts were larger, filling with milk. "That's good to know," she said.

Irwin counted. "I want to say it has been three moons since you found out you were pregnant. That was day fifty-eight since your menses—give or take two days." He winked at her, but she didn't see it. "That means you are over a hundred-twenty days since conception."

"One hundred-twenty days?"

"It has been cloudy the last few days, so I am not sure how close we are, or if it already happened, but we began following KaryKaryn the day after the full moon. That would mean you are at least four moons into your pregnancy."

"One hundred and twenty days." Yace repeated, sounding happier. "I'm nearly halfway through!" She put her hands on her belly. "Oh Kipp, we're halfway through our pregnancy."

Yace had begun talking to Kipp as if he were there, able to answer her. It was unnerving for Irwin to witness this kind of madness. KaryKaryn and Turk tried to ignore the deranged-sounding pregnant woman. Irwin figured Yace was behaving this way because she missed Kipp so much.

"It be nine moons from beginning to end of pregnancy," said KaryKaryn.

KaryKaryn had confessed to being pregnant several times. She told them stories of her youth, how she was raped by men in her tribe and men from other tribes. Every pregnancy had ended with either a miscarriage or stillborn birth. She did not seem saddened by her stories, but Irwin sensed that she felt she was not meant to have children.

"I be here for other reason. Not for baby making."

"Irwin, you slept for two days." Yace reproached him. "We're far beyond four moons now. Look at how fat I'm getting! I'm already halfway through my pregnancy."

"Your math skills, Yace. When we see the moon next, we will know how far along you are."

She placed Kipp's hand on her belly. "Soon we will be able to feel the baby kicking. Oh, I hope it has your eyes, your skin-color." She leaned in and kissed Kipp's forehead. "I wish you could be here with us, Kipp. Oh," she whimpered.

"You were just talking to him like he was here, and now you are saying he is not? Get a hold of your mind, Yace, please—for the rest of us."

"He's not here, Irwin. I want him to be, but he's not!"

Do not provoke, leave her alone. But this is madness. I could help him, but she will not let me. Maybe she wants him to die, slowly at that, and then blame me.

He walked away, grabbed a brush, stepped over to Bodi and began grooming the tall horse.

Yace asked, "Kary, how far is Ozaroton from where we are?"

"Not far. Maybe half moon walk."

"Good," said Yace. "I'm ready for a hot bath, home cooked meal, and a real bed!"

"We take easy route."

Yace asked, "What's Ozaroton like, Kary? Is it a large town? Is there an Inn where we can stay?"

"Town be large, yes. They be wary of new people. You may stay at Inn at front of town."

"Front of town? Is that close to the Healers' Hall?"

"Healers Hall?"

"Yes. Healer's Hall. That's where healers live and work."

"No Healer Hall. Hammond live next to Hospital."

"Hammond? Hospital?"

"Hammond be Doctor, teacher at hospital."

"Hospital sounds like a term used in seminary school."

"Seminary school? No. Words printed on building say Hospital. It be—"

"Alright, alright," Yace waved a hand. "I'll take your word for it."

From across Bodi's back, Irwin commented loud enough for KaryKaryn to hear. "That sounds like a place I would go to, to learn more about healing."

"Yes. They teach much. They treat injured, two and four-legged animals."

"You are saying they could teach me how to heal horses and donkeys too?"

"Yes. They heal chicken, goat, and everything!"

Yace's eyes widened. "Would they be able to heal Kipp's brain?"

"Maybe," KaryKaryn shrugged. "They heal many; babies, old, injured, pregnant. They be like Shaman, but there be many healer learn there."

"How many times have you been to the Hospital, KaryKaryn?" asked Irwin.

"Few time. Shaman help more. I stay close to him."

"Why doesn't Shaman live in Ozaroton?" asked Yace. "He could help a lot more people if he were there, don't you think?"

"He did. He not like it. He not like living close to many people."

Irwin continued to ask for information. "Are there many people in Ozaroton?"

"Five, six hundred."

"Only five to six hundred?"

"No, many more."

Yace corrected him. "She meant fifty-six hundred."

A bubble of anxiety rippled up his spine.

I hope there is not a copious amount of metal there. Of course there will be. Prepare for it, and everything will be fine.

"I really hope they'll fix Kipp."

He brushed Bodi's rump. "I can probably fix Kipp if you would let me."

"If you touch one fuking hair on him, Irwin, I'll kill you."

I would like to see you try.

He looked at their emissary. "KaryKaryn, are there laws in Ozaroton?"

"Yes. No kill, no rape, no thief, ahhh no ...."

"How do the people of Ozaroton feel about Telepaths?"

"Many live there, many be mix blood."

He eyed Yace. "Do they rule the land, so to speak?"

"No. Ozaroton people be equal. No one better; no one worse. There be many Clan-Duin, Erthin, Cyclops, and others."

"So, there are other creatures that live in Ozaroton, besides the typical faces we usually see."

I wonder if there are any Metalists.

"Yes, many rarities live Ozaroton." She smiled at him.

"Have you ever seen or smelled anyone like me?" KaryKaryn shook her head. "Would the people of Ozaroton condone a Telepath exchanging souls between bodies?"

KaryKaryn stared at him, clearly perplexed. "Huh?"

Yace hissed, "Shut up, Irwin."

"I would like to know what the repercussions are if someone transferred a soul, or consciousness, into someone else's body."

"I'm not going to do that!"

"You wanted to do it only a few days ago." His eyes settled on Yace. "I have noticed how you have minimized your engagements with Turk, doing things for yourself. I think you are trying to figure out how to do it without being caught."

Yace scoffed, "I wouldn't."

"Your father did the same thing to you. Why would you be any different? Once a Telepath, always a Telepath."

KaryKaryn said, "What you say Yace do?"

"Yace wants to take Kipp's soul and put it into Turk's body."

"I was just saying it! I'm not going to do it."

Again, he thought he heard her thoughts. "Not now, not while we are awake."

Yace spat, "No, Irwin, that's what you do!"

"You are hoping to do it during the night, but you do not know how long it will take." He could see the guilty thoughts in her eyes. "Maybe you are hoping to do it on a night that KaryKaryn is away hunting."

"I not understand Irwin; what she do?" KaryKaryn's eyes were pleading.

"Yace wants to place Kipp's consciousness, his soul, into Turk's body, and then make him into Kipp. She says she can change Turk—make him look like Kipp with a few telepathic tweaks."

"Irwin, shut the fuk up!"

"Turk not want that. If you do what Irwin say you do, I speak at Ozaroton council. They banish you, or worse." She wagged her finger. "You cannot manipulate for personal gain—that a rule."

Irwin studied KaryKaryn.

Yace replied, "I'm not going to hurt Turk. I only want what's best for Kipp."

Everyone glared at her. Even the animals seemed agitated. Yace's contempt for Irwin was palpable.

"We'll only sleep a little while tonight," she said. "I want to cover as much land as we can. I'm ready to be in Ozaroton." Her nostrils flared and her hair flew around her body as she turned and waddled away from the campfire, into the tent, grumbling the whole time.

"We keep eyes on Yace," whispered KaryKaryn.

Irwin touched her shoulder. "Thank you, KaryKaryn. She needed to hear what you said."

I wish Yace was the old Yace and not this devious, smarmy, pushy woman. I dislike pregnant women. But is all this hormonal, pregnancy stuff? Or is Nonbry correct? That indeed Yace is being controlled. If it is true, can we un-mesh her and Dephen, or whomever?

Breathe.

We cannot get to Ozaroton soon enough.

<h1 style="text-align:center">31</h1>

Forgiving and Forgetting

The walk down the long and twisting slope had its moments of both treachery and reward. Once they were confronted by a mama grizzly bear with three cubs. She didn't want to back down, but Irwin's Metalist scent forced her and her cubs to retreat up a tree. The party kept themselves exposed, not wanting to startle any other native species as they passed through open glens, dense forests, and wide meadows.

They had to go around an area that had recently been covered by a mudslide, costing them half a day northward. Two days later, they walked through an area recently scorched by fire—possibly caused by a lightning strike. The blackened ground spread out for many kilometers—up into the forest and down toward the jungle canopy—and only an occasional green sprig dappled the charred area.

Turk was becoming an expert at catching ground rodents, and they ate many rats, squirrels, chipmunks, and other creatures Irwin could not identify. He did not want to know. They followed a herd of deer migrating westward. KaryKaryn took Turk on a hunt in hopes of bringing back a more substantial meal for supper.

They lived from moment to moment, day to day. Though their relationships were tumultuous, the landscape often matched the attitude of the group, jagged edged, bent and broken by the wind, and sometimes smooth as a well-worn rock.

After KaryKaryn's deer kill, the foursome enjoyed their meals for many days—allowing them to focus on the hike and not their growling stomachs. They drew closer to Ozaroton; but until they arrived, they had to contend with rainy days and a hormonal Yace.

"You know, I never thought I'd say this, but I'm happy to be pregnant. When we arrive in civilization again, I want us to get a cart or a covered wagon. We'll stuff it full of blankets, pillows, you know, things of comfort. I miss my blanket Ede made for me. It's so much softer than this one Kipp found." Yace sighed deeply.

"I wish I had some knitting needles and yarn. I would make the cutest booties! I wonder if we're having a boy or a girl. What colors should I use? Green? Yellow?"

From thoughts of the baby to thoughts of food, Yace's lips never remained shut for long. Neither did her imagination. "I can't wait until we get to Ozaroton. Do they have a bread shop? Do they have sourdough bread? If they don't, they probably make flour, and maybe they'll have some yeast. Oh, maybe a sourdough start! I know, Irwin, you could make me some bread."

He wanted to remind her that they were going to separate once in Ozaroton. He wanted to be bitter, like she had been with him so many times, so many days. Instead, he remained silent.

If you cannot say anything nice, say nothing, just bite your tongue and be quiet.

"Oh, I know. We can have a sod roof on our cart so we can grow herbs and vegetables. And barrels on the sides to catch rainwater. Oh, I know, we'll do just like Patrice did: have a lemon tree in a barrel on the back. Oh-Oh, an apple tree too! Then we can make pies. Oh, and lemon on fish. Oh, Patrice makes the best lemon and butter fish!

"And I want to get a cow—maybe a goat too. Then, we can have warm milk and cheese. Oh, and the thought of butter, yum. I know that if I'm fat, my baby will be happy."

Demanding more and more from those around her, Yace said, "Kary, massage my lower back. Irwin, make me some tea—extra mint this time."

One evening, after Yace had fallen asleep, Irwin asked, "I have noticed she is being flightier. Her mind is in this whimsical mode, and it is making my mind hurt. Do you know why she is being like this?"

"Baby make her like this," KaryKaryn said. "She be like this until last moon; then she go back to bitter."

"Why do women choose to have babies if this is what pregnancy is like?"

KaryKaryn shrugged, "I never choose baby. Some women want baby. Not me."

"Are all women like this when they are pregnant?"

"Some, yes. Some be nicer than Yace."

"I never thought anyone could be so moody, so unpredictable, so thoughtless!"

"Yes. It be rough. Some women want pregnant, they pregnant many times." She made a face of disgust.

He shook his head. "I cannot imagine wanting to have lots of children. I know I was not easy to handle. My elders told me that often."

She patted his shoulder. "You be too nice to be bad child."

"I know I did things to make them mad. I did not like my life as a child. My family had no love for me."

"I understand. Being rarity is hard. We demand much from family and friends."

"I've been thinking of names." Yace broke the silence during their trek one afternoon. "If it's a girl, what about River or Rainbow? But if it's a boy, I was thinking of Forest, or maybe Cedar. What do you think of those names, Irwin, KaryKaryn?" No one had any opinion, and with how far along Yace was, she had plenty of time to contemplate many names.

Her attention never stayed focused for long. Her mind bounded back and forth, surprising Irwin to no end with what she might say. "I've been thinking that maybe instead of going to the Gypsy, they come to us. I've traveled most of my life, and though I've seen many sights, I've always wondered what it would be like to live in one place. I know Kipp does too. He's always wanted to be stationary—ever since leaving his childhood home. I've often wondered what it would be like to have a home, a garden, access to fresh water all the time and to not be constantly on the move.

"I know that moving around can be hard on infants. I remember Patrice's son, Bay. He was colicky all the time as an infant. But when we stopped for a two-moon reprieve, he stopped fussing. I think it's because Patrice had been working so hard—making sure the rest of us were fed while we were driving—she didn't have time to focus on him. But when we stopped, she had a lot of time to focus on him.

"Babies need so much time and care. I'd like to think that Ozaroton's the ideal place to live. I mean, if the Cyclops live there, and no one minds them, it sounds like a good place to live. Why not encourage the Gypsy to come visit?" Yace went on and on, addressing no one in particular.

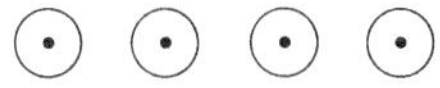

Five moons into her pregnancy, Yace grew large with swollen breasts and stomach. She had difficulties climbing in and out of the saddle now, but she didn't want to walk—citing her many pains and aches. There was no end to her fantasizing and whining. But one day Irwin noticed something peculiar.

He was scared to ask Yace about it. Instead, he approached KaryKaryn, pulling her aside. He kept contact on her forearm, so Yace would not overhear their conversation. "I think I saw blood on her skirt, Kary. It looks like the same type of stain she had when she began her menses."

They looked at Yace, in her own world, attending to Kipp.

"This not good," said KaryKaryn. "I go speak to her."

KaryKaryn approached Yace and spoke in hushed tones. Yace raised her skirt—blood was smeared across her crotch area.

"No. No. NO! Oh no! Oh, no Irwin! Irwin." She rushed to him. "Irwin, I-I need you to heal me. You need to heal me now!" She stripped naked, revealing her swollen breasts and bulging belly. "This can't be happening."

"You will be alright, Yace."

"NO! I'M NOT ALRIGHT IRWIN! This can't be happening. I don't want to die!"

"I think you are overreacting, Yace."

"You don't understand, Irwin! Something is wrong with my baby." Her face smudged with tears, she screamed, "I need you to heal us. Now!"

"Heal your baby? But I know nothing about healing babies. Yace, I do not know what to do here."

"Something's wrong, Irwin!" Fear rattled her voice and shook her body. "You can't let this happen! I need you to fix me, fix my baby. Now!"

"How do you know something is wrong?"

"Women don't bleed when they are pregnant, Irwin. We're not supposed to bleed. Blood is bad; do you understand?"

"I will see what I can do, but I know nothing about babies." Sweat beaded on his brow, and his throat tightened. "Can you please lay down?"

What the shit? After all this time of not giving me the light of day, she now summons me to do something I know nothing about.

Does this mean I am absolved of my previous blunders?

"You'd better fix us!" Yace laid her dress down on a blanket of moss and then herself.

Irwin's hands shook. Yace's blue eyes watched intently as he tried to figure out what he needed to do.

KaryKaryn came to his side. "Baby sit here, stomach here."

He was completely innocent of the ways of babies. He knew how they were made, but everything else was a mystery. "What do you think is wrong?"

"Baby be stillborn."

"NO! I know it's alive. Irwin!" Yace reached for his hands and placed them on her bulging belly. "I need you to work your magic. Heal us! Just give us your magic. Pleeeeease."

He wanted to talk this through before doing anything that might have drastic consequences. "Kary, do you hear a heartbeat?"

"Only Yace."

"My baby." Yace was inconsolable. "My baby."

"Then I should just heal her, correct?"

KaryKaryn shrugged. "Baby maybe hurt. Yace maybe hurt. I not know."

Thank the heavens that Kary knows the symptoms of a miscarriage and still-birth.

"Did you bleed?"

"Yes, every time. Longest time I with baby be seven moon. That hurt most. Shaman heal me; say I could die if he not there."

Yace could die!

His guts twisted. He held his breath. "What does stillborn mean?"

KaryKaryn said, "Baby dead inside. Miscarry is same."

"Stillborn happens at birth; I thought you knew Kary." Yace snapped.

KaryKaryn snapped back. "I be seven moons when stillborn happen to me. That be worst."

Irwin stared at Yace's nakedness, fearful of making the wrong decision. "If the baby is dead inside of her, should I extract it?"

KaryKaryn shook her head. "Baby come out."

"My baby's not dead! I don't want him to be dead."

"It be painful, every time," said KaryKaryn. "Yace, you be painful?"

She did not respond.

"She did not know she was bleeding until we told her," Irwin said, logically analyzing the situation. "I am guessing she is not in pain yet."

"Miscarry. Stillborn. Body reject dead baby; soon it comes out. Much pain then."

"I want a family." Yace was choking on her tears. "I don't want this! Kipp-Kipp, I need you, please." She used her telekinetic power to slide him closer to her so she could grasp his limp hand.

Irwin stared at KaryKaryn. "I think we should give her milk of the poppy. It would sedate her, help her sleep—cut the pain."

"No. Shaman said no milk of poppy for pregnant one." KaryKaryn said. "We have valerian, burdock, chamomile. We make tea, sedate that way."

"But if the baby is stillborn, it will not matter if we give Yace milk of the poppy." KaryKaryn shrugged. "Maybe baby alive."

He realized that she may have been speculating. "Did you even listen for the second heartbeat? Could you please?" He moved out of the way. KaryKaryn knelt and placed her ear on Yace's belly.

She concentrated, eyes closed, breathless. "I hear a faint rapid beat." KaryKaryn sat up. "Maybe small drop poppy milk."

"You think that will be safe for the baby?" He did not want to make the wrong decision.

KaryKaryn shrugged again.

"Just heal us," Yace whispered.

He held her hands, searching her watery blue eyes. "I do not know what I am doing, Yace. I do not want to hurt you or the baby."

"I trust you." But he heard her mentally whisper, *I don't trust you.*

He dropped their contact. "KaryKaryn, how far away are we from Ozaroton?"

"Um, I not sure, maybe two days."

But possibly longer.

Again, he thought he heard thoughts; this time they were KaryKaryn's. He dismissed the notion, barked orders. "Yace, get dressed. KaryKaryn, get the medicine bag. Turk and I will make another stretcher."

KaryKaryn returned to Yace's side and rolled her over in a heap of blonde hair and nakedness. Yace calmed down enough to dress. She took a small drop of poppy milk onto her tongue. She had wanted to argue with KaryKaryn, but the Clan-Duin woman was steadfast in what she believed should happen. No one wanted Yace to lose her child—or die.

Before long, Yace was asleep. By late that evening she was fastened to a second stretcher pulled by Nee Nee. KaryKaryn took up Bodi's lead, and Irwin walked next to Nee Nee; Turk brought up the back.

Before they embarked, Irwin made an agreement with KaryKaryn. "We cannot, will not, stop until we get to Ozaroton. I do not care how many days we are from there. My friends are on borrowed time."

I hope this does not get worse for any of us. I do not care what Yace says; I do not want to leave them. We are a family. We might go through tough shit, but I am learning it is better to go through this stuff with people you like than those you do not—or worse, by yourself.

32

OZAROTON

As soon as they exited the jungle, the last ray of sunlight vanished. They found the road, the only path into Ozaroton—or so KaryKaryn insisted. Now they were closer to civilization. They had crossed marshes, chased away wild boars, Irwin moved gnarled trees and underbrush, and laid smooth rocky areas—they all had worked hard to find the road.

"We arrive Ozaroton tonight," KaryKaryn said, and Irwin thought he saw her smile.

There were several more kilometers to go. At least the path they were now on was even and easy to navigate. They marched with purpose, jogging at times, along the last stretch of their journey to Ozaroton. They were close enough to smell wispy scents of fires and food being cooked.

The road was wide enough for two wagons to pass side-by-side—they walked in tandem. Slowly, the moon ascended, shining through the patchy canopy and casting shadows.

By the time they reached the edge of town, the moon was a quarter of the way across the night sky. It was nearly full, waning by two days. Tonight, the bright sphere lit the wide roadway that appeared to end just ahead. Seven wooden buildings popped up out of nowhere; three were businesses, one a long barn, and various shaped homes all situated in a semi-circle surrounded by thick underbrush and trees. Did the road end at the barn? None of the businesses were open—only the homes were lit.

Irwin wondered aloud. "This is Ozaroton? Where is the hospital?"

"Yes, no." KaryKaryn pulled Bodi to a halt. They stood in the center of the semi-circular line of buildings waiting for KaryKaryn to figure out what to do next.

"Kary, where is the hospital?" He pressed—angered, hungry, and tired.

"It be here." Her green eyes studied two of the homes standing next to each other. One was three stories tall, and the other, a meek one-story home.

"Where? I do not see the building with the word Hospital on it." He could feel metal, heard it calling from close-by and farther away, beyond the trees. This cannot be all of Ozaroton.

KaryKaryn muttered, "I don't know who I speak to."

"What do you mean, who do you speak to?"

She dropped Bodi's lead line. The large horse stood patiently as she left its side and headed for the closest porch.

"KaryKaryn, where are you going?"

"We need permission. Stay." She put her hand towards his face.

"Permission? What kind of place is this?"

Turk was still in his canine form. His bristly fur brushed against Irwin's leg. They watched KaryKaryn step up to the front door of the largest house and knock. Shadows moved behind closed curtains. A female opened the door. She motioned for the mostly naked Clan-Duin woman to come into the home.

Irwin turned his attention to the animals and the stretchers tied behind.

There was a loud commotion inside the house. Then the woman who had opened the door followed KaryKaryn to the group outside. Irwin was practically asleep on his feet. The older woman approaching looked to be Clan-Duin and Telepath—dark hair, light skin, and dark blue-grayish eyes. She went to Irwin first.

Extending her hand, she said, "I am Jule. KaryKaryn says you have injured friends." He could tell that she wanted to make contact with him—wanted to telepathically probe.

He refrained from her contact. "Yes. They need to see a healer, now, if possible."

Jule glanced at the two lying on the stretchers. "A Clan-Duin and Telepath."

KaryKaryn said, "Yes."

"They can pass. I will let Hammond know you are coming to the hospital." Jule placed her left hand to her temple and closed her eyes. When she reopened them, they settled on Irwin. "Now you, young man, are you Talented?"

KaryKaryn snickered. He glared at her and said, "Yes. I am Erthin."

Jule glanced at KaryKaryn, then looked Irwin up and down, and said, "You don't look Erthin."

"I am not very powerful, but I can harness several of the elements." He snapped his fingers and created a spark of fire. "Is that satisfactory? Or shall I whip your hair around?"

"That spark's satisfactory." She glared. "Just so you know, Ozaroton does not allow people without Talent beyond this area." She pointed at the buildings that surrounded them. "You might be harangued for not looking, well, you know. It's possible you'll be challenged. There's a no killing rule here, but the men like a good challenge. In reality, they like betting on a fight! If you like to fight, don't shy away from one. We've got wonderful healers at the hospital."

He bowed his head. "Thank you for allowing my friends, and myself, within your quiet town. I will respect all."

Jule added, "If you had no power, you'd stay with me."

"Thank you for your kindness." He bowed.

KaryKaryn took Bodi's lead line and led the troupe once again. Turk stayed at her side. Irwin followed along with donkeys on either side. She followed the road as it wound around the long barn, through a mass of tightly knit trees, between hedges of fruit-bearing bushes, and down a small embankment. As they exited the dark underbrush and started down the short hill, the sight of so many houselights reminded him of starlight shimmering on a still lake. But this was the bustling town of Ozaroton—albeit sleepy now.

"Thank you, KaryKaryn, for getting us here," he whispered to her as they entered the unseen part of the small city.

The road transitioned at the base of the slope from hardened dirty gravel to cobbles. One and two-story buildings lined the major thoroughfare, weaving into town. Although stores were closed, he noticed ceramic and quilting shops, a store full of children's clothing, a bread store, and more. Above many of those shops, light shone through sleepy windows. Some were still awake.

The cobbled road was angled—a small channel cut through the center for rainwater drainage. KaryKaryn led them to a large three-story white building. It took up an entire block. The word HOSPITAL was painted in red across the top story and on every side of the building. The main entrance was a covered drive-thru that stretched into the roadway. It was large enough for a wagon and horses to park out of the elements. Held up by six enormous stone posts, lanterns were lit around the entrance, welcoming all who were injured or suffering. No other lights were on. It was dark and quiet.

A large residential building that must have housed many families was across the road. There was a tall atrium in the center with long lit windows—probably for people who would be coming or going during the night. The front double doors flew open. A large Erthin with thick mutton-shops that blended into his short red hair hustled over to where they stood at the hospital entrance. He waved at KaryKaryn, calling her by name. "Why are ya here tonight?"

"She miscarries; he head injured."

The man stopped. "Well, that isn't good. Jule only said there were two injured people coming my way, but she didn't mention the extent. Well shoot, I need my students." He chuckled and sighed. "I had just sent the last one home for supper. I guess that's how things go sometimes, huh?" Hammond clapped his hands, and everyone turned to him. "Alright. We can bring them in one by one. Leave the head injured one. A miscarriage, depending on how far along she is, can lead to death. Brain injuries, yeesh, we'll deal with that soon enough."

Irwin wasted no time disconnecting Yace's stretcher. Hammond said, "You did an excellent job of slinging them, young man. You'll have to teach my students how to make these stretchers."

Irwin's focus was on getting help for his friends. They hoisted Yace up and carried her into one of the Hospital rooms. Kipp was taken into another room across from Yace.

After Irwin released his friends from their bindings, a stream of Erthins rushed into the hospital. Seven pupils, along with Hammond, were ready to use their healing powers. Many assured Irwin that he had nothing to worry about now that the Healers had arrived.

Hammond questioned Irwin about Yace and Kipp. He needed to understand exactly how each one had come to their current condition. Irwin noticed all eyes were on him. He stepped from side to side. His throat tightened, and he said, "I believe it was three nights ago when Yace dismounted from Bodi, and I noticed a bloodstain on her skirt." He had been awake for many days, had forgotten how long.

"Well, there's the problem," Hammond said. "She shouldn't have been up on a horse. Women shouldn't spread their legs for very long while pregnant. Maybe a few minutes a day with their partner, but not hours at a time on horseback." A few of the students chuckled. "Her cervix was probably bruised, or a tear in the uterine lining probably occurred. But we'll make sure the fetus isn't compromised." The students were awed by his assumption.

"What about your other friend?"

"Kipp was beaten near death by about twenty Roha tribesmen and women."

"Roha? I hear they're awful creatures. I'm amazed he survived."

"I was close by when it happened and began healing him immediately."

Hammond chortled, "You healed him?"

"Somewhat."

"I pegged you for a Telepath, not an Erthin. I don't sense Erthin powers in you." Hammond laughed loudly, and several of the students joined in.

Your cynicism does not amuse me.

"I might be weak, and not look like an Erthin, but I can tell you Hammond that your only Erthin power is healing," Irwin smiled as he snapped his finger making and presented his fiery spark—proving that he was part Erthin.

We are not here to compare powers.

"I tried to heal Kipp, as best I could, but he was badly broken. KaryKaryn took us to a healer named Shaman, who—"

"Shaman! You took him to Shaman?! Oh, Kary, you know better than to go to that man."

"We be far east of here when Roha comes," said KaryKaryn. "We do what we must."

"Shaman doesn't know how to heal, Kary. You know this. Come on, he believes the patients can heal themselves. But when your injury doesn't heal, or you have a loss of feeling in your limb and it turns a lovely shade of green and gets a funky smell, you come to me." He stared at KaryKaryn, possibly pointing out reasons for her previous visits to the hospital. "Kary, you know better than to trust that idiot!" She glowered, hands on hips, but didn't dispute Hammond's opinion. He turned to Irwin and said, "Let me guess, he did a minimal amount of healing on your friend and then pushed you out of his cozy hollow."

"Yes."

"Of course," Hammond snarled. "Shaman's bedside manners are horrid. That man lacks social skills. That's why he's no longer allowed to step foot in Ozaroton." Hammond studied the Metalist like a Telepath would and then hopped to the business of saving Yace and Kipp.

Hammond turned to his pupils. "We need some paperwork done, vitals, blood work, and case study information on both head trauma and miscarriage. We'll be adding to the details as we go. These two also need to be cleaned. Their body odors are less than pleasant."

Irwin felt bad for not taking better care of his friends. He knew he didn't smell that pleasant, either. "I know I should have changed and cleaned them more often."

"You did what you had to do to get them here before the female died. As it is, she will live along with the baby." Irwin hung his jaw as he swung his head toward the doctor.

"Whether it was of your doing, or the lady's, the fetus is alive and thriving. We will check to make sure there isn't anything else wrong with the lady's uterus—make sure she makes it through all the stages of pregnancy. As long as she follows a good bedrest routine, the baby should be born happy and healthy." He was trying to put Irwin at ease. "Oh, and for records sake, what are their names?"

"Yace and Kipp, Sir." He revealed only their first names. No one needed to know any more about them than they already did. "They are both twenty-two years, no, probably twenty-three now. I believe Yace is older, but I'm not sure by how many moons, and they have the same blood type."

"Oh, they do, do they? And how do you know this?"

"Shaman told us that Kipp needed a blood transfusion, something about a blood born pathogen." Irwin pointed at the young naked Tropogagi man hiding behind KaryKaryn. "He used Turk and Yace's blood."

"The audacity of that man," Hammond bellowed. "And I bet he used bamboo as their needles again, didn't he?! What an ass."

"Actually, they were metal." Irwin said, hoping to save some face for the grumpy old Shaman.

Hammond was a jolly man, laughing at nearly everything. "Metal needles? How'd that old fart come across metal needles in the middle of a jungle?"

"They are mine. I have them in my medicine bag."

"You carry needles for blood transfusions in your medicine bag?"

He glanced at KaryKaryn—she was smiling, amused. "I also have flesh sewing needles."

Hammond looked Irwin up and down, then to KaryKaryn. "What other powers do you have?"

Irwin knew to stay meek, humble—hidden. "I am an Elementalist, but I usually just say, Erthin. I have noticed that people are intimidated by Elementalists." He moved out of the way as a student stepped between the two men and their lively conversation.

The students were retrieving items to take care of Yace.

Suddenly, all seven filed into Yace's room. The last one brought a wheeled tray-table with various medical supplies on it—most were metal. The wooden wheels rubbed against a metal axil as the cart rolled past Irwin. He tried to ignore the high-pitched screech that only he could hear. All the metal tools were laid out with a bottle of pungent alcohol. Yace was lifted off Irwin's bamboo stretcher and positioned on the bedsheets. Her clothing cut off, two students began to sponge her dirty body clean.

The stretcher was given to Irwin. "Here you go," said a young partial Clan-Duin/Erthin man. He sounded as if he was plugging his nose, and he didn't make eye contact with Irwin.

Irwin stepped out of the crowded room into the hallway with the long stretcher. It had been dragged along many a rough road.

What do I do with this?

KaryKaryn stepped up to Irwin. She peered into the room as they were rolling Yace over, pulling her clothing out from under her—all soaked with excrement and blood. Another student began drying Yace with a large cloth. "Turk and me take animal to barn." She pointed in the direction they had come. "Back soon."

Apprehensive about staying in a place so foreign, hearing all the metallic songs, he asked, "Do you want any help?" He placed the stretcher against the wall behind him.

"No. You stay. Turk help me," said KaryKaryn. Turk had stepped outside and was waiting with the animals.

Irwin walked with KaryKaryn to the front door, opened it for her, and held it open. "Turk, if you want, you can wear my clothing. Just look in my saddle bag; take whatever you need."

"Thank you, Irwin," said Turk.

"I wear Yace dress."

"I do not think she will mind."

"We eat after."

"Okay. See you two soon." Irwin waved them off, sighing to himself. He turned around and walked back inside the hospital.

33
<u>Doctor Hammond</u>

There were seats in the main entry room of the hospital for family; they were pressed against the walls. Dozens of pictures hung above the seats; some hand-drawn and others painted. All were of bodies, bones, muscles, bi-peds, and quadrupeds. Horse, cow, chicken, goat, sheep, and pig hung along with adult bi-peds, male and female, and one androgynous child. Another picture depicted a pregnant female. The gestating baby looked to be half-way through the process of growing in the womb. There were smaller pictures leading up the stairs, and there was a display of various skulls—animal and human—along the back wall. He stared at a skeleton painted next to a muscled body. All the parts were identified in fine handwriting. The collection was mesmerizing.

Irwin perused the walls before he sat in one of the chairs. He stared at the painting across from him while listening to his stomach growl and the murmuring students. Students chatted with 'Doctor' Hammond. Irwin sat there for a while, nodding off, when suddenly he heard his name being called by a female.

Perking up, he opened his eyes—forcing them to stay open—he called out, "Has something changed? Is everything alright?"

"Yace is awake and asking for you," A female healer said. She was older than him, but only a few years, he guessed. Her red hair was in ponytails, and her face was tanned and covered with freckles. Her bright green eyes studied him.

He blinked and stood. "She is? Thank you."

"My name is Olivia." She smiled at him and led the way.

There were three others in Yace's room, but they all left when he stepped through the doorway. She looked up at him groggily. "Irwin! Is this real?" She reached for him.

She appeared to be under the influence of drugs. Irwin could tell that Yace wanted to make sure this was not a telepathic dream, or something worse. He moved to her and touched her hand. "Yes Yace, this is real."

"Ah, I can feel everything!"

"Yace? Are you alright? What just happened?"

Hammond entered the room. "How you doin' my dear?" He walked toward them. "You alright with him?"

Yace snapped, "Yes. Leave us. Please."

Hammond looked the two of them over and then heard his name called from Kipp's room. He went back across the hallway, but stayed only at the doorframe, close enough to look back in on Irwin and Yace.

"I don't trust that man, Irwin." Yace whispered. "We need to leave here. Now!"

"We cannot leave. They are healing Kipp." He said sternly, then lightened up to ask, "How are you feeling?"

"Awful." She said with a pained look upon her face.

"They said your baby will live."

"But I'm in awful pain—more than before."

"You almost had a miscarriage, Yace. Of course, what you are going through is painful."

"You don't understand, Irwin." She winced in pain. "Maybe what that man did to my head and body was a good thing." She turned onto her side, doubled over from the pain. "Please get that asshole of a telepathic Healer back here, Irwin."

"Hammond," he called.

Stepping back into the room, Hammond said, "How'd you remove my telepathic spell, young man?" He did not approach, obviously put off by Irwin—by his appearance.

Yace said, "I shook it off. I'm sorry. I didn't like it—didn't feel right—but now I hurt, so if you'd please."

Irwin released Yace's grasp and stepped back from her side. Hammond placed one hand on hers and the other on her forehead, recreating his telepathic spell. Irwin watched the healer, yet kept a hand next to her exposed leg. "What are you doing to her?"

"A moment ago, she was not in pain, then somehow she shook off my spell." Hammond eyeballed Irwin. "The telepathy I do dulls the nervous system, allowing the patient to be aware, but not in pain. She can talk to you. It just feels weird for her to move. At this moment, Yace isn't entirely aware of her own body."

Yace let out a sigh of relief once the spell had been replaced. She was able to lie flat, and no longer looked pained. A drugged smile grew across her pale face.

"You are using telepathy to dull the senses instead of poppy milk."

"Yes. It's better for both patient and doctor. Besides, since she's still with child, poppy milk isn't something her child needs. Your Clan-Duin friend is under my telepathic narcotic too."

"I'm feelin' pretty good right now," Yace slurred and giggled. "Definitely good."

Irwin pressed the doctor for information. "How is Kipp, Sir? Will he be alright?"

"Oh, yes. I want to talk to you about your Clan-Duin friend." Hammond glanced over his shoulder to the other room. "Looks like he'll make a full recovery, if only because someone did some extra healing." His look turned stern. "This is not something Shaman would ever do, so I'm guessing that was you."

"What did I do?"

"It appears that you created what's known as a ribbon-effect. A residual layer of healing energy which oscillates throughout the body. I'm not sure how you knew to make it, but it has kept your friend in a type of stasis."

Yace muttered, "I told you not to touch Kipp anymore."

"I have not healed Kipp since I got in trouble for it. I have respected your wishes, Yace. I have not healed Kipp since that one day."

Hammond was intrigued. "How long ago was that? Do you remember?"

"About two moons ago, since the last time I tried." He glanced at Yace.

"Do you know what a direct tap is, young man?"

"Yes. Shaman showed me."

"But he didn't teach you how to use it other than to oscillate energy, did he?" Irwin shrugged.

"Well, you summoned a direct tap to the Ether, thus waking your friend, but he probably wasn't coherent."

"He did wake. They said he did." Irwin looked at Yace.

"He probably couldn't do much," said Hammond.

"He muttered and drooled, a lot!" Yace said, "But then he went back to how he was."

Hammond looked at Irwin. "Had you continued using your powers, summoning more energy into him, you would've brought your friend back to a fully conscious state. It's obvious to me you didn't know what you were doing." He chuckled. "You were just flooding him with healing energy, not directing it to any one spot, and that's why it didn't fully work. And you were probably drained of energy after doing that, huh?"

"Yes." Irwin yawned, feeling as tired now as he had been that day.

"You fell asleep healing him," said Yace.

Hammond said, "It can be a dangerous venture, young man. Tapping into that power if you don't know what you're doing is the quickest way to die."

Yace said, "I remember kicking you. I thought you were dead."

KaryKaryn knew I was alive. She wanted to stay, and so did Turk. But you left me there because you were angry that I went against your word. I knew what I was doing would heal Kipp, but you had no faith in me.

Hammond patted Irwin's shoulder. "That small tap you created did a decent job of keeping your friend from getting worse. What Shaman did ... that man ... I'm just glad you made it here. Kipp is an excellent case study for the students. They are learning a lot about head trauma from him."

A blueish-white light emanated from Kipp's room, and the hallway glowed. Irwin moved toward the door. "What are your students doing?"

"Their working their magic. The seven of them will finish soon. Then we'll have someone with him until he comes to. Once awake, we'll see if Kipp can get to his feet. Most likely there'll be a few things in his body we'll have to rework before he'll be ready to leave the hospital."

"Rework?"

"A few of his bones might not have set fully, or properly, and he's got atrophy happening in all his muscles. So, we'll have him move around, go through a few physical activities, see if there are any outlying issues."

"Outlying issues?"

"Scar tissue formations, tendons that have shortened, bones that didn't lineup correctly, or any other hitches in his giddy-up, so to speak." Hammond patted Irwin's shoulder again.

This time, he stepped back from the contact.

"I'd say, in about two to three days, depending on how Kipp and Yace heal, they'll be ready to leave the hospital." He looked at Yace and smiled. "And on your feet, not on stretchers."

Irwin was impressed by the workmanship, the professionalism, and the humanity these people represented. He asked, "How much do I owe you for healing my friends?"

"Around here, in Ozaroton, people work off what would be considered payment. We don't do money. It corrupts the mind. If you want, there are linens that need cleaning."

"I can do that." He was quick to assess what else he could do for the hospital. "I can also make needles for extracting blood, sewing up flesh, and such."

"That would be an acceptable trade. We'll take your needles for healing your friends." Hammond added, "Of course, that depends on how used they are."

"Everything I make and use is completely sterile. And I do not share needles without them being boiled thoroughly. How many would you like?"

"I figured you'd have only one, well maybe two, if you know how to blood-let."

"I can make you as many as you want."

"You know how to make them?"

"Yes, I do."

"I didn't see you as an iron worker!"

"All I need is a fire, metal, and time."

"Well then, we'll take as many as you want to make. Tomorrow, you can go to the Blacksmith's hearth and see about working with him and his cronies."

"Sounds fair. Thank you, Hammond. sir."

Irwin's stomach grumbled.

"When's the last time you ate, young man?"

"It feels like days," said Yace. "I'm hungry."

Hammond looked over at Yace. "We'll have some sort of pudding for you, young lady, coming in a little while." He returned his attention to Irwin. "The most taverns are done servin' meals. And The Kitchen's been closed since just after dark, but you might visit the Gentleman's Club. It's down the street, around the next block along the river." Hammond added, "KaryKaryn will probably end up there tonight. You should follow her."

"Why would she go to a Gentleman's Club?"

"Cause she ain't no lady."

34

<u>The Gentleman's Club</u>

Tired and starving after leaving Yace's room, Irwin sought KaryKaryn. Wondering if she had not forgotten about him, he walked out of the hospital and enjoyed a breath of fresh air.

A woman holding two babies against her chest swiftly approached the hospital doors from the residential complex across the way. She was a young blonde-haired, blue-eyed, obvious Telepath in her mid-twenties holding what appeared to be twin babies. One child was asleep, swaddled against the woman's chest in a cloth wrap. The other moved busily in her arms. Irwin held the door for her.

"Thank ya," she said, gripping the fidgety child.

"You are welcome." He reciprocated her smile.

The child squirmed toward Irwin, almost falling from the young woman's grasp. "Oh, Zamantha. You gotta stop doin' that. I swear!" She blushed, noticing Irwin's curious eyes on the year-old child.

The baby looked at Irwin and giggled. He watched the woman walk further into the hospital. "I hope your night is well."

"You too, thanks."

KaryKaryn startled Irwin when he turned right into her. They chuckled at each other, and he asked, "Where is Turk?"

"He stays with animals. He nervous here. Smells, sights, sounds be powerful to him."

"I understand." He knew how Turk must have felt. Irwin had been aware the moment they stepped into the town of Ozaroton exactly where all the reserves of metal were kept. Every stable yard and smith shop rang in his psyche. "Coming back to civilization, if it is too crowded, can agitate me too."

"You hungry, thirsty, want to sit with friend?"

"Yes, to all of that." He said, tired, and ready to be idle. "You look good in that dress."

"Did I tie good?" She turned to show the bowtie she made with the two girth strands around her midsection. It was something Yace had shown KaryKaryn how to do.

"Yes." He noticed a happiness in KaryKaryn not seen before. "Where are you going to take me?"

"Gentlemen Club."

"Is that a tavern's name?"

"No." KaryKaryn replied, "You see."

They walked side-by-side. KaryKaryn kept smiling, looking at Irwin. He asked, "What is the Gentlemen's Club, if not a tavern?"

"A place men meet women."

"Then it is a brothel."

KaryKaryn made a face. "Brothel?"

"A place where men meet women to have sex."

"No, Gentlemen's Club not that. There be food, drink, dance, music, games; women live there, men come meet them. If they like each other, she move from Club to man house."

He was trying to understand what type of place she was taking him to. "So, the women live there, but men can only visit. The women entertain, but do not solicit sex. And if a man sees a woman he wants to take home, he does so. Is that right?"

KaryKaryn nodded.

"Then the women are for sale?"

"No. The women be free, no sale. Safe place women live, no men live there." She raised an excited eyebrow to that fact.

They turned left at the next block and followed the street until stepping up onto a large porch. The outside area was covered with tables and benches and chairs for people to sit and enjoy the outside air. Inside, the home looked warm with a large stone hearth and raging fire. A few candles flickered in the middle of the long table where a horde of women in bright dresses gathered. Above the crowded table hung a wagon-wheeled chandelier with many candles shining as bright as the fire. There was only one man in the room.

Irwin counted fifteen ladies. They looked like an arrangement of colorful flowers—their dresses vibrant—sitting around the large table. At the far end sat a well-dressed Erthin man; he appeared to be in his late thirties—graying hairs around his ears stuck out like animal whiskers. Everyone was playfully engaged in a card game, talking with lively banter.

KaryKaryn pushed open one of the closed front doors and entered the loud room first.

"Kary?" The eldest woman at the table sat tall and put her cards down. "Oh, Kary! I've been hoping .... It is so good to see you, my friend." She rushed around the table to embrace KaryKaryn.

More ladies at the table shouted KaryKaryn's name. It looked like their game was almost over. Irwin held back out on the porch, startled to see so many women and only one man in the large room. He noticed the fabric couches, chairs adorned with crocheted comforts situated around a hearth, a four-person gaming table with dice, and several smaller two-person tables along windows. Behind the long table of pretty ladies, there was a long bar paralleling the far wall—tall stools tucked under the oversized counter.

KaryKaryn's older female friend looked over her shoulder while hugging her and asked, "Kary, have you brought a man to my establishment?" She pulled away from the embrace to greet Irwin. "Good evening, young man. Are you hungry or thirsty?"

"This be Irwin." KaryKaryn said.

He stepped close to the gray-haired woman and bowed his head. "Hello, I am Irwin Miner." He peered into the room, intimidated by so many happy female faces.

He realized how messy his hair was. His clothes had layers of mud, and he was unshaven. He had not bathed in many days—his odor was very metallic and would offend all the Clan-Duins in the room. Had he known he would be in a room full of women, he might not have followed KaryKaryn. All he could do was fix the Metalistic stench, making the iron inside him into tiny rocks. He let those small metallic rocks fall onto the porch before entering.

"Good evening, Irwin. I'm Miss Gracie. Please, come on in. Welcome to the Gentlemen's Club."

"I be hungry an' thirsty, Gracie."

Miss Gracie kissed KaryKaryn on the lips. "Of course I'll feed you, my sweet."

"Thank you, Mam."

"We have some food left over from tonight's meal that you two will enjoy."

"At this point, I will eat whatever you provide," he said.

Miss Gracie snickered, "So you're like Kary. You'll eat anything?"

"Yes, at this point I would."

"How about grubs?"

"Grubs?" He chuckled. "I will eat them; I might not like them. But the smell I smell is not cooked grubs. It smells like chicken or turkey."

"It's goose." Miss Gracie quietly asked KaryKaryn, "Is he the reason you left for Daos?"

KaryKaryn nodded.

What? Did KaryKaryn come to Daos for me?

She tossed a coy smile at him and walked further into the brightly lit room.

Irwin was reluctant to follow KaryKaryn and Miss Gracie to the table. He assessed everyone there and noticed that nearly every female was close to his age; a few were maybe several years older. Only one of the females looked to be in her mid-teens—the youngest in the room—and she wore a bright pink dress and a gaudy amount of make-up. Her amber Clan-Duin eyes watched him move toward the table.

Seven ladies were Erthins, although two were mixed with Clan-Duin or telepathic traits. He felt all the Erthin powers in the room. The older gentleman at the table could heal and harness water. The other seven ladies were Clan-Duins, but two held telepathic traits—lightened features and bright blue eyes. Miss Gracie looked to be a Clan-Duin/Telepath.

At last, the card game was finished, and everyone laid down their hands. An uproar ensued.

"I win!" The man bellowed, and then looked at Irwin. "Hey, did anyone check this man's credentials?"

Miss Gracie looked at KaryKaryn, asked, "You followed protocol, correct?"

"I did, yes."

The Erthin man said, "You sure don't look Talented."

"I get that a lot." Irwin stopped several feet short of the crowded table.

"Oh, Thom, it's late and we don't need the council in here bustin' the party up," the youngest woman sneered. She had been watching Irwin since he stepped up to the doorway. She winked at him.

"Had I known where KaryKaryn was taking me, I would have washed up and changed."

A couple of ladies giggled; all of them were studying his every move.

Miss Gracie made a sweeping gesture with her hand. "Come sit down, Irwin. These ladies won't bite."

"Some of us will," said a bubbly red-headed Erthin with brilliant blue eyes.

"Vivian, please, be welcoming of our guest," said Gracie. "If he came here with KaryKaryn, that means they've both traveled far."

A dark-skinned Clan-Duin, whom Irwin believed to be telepathic because of her blue eyes, said, "Are you a world traveler, Irwin?"

One Erthin asked, "Where ya from, Irwin?"

Another female commented, "He came from Daos. Weren't you listening?"

Thom sipped from on a cup of wine. "You came from Daos? You don't look Daosian. I would know. We've got a few of them up in the mines. But you look familiar." He stared at Irwin like a Telepath would, hungry to know more about the new arrival.

"I am from up north."

"We've got a few Northies too," said Thom. "In fact, about a moon ago, a man claimin' he was from Kobiton moved into our town. Says he's a miner, but I think he's one lazy son-of-a-bitch." He cackled. "That man doesn't take kindly to being ordered around. I noticed he prefers drinkin' and being dark and menacin' to everyone in Minersville.

"He's not a grateful bastard, either. But then again, most men in Minersville are self-servin'. They just want things their way, which, of course, is how most of the people of Minersville live. They forget that if you want to earn your keep, you must hold your feet on the ground and be good with your hands—or other body parts." He chuckled drunkenly. "Laziness isn't welcome anywhere around here."

"Oh, Thom, you've had your time to talk," said one of the older ladies who was not interested in him. She turned her attention to the newcomer. "Please, Irwin, just ignore him."

"Hey, be nice to my future partner." The woman at Thom's side sneered at her housemate.

One of the Clan-Duin ladies inquired, "Why are you travelin' here, Irwin?"

The Erthin closest to him flirted, "You lookin' for a mate?"

"If you want, Irwin, I could trim up your beard," said another young woman of Erthin/Clan-Duin mix.

"I'm better at beard trimming than Bretta," said one of the Telepaths.

The Erthin nearest Irwin commented, "I can sew anything, and I'm an excellent cook too."

"Watch out, young man," Thom chortled. "These ladies are hungry for new meat. All they ever get are grungy old miners."

A Clan-Duin woman glared at Thom and said, "Or older men who have never wanted to settle down until now."

The youngest lady in the bright pink dress replied, "Miners aren't all that bad."

"Daisy," Miss Gracie spoke up from her position at the bar. She had been retrieving alcohol from a secret stash. "They're not allowed to give you metal trinkets to buy your affection. They must earn it by being dedicated to only you and no other. When you give yourself away for free, like you did, you demean all the rest of the ladies here."

"I go and fuk one miner and you just can't let it go, can you!" Daisy huffed, stood up, and stormed out of the room.

Miss Gracie spoke up so that Daisy could hear. "Some of you ladies are doomed to be whores if all you want are shiny trinkets and things that make you momentarily happy."

"Fuk you, Gracie. You're just making us into complacent housewives!" Daisy shouted from the hallway.

"She will learn this lesson the hard way, I imagine," Miss Gracie said as she and KaryKaryn brought two large jugs of wine to the table. KaryKaryn handed Irwin an empty glass and gestured for him to take Daisy's chair.

A Clan-Duin, seated at the far corner of the table, asked, "Is that the stuff from three years ago, Miss Gracie?"

"Yes, it is," she said. "It's the last two bottles." She smiled lovingly at KaryKaryn. "I told Kary I would hold them until her return."

"Oh, I'm all liquored up." Thom jubilantly replied. He placed a hand over his cup, refusing a refill.

As Irwin sat down, an Erthin in a pretty purple dress asked, "Why did you come from Daos? I hear they don't accept people like us. They kill us on the spot."

He blushed, "As you can tell, I do not look Talented."

Miss Gracie said, "Abigale, Harlin, would you two please bring our guests some food? I'm guessing you'd both be alright with goose wings, steamed vegetables, and bread."

Irwin's belly growled loudly, and everyone laughed. One of the two ladies being requested to retrieve the food rose from her seat. "Of course, Miss Gracie." The other female followed but said nothing.

Irwin watched the two walk from the room and then said, "My partner and I were on a journey to save his woman."

One of the ladies had not fully understood Irwin and asked, "Kary, are you his partner?"

"No," KaryKaryn shook her head and took Abigale's seat next to Gracie.

The Erthin to Irwin's left leaned in and asked, "You were on a journey to save someone?" Her eyes were emerald green and matched the dress she wore.

"Daos Territory." Miss Gracie said, taking a seat at the table.

"What an inhospitable land. You've made quite a long journey, my friend." She reached and squeezed KaryKaryn's hand.

They looked at each other with love. "Yes," said KaryKaryn.

The sweet Erthin dressed in green who sat next to him filled Irwin's glass and then her own with wine. "Thank you," he said, and then turned his attention to KaryKaryn. "Why exactly did you come to Daos, KaryKaryn? It was not for me and my friends. You just happened to be there when we were, correct?"

"Many moons back, the council ask me," she told him. "They spoke of change. They say change come." She stared back at Irwin.

He had a tough time swallowing his sip of wine.

What do you mean by change? Does this Council know about me?

Thom burst out, "Now I see it! You gotta be related to the Sampsons! You look like Jamie and Jowin."

"Sampson?" He felt his throat tighten more—his belly filled with butterflies.

"There's Hager and Hurwin Sampson; they're twins," said Thom. "And their sons, Otis, Edison, Jowin and Jamie, they're also twins. You look almost exactly like Jamie, but I know you're not him, 'cause he's got two little boys to deal with. There's no way he'd be down here without them. But you gotta be related to the Sampsons."

"Hurwin and Hager Sampson?" Irwin muttered; his interest perked. "My name is Irwin Miner. That was my father's name."

"You've gotta be related," said Thom. He leaned in, staring at Irwin. "You know, now that I get a good look at you, you look like the guy I spoke of earlier, the one who just moved here from Kobiton."

Fear rippled down his back.

Shit!

"What is his name?"

Thom replied, "I believe it's Alfred. No. Albert, yeah, Albert Miner."

The Erthin at this side said, "He has the same last name as you, Irwin. Maybe you're related to him."

Shit! Father is here!

Irwin sank into his chair. He needed to remain calm, but the alcohol in his belly spun his mind. "Are you sure his name is Albert?"

"Oh yeah, sure as day. He's one prickly pickle; if you know what I mean. The two interactions I've had with the fellow were rude. He's blunt," Thom said, "I don't see him bein' the fatherly type, but your face is—even with all that hair—is just like his, but younger."

Shit. I hoped he had died.

Irwin took a few deep breaths and saw a plate full of food coming toward him. Small muffins, a few slices of cheese, steamed vegetables, and goose wings. Seeing the feast helped calm his anxiety—for now.

Thom kept chuckling. "Yeah, he said he was lookin' for his cousins. Said he was related to Edgar Sampson, father of Hager and Hurwin. But Edgar's been dead a few years now. And those Sampsons don't come down the mountain all that often. They live high up somewhere." He nodded. "Yeah, you look just like Jamie. You're probably his age too."

Food was placed before Irwin. He looked over the warm plate, smelled the scents of meat and muffins. His thoughts were rampant.

I cannot believe that father is here! What should I do?

He sat like a carved stone.

The Erthin at his side was curious. She said, "Are you related to the man Thom's talking about?"

He thought about what to say. "That man sounds like my uncle. He is a crotchety old bastard. I remember him mentioning something about going to find family. My father, Samuel, died unexpectedly about a year ago." His heart sped, pounding the inside of his chest like his father had pounded him so many times. "That is why I set out on my journey."

The green-eyed Erthin said, "Are you thinking about going up to Minersville, ya know, to see your family?"

No. But maybe I should? I have always wondered about that side of the family. I never knew about them until Jebadia's death. I wonder if they are as crazed as father.

But if I go … if I go and I see father, guarantee he will try to kill me again. I know it. I was his biggest disappointment. Maybe I could vaporize him. No, he would be able to deflect my Erthin abilities—only a cave-in can kill us.

"I do not know."

"You look like you're contemplating it," she said.

35

A WHIRLWIND OF STORIES

One of the ladies spoke up. "What are the Sampson boys like, Thom?"

"Are they of coupling age?" Another lady pried.

A Clan-Duin, dressed in blue, said, "Are they rude, like most miners?" She looked telepathic, with blue eyes and pale skin, but her hair was dark brown—a Clan-Duin trait.

"Yes, they're all of couplin' age. But I'm not sure I'd approve of any of them for you fine ladies."

"Why not?"

A Clan-Duin several seats down asked. "Are they ruggedly handsome, like Irwin?"

Another woman asked, "Do they all really look alike?"

"Yes, they all have the same family traits, like Irwin here. The long nose, long brow, and thick eyebrows—well, mostly alike. Hager's boys are coupled with Clan-Duin blood, so they're a bit musty around the collar, if you know what I mean." Thom chuckled. "Harwin's boys, well, they're just a bit different. I don't know if the mother drank while pregnant, or if maybe they didn't get enough oxygen in the womb. Really, they shouldn't have been born, but one of those young dummies mated about two years ago with one of the local whores and had twin boys."

Jenna gasped, "All of them are twins?"

"Yes, it's probably a trait carried down on the father's side of the family."

"Did they all come from the north?"

"I don't know. The Sampson's have lived up in Minersville as long as I've served the people there—over a dozen years, now." Thom leaned against the table, confessed a secret. "Jamie's woman was actually pregnant with three babies."

"Three?" They all replied in chorus.

Irwin tried not to appear involved with listening, although he was intrigued. He ate everything on his plate.

They were all excited. "Triplets!"

"Oh, the poor mother." One woman commented. "How would she manage feeding three when we only have two breasts?"

Thom snickered, "You all know Verona, Hammond's wife."

"She's a twit!"

"Be nice, Lucile. Verona is just misunderstood," Miss Gracie said. "As some of you know, being telepathic is not easy. We must make sure that we respect everyone equally."

Thom continued with his story. "You know how she's got them two babies." All the other ladies, except Miss Gracie and KaryKaryn, leaned into the table's edge—staring at Thom. "One of them ain't hers."

The Erthin nearest Irwin insisted, "It's the one she claims looks like Hammond, but it doesn't. Am I correct?"

One woman said, "That dark-haired child. She's the one who has no thoughts, but you can tell that baby is thinkin' somethin'."

The woman next to her said, "I think there's somethin' mentally wrong with that child."

"Yessirreee," Thom boasted loudly. "She kept one of the babies."

The Erthin nearest Irwin said, "That's stealing! That's not allowed in Ozaroton."

"Well," Thom licked his lips. "She didn't exactly steal the baby. See, the mother wasn't doin' very well. Verona stepped in to help feed the babies."

One of the ladies interrupted Thom. "Was the mother dying?"

"Yes, she was. She had been hemorrhagin' long before Jamie brought her to me. And then one of the babies was breach, which caused other issues. That mother should've aborted one of the fetuses instead of goin' nine moons with all those babies inside her. Yep, I tried all I could do, but she was in shock and slippin' away fast. Let's just say it was a dangerous scenario for the young woman."

"Oh, those poor babies!"

"I can't imagine!"

Gracie said, "One of every three pregnancies ends in deception. You don't get to keep all the babies, ladies."

Jenna rolled her eyes. "You're not gonna give us your miscarriage lecture again, are you, Miss Gracie?"

One of them said, "But I thought everything could be healed!"

Thom explained. "When it first happens, of course. But this poor woman had been tryin' to push a breach child for half a day before she was smart enough to stop. And then it took a full day for her to get to me." His expression was solemn. "She was with men who didn't know anythin' about child delivery. They only came to me after they'd been tryin' to cut her open to pull out the babies didn't work."

The same woman kept saying, "Oh, I can't imagine!"

"Wait a moment. I remember Hammond telling me this story a while ago," Miss Gracie said. "Didn't the father kill the mother and take the two boys?"

There were many gasps. "He killed her?!"

"Those poor babies."

"Maybe it's good that Verona stole that little girl."

The lady, leaning on Thom's shoulder, sniffled, and said, "That just makes me so sad. Why didn't they come to you when she was first in labor, Thom?"

"They just didn't know. I think endin' the mother's life was a mercy killin'," he said. "She had bled for nearly two days before arrivin' at my place. I was keepin' her alive as we rushed here. I hoped Hammond could help save her. I'm fairly sure Jamie knew he had wronged the mother of those children. What she did for those babies was above anythin' I've ever seen a mother-to-be do. I feel like she held on so they could be delivered." He was clearly saddened by his story. "At least while she was in my care, and in Hammond's, we made her as comfortable as we could. But I knew she wasn't gonna make it. Sometimes the decision to consult a Healer happens after things are already bad."

Someone commented, "That is just the worst thing ever!"

Audry looked at Thom. "What type of man would do that?"

"The Sampson family are quite reclusive," he said. "They don't visit Minersville every day, maybe once a moon. I believe they live about a two-day hike from Minersville and only come down for rations and such." He was watching Irwin. "Although Harwin's other son, Jowin, I've seen him a lot in town lately. He's been goin' to Master's Saloon, enjoying the ladies there. I was hopin' he'd come on down here to Ozaroton, find himself a proper woman. But most likely he'll proposition one of those whores to be his wife."

Audry pried, "Why did Verona get to keep the baby girl?"

Thom said, "She was nursin' it when Jamie took his boys. I'm not so sure he knew there were three babies. He wasn't around for much of the delivery process.

He was angry and took off after arrivin'. It was obvious he was under much duress. He needed to walk off his anger."

"Did the mother ever see you before she gave birth?"

"Yes, she did. I believe her name was Suzy, or Summer. She came to me after discoverin' she was pregnant. At that time, I only heard two heartbeats. It was only when we brought her to the hospital for emergency delivery that we discovered the third one."

"I always wondered how Verona got that second child." Jenna said, sipping her glass of wine. "She never looked *that* pregnant."

The young Clan-Duin next to Jenna said. "And if you remember, Ashlee was a moon premature."

"Verona didn't take care of herself during her pregnancy," one of the telepathic ladies said. "She always ate whatever she wanted and just sat around moaning all the time."

Another Clan-Duin, a huskier woman in an indigo dress, said, "Oh, to be a healer's wife." She stared at Audry, the woman who was hanging on Thom's shoulder.

"High blood pressure, numbness in limbs, even gestational issues are a pregnant woman's nightmare, ladies," Gracie said. "It can happen to any of us. That's why I stress that you all get enough exercise and to eat healthy every meal."

"But your cakes, Miss Gracie."

"Your carrot cake!"

"Her apple pie!"

Thom said, "You make food that is too temptin' for anyone to stay thin, Miss Gracie."

Miss Gracie smiled. "I've gotta give all you men a reason to come in here and meet these lovely ladies. And I need to teach them all the ways to please a man—first, and foremost, through their stomach."

A Telepath said, "They do come for us, Miss Gracie."

The darkest skinned woman at the table said, "No, it's her food. That's why they come."

Miss Gracie spoke over her boisterous housemates. "I believe Verona was allowed to keep Zamantha because she was so close in age with Ashlee, and because she had already bonded with the infant. I know that little girl would have been adopted by anyone willing to put up with—"

A younger Telepath interrupted. "I couldn't! That baby has no thought at all."

Miss Gracie continued, "a deaf, dumb child."

"She's not deaf, Miss Gracie," one of the older female Clan-Duins said. "Just dumb."

Another Telepath said, "she never pays attention to me when I play with her."

Bretta, a telepathic/Erthin to Irwin's right, spoke over everyone, "I don't think that baby likes any of us Telepaths."

Jenna, another Telepath, said, "Why wouldn't she? Her mother's one!"

Bretta sneered, "She doesn't like Miss Gracie, or me, or Wendi either."

Jenna added, "I think she has mental problems. She never wants to engage with me, practically acts like I'm invisible."

The alcohol was flowing through Irwin. "Maybe she has powers no one knows of. Maybe that is why she does not like Telepaths."

"Well, if you are anythin' like those miners," Thom said, "then you could tell us about her powers. I know those men aren't mortal. Some of the men complain they stink like Death, but then again, most of the men in Minersville smell bad. And the fact that you look like them ...."

"I have never seen this child," said Irwin. "Does she look mortal? Because I am mostly mortal, with just a hint of Erthin power."

The young Telepath next to him said, "But your mind is just like hers. I cannot hear your thoughts."

"At this moment, I have no thoughts. I am too exhausted." He stared at the Telepath.

There is a little Metalist girl here in Ozaroton!

I need to talk to Yace.

"You've had no thoughts since you walked in?" The young Telepath's blue eyes were focused on Irwin.

"Babies think a lot, actually," Miss Gracie said. "But they are more linear thoughts, like, I'm hungry. I'm tired. What's that? I pooped myself." Everyone chuckled. "But there is something different with Zamantha; I've seen it. She pays attention to different things as opposed to her sister, who is easy as pie to play with."

"Irwin, rarity," said KaryKaryn. "Show your metal."

All eyes were now on Irwin. Thom asked, "You've got a Talent with metal?"

Irwin spoke his memorized lines. "Yes. I am good at sculpting it, molding it, with a hot hearth that is." He chuckled nervously, tossing a glare at KaryKaryn, hoping that she would remain quiet about his rare powers. He pulled from the back of his pants—from his flesh—a small dagger embellished with woodland reliefs. "This is one of the last things I made before setting out on my journey." He handed it over to the female Erthin next to him. She marveled at it.

Her green eyes grew wide. "You made this?"

"Yes. It is one of my prettier possessions." Several of the ladies chuckled at his choice of words.

"Irwin." KaryKaryn knew he was withholding information.

He redirected the conversation. "Kary, show them the dagger I gave you as a token for bringing me and my friends here to Ozaroton."

The green-eyed beauty next to Irwin said, "You've friends? Not that you wouldn't have friends. Where are your friends?"

"In the hospital."

The ladies burst with concern.

"Oh, my!"

"In the hospital!"

"What happened to them?"

All eyes and ears were on Irwin, as he wanted. He did not need KaryKaryn to disclose information about him—information no one needed to know. "Well, my female friend, Yace, is pregnant. She began bleeding a few days ago. We were all worried that she was miscarrying, but Hammond says the baby is alive and my friend Yace will make a full recovery."

All the ladies at the table made some sort of sound or remark, feeling bad for a woman they had never met before.

"What a horrible nightmare."

"Is she going to be alright?"

"How far along is she?"

"That is just awful, I cannot imagine!"

Irwin nodded in agreement. "Yace is over five moons along. Hammond said the baby is doing well and will make it to birth."

"Do you know what caused the bleeding?"

"As I have told you all," Miss Gracie spoke up in her motherly tone. "Miscarriages can happen for no apparent reason other than the fetus isn't developed enough or is not strong enough to live. That is not to say that your next pregnancy will end the same way. I believe the souls of our children pick us to be their guiding parent. Much like all you ladies who decided to live here and further your ambitions and learn to be independent rather than pregnant at fifteen."

One of the Clan-Duins rolled her eyes. "Ugh! Not the miscarriage lecture again." She drank the rest of the wine in her glass.

The female next to Irwin said, "Hammond is the best healer. He will make sure your friend makes a full recovery. He's an amazing doctor and teacher. My cousin Olivia has been learning from him for the past year and is making amazing progress. She told me that at some point she wants to be a doctor too."

"I have met Olivia; she seems quiet."

"Yeah, she is." The red headed Erthin at his side stared lustfully at Irwin.

"Hammond believes that Yace being on horseback is what caused the issue. Said something about a puncture in her uterus. But he said she and the baby will live."

An uproar of praise erupted from the drunken table.

"Now my friend Kipp, he got into a fight with the Roha, and ...." He confessed his tale.

Irwin enjoyed his food and wine and shared a few stories of their journey from Daos to Ozaroton. With the alcohol flowing freely, and him feeling at peace with where Yace and Kipp were, he allowed himself to let loose for the first time in a long time.

After the conversations ceased, everyone was noticeably tired from the late night. Many of the ladies watched as Thom gave Audry a passionate kiss and asked her, "Will you be goin' to Minersville with me tomorrow?"

"I need to think about it," said Audry, glancing back at the table full of her friends.

"I'll be back tomorrow mornin' for your answer." He brought up the back of her hand and tenderly kissed it. "Remember, there is no need to rush. I'll wait for you." His hazel eyes held Audry, but at the last second, he glanced at Irwin who was also watching their romantic exchange.

"Good night, Miss Gracie, Mistress of the manor." Thom went to Gracie and kissed her cheeks. "Good night, friends of Audry, it was my pleasure to get to know you all better."

All together the women said, "Good night, Thom."

Once Thom left, most of the ladies stood and took silverware, plates, cups, and empty jugs to the kitchen. The two tables that had been pushed together were now separated, and chairs were being stacked on tabletops for the night. Rags, brooms, and dust pans were pulled out and put to use. Irwin had finished his meal, his plate was taken away, and he found one of the stuffed chairs to relax in near the fire. He watched the ladies do their work in that large living room. He was slow about leaving, hoping to go with KaryKaryn back to the hospital.

She came to him and gazed into his tired, drunken eyes. "You go see Yace an' Kipp. Maybe sleep at hospital; they have many bed. I stay with Gracie."

Irwin nodded and yawned. "Thank you, Miss Gracie, for your hospitality."

"You just happened to be here at the right time, young man." She smiled. "I'd offer a couch to you if it wasn't against house rules. There is Spring's Inn up the road, or Jule's place back at the beginning of Ozaroton. But it's possible the hospital will put you up for the night too."

"Thank you for your kindness, Miss Gracie. I think I will return to the hospital to see how my friends are doing."

"It's late into the night," said Gracie. "And if they are injured, guaranteed they'll need sleep, much like you."

"What do I owe you for the food and drink?"

"You owe nothing. Like I said, you and Kary just happened to arrive at the right time. We knew Thom was coming. He's been courting Audry for the last five moons. Tonight was a special night. They all got to see the real Thom for the first time. No lies, only truths."

The three young ladies who were wiping down the room and sweeping up commented to one another.

"That man's got an ego."

"I don't know how Audry can stand him—he's so full of himself."

"I don't know, I think I'd date him if Audry wasn't."

"You're too good for him, Harlin."

"It is Audry's decision to be with Doctor Thom, no one else's." Miss Gracie spoke over her shoulder, then told Irwin, "If you feel indebted to us for the meal and drink, we could use some help adjusting the lighting tomorrow. That is, if you can support the weight."

Irwin looked up at the wagon-wheel chandeliers. The candles were mostly burned down. The chandeliers looked heavy, hanging from chains that went through a metal loop at the ceiling and attached to weighted pulleys secured in placed along the far wall. To move the heavy wheels, it would take strong and steady arms. Most of the candles had melted all the way and would need replacing. "I should be able to help," he said. "When shall I be here?"

"Oh, either before or after the midday break. We're busiest at that point with meals and such. You should come for the lunch break; we are serving goose that you can have either on lettuce wraps or flat bread. I have a spread that's spicy; most the men like it. I think you'll like the wraps; they got everything a manly body like yours needs to work through your daily chores." She patted his chest, and Irwin stepped back.

"Thank you, Miss Gracie. I might take you up on that offer. Right now, I do not know what my tomorrow holds, but you will see me sooner than later to help with those chandeliers—most likely morning." He bowed, instead of kissing the older woman on the cheek like Thom had done. "Thank you for the wonderful meal and conversations. KaryKaryn, I will see you tomorrow."

KaryKaryn smiled. "Sleep good, Irwin."

36

The Walls Are Closing In

It was starting to sprinkle when Irwin found the main entrance to the hospital. Several of the interior lights still glowed, and he saw the healer named Olivia leaving Kipp's room as he walked into the sitting area. She acknowledged him with a nod and went down the hallway away from the patients' rooms.

He heard Yace giggle, and a smile parted his lips. She was awake and seemed to be in good spirits. As he stepped into her room, he saw the young telepathic woman and her two babies talking with Yace.

"Hi, Irwin!" Yace said and outstretched her hand for him.

He was cautious about entering the room. The blonde female greeted him with a wide smile. "Hello there, I'm Verona." She also reached forward for his hand.

He went to Yace who told Irwin as they made contact, *She's telepathic.* He had also said it, but Yace did not hear his words. She continued to guide her friend, *Be cautious of her, Irwin. She wants to know about you. She cannot sense your mind—she is one of those Telepaths.*

He leaned in and kissed Yace's head. "I am glad you are doing better."

Yace, we need to get rid of her. I need to talk to you.

Again, Yace telepathically cut him off. *One of those children isn't hers. She's like you, a Metalist.*

They stared at one another. She said aloud, "Me too. Did you hear? Doctor Hammond says my baby will live."

"That is good."

Yes, I know. Please, Yace, we need to get Verona and that child out of here!

He took the seat next to her head and remained silent, almost stoic.

Verona said, "I had two miscarriages before Ashlee and Zamantha came along. Hammond says that miscarriages reset our bodies, gettin' them primed for the real baby you're gonna have." She looked down at her nursing child. "You're lucky you're still pregnant."

He looked at his friend. "I agree."

Please, Yace, get rid of her.

One of the babies was asleep between Yace's legs, the other was suckling on Verona's breast. He kept his left hand on Yace's shoulder, smiling at her in adoration. He used his eyes and his physical gestures to make Verona believe they were intimate.

Get your hand off my shoulder. She'll suspect something if she can't hear my thoughts.

"How is Kipp, do you know?" Irwin lifted his hand off her shoulder, resting it in his lap. "I noticed the door is closed."

"They said he needs to rest," she said.

Verona said, "He's got a healer in there, doin' continuous healin'. If he's got head trauma, that's what they do 'til the person wakes up."

Yace said, "I hope he wakes up."

"He will." Irwin patted her hand. "They have wonderful healers here."

Yace looked at Verona. "How old did you say your girls are?"

"Just over a year old, but I like how thirteen moons sounds. Makes them sound older."

"Zamantha acts older than Ashlee," said Yace, "She has a lot more hair, and is more mobile than her sister."

"Zamantha is older," said Verona. "She was born first."

"They do not look alike." Irwin saw the differences between the two little girls. It was like day and night; Ashlee had short and wispy blonde hair and was pale-peach in complexion; meanwhile, Zamantha had darker hair that was longer, thicker,—not quiet brown, but not blonde either—and her skin was a darker ashen-gray, her eyes held a gray-silvery hue; just like Irwin.

"That's 'cause they're fraternal," said Verona. "I think Ashlee looks more like me, while Zamantha looks like her father."

"Who is their father?" asked Irwin.

"Hammond," said Verona, as if it should have been obvious.

"Zamantha does not look like Hammond," he said. The babe suckling on Verona's breast stopped and dropped it. Her eyes opened and were on Irwin. She giggled, making milky bubbles on her lips.

Yace glanced at Irwin. "You look tired, Irwin." She put her hand on his. *Did you see how Zamantha just looked at you?*

"I am." Irwin yawned.

Yes. We need to talk. Now!

Then Yace yawned. "I'm feeling tired too."

Verona looked at the sleeping baby on the bed. "Yeah, I'd better get going. Now that this one's done eating, she'll fall asleep soon. Well, it was nice meetin' you Yace." Her smile flattened as she acknowledged him, "Good night, Irwin."

"Would you like some help with the door?"

"Yes, thank you! That'd be nice. Doors are hard to open when you've two sleepy children."

She tucked Zamantha into the body wrap large enough for one child, and then picked up Ashlee, placing the sleeping babe on her shoulder. Zamantha made a noise and began to move, so Verona pushed her exposed breast back into the child's mouth.

Irwin walked ahead of Verona all the way to the main door of the hospital and opened it for her. "You have a good night, Verona."

"Thank ya," She thought, and then added, "you too!"

He smiled but dropped it the moment her back was to him.

He returned to Yace's room. He pushed the door closed and used his Metalist power to bind it, locking them within so they could converse undisturbed. He took the seat at Yace's side and put his hand on her shoulder.

"Yace, I am not sure I want to be here anymore."

"You're acting like you've seen your father." Yace stared, possibly wanting to telepathically probe. "What's gotten into you, Irwin?"

"It appears that I have four cousins and two uncles that live in Minersville. One of which is that child's father whom I understand I look exactly alike."

"How do you know this?"

"And my father is here, I mean there, in Minersville. He arrived about a moon ago, saying that he was looking for his cousins. I do not know how he knew they were here, but it appears that my whole family is upslope and-and this is too much of a coincidence for me to not have anxiety." He looked around her hospital room. "I feel like Albert knows I am here."

Yace continued for Irwin. "Meanwhile, Verona is pretending Zamantha is actually her child; that child looks like she could be your daughter, Irwin!"

"Her father is my cousin, Jamie. It seems he does not know because she was stolen, so to speak, from her dying mother. That child ..." He pointed in the direction that Verona had gone. "... she would be my second cousin."

"How do you know all this?"

"KaryKaryn took me to the Gentlemen's club for an evening off, and I got less than that. I got an earful. There was this arrogant Erthin Healer by the name of Thom who just happens to live in Minersville. He is down here courting one of the ladies in that place. He sure enjoys talking. Oh, the stories that man told."

Yace inserted, "Verona said that Zamantha's her daughter, but I could tell right away that child wasn't hers. She's just like you, Irwin. That little baby, Zamantha, I can't read her thoughts—she's just like you!" Yace's blue eyes were wide.

"Yes, I know. And the only reason Verona claims that child is hers is because Zamantha bonded to her when she was born. Verona was in the hospital when Jamie came here—thirteen moons ago—with his pregnant wife. She was pregnant with three babies."

"Triplets?!"

"Supposedly, Zamantha has two brothers." Yace's brow wrinkled. "See, Jamie thought there were the two boys, which he took back to Minersville. But before leaving here, he killed their mother. Thom said it was a pity killing; Zamantha's mother was beyond healing. But I think Jamie killed her because she knew too much about him—about our powers. My father has always been strict about us not talking about, or showing off, our Metalist powers. I understand why he did not want to, but now I want to know about my family. I have so many questions."

"Like?"

"There has never been a female in the mines, that I know of, except my mother. And I was told that she died right after I was born. I have no sisters, no female cousins, no aunts. I never questioned why. But now I want to know why. Are all the men in my family afraid of women? Or is there something else? Maybe they take pleasure in killing women. Or maybe they are all like me and prefer men, but have sex with women to promote the next generation of miners. I am so confused and suddenly feel like I do not know my family."

"Did you drink some wine tonight?"

"Wine has nothing to do with this, Yace."

"How do you know, for sure, that you don't have sisters or female cousins?"

"There have never been any on my side of the family—that I know of. Father nor Jebadia ever mentioned females other than what they thought they were good for."

"Well, your father—"

"Thom talked about the Sampsons—how they were all twins. How they were only boys, never any girls, until Zamantha. Now I want to know why there were never any girls in my family. Because there sure are a lot of females on Urthis, and it is not like people can say I am going to have a girl and then have a girl—it is all random what type of child anyone would have."

"You're right about that."

"Miss Gracie told me that Thom could not lie tonight." Irwin confessed. "I am guessing that she did something telepathic which made him talk only truths."

"Who is Miss Gracie?"

"KaryKaryn's lover."

"Wow, you have had quite a night, Irwin!"

He crossed his legs and leaned into Yace. "Should we stay in Ozaroton?"

"We have to stay," she said. "I have to talk to the Cyclops after I'm all healed up. And I don't know how long that'll take. Cyclops are fickle creatures, and that's why it's been so hard for the Gypsy to find them."

"Should I stay?"

Yace looked into Irwin's eyes; both of them were tired. "I don't think there's anything to worry about, Irwin. If your father's up in Minersville, there's no way he'd come down here. Minersville's probably a dream for him." She paused for thought. "But you think he's only there temporarily?"

"Why would he seek our family?"

"Maybe because he left you and realized that family is worth something," she said. "But that's probably not the case." She continued to watch Irwin with an uncharacteristic intensity. "You think it's something else?"

"Part of me wants to go up to Minersville and confront him."

"Why would you do that? You're free of him—from his tyranny. He doesn't own you. And you don't owe him anything, Irwin. Remember that!"

He shrugged. "Maybe to show him that. Maybe to seek answers to my questions."

They fell quiet.

"I don't think you'd get any answers from Albert. Your father is an arrogant asshole, bent on hurting those around him—especially those closest to him. He doesn't want you, Irwin, therefore, you shouldn't want him." She stared into his tired eyes. "You deserve better."

"You are not suggesting Nonbry be my surrogate father, are you?"

"No," she said. "You are your own father, Irwin."

He cackled, "How does that work?"

"You know what's best for you. You're great at taking care of yourself and those around you. I mean, come on Irwin, you kept Kipp and I alive. I could have died, but you did what you knew to do. And I've-I've been foolish in not acknowledging all that you've done. I was selfish and petty with you." Her hands were icy as she touched his. "I am so sorry for being a bitch. You were the one thing I needed all along, and I just shunned you. You could have left us because of me, but you didn't." Tears dribbled down her cheeks. "I am truly sorry for how I was with you."

He wiped away her tears.

"Irwin, I am so lucky to have you in my life."

"Thank you, Yace." He watched her yawn. "Maybe it is time for us to sleep."

"You deserve a good rest."

"Should I worry about my father?"

"No."

"Should I worry about the people in Ozaroton?"

"Why are you suddenly so worried about everything?"

"KaryKaryn." He stared at Yace. "Did she ever tell you how, or why, she came to our rescue so quick?"

"No. Why?"

"Did you ever hear her think anything about me? Anything bad?"

"No. Why, Irwin, what's wrong with KaryKaryn?"

"She told me she had come to Daos looking for change, and then she stared at me, exactly like a Telepath would. KaryKaryn is not a Telepath, is she?" He wanted confirmation.

Yace shook her head, "Not that I know of."

"KaryKaryn said she was sent to Daos by Ozaroton's Council."

They gazed at each other again before Yace responded. "I don't recall KaryKaryn saying any reason she had come for us, only that she was glad she could be there for us. I don't think you have anything to worry about."

"She said she was sent to see the change, that I am the change. Do you think the Telepaths here know what I did in Daos? Or Nuaki Village, or any of the other places I have destroyed?" His toes wiggled in his boots. "I know I have changed many places and people's mindsets."

"I think you're worrying about silly stuff, Irwin. KaryKaryn just happened to be at the edge of Daos at the right time. I know you've destroyed many places, but do you really think you had that much of an impact?"

He did not reply, and gazed off at nothing.

"I wouldn't worry about any of it, Irwin. We're safe here in Ozaroton; this place is a sanctuary for people like us."

"So was Nuaki Village."

"Nuaki Village is where the worst of the worst live, Irwin. If you truly destroyed it, you did the entire planet a favor, I think." She looked into his reddened eyes. "You look like you need some sleep. How many days have you been up?"

"Two, I believe." It was three exceptionally long days—he was suffering from sleep deprivation.

"Yeah, you need sleep." Yace reached out for his hand. "You're not thinking straight. You're over focusing on stupid stuff."

He tried to shake off the feeling that his world was about to crumble. "Thank you for listening to me."

"That's why I'm here."

"Goodnight, Yace." He leaned in and kissed her forehead. "Sleep well."

"Will you check in on Kipp for me, please?"

"I'm going there next." He squeezed her hand and stood, stretching his weary body. He unlocked the door, summoned it open, and walked away, leaving the door open so she could hear him visit with Kipp.

He stepped across the hall and studied the closed door. He wanted to go in but was afraid to disturb the healer who was working their Erthin magic on Kipp.

"Knock already," barked Yace. She startled him and immediately his fist flew, beating on the door.

"Come in." A male healer sat inside the room. He was part Erthin and part Clan-Duin with darker hair and skin, brown eyes, and freckles scattered across his narrow nose.

"How is Kipp?"

"Well, his frontal cortex is responding well to my subjective stimuli. He's still unconscious, but when I get him to mentally respond to innate reflexes, his neurotransmitters are working effectively, which is good. And his synapses brighten when asking for basic memories such as walking or talking, but we will see how it all is working once morning comes."

Irwin did not care for the heady talk—just the basics. "I see he is still asleep. Do you have an idea when he will wake up?"

"The morning shift plans to do that. I'm here with him until about first light, and then I believe Olivia will be back to sit with him and help Yace if she needs it."

Irwin sighed, relieved. "Good to hear. I am hoping to sleep for a little while. Is there anywhere I can do that beyond those chairs in the front room?"

"Yeah, they're about as uncomfortable as a chair can get. Upstairs, there's a sleeping area with bunk beds and a room to lounge in. There's also a small bathroom, no tub, but there's a washbasin and a toilet. And if you want, you can change into our medical clothing; it's all clean and folded. It's located in the cabinets in that room." He was obviously put off by Irwin's stench.

"Thank you for the offer of clothes and a place to bathe. I know I smell; we have been going for many days and had no time to clean."

"I didn't want to be rude."

"Thank you for everything. What was your name again?"

"Devin. Devin Hammer." He chuckled, "You can probably figure out what my father does."

"Make things like hammers?"

"He prefers to swing them—building things and such."

Irwin yawned. "Thank you, Devin, for taking care of my friends tonight."

"No problem."

"Irwin, Irwin Miner."

"You're a miner?"

"Yes."

"Explains the smell."

He rolled his eyes.

"Take the stairs in the entry room and go up to the third floor. To the left of the stairway is the lounge room, there is the sleeping area and bathroom. You should find everything you need, although you might want to take a light from the hallway."

"Thank you. Have a good night, Devin."

"You too. Sleep well."

Irwin went out into the hall and glanced back into Yace's room. She looked to be sleeping, but was still awake and listening.

"Thanks, Irwin." She said, eyes closed.

"Good night, Yace."

Yace whispered, "Good night."

He was beyond tired. As he hiked the stairs, he could feel his body demanding that he stop moving and just lay down. It was quiet on the third floor. He stepped into the lounge and found the attached bedroom. He laid down on the first bunk and fell asleep quickly, but not before ruminating about Yace, her moods, and their relationship.

I need to find a qualified Telepath tomorrow; ask them to look into Yace's mind, find out if she is herself, or if Dephen has completely taken over. But how would they know? How could they tell the difference? Nonbry said the only competent Telepaths he would trust would be here. But will they be able to eject Dephen from Yace if he did live within her? If she has given herself over to him, allowed him unequivocal access to her, there would be no separating them.

How she has acted towards me these last few moons …. And then she acts completely different when around new people. It is all a game—seems to me. All reminiscent to Onj Raha and the telepathic web she created there.

But it could be hormonal. I know nothing about women during this time in their lives. And KaryKaryn said that women run the gambit of emotions while pregnant. It is so hard to tell.

I wish I were a Telepath. Then maybe I could tell the difference.

37

REMEMBERING PAPA EDWIN

He sat in a wide field filled with pink, yellow, and white wildflowers rippling in the warm afternoon breeze.

"There you are!" Shouted his great grandfather Edwin as he exited the forest up slope. The old man hobbled over and sat with the youngster.

Irwin wiped away tears and snot from his face. He had stopped crying but was still mad. "I hate father."

"He should not have said what he said. But you cannot hate him."

"Yes, I do! I want papa Jeb and father to die." The tears began again, blurring the serene landscape.

"Those are some angry words coming from your young mouth. You should think about what you say before speaking it. If you do not, you will be slapped."

Irwin scrunched his face and folded his arms.

"Your father does not want to get attached to anyone like he was with your mother. It is a sore conversation, but your father loved your mother. Deeply. He was attached to her like a leaf to a tree."

"Leaves fall. I wish I was with mama."

"Do not say that. Never say that! Do you hear me? She died to save you."

"I wish I was my twin."

"Do not say that either." Edwin went from firm to kind in an instant. "Look, Irwin, your father just wants you to have more brothers."

"He said he would replace me."

"He did not mean that."

"Yes, he did. He is a meany."

"You might be correct about that. But your father just wants the family to succeed. He and Jeb believe that if they find a good woman, she will bring into the world good, healthy children. Good little boys, little brothers, just for you."

"Am I not good? I try. I try." He began to sob.

"You want little brothers to play with?"

Irwin sniffled. "I want a girl like mama."

The old man turned rigid. "There will never be a girl in our family." He brushed Irwin's ragged hair back from his moist silvery-gray eyes.

"Why?"

After a deep inhale, Edwin blew out the words, "It's complicated."

Being four years old was not old enough to understand adult concepts, but Irwin had no siblings. He lived with adults and was held to higher standards than most children should be. For the most part, Irwin acted more like an adult than his father and grandfather—this he already knew.

Irwin saw the hard lines wrinkling his great grandfather's face. He asked, "Where do women come from?"

A smile lifted Edwin's thin lips. "Women live in many places. They prefer cities and villages. The mountains are not a place for women. As you know, it is hard to live here. They are delicate. They would wither like picked mountain flowers in such harsh conditions."

Irwin stared at Edwin. He was trying to understand. "If a baby girl was born here, would she die?"

Edwin nodded.

"Can we move to where women are?"

Again, Edwin blew air from his lungs. "We are miners, Irwin. We do not live in cities or villages; we live in the mountains. It is in our blood to mine. That is why we were created; it is what we are meant to do. There is nothing else out there for us." Edwin pointed toward the distant, jagged mountains.

"I want to be a goat herder."

"If you had your way, you could be a goat herder, but that is not how life works. We do not always get to do what we want."

Irwin snorted, "Grandpa Jebadia said that to father. He got angry."

"He was right to do so. Your father is stubborn, but he knows that us Miners must continue on creating the next generation. Our bloodlines must continue."

"Why?"

"Because that is what you do when you are an adult. Tomorrow, Albert and Jebadia will leave with the coal and go to Chinochi, where they will stay for a few days before returning with supplies—possibly a woman. Then you will get to see what a woman looks like."

"But-but a woman will die here. You just said it. And Father says women are weak. You say they are delicate. A woman will die here!"

"It takes time to find a woman, Irwin. Besides, we will make this place habitable for her. We did that for your mother."

"But she died."

"Yes. She died right after you were born. There were complications. Things we did not account for. But women die in childbirth all the time. I am sorry to tell you, but that is how life works. Men outlive women."

Tears dribbled from Irwin's eyes once more. "I do not want father to find a woman."

"You do not want siblings? Little brothers?" They stared at each other. "I know you do. You would have so much fun with two younger brothers."

Irwin finally nodded. "But I want a girl sibling and a boy sibling."

Edwin took a long moment to respond. "That would be fun. Huh. One of each. But that would never happen."

"Why?"

The wind whipped strands of hair into their eyelashes and continued to press the smell of wildflowers up their noses.

"You say we are always born with a twin. Why has there never been a girl twin?"

He stared at the youngster, eyes watering.

"Your mother was soft and caring. She meant the world to your father. He would have done anything for her, for you and your twin. She sacrificed everything for the two of you. Unfortunately, you were the only one who survived. Your mother's death ruined your father."

A flock of geese honked at each other as they flew overhead in perfect formation. They both watched the V-shaped flock ripple across the blue horizon like waves lapping along a beach.

"I want you to know that I believe women are powerful. They must be to live in this world. Some of them are not powerful enough to live with us. As you know, we miners are hard to live with. But that is not to say that women cannot live in the mountains; they can if they choose. I believe women are smart enough to know not to. Did you know that women must be strong to be able to create and hold a child within them?"

He blinked. "They do?"

"Yes, they are stronger than us men who pretend to be so strong." He attempted to flex a saggy arm muscle. "Only women can have and hold babies. No man will ever be able to do that. Never."

"Your arm is saggy." The young Irwin pointed and laughed.

"Yes, it is. You know, at some point you will be old and saggy, just like your papa."

Edwin tickled Irwin, trying to keep his frown and attitude right side up.

"Now, your father and Jebadia might try to teach you that all women are weak. Both of them have their own issues with women. Beyond intimacy, your father also hates weakness of any kind. And he believes everyone should be as smart as he; that his way is the only way; that you should know what he wants, how and when he wants it. Which was taught to him by Jebadia. And I am the one who taught him. But here I am trying to break that cycle."

"Father is not smart. He cannot read. I can read!"

"Yes, you can. And I am proud that you can. That will make you a better person, being able to read—to learn new things. You might even learn to have empathy for others."

"I hate how he says his way is the only way."

"Yes, well, Jebadia has always been a bad influence on your father. Together they stir the pot of anger, of hatred towards all—they are egocentric assholes. I understand why it is hard to find a woman willing to put up with us. Your mother was a goddess of a woman. And she did not put up with Jebadia's shit—at all. She put him in his place. She was the only woman to do that. Of course, she cooked the best meals and used that as an influence over him. He would do nearly anything for her food.

"So much has changed since her death. But not Albert and Jebadia. They are much the same in every aspect. Especially when it comes to ideals. They are thick-headed, strong willed. That is one of the reasons Jebadia and I do not speak to one another except when it comes to you. But even then ...." The old man trailed off.

"Father hates women?"

"Yes. He thinks they are weak. And he does not appreciate Jebadia's insistence with him breeding again. But we must keep the family lineage going."

"Why?"

"We are the last of the Metalists." He paused for a long time before adding, "Jebadia and I are too old to reproduce. Your father is of the right age and will be until you are old enough to breed. In due time, you too, Irwin, will breed with a woman." Irwin made a face of disgust. "When you get older, you will understand."

Irwin stuck out his tongue. "When I get older," he mocked, "when I get older. Bah! Father says that all the time."

"He is making a point. You are too young to understand many things, but when you get older, these things become easier to grasp." He paused again. "I too have things I want to tell you, but you are just too young to understand." There were tears in Edwin's eyes.

"What if I was born a girl?"

"You would not be alive."

"Why would I not be alive? You say girls are powerful."

"They are! They are more powerful than any of us ever realize until sometimes it is too late." He wiped a few tears from his eyes and looked in the direction of the almost invisible flock of geese.

Edwin's voice grew raspy, and he coughed a few times to clear his throat. "My brother, Edger, and I and so many other men were raised by our grandmother, Baena. After leaving our mother's tit, she was the only female we had contact with.

"In the mines, there were no other women—only our grandmother's haunting voice. She was always there telling us what to do. Even if we did not see her, she was there, in our thoughts, watching our work. We were there for one purpose, and that was mining. It was not until we were men like your father before we saw female Metalists again. And the only reason we saw them was to breed.

"All the Metalist females born were raised and kept separate from the boys. They were kept for one purpose. I remember how meek they were. The one I was forced to ... her tongue was cut off. Only Baena was allowed to talk to us. And when she did, she held us all in her power. We would have done anything for her."

"Wow."

"Indeed. You must know that female Metalists have a power that is unlike the power you will wield one day."

"Why?"

"I guess to keep us men from doing something bad. The thing is, she could instruct us to be bad and we would not know the difference."

"Why?"

"Her power over us kept us compliant. All the men—our fathers, cousins, and uncles—we worked the moment we discovered our powers. We worked long days, many of them without food or water. We never saw the sun, the outside world. Because of this, our family members died young. We were not taught how to harness our powers properly; we were only told to do it—no questions asked."

"Why?"

"Baena commanded, and we obeyed. But after a while, I began to question everything. The breaking point happened when my favorite uncle fell over dead." Edwin stared off at the mountainous scenery. "He ceased living right there in front of us."

"He died!?"

"Yes. He over-used his powers." His old eyes came back to Irwin. "It does not matter that we can heal; if we give too much of ourselves, work too hard, we can die that way too."

"Father says only old age or cave-ins kill us."

"Being overworked is another way to die. But it takes many days and ignorance for that to happen."

"I am smart."

"Yes, you are, Irwin."

Irwin beamed at his great grandfather.

"That is why you have all the lessons. I am training you to be smart about the decisions you make regarding your power once it does come to you." Irwin stared at his elder in awe. "It is also the reason we live here and not in GnSaan anymore."

"GnSaan?"

Edwin nodded. "That is where we are from, although I do not believe we are from there or here. I believe we came from somewhere else in the cosmos."

"Wow!"

"Indeed."

"Where is your brother now?"

"My brother lives far south of here and probably with many grandsons and great grandsons. I imagine he is feeling old these days. I know I am." He stared at Irwin with love in his eyes. "You are the reason I have changed so many of my ways. Without you in my life, I would have died long ago."

Irwin pleaded. "Do not die."

"I do not plan to—not anytime soon." Edwin held Irwin close and kissed his forehead. "But there will be a time when I am not around. And when that happens, I will need you to be strong."

He hugged his elder tightly. "Please do not die!"

"If I can, I will stay alive forever … for you." He held onto Irwin for a long and tender moment.

"What happened to Baena?"

"She died."

"How?"

"She was old when Edge and I escaped. I am sure she has been dead for a while."

"Did you kill her?"

Edwin shook his head. "I wanted to. I held much anger and resentment toward that woman for what she had made us do. All that she had done. How she made our people suffer. I felt that way for a long time—that is, until the day you were born. Though she had been dead for a while, it was not until you were in my life that I made amends with Baena."

"How?"

"I forgave her. After you were born, I had much time to reflect upon my life while looking at you, watching you grow every day. That was when I understood Baena and how she came to be. She was doing what she knew and behaving the way she did because that was what was taught to her. She had been used by others—she did not know any better. She grew up surrounded by misery and slavery, and that was her existence. Her death was a bittersweet ending to a life she was forced to live. We were all slaves—forced to mine manganese."

"Does your brother have babies?"

"Yes. I am sure of it."

"Where do they live?"

"South of here, probably. And in a dark old mine like ours."

"Do we always have a twin?"

Edwin nodded. "It is the one family trait that carries through to every new generation. Though sometimes the twin is born dead, like your twin." Edwin paused.

Although Irwin was only four, he sensed a change in Edwin's demeanor. "The same thing happened to your father too."

"It did?"

"Yes, his twin died too."

"Father compares me to my twin."

"Yes. I hate it when Albert compares you to a dead being. You are alive and very capable. You are just not the son he wanted, which is sad. He should accept you as you are and not try to change you." He embraced Irwin. "I accept all of you, Irwin. You are an amazing little being."

"I wish my twin was alive. Father could yell at him."

Edwin chuckled. "If your twin had lived, you two would always be in trouble. There would be much more yelling. I am glad you are a single child. Had there been two of you, Jebadia would have left us by now."

Irwin put his hands together and closed his eyes tight, to make a wish.

38

<u>Baby Zamantha</u>

That dream left Irwin feeling like he had not slept.

It was early morning, and the room was still dark. His body woke, and he was ready to go as he had for many moons now. He couldn't force himself to sleep more, but he lay there contemplating his life—ruminating over his dream.

How could female Metalists have such power over the men? There must be something about them that makes them different. Maybe that is why I never knew of any. Maybe they are killed the moment they are born because they are more powerful than any other—like Edwin said. If that is the case, my whole family is seriously messed up!

He remained idle for only a brief time. Soon, he was on his feet and back in his dirty clothing. He left the quiet third floor and crept down the squeaky wooden staircase to the main floor. He walked toward Kipp and Yace's rooms, but they were both closed.

I need to talk to Yace. That dream .... But I do not want to wake her; she needs to recover.

He went to the front doors instead.

Irwin's mind was buzzing from the metallic songs ringing everywhere throughout Ozaroton. Beyond his troubled thoughts, he tried to ignore the metallic humming that only he could hear. As he exited the hospital, Irwin almost bumped into Verona. He moved to avoid the young woman, but her covered basket—full of freshly baked muffins—swung around.

"Oh!" She grabbed the basket to stop it from rocking. "Well, good mornin', Irwin, was it?" She said with a touch of attitude.

"Good morning, Verona."

"I've breakfast for ya'll. Hammond suggested I get muffins." Irwin took a step back and opened the door for Verona. "Thank ya." She smiled. He waited for her to cross the threshold and then followed her into the hospital. "I got blueberry with walnuts. They're my favorite, and I thought since ya'll had been gone from such good eats for so long, I'd bring ya somethin' warm and refreshin'. They were baked this morning down at the Alcove Bakery."

She walked ahead of Irwin, straight up to Yace's closed door. As her left hand reached for the doorknob, he said, "I think Yace is asleep."

Yace must have heard their approach, and called out, "Be cautious when opening the door. Zamantha is near it!"

Verona held the handle, ready to turn it. "Would ya mind pickin' up my Zamantha? She's a fast one. I guarantee she'll be out that door the moment I open it."

"I have never held a baby before," he said.

"Oh, don't worry about it. She don't bite, much." Verona opened the door. Sure enough, Zamantha was there and waiting for an opening so she could take off on her fat little legs. She was rambunctious for her age and tore out the doorway toward Irwin.

Verona stepped into the room as Yace said, "Zamantha didn't want to stay on the bed for very long."

"I told ya she's an armful," Verona giggled. "She's an explorer, that's for sure."

Irwin stood in the hallway. Zamantha ran for him, and he backed away through the main room, and hit his back against the stairs' wooden railing. Her arms were out, fat fingers wiggling—she giggled wildly—and she grabbed his pant legs.

"Irwin, did you get her?" Yace shouted from her bed.

Zamantha wrapped her arms tight around his legs and began to squeeze. Irwin felt an electrical charge of energy ripple up his body. He was momentarily paralyzed—like a statue made of stone. He could only stare at Zamantha.

Verona called, "Don't be afraid of that little rascal! You might have ta chase her."

Irwin could not speak—his body would not listen to his internal demands. He wanted to get away from Zamantha. His heart raced; he didn't know what was happening as that electrical charge surged throughout his body.

Zamantha kept on hugging Irwin with apparent delight.

What is happening to me?

He could do nothing; say nothing. He wanted to close his eyes, but his whole body was unmoved by the binding energy.

Verona came to Irwin's rescue and pulled her insistent child off his legs. "Zamantha, let him go." The toddler wailed.

He was able to breathe now, inhaling deeply, but felt winded nonetheless.

As Zamantha cried in her mother's arms, a compulsion grew within Irwin, bubbling through him like hot water, and insisting he go and take the child from her mother's arms. He knew to ignore it, to withhold, but the urge to rescue the distressed child was nearly overwhelming.

What did that child just do to me? What type of creature is she? I need to speak with Yace, alone, now!

He quivered, continuing to refrain from grabbing Zamantha from Verona's arm. Instead, he walked over to the doorway into Yace's room and held onto the door frame. His fingernails pushed into the wood. He was afraid to enter the room. His voice rattled, "Good morning, Yace."

"Irwin." She reached out for his contact. "How'd you sleep?"

"Decent." He replied, taking one step at a time toward Yace's bedside. Zamantha was flailing around in her mother's grasp. Verona was having a challenging time taming her toddler, and he was having a tough time not rescuing the inconsolable child.

The moment Irwin touched Yace's hand, he told her; I need to talk to you. Alone. NOW!

"I don't know what's gotten into her," said Verona. "It might be nap time, although it's earlier than usual."

Between Yace's legs, Ashlee was quietly playing with a beaded necklace, completely content and ignorant of her suffering sister.

Zamantha continued to thrash, screaming in her mother's ear. Verona set the insistent child down. She toddled over to Irwin and reached for him. "Up, up," demanded the little child.

Irwin looked at Yace.

I fear this child.

Yace nodded at him. "It's alright, Irwin. You can pick her up."

Verona said, "I've never seen Zamantha so demanding!"

Irwin looked at Zamantha as if she was an explosive ready to detonate. He wanted to run away from her, yet he wanted to pick her up and hold her tight.

I must resist all urges. Breathe.

"I have never held a child, a baby, before."

"Don't worry, Irwin, you can't break her." Yace said, then chuckled. "Well, actually you can, but you'll be fine."

The look Irwin gave Yace told her that he had more important matters to deal with than picking up a child that had just physically shocked his soul. Yet, he did not want to disappoint the toddler. Zamantha cried harder, waiting for him to do as commanded. Finally, he succumbed, picking her up and held her at the end of his reach—as if this baby could eat his face. Zamantha's attitude changed. She smiled and giggled at him.

Verona laughed. "That's not how you hold a child."

Yace chided, "Irwin, you don't have to be that way."

He closed his eyes and huffed. "Yace, I did not sleep very well. I was hoping to have a moment alone with you." He looked at Verona, walked over, and handed off Zamantha. "Here is your daughter."

"Oh." Verona sneered, "Well then, we'll come back later."

"Irwin, you're being rude." Yace snapped at him. "Please pardon my friend, Verona. He is obviously still weary from our travels. Thank you for the muffins. They smell scrumptious!"

"You're very welcome, Miss Yace. We'll come back later, after a nap perhaps." She glared at Irwin.

"Sounds good," said Yace.

Verona had to place Zamantha down so she could wrap Ashlee. The child went back to Irwin and looked up at him, smiling. He ignored her. Once Ashlee was settled into the swaddling wrap, Verona picked up Zamantha. The child began screaming again as she was taken away from him.

The moment Verona left Yace's room, Irwin summoned the door to close, locking them in.

"That was very rude of you, Irwin. You need to be nice to the people here, but especially Verona, she's Hammond's wife! Besides that, she has two children, two! Imagine dealing with all that energy."

Irwin wiped his face, unable to summon an apology for his attitude toward Verona and her girls. Instead, he went to Yace and placed his hand on her shoulder.

Something happened.

"What's wrong now, Irwin?" She sounded almost bitter.

There are a lot of things. Where do I start?

"I had a dream," Irwin said, knowing he had much to talk about. He knew the memory of his dream was fading. The recent jolt to his psyche, however, would not. "It was a disturbing dream, but I do not think it was a dream. I am fairly sure it actually happened."

"What do you mean?"

"This dream was of Grandpa Edwin. But I know it was not a dream, it was a memory from long ago."

"A vision, perhaps?"

"What I dreamed happened to me; I think I was about four, five maybe. But I remember it like it was yesterday. Father had told me he would replace me with new boys. Edwin came to console me. We sat in the field where my mother always sat. Every time we would sit there to play games, or read, or learn, he would tell me so." He exhaled, looking at the far wall, recalling the meadow. "In this memory, Edwin confessed that he and his brother used to live in a place called GnSaan where they were ruled by my ..." He counted on his fingers. "... great, great, great grandmother Baena. That she had a power over all the Metalist men. That they would work themselves to death because she said so. Papa Edwin and his brother escaped from there, from GnSaan. Saving themselves and future generations from eternal enslavement."

Yace looked at him skeptically. "How certain are you of this?"

Dreams are just dreams, Irwin.

"Don't you think this dream is a little too coincidental, especially after finding out that your uncles and father are all upslope? Maybe you're just processing everything you learned last night!"

"There is more to this dream, Yace."

This is a memory, not a dream. I remember it happening!

"It turns out that the reason there are no females in my family is because they are stronger than the men."

"If the females are stronger than the men in your family, don't you think they would be alive, and all you men would be dead?"

He stared at Yace, contemplating.

I think they are killed when they are babies, still warm from the womb.

"I want you to look into my memories."

"I said I'd never do that to you again."

"I need to find out why all of this is happening."

"Why all of what is happening?"

Look into my mind, please!

"You seem agitated, Irwin. What's really going on?"

He pointed in the direction of Zamantha. "That little child shocked me."

"What do you mean, she shocked you?"

"When I was out there, and you told me to catch Zamantha, she caught me. She grabbed onto my legs tightly and sent an electrical jolt up my body. It stunned me. I could not breathe; I could not blink. She shocked my soul, Yace." His voice cracked. They stared at each other, and then Yace placed her hands on his temples and took a hold of Irwin's mind. He felt her there inside his mind. They flashed to the moment when he was in the waiting room with Zamantha. They both felt her charge of energy.

Her hands pulled away from him. Her eyes watered with fear. "Irwin, this isn't good." Yace's voice cracked. "She claimed you."

"What?"

"That was her making a specific connection to you. She made a link. That electrical charge was her laying claim to you, bonding you to her. It's like the bond Kipp and I have, but different." She paused. "It's the type of bond that makes you do as she demands. You know, play with her, coddle her, feed her, and such."

Irwin tried to shake off the feelings he had. "When she was crying, just a few moments ago, I wanted to take her from her mother and soothe her." He shuddered. "It was the most insane impulse I have ever had."

"I'm glad you didn't act on impulse. Kipp would've."

"Will you look into my head?" He sat facing her. "Maybe fix that thing Zamantha did to me. Please!"

"I'm not sure I can fix what she did to you, Irwin. She bonded you."

"Then telepathically make it so I am not susceptible to her."

Yace laughed at Irwin's insistence. "This is a first."

"And it will be the last. Trust me. After this, I am not allowing myself physical contact with anyone ever again."

"You're being brash."

"Just fix me, Yace." His eyes closed, waiting for her to use her telepathic magic on him—to make him feel better.

Her hands were chilly when they touched his skin again.

She took them both back into his dream he had woken from. She saw Edwin, his caring ways, heard his voice, and now understood more about Irwin's family. But as they flew through the dream, it triggered another memory that was so virgin, Yace and Irwin followed it.

It was snowing. Everything Irwin saw was blurry. He was moving back and forth, being jostled around. He faced forward, felt an icy wind, but also warm sun. His eyes had not adjusted enough to view the bright environment. He felt a warm body against his backside. A frantic heartbeat vibrated through his body that was not his own. There was loud screaming in his right ear. He tried to move, but was tucked in tight.

Abruptly, the world before him went dark. Irwin felt cold snow on his face. He was being smothered by the body he was attached to. The heartbeat that had once beaten against his backside had ceased its drumming, and the screams coming from his right side were now louder. Irwin began to cry.

Daylight was bright in his eyes once more. Two faces crowded around him. He cried a few more times, but then quieted. Meanwhile, the other baby never ceased wailing. Irwin took in the faces—recognized them. It was his father and grandfather. They looked much younger—their faces riddled with anger.

Albert was annoyed. "What should we do with this one?" He pointed to the wailing babe at Irwin's right side.

Jebadia said, "Metalist females are not allowed to live; you know this. Since I killed Charlotte, you must kill her. Do it quick." He bent down and picked up Irwin, who started to sob.

"I just want to leave her to die." Albert grimaced.

Jebadia growled, "In the snow? You are callous. Kill her already! We will return home now."

Albert's shoulders slumped as he turned away from Jebadia and Irwin. The older man wrapped up Irwin into a secure bundle. He listened to his sister bellow, but suddenly her insistent cries were silenced.

The icy tundra was quiet. Irwin cried again—softly this time. Everything felt different, including the heartbeat he now heard. He continued to cry.

Yace's room came back into view, and Irwin realized he was sobbing. He wiped away the tears, saddened by the vision they had just witnessed. Yace shed light upon Irwin's first moments of life. She cried too, but was quiet about it. Her hands recoiled from his temples.

"You had a sister."

"I bet my father did too."

"Oh, Irwin!"

"That explains why Edwin had a tough time talking to me, telling me the truth. He knew the truth. He probably made Jebadia kill Albert's twin. My family is so messed up."

"Do you think the females have a power like telepathy? Is that why the men will do whatever they command, no matter what?"

"I guess, maybe."

"This morning, Zamantha was playing with my metal tattoo while Verona went to get the muffins. She pulled at the metal, pulled with her powers—not physically with her fingers."

"She can use her powers?" He gasped. "When were you going to tell me?"

"You've been able to use your powers since you were born, right?"

"No, Yace, I was six ..." He shook his head, misremembering. "... seven, when I heard the metallic call. But you are telling me that little baby was playing with your tattoo with her powers? This is not good, Yace."

"Irwin, tell me, what is the worry here?"

"Beyond the fact that it took me until just recently to master my abilities. She has no one to guide her, no one to show her how much fun our power can be if used correctly. She could hurt people; she could hurt her sister or mother. Maybe I should go and check on her."

"Sounds like you're feeling impulsive again. Besides, you don't even know where she is."

He walked around Yace's bed. The smell of blueberry muffins was potent. His stomach growled as he passed the basket. He went to the closed window and opened the curtains, exposing the room to morning's light. It was bright outside—another sunny day.

He pointed at the building across the way. "She is on the third-floor, second window over."

"Fuk, Irwin! You can feel her?"

"Yes. Now maybe you understand why I am having such anxiety right now."

"This can't be good. Are you gonna be alright, Irwin?"

He was trying to shake off his anxiety. The blueberry scent was enough to overwhelm and force him to pick up a muffin and eat it. "I am now." He took a bite.

"Can I have one?"

He tossed her a muffin. "Are you really going to be alright, Irwin?"

"I do not know. Beyond having a female Metalist lay claim to me, and finding out half my family lives a day's travel away, I am not sure. Oh, and my father is there too. Oh, and the person who brought us here was sent to find me by the council of Ozaroton. Yeah, I do not know why I would be anxious."

"Like I said last night, I don't think you have much to worry about. KaryKaryn's intentions have always been true. She was our guiding light, even if we did get mangled along the way. It's called Tropogagi land for a reason—the land of cannibals!

"Now your father ... maybe he wants to be closer to family. Maybe he wants to be a grandfather. Or maybe he's hoping one of his cousins will father some twins for him to take parental ownership of ... although that just sounds scary! That you survived your upbringing and didn't kill yourself ....

"And Zamantha bonding to you is just a fluke, a minor problem you don't really need to worry about."

"She bonded to me against my will, Yace!"

"And once we leave here, that bond will die." Yace assured, "If you don't engage the bond, it dissipates over time. It happened with Kipp and I."

He stared at her; she could not stop his worries. There was much for him to contemplate with so many family members living this close to Ozaroton.

But his suspicion about Yace not being herself disappeared from his mind. Those thoughts were tossed aside—made unimportant.

The last thing I need to see is my father.

And if he finds there is a female Metalist here, she will not be safe. No one will.

"I hope you are correct about that." His mind still raced.

I must find other things to do to keep my mind calm or all I will think about is Yace's irrational behaviors and my family.

"So now what? What are you going to do with your day?"

"There are linens to be cleaned, and I said I would trade those metal needles we used for the blood transfusion—for your care."

"That's very nice of you, Irwin."

"If I help, then I will leave a good impression. From what I understand, my cousin Jamie did not."

"You might not want to talk about that out loud. Especially now that it's daytime."

"You are probably right." He took another muffin and bit into it. "These are good. Yum! I think I will work here first, then go clean the stalls. I have been asked to help at the Gentlemen's Club too. I will probably go there after the stalls. Then I will offer my hands and back anywhere else."

"Helping at the Gentlemen's Club? Are there any men there which turn your fancy?"

"Only women live there, Yace."

"Well, that is very sweet of you to help those ladies out, Irwin." Yace yawned. "I need to rest."

He gasped, remembering, "I took off the telepathic spell again. I am sorry."

"You did it last night." Yace did not sound angry, only pained. "I've been without mental ease all night."

"I am extremely sorry, Yace. I did not mean to—"

"You forgot; I'll forgive you this time."

They finished their muffins.

"Would you like me to check up on Kipp again?" Irwin licked his fingers.

"Please, yes." Yace closed her eyes. She took several rhythmic breaths, her hand under the covers rubbing her belly—the other hand cradled a partially eaten muffin.

Irwin left her room, leaving the door open. Devin was departing Kipp's room. Olivia settled into the bedside seat, getting ready to work her healing magic. He saw her but followed Devin away from the patient rooms down the hallway. "How is Kipp this morning?"

"He's doing well. Like I told you last night, the plan for today is to get Kipp active when Hammond arrives. We'll then see if there are any speech problems or physical issues and then make up a plan to keep him moving and get you all out of here."

"Thank you for the reassurances. I was told there would be work for me to do today."

"You're ready to work?"

"Yes, please."

39

Making New Friends

There was a line of rain barrels in the hospital's courtyard. That was where Irwin would clean the linens. Thick cords of rope were strung up high between buildings. He stood on a five stepladder and used wooden clothespins to affix different size linens to the overhead lines. He finished putting the laundry up to dry in no time after using his Erthin Talents to wash and rinse. Everything would be dry by midday. The air was already warm. He went back to the hospital and looked in on Kipp and Olivia. She smiled at him but remained focused on Kipp. He paused at Yace's door. She was sleeping on her side, facing the door. He continued with his morning missions to help out as much as he could.

He retraced his steps from the night before, back up to the barn. He passed the Alcove Bakery and its sweet bread aromas. There was a place called The Kitchen that was currently closed. In the same place there was a child's clothing shop with dressed up wooden dolls on display. The road transitioned into gravel on the hill that slithered into dark, dense brush. It appeared that the roadway ended at the prickly bush, but it slithered between bushes and came around the backside of the barn, where the shrubs spilled into the large circular space at the front of Ozaroton.

The barn's front door creaked when he pulled on it. Irwin hoped to see Turk and KaryKaryn, but there were only animals—several horses, about thirty chickens, and a pig with a dozen piglets. It was so noisy in there he did not see the man at the end of the walkway feeding the animals.

"Hi-ya!" A tall Clan-Duin called to him. "You with Kary?"

"Yes. I am Irwin."

"Zilio."

"Do you know where KaryKaryn and Turk are?"

"You missed 'em by a horsehair! Kary's taking Turk to a half-way house for Tropogagi. She's going to make sure he's set up with a room and gets to meet others like him."

"Ozaroton has a halfway house for Tropogagi?"

"Doesn't every town?" Zilio chuckled.

Irwin rubbed his neck. "I am here to clean up after my animals."

"You are, eh? Do any of them know how to drive?"

"Wagons and carts, yes. They all can."

"We might use them today, if that's alright?" Zilio sounded very lighthearted. "So, ya wanna clean some stalls? The shovels over there; the hauler there." He pointed at each tool. "I just checked their water and tossed bundles of grass to your three."

"Thank you, Zilio."

Cleaning the stalls gave Irwin time to focus on the task at hand. It was a pleasant reprieve for his whirling mind. But when he was done with his own two, he felt he needed to do a few more. It took five stalls before his nerves relaxed.

He was thanked for the hard work and retrieved his personal luggage, along with Yace's and Kipp's clothing bags. He slung the bags across his shoulders and set off toward the hospital.

Before leaving the barn, Zilio had told Irwin where he could get himself and his clothing washed up. He also told him of all the work that would be done that day—making it sound like they would need another pair of helpful hands.

"If I have time this afternoon, I will come and help." Irwin offered. "For now, I want to see how my friends are doing and get cleaned up a bit. I know I smell bad, an understatement, right?"

"Didn't want to say anything."

"No one ever does, but then they all suggest by expression that I need a bath."

Zilio chuckled, wiped away a tear, and said, "They'll have bathing supplies at the Bathing Club: soaps, scrub brushes, and such."

It was nice that Ozaroton had all the luxuries Irwin had come to enjoy when visiting larger towns or cities.

He returned to the hospital and delivered the needles in a hard leather satchel. Hammond was not yet there. Yace was still asleep. Kipp looked peaceful, but still unconscious. A wool blanket stretched across his body up to his armpits. His arms and hands were out and folded across his belly. It was still early for most people to be going about their day. Most businesses were not yet open—only the bakery and a forge. Irwin heard the distant ringing of metal being hit by a hammer.

He wandered down the street to where it T'd into the main road that followed the river up to Minersville. To the east was Luellen's Laundry and the Bathing Club next door—a large three-story building—and several other small shops. None of the buildings had residences above—most were only one-story tall. The houses were built beyond the main thoroughfares—away from places of commerce. To the west was the Gentlemen's Club standing tall a block away. He saw the large, covered porch. The building was enormous, with a lookout tower four floors above the road. There were many businesses between here and there, including a stinky butchery he had smelled last night.

Irwin stood at that intersection to contemplate and felt he was being watched by a pair of Clan-Duin men. They rounded the corner, heading the way Irwin had already come.

They are probably going to work or to the bakery.

He went to the Gentlemen's Club and wondered if they would accept his help now or if he should continue on with his day. When he knocked, he was not turned away even though the house was locked up. The green-eyed Erthin who had sat next to him last night welcomed him into the grand gathering room.

"Irwin!" She was clearly happy to see him. "You're here early. Come on in, it's good to see you!" She locked the door after he entered, urging him further inside.

"Good morning. I did not catch your name last night."

"My name is Safina, but all my friends call me Sunny. You can call me Sunny!" She was clothed in a pretty green and blue floral-patterned dress, and she held a radiant smile. Her emerald-green eyes were hypnotic. "Are you hungry? Laurel and Harlin are busy making breakfast. There's always enough to go around."

"I have already eaten, but thank you, Sunny." She smiled brightly again when he said her name.

"Are you here to help with the lights? Miss Gracie usually instructs how to do those. She has a way to do things around here and prefers to be present when we are moving those big candle racks around."

"I stopped by to help with the lights, but I also remember a few of you ladies saying you were good at shaving. I was hoping to get my—"

"Oh yes, please let me shave you. Please, please, please! I could give you a handsome facial trim and fix your hair too." She reached over and tucked a strand behind his ear. "Oh, and if you have anything to mend, I'm good at stitch work. And I can clean clothes quicker than anyone else here!" She was eyeing the baggage slung across his shoulder.

"Thank you. I would love to have you trim my hair."

Her eyes grew brighter, and she danced around. "Let me go get everything I need." Sunny dashed out of the room.

From his left periphery, he noticed another female enter the room the moment Sunny left through a side door. "Oh, hi!" It was the Erthin woman who had sat on his right side the previous night, Bretta. Her blue eyes were firmly on him. "Irwin, correct?"

"Yes! Good morning."

Bretta's blue eyes never moved, even though her bouncy red hair and tall, slender body did. "Have you been here long?"

"No."

She stepped close to him. "Is there a reason you're here?"

"To help with the heavy candle racks." He pointed to the ceiling. "And to get my face trimmed." He didn't need to point out how mangy he looked.

"Can I get you anything else?" She tried a coy smile. "Tea, breakfast, a hot bath? I'm good at massaging your aches away too."

She was trying to lure him in, but Irwin knew this vixen's game. "No, thank you."

Bretta pressed, "Does Miss Gracie know you're here?"

"No. But I believe Sunny is going to get her."

"Oh, she is?" said Bretta, a bitter tone in her voice. She recoiled slightly, but continued to slither around him. "Miss Gracie's probably sleeping in with Kary. You should probably leave until she's up."

"Sunny said she would cut my hair."

"Sunny, cut hair?" Bretta scoffed and rolled her eyes. "She couldn't cut a straight line to save her life. I wouldn't trust her to shave you either. She's too young for those types of things. What you need is a real woman's hand to do that. Sunny is only eighteen. She doesn't know much about a man's needs. I know …" She moved closer; her telepathic eyes stuck on him. "… you need a steady hand. One that has shaved faces and trimmed beards before. I wouldn't trust Sunny with a blade. The one time she did it, she cut that man's neck. She might cut yours too, but I would never hurt you."

Irwin took a step back. He could see that this Telepath was using her words to manipulate him. "I am Erthin, Bretta, and can heal any nick she gives me."

"You don't look or feel Erthin."

"I know you possess water and earth Erthin traits, so you cannot heal me. And I am immune to your telepathy, which is why you are drawn to me."

Bretta's eyebrows came together, analyzing. "What type of person are you?"

Sunny stepped into the room and shouted at her housemate. "Bretta, what are you doing here?!"

"I saw Irwin and wondered why he had been left all alone. You know Miss Gracie doesn't approve of men being left alone in the house. It's a rule, and you broke it. I'll be telling Miss Gracie the minute I see her."

"I was coming right back, Bretta." Sunny sneered. "Besides, Irwin doesn't seem like the type of man who would break or steal anything."

"How do you know what type of man Irwin is? You're not a Telepath!" Bretta turned and snidely added, "You see, Irwin, it's one of Miss Gracie's policies not to let a man be alone in the house."

"And we're not allowed to be alone with them, Bretta."

"You were with him alone before I was," Sunny scoffed, and Bretta added, "Of course, maybe I don't tell Miss Gracie, and I do the job, and you watch a skilled woman shave a real man's face."

Irwin said, "I do not appreciate how you are treating your housemate, regardless of the rules. They are rules I did not know of, but would have followed if someone had clued me in. Besides, I trust Sunny to do the best job she can." He smiled at Sunny. She held a leather pouch full of hair cutting utensils—he felt the metal pieces inside the purse.

"You know what? I'm going to notify Miss Gracie that you're here, Irwin. I'm sure she won't allow Sunny to give you a trim."

Sunny put her hands on her hips. "Fine, call for Miss Gracie. We'll talk to her about it!" She winked and smiled at Irwin.

Before long, Miss Gracie stepped into the room. "Good morning, Mister Irwin. Are the ladies behaving themselves?"

"Sunny offered to trim my hair."

She beamed, but Bretta snapped, "She'll cut his ear off. Let me do it."

"If he prefers Sunny's hand to yours, you should allow it."

Bretta stormed out of the room.

Miss Gracie turned to Irwin. "She's one of the few, Irwin, who I believe will live in an old maid's house, bitter and lonely." She turned her attention to the eager-to-please lady. "Well, Sunny, if you're going to work on Irwin's beard and hair, you'll want him on a stool. The bar is the best place for that. You've got the mirror on the other side for him to watch what you do—let you know if he approves."

"Thank you, Miss Gracie."

With a nod, the older woman said, "I'll send Wendi in to help. She can steam a towel for his face. Maybe help wet his hair for you."

Sunny winced. "What about Jenna? I'd prefer her here, instead. Please."

"I know Wendi likes you more than you like her. You need to work on being assertive. It's okay to say no. Remember, this is the only safe place in town where you can be forward with your roommates and not be kicked out for being so." Miss Gracie turned to Irwin. "Wendi prefers women to men. She came here years ago, hoping to find a man, hoping to make her family proud, but she's not interested in the opposite sex."

Wendi's story was like Irwin's, but at least she had a safe place to explore herself. He never did.

Sunny said, "She really started liking me after this one night we, um ...." Her face flushed and her eyes darted away from the others.

Irwin asked, "How long do most ladies live here?"

"This is a halfway house, so to speak, for women who don't live well with their families," said Miss Gracie. "Or ladies who just want to be independent and learn to do things for themselves apart from their family. Most of the ladies live here no longer than one or two years. They usually find a partner and move out. It's only every once in a while, when a young lady moves in who is too stubborn, like Bretta, or if they enjoy female comforts instead of male comforts, like Wendi. There is nothing wrong with personal preferences, but I know those ladies are not long for my house. They are here to find their way, their place in life. I'm just a safe stone to step on to help them along their life's journey."

Jenna came in, yawning, her feet dragged across the wooden floor. "Yes, Miss Gracie."

"You look hung over, Miss Jenna."

"I am, Miss Gracie." Jenna blinked a few times. Her eyes were swollen—she still looked intoxicated. "I love the wine, but the wine never likes me."

Sunny asked, "Will you help me clean up and trim Irwin's face?"

"Only if I can have some tea." Jenna yawned again.

"I'll make sure some is ready." Miss Gracie left the room.

A tea kettle and three matching cups were placed on the bar counter. It was a bitter black tea made from roots, but it had a caffeine kick Irwin had never felt before. He enjoyed the tea but was definitely trepid about Sunny's shaving abilities. Her hands shook a few times when she began going at his face with the sharp razor. And being a Metalist, he worried about the blade melding with his flesh. He had to resist the urge to allow the metal to merge with his skin as it scraped across it with each swipe.

Jenna offered help when Sunny was stuck in a bad angle. She nicked Irwin a few times, but only a little blood trickled out before the wound healed. Every time, Sunny was profusely sorry. She did a great job cleaning up his face—a job he was often tired of doing and didn't mind having someone else scrape his hair off.

Kipp usually does this. I miss him.

There was a trust created by the three that day. Irwin felt and looked cleaner from the neck up. The rest of him was still gritty from all those days of journeying through harsh lands. All he wanted now was to submerge his body in a hot bath and to soak undisturbed. Thankful to be clean-shaven and lighter on top, Irwin offered to help lower the wheels of lights to allow the women to change the burned down candles.

40

<u>Kipp Is Up!</u>

He spent most of the morning at the Gentlemen's Club before returning to the hospital. He arrived right behind Hammond. Olivia was talking with the Doctor about Kipp's progress. They stood in the hallway between Kipp's and Yace's rooms. All seven of his students wore the same light gray uniforms and were on-hand and ready to help get Kipp moving. Irwin listened in on the conversation while staying out of the way.

He was still tired; he felt like he hadn't slept enough. He took a seat and waited to hear his name called. He watched two female students go into Yace's room. They woke her to change the bedding and then they went outside to wash the dirtied linens.

He closed his eyes to rest for what seemed only a short time.

"Kipp is up!" someone shouted.

Irwin had fallen asleep. He jumped from his seat and rushed to see his best friend. It was crowded in Kipp's room. Four healers gathered around his bed, including Hammond. The other four stood at the doorway, watching intently. Irwin stepped between the students.

Hammond sat next to Kipp's bed. Olivia held a small cup of water for Kipp. He was clearly groggy. His eyes were closed, but he turned his head slightly and sniffed the air.

Kipp's voice was weak when he said, "Irwin." His eyes fluttered opened and then closed, though he was trying to keep them open. Slowly, weakly, Kipp's hand rose, reaching for him.

Irwin stepped around the foot of the bed and held his hands tight across his abdomen. He was afraid to grab Kipp's extended hand and shed whatever spell Hammond had placed. "I am here Kipp."

The Clan-Duin's voice was weak—as if it hadn't been used in over three moons' time. "Where are we?"

Olivia stood from the chair next to Kipp—motioned for Irwin to take it. He remained on his feet, hovering over his friend. Everything became blurry.

"Ozaroton, my friend. We made it."

Kipp's brown eyes were finally all the way open. "Is this real?"

"Yes, my friend, this is real. You are alive. I am glad to see you, my friend."

"I thought I'd lost you."

"I am here. I will always be here. Never will I let you go." Irwin wiped away his tears.

They stared at each other for a long moment before Hammond's chortle broke their concentration. "Of course, this is real. This place ain't a dream, though sometimes it seems to be with all the wonderful weather and fertile soils."

"Who are you?" Kipp flinched at the outburst. He looked around the room. "Irwin, where is Yace?"

She called out to him from her room. "I'm in here Kipp!"

The sound of her voice startled him. "Yace!"

"Kipp!"

He tried to sit up, but his body didn't want to move. The telepathic nerve-dulling spell made Kipp appear intoxicated. "What's wrong with me? And why is Yace not in here?"

"Would you like to see your female friend?" Hammond leaned in, trying to get Kipp's attention. "If you're motivated enough, I'll fill you with some endorphins and we will see how healed up you are." He paused. "You ready?"

Kipp reached for Irwin, grasping his forearm. His brown eyes grew as the telepathic spell grounded out of him, "What's going on?" His eyes fluttered, he stammered, "What's going on?" Then he passed out.

Shit!

"I am sorry," said Irwin.

Kipp's arm dropped to the bed.

Hammond growled, "How'd you ... what'd you do there?"

"I am sorry. So sorry. I do not know what I did. I am still getting used to my powers. I do not know what I am doing most of the time. So sorry." He shrank away from the bedside. He knew it was his Metalist power that grounded out the telepathic spell, yet pretended to be ignorant.

Hammond glared at him. His hands went to Kipp's forehead and right hand. He summoned the Clan-Duin to wake once more.

Kipp struggled for breath as his eyes bolted open. "Irwin." He reached for his friend again, but Irwin crossed his arms tight across his chest, leaned back.

"I cannot touch you right now."

"What happened?"

"Do you remember the battle with the Roha?"

"Battle?"

"Do you remember the Tropogagi?"

"Huh?"

"What do you remember, Kipp?"

"I don't ... Irwin." Kipp tried again to reach for his grounding contact. "Where are we?"

"Ozaroton. We brought you and Yace here as quick as we could."

"What happened to us?"

Irwin looked at Hammond and asked, "Is the reason he cannot remember anything because of brain damage?"

Hammond raised a curious eyebrow. "Well, I was curious to see what all he knew too. It appears he was not only kept in a physical stasis by your powers, but your telepathic friend did an impeccable job protectin' his brain from worser damage. There were many different spells at play here, in keepin' your friend alive and safe."

"Telepathic spell? But Yace said his mind was barren of thought, of dreams. How is it that he can remember anything at all?"

"There were many things at play here with keepin' Kipp alive. Many power sources are wrapped together. I know that none of them were Shaman's, or at least if they were, they had been altered by you and your friend, Yace. But even then, sometimes our brain is smart enough to protect our inner self from what has happened to us—especially if it's traumatic. It's possible that all Kipp's memories will return, but it'll take time. Though we do have Telepaths who can help reclaim memories. If you want, I can call for one to come and help clear up—"

"I want Yace to do it." Kipp sounded more awake and alert. He shouted, "Yace, why aren't you here? Yace come here!" He was hyperventilating.

"Kipp, I need you to let Doctor Hammond help you," she loudly instructed from her bed. "He's a good healer, and we're in a good place. I promise!"

Kipp kept reaching, wanting to contact Irwin. "Do you trust them?"

"Yes. I trust them—all of them." He surveyed the room and all the Erthins. "They healed Yace too. Right now, she is recovering in the other room."

"Yace." Kipp's lower lip trembled. "What happened to her?"

Hammond leaned in. "Maybe you should get up and go ask her."

Kipp grasped Irwin's forearm. He did not want to melt Doctor Hammond's spell again and flushed a healing energy throughout Kipp when he made contact. He watched Kipp's eyes grow wide and moisten.

Kipp whispered, "You saved me, didn't you?"

Irwin hesitated and then nodded. Their eyes locked. Irwin noticed Kipp's eyes turn golden.

"... love you. Thank you."

Irwin left the room as the healers stepped around Kipp's bed again. He watched from the doorway as they combined their powers, holding hands. He felt them charge up their Erthin powers, combining them into a large blast of healing energy. Hammond focused all that power on Kipp, flushing him with endorphins, pushing him up and getting him to move.

Fear boiled in Kipp's eyes; he could hear the distress in his voice when he pleaded, "Don't leave me."

"You will be fine, Kipp. I trust these people. They are good people. We are in a good place. I promise."

Kipp slowly climbed out of the bed—clumsy on his feet. All his muscles had atrophied during the three moons of unconsciousness. But as he walked, all eight healers thrust his muscles to fill with mass. By the time the Clan-Duin made it to Yace's bedside, some of his physical limitations were partially healed. Irwin witnessed Kipp's weakened body grow strong and fill out. He looked like he had before the attack, except for the new scars.

From outside, a loud bell rang down the street—that large piece of metal Irwin had felt upon entering Ozaroton last night. It echoed around the township. The iron bell rang three times, signaling that it was time for a midday break. Everyone working in the lumber yard, out in the fields, down at the foundry, or at the mill was allowed time to eat lunch at one of the eateries in town.

Almost immediately, half the students left the hospital. Hammond instructed those who remained to continue working until their peers returned. Doctor

Hammond backed out of the room and into Irwin who stood in the hallway watching and listening.

"It's mealtime!" said Hammond. "Why don't ya come with me to my favorite place and enjoy a well-cooked meal."

Irwin caught Kipp's scared eyes. "What about my friends? When will they get to eat?"

"Oh, don't worry. Britz'll be getting them some gelatin soon." Hammond patted Irwin's back, trying to turn him toward the front doors. "We prefer not to feed too much solid food; it makes more of a mess to clean up later. But I guarantee, by tomorrow mornin', after a good night's rest, your friends'll be ready to leave this place."

Irwin flinched from the hard pat. He glanced back at Kipp and stepped aside for the doctor to take the lead. "Good. But that means I must find us a place to stay."

"Well, there's Jule's place back at the entrance to town." He pointed. "It's cozy there, but she's only got three rooms to spare for outsiders." Hammond walked up to the double doors and stopped. "Then there's Spring's Inn. It's upslope from town. Usually those who come down from Minersville stay there.

"Now, dependin' on how long you're stayin', there are lofts above the markets." Hammond opened the door and Irwin walked out, but the doctor never stopped talking as they strode away from the Hospital. "And then there are halfway houses that take in people like your friends. But there are rules for those places. Each residence is different about who they allow in. Comingling isn't allowed in any halfway house. So, your two friends would probably live in a loft. But you-you'd have the option of stayin' at an Inn or movin' to a halfway house."

Irwin did not like the thought of not living with Kipp and Yace.

"There are some things you need to know about Ozaroton ...." Hammond droned on as he spouted information Irwin already knew about sanctuary towns and cities. Hammond implied Irwin appeared too mortal for a place like this, and that he would have to prove he was worthy to be allowed to stay.

He tried to shake off the suggestion that he would not be allowed to stay. Hammond took him up the slope to Spring's Inn. They startled an older woman as they entered the large house. She welcomed Irwin and said she was pleased to put him and his friends up in rooms for however long they wanted.

Gracious to be so welcomed, Irwin asked what he could bring for supper. "A big fat rabbit!" Miss Spring said, and then laughed. She was a bright-eyed, older

Clan-Duin/Erthin woman who seemed to have extra of everything, including giggles. "And maybe a basket of apples. I'll bake a pie for you if you do." She winked at Irwin, flirting perhaps, but clearly delighted to be cooking for someone other than herself and her two grown daughters.

After leaving the Inn, Hammond and Irwin walked to the Gentleman's club. He did not want to eat with Hammond, but now he was stuck. They were led to sit at the same table, even though Irwin wanted to be alone. To his chagrin, Sunny was their server. The other men at the table badgered him about his appearance.

He had to demonstrate his power, using the knife trick and memorized lines. This was getting old. He wanted to show more of himself, knew they would accept him maybe if he appeared encased in metal.

That was Kipp's idea. Maybe there is some validity to it. I am so glad he is alive.

While eating his meal, enjoying the sight of so many people of Talent walking the streets freely, Irwin was asked to help clear a field of downed trees. He agreed and offered the use of his donkeys. The two men who needed his help were long-standing members of the community. One was a talker, the other kept quiet, but both had been impressed by his show of powers at the lunch table, and later that day when they came across a local elderly man who had been hurt Irwin once again showed some of his Talent.

Although he felt anxiety over his family living so close, Irwin wanted to prove himself to these people—he wanted a place to belong. Ozaroton seemed to have everything he wanted.

If I show my true self, hopefully these people will see me as an asset to their community.

During his day of working, he forgot his worries and rested his rampant mind. He had learned much about the town and its people. When he was done toiling—like other workers—he went to the market and did not have to buy the food for the nightly meal Miss Spring promised to cook. He was asked only how his day went and was wished a happy evening when he left the busy marketplace, a dead rabbit in one hand and a bag of apples in the other. Prior to visiting the markets, he had paused at the hospital and found both Kipp and Yace napping.

I am glad they are being cared for. Even more thankful to know that I will enjoy another home cooked meal tonight.

He arrived at Spring's Inn and passed off the dead rabbit. Miss Spring took Irwin to a wooden bathtub out on her back deck. It was already filled with chilly water. She warmed it before leaving him to soak. The place and the tub were serene, and there was a view of the river and the sun's descent. Irwin felt he deserved this time, these moments of beauty. It felt good to scrub away all the grime from the jungle of cannibals. Once he dressed in clean clothing, a sense of ease came over him.

I feel like I have finally found a place where I belong. I want to stay here. Now I just have to figure out how to make them accept me. How truthful should I be? Do I show them all my powers? Do I let them know what I am truly capable of? Do I tell them what I have done?

Just be truthful, be yourself.

The sun had set by the time supper was served. Irwin met Jasmine and Lily, Mistress Spring's daughters. They were bold and held nothing back. They laughed with wide mouths full of food. They obviously didn't care what others thought of them. They said what they wanted to say; they expressed their feelings to a fault. Irwin enjoyed the entertaining night with the older women.

This must be what it is like to have aunts and a grandmother.

He listened to the women jabber on and on about the locals and the food.

After supper and apple pie for dessert, Irwin 'found' a gift for Miss Spring in his baggage. Using his remaining metal, Irwin had created a lovely metal candle centerpiece for her table. The light reflecting off the metal surface brightened the dining room.

"Thank you, Mister Irwin." She hugged him; he allowed it to happen—only for a second or two.

"Thank you, Miss Spring, for allowing me to stay here. You have a lovely home. I am sure my friends will enjoy it as much as I do."

"As I said, you can all stay as long as you want."

Exhausted from his day, Irwin retired to his bedroom early that night. He was finally clean, full of food, and happy to be in a place so welcoming to people of Talent.

Tomorrow will bring even better things. I know it.

He drifted off to sleep and fell into a dream that felt, once again, real.

41

<u>DEADLY DREAMS</u>

lbert Hegwin Miner sat in the middle of a barroom. It was midday. With a jug of whiskey on the small table in front of him, Albert poured an ample amount into a ceramic cup. His eyes were firm on the front entrance of the saloon.

The bar owner kept a watchful eye on the newcomer. No one knew anything about Albert other than he was a sour-faced grouchy miner. One of the barmaids brought over a tray of cheeses and smoked meats for him to pick from. He took his fill before she moved on.

At the table behind Albert, four Erthins were playing a game of cards. They were hecklers and drunk before the midday meal. There was a table of elderly men, all Clan-Duins, over in the far corner of the large barroom. They were drunkenly arguing over stories from their heydays. At two other tables sat two couples—one couple engaging with the barmaid, the other in a corner booth speaking in hushed tones.

A handful of younger men entered the gritty establishment before the midday rush and claimed one of the larger tables. A moment later, several females followed the men into the barroom, giggling and talking amongst themselves. They took up all the remaining seats at that large table and the volume in the room increased tenfold.

A haggard looking Erthin man was seated near the front door. His clothing was dirty—beard and hair ratty. He watched Albert intently but tried not to be obvious about it—unlike the barkeep's beady, blue-eyed stare.

The midday bell rang. Albert shook his head at the sour ringing notes the metal bell created. He tossed a drink down his throat and poured another. He was almost done with the bottle and his time in the saloon—until he felt a Metalistic pull.

His eyes were drawn to the open doorway as his cousin, Hager, two adult sons, and their cousin stepped into the Saloon. Hager stopped at the doorway, throwing his hand up to halt the younger Metalists. They all noticed Albert sitting at the table.

"About time we saw each other, cousin."

Hager kept his arm out to protect his sons. He looked at the Erthin by the door. "Wyatt, why did you let that ragamuffin in? He should not be allowed in this Saloon."

Wyatt shrugged. "You ain't gonna brawl are yas?"

The two elder Metalists stared at one another. Hager turned to engage his adolescent children. "Hold off on going to see the ladies, boys."

"But that is why we came here." The son on Hager's left complained.

"We have other reasons for being here too," said Hager. "Stay close."

The son on Hager's right said, "We are not going to sit with him, are we?"

"I am heading up to see Ezy." Their cousin said. "She knows I am coming for her today." He moved around his cousins toward the stairway behind the bar.

"I told you to stay! Do not be gone for too long, Jowin." Hager glanced around the barroom.

"Lousy miner." Albert grumbled. He remained in his seat and tossed another drink down his throat.

Hager said, a softer lilt in his tone, "Edgar told us we had family. It is nice to meet you, cousin?" He stepped up to the table where Albert sat drinking his whiskey. Hager's two sons were hesitant to follow, but did.

"Save your pleasantries for someone who cares. Where is Edgar?"

Hager said, "He has been dead for years."

"Good. And your father and his brother?"

"My father, Adrik, is at home being a grandfather."

"Does your family suffer the same fate as mine?"

Hager's lip curled up with disgust. "What do you mean?"

"Little girls? You are killing them as was taught, correct?"

"We have never had any Metalist girls born to our name."

Albert waved his hand, "As long as you are murdering the baby girls, that is all that matters."

Hager glanced around the barroom. "Why are you here, cousin? What do you want?"

"I came here to find the rest of my family."

"You found us."

"You a grandfather yet?"

"Not yet, but hopefully soon. My boys, Otis and Edison, have been learning about women by coming here."

Albert snarled. "Those are weak names. They have probably disappointed you over the years, I am sure."

"My sons have never disappointed me."

"Oh, I am sure they have. You just do not have the courage to tell them."

Hager's silvery eyes stared at his ornery older cousin. "I would think you would have a few boys of your own by now."

"No." Albert shot down another cup of whiskey.

"Good. We would not want your angered blood to have been passed on, you fuking sour cuss."

"Says the one who bastardizes our blood by breeding with a Clan-Duin. Your bastard children are not suitable for miners' work. They might as well herd goats."

Edison and Otis held close to their father's side. They were just as tall as Hager, but lanky like Irwin. It was obvious that they were intimidated by their father's cousin, averting their gazes to the floor. Hager put his hands upon his son's shoulders. "Did you come all this way to boil our blood, cousin? Because, if you did, I am going to ask you to go back to where you came from."

Locals streamed into the saloon wearing grubby clothes. Some of them smelled as if they had not bathed in days. Most were Clan-Duins, but there were Erthin men and women too. Many worked in the fields and gardens, helping feed the small but thriving community of Minersville.

Hager's son, Edison, asked, "Papa, can we go upstairs now? I would like to see Misilu before anyone else sees her." There were several men heading toward the stairwell for a midday romp with a whore before having a meal.

Albert shot down another glass and emptied the jug into his cup. The last bit of whiskey stopped at the lip of the ceramic vessel. Albert tossed that drink in his mouth, then slammed the cup down. "I am not leaving."

"You will leave, cousin. Your kind is not wanted here."

"My name is Albert, not cousin. And your name is Bastard!" Albert chuckled. His eyes swirled from silver to gold as he stood up. All four Metalists in the barroom danced from side to side. Only they could feel Albert's magnetic powers being flexed.

"I am not a Bastard. I am Hager Sampson, son of Adrik Sampson, son of Edgar Sampson. You, Albert, are the bastard, the miscreant Minersville does not need," said Hager. "You should go back to wherever it is you came from."

"Is that a challenge, Bastard?"

Albert took a step forward, oscillating his Metalistic energy. Their powers pulsated. Each man was trying to pull for the other's personal stash of metal located deep within their flesh. Hager used his power to repel his sons away from the magnetic game being played. He then coated his flesh in iron ore.

"I thought your elders would have taught you better." Albert knew to never show his power in public.

The barkeep shouted, "Take your fight outside!"

The chair where the Erthin sat, next to the main entrance, squeaked against the wooden floor as he stood up and moved toward the family clash. At the same time, one of the Erthins at the table behind Albert decided to make it a more interesting brawl. He outstretched his reddened hand, reaching for Albert's backside. He was attempting to ignite the angered Metalist. What that Erthin did not know was that Albert could absorb the energy.

That one act was a game changing move.

A good fight was always pleasurable to the men of Minersville, but this fight turned deadly that instant. Albert made a dagger appear and turned to slice the Erthin's jugular vein. As he sliced and blood spewed, Albert shouted, "I shall not be distracted!"

Hager took that moment to assault Albert. He threw several hard punches at his older cousin's face. Hager wanted to keep the fight amongst the family. No one else in the Saloon needed to feel a Metalist's wrath.

The moment the fire wielding Erthin fell to the floor, blood flowing across the wood slats, his comrades jumped up from their seats, ready to fight. The Erthin bouncer at the door also advanced and together all the Erthins tried their tricks of incineration, drowning, wind whipping, and shoving long knives into Albert's back. None of them understood that they could not destroy a Metalist this way. Albert was livid. He returned their blades with deadly accuracy. And now there were five dead Erthins on the floor.

Hager continued his assault. Otis and Edison, who looked no older than sixteen, hid under a table near the front door. Townsfolk coming into the saloon for a meal stopped at the doorway to watch the deadly bar fight.

Hager tried to beat back his older, ornerier cousin, but Albert had years of practice beating Irwin. He showed Hager no restraint. No remorse. Hager fell back, dazed, and weakened onto his knees. Albert tossed one final blow to Hager's temple. He hit the ground, hard. His head bounced. Hager was unconscious.

Albert shouted and beat his chest. He acted like he had conquered something great; in reality, he had just beat his cousin into a bloodied pulp.

Otis and Edison sat back in horror of their father's cousin. They had never seen anyone be that hard, brash, and uncaring. The twins flinched when Albert roared like an animal, and they crawled across the floor to their incapacitated father.

Albert looked around the barroom and bellowed, "Anyone else want to challenge me?"

The barkeep was a pale-skinned, blue-eyed Telepath with no hair. He shouted, "You're banned from entering this establishment ever again, Mister Miner!" He did not appear to be scared of Albert.

Albert chuckled while summoning a metal blade that hung above the bar. It had been on display for many years. That large metal blade flew into the Telepath's backside. Blood spewed out of his mouth as his body fell onto the wooden counter. The barkeep was dead.

Just then, Jowin stepped down the stairs with his woman, Ezy, in hand. She was a homely-looking Clan-Duin with large front teeth and a gap between. Her brown hair was unevenly cut, and her eyes were slightly crossed, and she obviously adored Jowin.

Although Albert had seen Jowin sneak off, this nephew looked exactly like his estranged son, Irwin. Jowin stared at his elder; fear shimmered in his eyes. He pulled his Clan-Duin girlfriend closer.

Seeing the familiar face stirred up old emotions in Albert. He sneered, "You are not allowed to water down our bloodlines by mating with a dog! Your choice disgusts me."

Albert shoved his hand out, twisted his fingers and extracted the four and a half pounds of various metals Jowin held within his body. It was a horrific experience for any young Metalist to endure. Jowin fell to his knees, screaming in agony.

Ezy immediately reacted. She was ready to protect Jowin. She jumped out of her clothes, mutating into a large feline. With sharp claws extended, she lunged for Albert's face.

"Ezy, no!" Jowin cried out.

Albert laughed wildly as he threw the metal he had just taken back at the young woman. Ezy's amber eyes were filled with anger, but she was no match for any Metalist. The pieces of metal sliced through her body. She fell to the ground, immobilized.

Albert cackled. He looked for more people to fight. His Metalist powers were flowing. He was hungry for more violence. Men and women tried to get in his way; some attempted to stop him, to fight him, but he tore through them with his Metalistic abilities. Albert enjoyed taking advantage of the weak. He stole the knives pointed at him, throwing them back into their owners with precision. He punched and kicked, threw chairs, tables, and people around. Many got hurt—writhing in pain—while twice as many were dead on the saloon floor.

Once Albert realized Hager and the three cousins had somehow escaped, he stormed out the main door. Other people's blood soaked his clothing, dripped from his fists. "I am coming for you, Hager!" He cackled loudly. "Tell Adrik and your brother they are next ..."

... Then I am coming for you, Irwin!

Irwin tore awake from a deep sleep. He looked around the dark and quiet room. He tried to shake off that dream. He rolled over and fell into another dream that felt different from the first.

42

Miners In Town

Yace awoke from a light slumber to the sound of hoofbeats echoing outside her hospital window. She heard the animals come to an abrupt stop, breathing and snorting hard.

Frantic voices rang throughout the hospital foyer. "Help!"

"Hello! Is anyone here?"

"Help! We need a healer!"

Three men clomped around the main entry. The eldest muttered, "Nobody is here."

"Ezy is not doing so good, uncle."

"Hello!"

"This is what is wrong with this town, boys." The elder criticized. "They only work when it is convenient for them. They do not think of others, only themselves."

"This is crazy! Why is no one here?"

What's crazy is why can't I hear your thoughts? Shit, I know why. They're Metalists. Fuk!

Before they rounded the corner, Yace summoned Kipp's door to close with a bout of her telekinetic power. She heard the men coming. They stopped at her doorway. Yace lay still, eyes closed, pretending to sleep. These newcomers did not need to know who all was in the hospital, nor did they need to know that Yace was telepathic. Before they had a chance to see her, Yace changed her outward appearance, using her Coterie powers, and transformed into a Clan-Duin. Her long platinum locks turned black, as did her eyebrows and lashes; her complexion darkened.

As she silently lay in the bed, she was telepathically communicating with her beloved across the hallway. *Kipp, it's Irwin's family. They are here in the Hospital. I need you to go get him right now!*

Kipp whined, *How do you know?*

Don't question how I know, I just know. If you were to smell them, you would know too. You need to find Irwin now!

But Hammond said I'm not supposed to mutate until I'm completely healed.

"There is someone here, but she is asleep,"

"Hey lady, where is the healer?"

Yace remained still. *Don't argue with me, Kipp. We need Irwin here. We both know what this family is capable of. He's the only one who can keep us safe.* She forced Kipp to rise, using her telepathically laced words. *Go find Irwin, now!*

Kipp jumped up from his bed, and—in one fluid motion—mutated into a bird. He swiftly exited his hospital bedroom through an open window. Yace was with him for that moment, seeing through his eyes, feeling his body lift high in a breeze. He flew out of the Hospital's courtyard and over rooftops in search of Irwin.

Yace then thought loud and clear, *Hammond. A family just entered the Hospital looking for help.*

Hammond's voice rang in Yace's head. *Devin, isn't there to receive them?*

No, sir.

Okay. I'll be right down.

They are miners, sir. Use caution.

Footsteps paced back and forth between the anterior room and hallway.

A young man shouted from the lobby, "I do not hear Ezy's heartbeat!"

Another young man said, "I am going outside to make some noise."

"Do not be foolish Otis, there must be a Healer somewhere around here. They would not have left that lady in the room alone."

"Unless she is dead! I am going out to make some noise."

"No, Otis."

"How else will we get a Healer's attention, Papa?"

"I will go walk through the hospital and see if anyone is here. Stay here with Jowin. Maybe check on your brother and Misilu. She is not looking too good either."

Jowin cried, "Ezy. Stay with me. I love you. Oh, Ezy ...."

Feet shuffled around the waiting room, and someone said, "Papa, someone is coming. Looks to be an Erthin."

Yace knew the sound of Hammond's boots. She had heard him come from his home several times that day and always with a heavy heal. He tapped across the cobbles up to the Hospital doors. His voice boomed, "Good evening. What seems to be the problem?"

The elder explained, "My nephew's girl got cut up, caught in a fight trying to defend us."

"Heal her!" Jowin demanded as Hammond entered the foyer.

There was a long moment of silence before Hammond said, "She needs a room." Feet shuffled down the hallway, past Yace's room and into the patient room next to hers.

"What's your girlfriend's name?"

Jowin sniffled. "Ezra, but I call her Ezy."

The elder said, "Doctor Thom was not in Minersville. They said he came to Ozaroton. She would have been healed by now had Thom been there, but ...."

Hammond pressed, "How'd Ezy get hurt?"

Jowin's voice shook, "She was defending me, jumped in the way of a crazed man throwing knives at people."

The elder spoke over his nephew. "We rushed her here as fast as we could. Can you heal her?"

Hammond's voice dropped, "She's dead, been dead for a while."

"What!" Jowin howled, "No! Not Ezy!"

"You cannot heal her?"

"Her soul has gone. I cannot bring that back."

"I thought a Healer could bring anyone back from the dead?"

"Not true. Depending on the afflictions, I can only revive someone who's recently died only a moment ago. Once the blood stops moving and the brain stops working, the soul leaves the body." Hammond explained. "Ezy's been dead for a while."

Jowin howled and danced around the room.

"She's broken ribs, lungs full of blood, and puncture marks everywhere."

The elder chided his adult nephew for throwing a tantrum. "Jowin, where are your manners?"

"He is unwilling to heal Ezy."

"She is dead, Jowin! Clean out your ears." Jowin stomped a few more times before the elder insisted. "We should probably leave him. There is also Misilu. She ..." He began walking out of the room, apparently hoping Hammond would follow. They walked past Yace's door toward the outside covered entry where the donkeys stood, one holding a woman on its backside. "... she got cut up too, had

pieces of metal piercing her body. We were able to get those out, but she is still
...."

Once outside the Hospital doors, a donkey brayed at the doctor as he stopped
and quietly talked to the young woman. She screamed when he pulled her off
the animal and was told not to squirm while being brought into the Hospital.
Hammond and her boyfriend were gently walking with Misilu in their arms
clasped with one another, cradling her like a chair.

Yace saw through her eyelashes the bloody trail the young woman left as she
was taken into the room next to Kipp's. She screamed again when they laid her
down. The young man accompanying her darted from the room and went to his
father who stood just beyond Yace's door.

"She looks horrible, Papa."

"Misilu will be all right Edison. This man knows how to heal. We must trust
he can restore her."

"He said she lost a lot a blood."

From the other room, Hammond shouted. "Can someone come in here and
tell me exactly how this woman got so cut up?"

Hager went and explained, "Well, you see, Misilu was upstairs in the brothel
when the fight broke. There was a lot of metal flying, and she took a piece straight
through her. Then others just ended up inside. We were able to extract all the
metal, but she is cut up bad."

"Extracting the metal? How'd you ...? You probably cut her up more doing that
than just leaving it for me to pluck out."

"You would have had a tough time. There was a piece in her back."

"You shouldn't have done anything other than bring her here. You're not a
healer. That is my job."

"How bad off is she?"

"I've got her sedated, but the extent of her injuries isn't good. She's lost half
to two-thirds of her blood. Many of her internal organs suffered some sort of
damage, and she's lost her gallbladder and parts of her appendix, intestine, uterine
lining—she's all torn up. Most of that probably happened when you extracted the
metal. There are tools I would have used, not my hands, or a stick, or whatever
you used." Hammond took a deep calming breath. "I will call my students in to
help me work. I don't know how long it'll take, or if she will be fully healed. She
lost many parts of her body today because of assumptions. Next time, consult a
Healer before making drastic, life-altering decisions."

"She would have bled out."

"Less so if you'd left the shrapnel alone."

Yace propelled her psyche into Kipp's eyes—she could do that through their bonded link. *You haven't found him yet?*

I'm trying, Yace! There's Metalist odor all along the main road down from the mountain, up to the hospital. Smells like his family. And I can tell Irwin was all over town today. His scent backtracks everywhere on this side of the river.

Keep looking!

There was a loud bang in the room next to Yace's. The sound jolted her back into her body. She almost sat up, but restrained herself. She did not want to appear awake; she did not want to be bothered. She only wanted to listen—to be a witness.

Jowin bemoaned the fact that Ezy was dead, growling, thrashing around in that room. Otis was there at the doorway. He walked into the room, past his cousin. "Get the fuk out of here!"

"You feel that, Jo?" asked Otis.

"I do not want to feel anything right now."

"There is someone in that building across the way; someone like us."

Jowin paused his tantrum, stepped over to his cousin. "You think it is our crazed elder, Albert?"

"I think we should find out!"

43

ALBERT'S REVENGE

Irwin tossed in his sleep—one nightmare shifted into another.

It was dark. He lay on his back, eyes open. He felt tiny, looking up at the sides of a wooden crib. There were soft things all around him. Irwin rolled over, and the bassinet rocked side to side. He heard a noise and noticed a dull light emanating from the hallway beyond a partially open bedroom door.

Voices argued outside the room, sounding familiar. One was Verona, the other two voices were manly—aggressive. Those manly voices Irwin had heard somewhere before, but he could not place where.

There was a muffled scream, and then something heavy hit the ground. Footsteps tapped down the wooden hallway, and then a shadow stood still at the doorway. The body shape did not look familiar—it was not Verona. A child began crying in a crib next to Irwin.

A young man stepped over to the cribs. He looked at Irwin—at Zamantha. "You are a Metalist, baby girl!"

It was Irwin's cousin, Jowin! He loomed hungrily over Zamantha's bed. Then he dug his hands under the bedding, picking her up to carry away.

Zamantha cried out. Her cries rang in Irwin's psyche. He woke up, tossed off the bedcover and rushed to put on his clothes. Her cries continued to echo in his mind. She was telepathically summoning him to leave Spring's Inn and rescue her. It was an impulse he could not ignore, especially with Jowin's face and voice fresh in his mind from previous dreams.

Taking the stairs two at a time, Irwin flew out the front door. He forgot to shut it as he bounded off the porch. Never had he run so fast except when the Roha had been chasing. Irwin sprinted. He knew the quickest route from Spring's Inn to the backside of the residential complex across from the hospital. His day that took him all around the town of Ozaroton paid off.

A bird flew alongside him. It tweeted, and he slowed to study it.

Is this real or is this a dream too?

He did not feel winded from his running, nor sweaty. The surrounding air was neither hot nor cold, and he felt incredibly energetic.

The bird flew ahead of him, leading the way, going the same direction Irwin had already plotted. He raced up to the back door of the apartment complex and felt a Metalistic spark in the air. He threw the door open and saw his cousins, Otis and Jowin, stepping off the stairs. They paused to see Irwin step into the lit atrium. Jowin's silvery eyes glistened. He smiled greedily and tried to hold the crying and flailing Zamantha in his arms.

Otis shot metal daggers, and Irwin absorbed the flying pieces. He pointed at Jowin and said, "That is not your child."

"Jamie?!" Jowin looked fearful. "I felt her, and then I found her. She-she looks just like Karl and Korwin. You had said there might be another. Here she is. I got her!"

"I am not Jamie. And that is not your child."

"Who, who are you?"

Irwin stepped up and took Zamantha from Jowin. As soon as she was in his arms, she cooed and touched his face and hair.

Otis stammered, "I-I was told our people were forbidden from living in Ozaroton?"

Irwin looked Zamantha over, making sure she was not hurt. She giggled at him. He looked at his cousins. "Go back to Minersville."

"How do you know where we are from?"

Jowin said, "Who are you? And why do you look like my brother?"

Instantly, all the Metalists in Ozaroton heard and felt a metallic ringing that no one else could. Even Zamantha was affected by it, and she began crying. Irwin held her tighter. They all turned in the direction the metallic resonance had come from.

Irwin knew that sound. It was Albert's magnetic energy boiling up, ready to be released. He had not heard or felt that in a long time. He shuddered, knowing things were about to get much worse.

Every Metalist in Ozaroton could feel exactly where Albert was and in relationship to where they were.

Shit! He is at Miss Spring's Inn. He felt the candle holder I made her. An accidental beacon. I am so sorry, Miss Spring.

Irwin turned and saw his cousins staring in the same direction. They glanced at each other.

None of us are safe.

Otis and Jowin also knew what was happening in the distance. "You feel that?"

"You need to go," Irwin said. "Get your family out of here now. Do not stay at the hospital. You need to leave Ozaroton immediately."

"That is our crazed elderly uncle who we just met today. Papa seemed to know about him; called him Albert the Enraged." Otis's body shook. "I never knew he existed until today. Papa never spoke of him."

Jowin growled, "He killed my Ezy. And Edison's girlfriend, Misilu, is all cut up because of him!"

"I know all about Albert," Irwin coolly replied. "He is my father. I would not fight him. I would run away. Draw him away from this place, these people. They do not need to know his wrath."

"He is your father?!"

Otis spoke over his cousin. "He blew up Major's Saloon. Must have killed at least twenty ... thirty people. Even Erthins! I have never seen .... Papa never told us ...."

"I know what he is capable of. Do not worry about me. Worry about you and your family. You need to leave Ozaroton, now."

Otis asked, "What are you going to do?"

"I am running away. If we are not here, he will not stay. He has come for us." He looked at Zamantha. She was contentedly staring at him. "She is not safe here. If he knows about her, he will kill her too. He will try to kill us all. We must leave. Keep the people of Ozaroton safe by drawing him away." He placed a kiss on Zamantha's forehead.

Otis moved toward the front doors—toward the Hospital. Jowin was three strides behind and shouted back at Irwin, "Be safe, cousin."

Irwin turned and leaped toward the back door with Zamantha in his arms. He held her tight against his chest as they raced out into what was now the dark of night. Many of the houses he passed were dark. No one knew of the impending doom that would befall the town—unlike Irwin. He knew he had to get himself and Zamantha out of Ozaroton without Albert seeing them. There was no time to prepare a horse, pack clothing and food, or tell his friends. He had to trust his legs to take himself and the child far away, and quickly.

He raced down a side road he had taken earlier that day that wound around the buildings at the entrance to Ozaroton. Where he exited, it appeared overgrown and spilled out onto the main road. He didn't slow to catch his breath. He was running to save them. Zamantha giggled as he raced.

We are running for our lives, and she thinks this is fun.

The bird had never left his side, flying above him—just out of sight. But then suddenly it dove in front of his face, forcing him to stop. The small bird transformed into Kipp. "How do I kill your father, Irwin?" It was Yace speaking through Kipp.

"I would not fight my father, Yace."

"Tell me how to kill him! He's stunned right now."

"Get out of there, Yace. He will kill you!"

"Tell *me* how to kill *him*!"

"Cave in! Cave in or old age."

Kipp blinked. He stood naked in the middle of the road. He weakly called and reached out. "Irwin." Kipp moved as if intoxicated; he was struggling to stand and then sat down.

Irwin rushed to his side. "Kipp. Yace does not stand a chance against my father. He will kill everyone in his way. I told my cousins to draw Albert away from the people, away from Ozaroton. I cannot go back, Kipp. If I do ...."

Kipp closed his eyes. He was obviously in pain. "Yace made me find you. Doctor Hammond said I should rest, recover, not move. My everything hurts."

Hand on Kipp's shoulder, Irwin gave his friend an enormous boost of endorphins.

Kipp gasped as if catching his breath, feeling the powerful boost. He rose to his feet, his mind clearer than before. "What are you doing, Irwin? Did you steal that child?"

"She is a Metalist, Kipp, the only female Metalist I have ever known. She is rare. We must keep her safe. My father will kill her if he finds her."

"What are you gonna do?"

"I cannot stop my father. I know my powers will not work on him." He shook, partly from endorphins but mostly from fear. "I am running away."

"What about Yace?"

"I hope she is able to kill him—for Ozaroton's sake."

Kipp glanced back toward town. "I think I'm safest with you."

Irwin nodded.

44

<u>No One Is Safe</u>

Yace could hear Devin, the student-healer's thoughts, as he frantically came into the hospital from a side entrance. He was ruminating over getting the patients their meals—hoping that Yace wouldn't complain again about what was being served. He hustled in her direction, but then stopped. Yace heard Hammond telepathically tell Devin about the injured people in the hospital. The wooden tray Devin held was set down, slapped against the wooden floor. She heard his boot heals race toward the main entrance.

"Who are you?" Edison boomed when Devin rounded the corner, startling him.

"I'm Devin. I'm here to assist Doctor Hammond."

Hammon met them out in the hallway. "Thank you for arriving, Devin."

"Sorry I wasn't here, sir."

The two Healers then went into Misilu's room and closed the door.

"Papa, what are they doing in there?"

"Probably healing her."

"I don't think so. I just hear them talking."

"Then they are talking. Let them do their job, Edison. Last thing I need is another lecture from the Healer that we did not do something correct." It was quiet for a moment. "Where are Jowin and Otis?"

"They raced off."

"Ugh! I do not need this." The older man stepped past Yace's room toward the entry and called for the missing young men.

Yace heard Edison gasp and rush to his elder. "Papa? What was that?"

"Fuk. That is our cousin, Albert the Enraged."

"What is he doing?"

"He is searching for us. Flexing his powers, feeling for us." The elder Metalist stepped through the lobby. "He is coming for us."

"What are we going to do?"

"We are going to leave this place. Where are those boys? Jowin! Otis!" Hagar continued to holler.

Edison frantically moved around his elder and down the corridor. Yace heard the young man open the door to Misilu's room, shouting, "Get off her!" He reacted as a loyal Clan-Duin would.

She heard Hammond shout out in pain. Devin barely made a noise. The sound of two bodies falling to the ground followed.

And then the elder Metalist raced past her doorway, back to the room where Misilu lay. "What the fuk have you done Edison?" He began slapping his child. "You fuking killed them. You dumb clot!"

"Ouch! But Papa ... they were—"

Otis and Jowin burst through the main doors into the Hospital, shouting, "Papa, Papa!"

"Uncle Hager!" They rushed to find the older man coming out of Misilu's room.

Their elder, Uncle Hager, snarled, "Where on Urthis have you two been?"

Otis tried to find the words, "I felt a Metalistic presence across the way, so we went to see, but then .... Was that Albert the Enraged that we just felt?"

"Yes. We need to leave Ozaroton. Right now. It is obvious that our cousin has a tough time letting go of arguments. I assume he has come for us," Hager's voice rattled. "We need to leave before he finds us."

Otis fretted, "Where can we go that we will be safe, Papa?"

"I do not know. But not here. There is too much metal, and if any of the townsfolk try to get involved, they will die."

"Yeah," said Jowin, wringing his hands and wiping his forehead. "I know."

"No one is safe from Albert, not even us. Right Papa?"

Edison asked, "Can he kill us?"

Yace peered through her eyelashes and saw Hager staring at the younger men as they walked past her door, heading to the entry room. "Us miners can die, but not from anything metal."

Jowin hit his fist into the palm of his other hand and spat. "I want to stay and fight."

"You will not stay behind, Jowin. You are no match for Albert. Rage like his cannot be curtailed."

Otis pleaded, "What about Misilu?"

Hager shouted, "In the time you were gone, Edison's Clan-Duin sense took control, and he killed the Healer and one of his students."

"What?!"

Edison's voice shook. "I-I thought they were killing Misilu."

"Obviously, he never saw a Healer work their magic before." Hager slapped his son. "And now he knows to leave Healers alone. Dumb clot!"

Jowin said, "I would have helped you, Edy. You should have waited for me!"

Edison pleaded, "We cannot leave Misilu, Papa!"

"We are not staying, not after what all you have done. Besides, the people of Ozaroton will take care of her," said Hagar as he marched them through the entry room. "It is better this way."

"But Papa?!"

"We need to leave, NOW!"

They pushed the door open and hurried to gather their donkey's lead lines. They shouted at their animals to get moving, but time had run out.

Albert's wild cackle preceded the echoing of his donkey's hoofbeats coming down the street. He aimed his mount straight for his estranged family and stopped a hundred feet before the hospital's covered entrance.

"You have no business being here, Albert," shouted Hager. "Return to wherever it is you came from and sow your anger there."

"You have dishonored our blood by breeding with low-life's cousin. Clan-Duins, Erthins, and their like, they are not suitable for our blood. You should know that. I would have thought Edger taught you better, you lousy miner."

"I hope you have not reproduced; you scum faced disgrace. Your side of the family should end with you!"

Albert laughed. "You are correct cousin; our family should end! End with you!"

Yace forced herself to move, to sit up and look out the window. She saw Hager keeping his distance from Albert. Albert's donkey took a few more steps forward and then stopped. He dismounted, left the reins on the ground, and the donkey stood patiently awaiting its owner's return.

Yace knew. *This is going to turn deadly, real quick.*

A show of force was unleashed, unlike anything any of the Metalists from Minersville had ever experienced. What happened at Major's Saloon was only a glimpse into the wrath that was now being wielded. Albert Hegwin Miner was exposing Metalists—their amazing powers—to the world.

All the metal inside Yace's room and beyond began levitating. She saw the glimmer of silvery utensils and ducked—sending violent pains through her abdomen but saving her life. Above her head, metal whizzed past and out the window. Albert was summoning all the knives, forks, spoons, trays, canisters, medical utensils, doorknobs, buckets, mirrors, hinges, jewelry, and all other metallic entities within a wide radius to tornado around him. He had pulled every piece of metal within the block to do his bidding.

All this clamoring had awakened the sleepy townsfolk. It was late into the night, and most were dozing until the shouting echoed around them. Those who watched from windows were impaled by flying debris as metal from within their own homes was pulled into the fight. Yace stood up enough to peer out the window, hearing the screams from people and their loved ones as bodies fell from second and third story bedroom windows; blood streaked down building facades, staining curtains, and the cobbles below.

Albert stood in the center of a Metalistic tornado, cackling wildly—amused by it all.

Hager was no match for Albert, but he had Jowin, Otis, and Edison close by. Combining their powers, the four Metalists were able to make a magnetic bubble that kept them safe from the flying metal debris. Building facades were chipped, glass windows exploded, curtain pieces fell to the ground like snowflakes—nothing was safe from Albert's fury.

Several bold Erthins ran from the apartment complex across from the hospital wearing robes and night-time clothes. They believed they could counteract what was happening, contain the wrath. Albert saw the people ready to fight him and cackled as they tossed their Erthin onslaught. He absorbed it all: fiery balls, windstorms, waterspouts, and the ground up-heaving. Albert flung an arm off his metal twister at the Erthins, striking their bodies, slicing them dead.

He spotted Misilu running from the hospital. She was pale, weak, and leaned against the donkey nearest her while holding her gut. She might have been far away from the fight, but not Albert's rage. He pushed his twister around the magnetic bubble Hager and his family had created, making a metallic hand fly toward the unsuspecting woman. Misilu screamed as she, and the donkey, were sliced into pieces.

Edison heard Misilu's shrill cry and turned to help her, leaving his family behind. The Metalists needed his power to deflect and defend against Albert's onslaught. As Edison raced away from the bubble, Albert sent a long piece of wood with several nails secure to the end—the only reason it could fly—and flung it straight into the base of Edison's head. With precision, the wood piece pushed through his neck, severing vertebra and bones, taking Edison's head off his shoulders. As his body fell forward, blood sprayed everywhere. Edison's head flew on the wooden piece and fell near Hager's feet.

Jowin screamed at the sight—Hagar did too—and his rage gushed. Jowin stepped ahead of the magnetic bubble, wanting to take on Albert himself.

Hager shouted, but too late, "No, Jowin!" He tried to grab for his nephew, but the agitated young man was out of reach.

Yace watched it all happen in slow motion. The metallic arm Albert wielded flew straight for Jowin's face. The same board, soaked with Edison's blood, slammed into Jowin's throat, slicing his head off his body. It landed at Hager's feet, next to Edison's head.

Now it was Hager and Otis. They stood together, trembling; still defending against Albert's energy. The boorish man laughed at the demise of his two nephews. He stared at the last nephew, Otis, who was part Clan-Duin.

Albert knew how to trigger a Clan-Duin.

Otis began frothing at the sight of his brother and cousin's heads laying before his feet. He, too, stepped beyond the barrier, ready to hurt Albert. Hager was so focused on Albert he did not see Otis step beyond his reach until he tried to grab for his son. It was too late. The magnetic sphere diminished every time someone left it, and now it was only as large as the one man.

Only one nail was attached to the board, and it spun as fast as a propeller. Hager watched as Otis was cut down by Albert's wooden board. The piece of wood was now much smaller and had splintered. Otis's head landed next to his brother's and cousin's. All three decapitated heads stared up at their elder. Hager fell to his knees. His magnetic barrier faltered, and Albert's rotating wooden piece charged up behind Hager. Head severed, Hager's body fell forward. His blood dribbled across the cobbles. The piece of wood had finally broken into shards and protruded from Hager's neck and head.

Albert stood in the middle of the roadway. "Irwin!" He shouted, "I know you are here. I feel your metal—I feel you. Show yourself!"

Yace hunkered down, hoping that Albert had not seen her peering out the open window. From where she huddled, she could see the Hospitals' covered entry with its stone pillars. She hatched an idea.

Again, Albert shouted for Irwin as he walked toward the Hospital's entrance. Yace concentrated on the canopy, using her telekinetic powers, and broke it free from the stone pillars—hurdling it at Albert. It hit him hard, shoving him down—stunning him. She heard Albert struggling under the wood, trying to break through. She hesitated in acting for only a moment—contacting Irwin to confirm how to kill his monster of a father.

She then broke loose the section of wall she hid behind, separating it from the Hospital's facade. She levitated that section of wall over the canopy and slammed it down on the slab of roof, already pressing Albert against the cobbled roadway. Two more times she took that wall, levitating it up high and bringing it down, smashing Albert flat—ensuring he was dead forever!

"There's your cave-in, Albert Hegwin Miner."

45

LEFT BEHIND

From far behind Irwin and Kipp came a loud sound, like that of an explosion. They both felt the ground move and looked back in the direction of Ozaroton.

Kipp put his hand on Irwin's arm. "What do you think that was?"

"I hope that was Yace killing my father and not the other way around."

"Yeah! Oh Hakra, I hope so."

Irwin could not remain still over his anxiety of his father's wrath, the terror the old man had instilled in him felt like a noose around his throat. His feet wanted to fly away from this place. Holding Zamantha tight, Irwin took off running again—racing away like he wanted to as a child—away from the devastation Albert wrought.

Pumped up on the endorphins Irwin had given him, Kipp stayed with his friend. Though after a while, the Clan-Duin suggested they leave the roadway.

The two disappeared into the overgrown jungle-scape and followed a narrow animal trail down to an inlet. The tide was low and the two men with the sleeping child crossed the shallow waters and made camp on the far side of an island.

Exhausted, they stayed hidden and fell asleep—the child nestled between them. Kipp and Zamantha slept more soundly than Irwin, who jostled awake several times. His dreams were violent and filled with being chased and killed by his father.

When morning lit the land, they all woke. Irwin and Kipp were wary of what this new day would hold; the child was content to be with them. They sought a fruit tree, bursting with food, and shared bananas with Zamantha.

"You look like you didn't sleep."

"Not very well, no." Irwin shook his head. "My dreams were filled with my father and echoes of childhood nightmares."

"Sorry to hear that."

"Yes. Me too."

"I wonder what happened, what that loud boom was about," said Kipp.

"You could always go and take a look. Make sure it is safe for us to return."

Kipp replied, "I could do that."

"It should not take you very long to see how Ozaroton looks. Make sure it is still standing. If it remains, then come back for us and we will walk the road there together."

"I don't know. After shifting yesterday, my body still hurts. I shouldn't have been forced to do anything other than recover. I mean, the Doctor said so, and you said you trusted them. But Yace .... I don't know if I trust her anymore."

"I can give you all the energy you need."

"I wish she were like you. But no one is like you, Irwin. You've always been true to your word, to everything."

Irwin's head cocked sideways. He watched Kipp intently. The Clan-Duin continued, voice shaky, "But Yace ... she's never been fully truthful with me. She's messed with my mind too many times to count. I know she wants me all to herself, to use for her devious demands, but ... but that's not what I want. And she's never cared about that, about me. It's always been for her—about her."

Kipp's brown eyes stared across the tranquil waters.

Irwin gazed at Kipp and recalled the last year of his life, full of memories with this man at his side. They had been through much together, discovering themselves and furthering their Talented abilities. He felt they were good for one another, a comfort to each other—mostly. But at the heart of it, they were attached to Yace—Kipp, more so than Irwin. For Irwin, Yace offered good council and a shoulder to cry on, but also harsh criticism—much like his father. And Kipp—Irwin knew—he was in love with Yace. He had heard Kipp confess his undying love to her and consummate their love dozens of times. But he also knew that Kipp had other desires, that Yace had not, nor would she be able to meet.

Kipp cleared his throat. "For the longest time, I've allowed Yace to do as she wishes with me, spinning my mind, forcing me to chase after her. We both know that she loves being fawned over, talked about, even stalked. And then you came along." There was a long pause before Kipp admitted. "I saw how she was with you, always flirting, wanting you, trying to use her powers to influence. And you resisted it all. You were the first man she tried all her tricks on, but none of them worked. At first, I didn't understand, 'cause who wouldn't want her, I mean ...."

Kipp's brown eyes turned golden, a look Irwin had seen only a hand full of times.

"There's always been something about you, something I appreciate more than anything else." Kipp heaved, "I don't want to leave you." He was slow to get on his feet.

"Then let us go to Ozaroton together."

He tapped the side of his head. "It's Yace. I sense urgency with her, but I can't hear her. It's like she's muffled too far away to .... You know what? Stay here. I'll make sure everything is good, that your father is dead and such. Don't worry, I'll be back before you know it."

Irwin placed a hand on his friend to make sure he was not being possessed by Yace.

"See you soon. Be safe, my friend."

"You too. You'd better wait here for my return."

"I will."

Something about him changed. He has never been like this.

Kipp looked at Irwin for a long moment, heaved a deep breath, mutated into a crane, and lifted into the air. His large white wings caught a breeze, and he sailed over the canopy of trees toward Ozaroton. Irwin watched his friend go and hung his head. He too felt pained—already missing Kipp.

Zamantha tugged on his pant leg; her face and hands were covered in remains of banana and sand. She squealed with glee, "Up, up."

Irwin wanted to cry. "I should not have taken you from your family. I should take you back. That is, assuming we are all safe and Yace indeed killed my father." He looked toward the sky to see where Kipp was, but his friend was already out of view.

"Up!" The child demanded and Irwin complied. She manipulated him using her Metalistic telepathy—but he was unaware. He was ready to take her back to Ozaroton, but she managed to switch his thoughts, redirecting him to the beach—to clean up and play in the still waves.

That first day alone with Zamantha, every time Irwin thought about returning to Ozaroton, she redirected his thoughts. By the end of their second day, he started to realize how powerful her telepathic hold was on him—he could not break that bond. Yet through that bond he began to understand the youngster better, understood how lonely she had been under the care of Verona and Doctor Hammond. She had constantly fought with her supposed twin sister and was ridiculed by every Telepath she met in Ozaroton. She also had learned that her mother had only wanted one child to attend, not two after all. The youngster would mutter thoughts, words that would only come from an adult—reminiscent of Irwin's childhood abuse.

On the third day, Irwin was depressed by this predicament. He now understood why his family would murder the girls at birth, but still condoned the idea of it. Zamantha was just trying to get her needs met. Yet it all was incredibly exhausting, especially when keeping up with the youngster. She wore him out with her demands and vast amount of energy. Luckily, he had learned to sleep when she slept, eat when she ate, and lived life with wild abandon. There was something humble about how she had taken to Irwin so quickly, which captured a small part of his heart, but the rest of him remained terrified of the youngster.

He sat on the beach, exhausted, worried that something had befallen his friends. He wondered if his father was still alive and searching for him—if the old man knew about the little girl. Irwin was still fearful of his father, scared to accidentally meet him and suffer the repercussions. Meanwhile, the child raced around playing catch with dragonflies or dancing with palm tree shadows. He was tired of eating bananas. He skewered a fish and started a fire to cook it. But then Zamantha found she could stomp out the flames. Irwin was angered that he was unable to cook his meal over a fire. Instead, he heated it with his hands, but somehow it didn't taste the same.

I messed up. I should not have left Ozaroton and my friends. I am a bad person. I should have stayed with my cousins, helped defend the town. Everyone is probably dead because of me, my inability to cope with my father. How could I have been so selfish?

I was selfish for her; I guess.

Then he glanced at the happy child.

I am glad I saved her from my father. But should I take her back to her family in Ozaroton? They would not be safe with her, especially as she gets older and her powers intensify. She might be able to pull for the metal, but she cannot manipulate it like I can. She needs to be with her actual family. They are the only ones who can teach her how to be safe with her powers. All I must do is find them, if they are still alive, and return her to them. After that, the bond will dissipate if we are not together. At least, that is what Yace told me. But like Kipp said, I do not know what to believe. She has run my mind around too.

All these telepathic women in my life ....

Zamantha jumped into his arms, and a coy smile spread her thin lips. Then she jumped out of his grasp, trying to goad him, and raced around. "I am so tired of all of this," He grumbled, but rose to his feet and dashed after the child—she loved to play chase.

Soon he felt one of his metal tattoos moving toward him. The tattoo was on the ground, racing down the lane, but then veered toward his position. He picked up Zamantha, and they walked along the beach over to where they had originally crossed. He knew it was Kipp. Eagerly, he searched the green foliage for his friend. His heart skipped when he noticed Kipp leading the donkeys from Bode's back. The packs looked fully loaded.

The tide was getting low, and the small sandy bridge they had taken days before revealed itself once more. The giant warhorse took high steps when first entering the warm water. The donkeys waded across, heads high and attached to the saddle.

Kipp's smile grew, and he jumped off Bode to hug Irwin. "I missed you."

"I missed you too." Irwin leaned into the embrace, inhaling the scent of his friend. "How is Yace?"

Kipp pulled away, appearing agitated. "She asked me to bring you all your stuff with extra food, and clothes, and a message."

"Thank you, Kipp. What is her message?"

Irwin waited, but the Clan-Duin looked for Zamantha instead. "Where's that little rascal?" He pulled out some clothing from a pack on Nee Nee's back, and a doll.

"What is the message Yace sent?"

"You really wanna know?"

"Yes."

Kipp closed his eyes. "She's leaving Ozaroton. She wants me to go with her, but ...." He wiped a tear from his cheek. "She's going back to Daos, at Nonbry's order."

"Why?"

"Control. It's always about control with Telepaths. You know that. I guess Nonbry and Ozaroton's council came to an agreement. They believe it's in the planet's best interest—this is what Yace told me—that they put someone of power into position in Daos, someone that can turn that country around. They don't want it to be forfeited to Hakran control. She seemed pretty pleased to have been given the opportunity."

"Huh. I thought she and you would return to the Gypsy, or they would come to Ozaroton. That she would help teach the twins how to use their power. What happened to that idea?"

"Things changed, I guess. It's not ideal, but maybe the twins would go to Daos too. I mean, they're all related to the Daosian empire, anyway. Like I said, it's all about control."

Irwin chuckled. "The ultimate foothold position. Of course. What a perfect position for Yace. And the Gypsy too. A whole territory where people of Talent would be welcomed ...." *Hopefully.* "... Unless she has some ulterior motive."

Wait .... Could this be what Dephen wanted all along? To have full control of Daos—the whole territory?

I think it is.

How could I have forgotten?

He did not want to believe Yace had influenced him to forget, but a trickle of doubt dribbled down his spine.

Dephen took control by taking over the bodies of his loved ones. I wonder if that was how Somer Ishik lived—through other family members. He did speak, using over fifty mouths. To be that powerful—to want to control the masses—requires something ....

Nonbry had warned that destroying the Ishik regime would have catastrophic consequences. Did he know of Dephen's plans all along? But how could this be perceived as bad?

I really wish I could have been in that meeting. I would have asked so many questions—would have asked to have Yace telepathically probed.

Now I kind of feel sorry for Yace. Did she know of Dephen's plan? Or did he 'convince' her?

It would have been easy to do. She is the kind of person who wants things handed to her. For fame and fortune, she would do anything.

Nonetheless, I must make it a priority to meet with one of the Telepaths in Ozaroton. Have my questions answered. Though it seems I already have found some of the answers. And ask them to look into Yace's psyche. Make sure she is who she is. This seems too convenient.

The Clan-Duin broke through Irwin's mental conversation.

"Yace says I have to go with her," Kipp said, his head hung low. "But I don't want to. I don't wanna be her pawn anymore. I've done so many things for her." He stared off, held a look—as if he had more to say.

Irwin chuckled. "You love her. You have said that you two were made for each other. And you two have a child coming."

"I do? Are we? Or was I manipulated by her to believe that, including her pregnancy? For all we know, it's that idiot Turk's."

Irwin's brow furrowed deep, like Kipp's, when he asked, "Did something happen between you two?"

Kipp's eyes turned golden as they looked at Irwin. "You. You changed everything."

I think you suffered brain damage, Kipp. You are not acting like yourself.

Irwin stammered, "What do you mean, I changed everything?" Kipp's gaze remained strong on him. Irwin put a firm hand on his friend's barren arm. "Are you all right? You do not seem yourself."

"Yeah. No." His attention drifted far off across the peaceful waters. "I don't know."

The sky was robin's egg blue. The air was filled with a sweet breeze. The horse and donkeys stomped and swatted their tails at the flies.

What are you not telling me, Kipp?

Zamantha came running up to them and saw the handmade doll in Kipp's hand. She squealed, pulling it free from his grasp. "There you are." She raced away with the toy, giggling, and tossing a look back at Kipp—hoping he would chase her. "Are you just letting her run around naked?"

"I cannot contain that child. Nor should I."

Kipp leaped into his canine form and began chasing the wild child. She screamed happily, flailing the doll around in her hand. Watching them playing brought a smile to Irwin's face. He tried to keep it there, tried to ignore the voice in his head.

Yace is going to take him from me. This is what she wanted all along. She said she would. What do I do? I do not want to live without him, but ....

Irwin turned away from the beach, from all the fun Kipp and Zamantha were having, and let out a sob. He had to walk away, to be by himself and grieve for what was about to happen.

46

TRUTHS REVEALED

Kipp and Zamantha came looking for him. He heard them and stood up, wiping away tears.

"What's the matter, Irwin?"

"You-you should get going. Yace needs you." He reached for Zamantha, an attempt to take her from Kipp's arms.

"What? No. Why?" Kipp held the child, not giving her up.

Irwin stared at his friend, confused. "Yace."

"I'm not leaving you."

"What?" Tears flooded Irwin's eyes. He heaved another sob.

Kipp moved with Zamantha in his arms and reached around Irwin. "I am not leaving you. She wants me to, but I can't."

Irwin shook.

"I made a promise a long time ago," said Kipp. "Do you remember it? It's the same promise you've made to me dozens of times now. I promised I'd keep you safe. You've done that tenfold and more for me." A tear fell from Kipp's eye. "You've always been so .... I can't leave you, Irwin. You are my family, more so than Yace ever has.

"To tell you the truth, I don't feel the same about Yace anymore. It's not that I don't love her, but I know her. Yace has led me to disappointment and jealousy. She's jaded me. And I don't want that in my life anymore.

"You've always been the better person, Irwin, a better friend than she could ever be, and-and ... and I need that. I need loyalty. I need a clan. A clan that would do anything for each other. And I've had that with you ever since the beginning."

Irwin sobbed, happy to hear Kipp's epiphany.

"I love you, Irwin." For once, Kipp was the one who held strong. Meanwhile, Irwin slowly crumpled in Kipp's arms. "I want you in my life. I want you to be my clan. I've had a tough time saying this to you in the past, but I-I … I love you, Irwin." He tilted his head sideways; his lips sought Irwin's.

Irwin was unsure of this conversation. It felt like a dream. He stared into Kipp's bright golden eyes. "But you like women."

"I like women, but I love you."

Zamantha put her hands on their faces, trying to make them kiss again.

"You can pick? I have never, I have always only liked men."

"Why should it matter? I love you." Kipp reiterated and kissed Irwin again.

This seems too good to be true.

Every kiss was like a blast of lightning to his lips. Yet Irwin fretted, "What about Yace?"

"Fuk her. I'm not going with her."

"Are you sure? She is pregnant with your child."

"I'm not sure it's my child, Irwin. I really …." They stared at one another. "I decided while packing that I wanted to stay with you. I don't want to deal with her anymore. I don't care that she's pregnant. She's got Turk. He's going with her too. And don't worry, I got all our stuff. We can start anew without her. We'll do whatever we want!"

Why am I afraid to trust him? Because of Yace.

I must remember that I have touched him many times now, and he has not changed. That means Kipp has made these decisions with a free mind.

Then, maybe, he does love me?!

Kipp's eyes shifted to Zamantha. "So, what are we gonna do about this little one?"

"Take her back to her family."

"You mean Doctor Hammond and Verona? We can't. They're dead."

"They are? Oh, no! That is unfortunate. Well … well then, maybe we take her to her real family, my cousin Jamie, up in Minersville. I know he and the rest of the family live somewhere in the hills near that township. I am sure we can find them within a day or two. And I can use my powers to locate them, so long as they do not think I am a threat. I just hope they want her."

"I don't know if your extended family's still alive. I mean, a lot of them died in Ozaroton, all of them that had come to the hospital—at least. Besides, do you think it's a good idea to find your lost family? Especially after what your father did?"

"I have to. I know nothing about raising a child. And she does not belong to me."

"Are we gonna do this right now?"

"No. We do not have to leave right now. But I want to take her back. Dealing with a child is not easy."

"Are you joking? They're fun, but especially at her age. They're so curious about everything."

They stared at each other.

Irwin rubbed the back of his neck. "I need confirmation that Yace killed my father, that they do not have him sedated through telepathy in a basement, or some other means, do they?"

"Yep, she killed him! Holy Hakra, she killed him the only way you've ever said how—a cave in. You should've seen the destruction. She tore the roof off the Hospitals' covered entry and broke it over him. Then she slammed the Hospital's wall into him too. She bashed your father into a bloody mess. That was that loud boom we heard. You should've seen all the blood and body pieces," He slapped his knee. "But it's all cleaned up now; I was part of the cleanup crew. That's what Yace wanted me to do. That's what was so urgent. It's why I didn't come back the other night. I was too exhausted after all of it—just passed out.

"But last night, Yace made me feel guilty for wanting to see you. She told me you planned to leave us back when I was still injured. I could tell she was lying. And earlier, I overheard her with one of the townsfolk saying that you were one of the casualties that we cleaned up. I think she's setting you up. I don't think she wants you to be able to live in Ozaroton. But I don't know why she'd do that? Do you?"

"Who was she talking to?"

"Some pretty Erthin woman. Olivia's cousin, I believe, but I don't know her name."

"Her name is Sunny."

But why would Yace lie to Sunny, of all people? What does she have to gain?

She does not want me to talk with an Oracle, a Telepath. Someone who might see through this charade. She is trying to keep the upper hand. Trying to manipulate the situation to her advantage. Worse yet, she does not want me to be happy.

He tried not to show his irritation over Yace. "I would never leave you, Kipp. Maybe Yace, but not you. I do not know why she wants me gone, other than the fact that I defied her orders and healed you. But had I not done that, you might not have made it to Ozaroton. And I could not live with myself if you had died. She demanded much of me while you were unconscious, and she made me wrong for so much too."

"It's alright, Irwin, you did your best. You always have."

"I would like to know why she lied to Sunny, why she told her that I had died."

"She's been saying and doing shady things, but especially ever since talking with Nonbry and Ozaroton's council. Another reason I'm done with her."

"Oh, I get it. She has told me that we are family, but I know she does not want me around. I am guessing that she does not want to share you—never has. And maybe she has known how you have felt about me all along. That is why she has twisted your mind. It makes sense. I mean, since I am not sexually attracted to her, she has no real use for me. The only reason she kept me around was because I helped keep her grounded. But now she has no use for me. She cannot telepathically control me. And since I refuse to bond with her, she will never have control over me."

"You think it's that?" Irwin raised a coy eyebrow at Kipp as he speculated, "I think it's something else. I mean, she's been moody ever since her meeting with Nonbry and Ozaroton's counsel. She made me sit through it all. I fell asleep a few times. I'm glad I wasn't grilled like she was. But she told them everything, and I mean everything, about you and your family.

"You know, I never realized how crazed your father was until …. I mean, you've told me stories. But what they said happened in Minersville was horrific."

"Yes, I know. He killed everyone at the local saloon after attempting to kill his own kin. My father is a wicked man, a murderer. He has never cared about anyone. He always enjoyed taking advantage of the weak and innocent."

Kipp's mouth hung open.

Irwin stared off. "I saw it all happen. I mean, I dreamed it. I dreamed of my father confronting his family. I am sure this happened on the day he came to Ozaroton. I saw the fight at the Saloon. I saw my father beat his cousin, Hager. He also killed many Erthins, and a telepathic barkeep and other innocent bystanders. That dream then washed into another and that was when I saw my father's cousin Hager and his sons arriving at the hospital after the fight. Their girlfriends were all cut up; one was already dead."

"Yeah, that's what they said happened."

It must be my Coterie powers which allowed me to see all that. Ugh! I do not want to be telepathic too.

He felt pained by his confession. "Did you bring any alcohol?"

"Yeah, of course." Kipp studied Irwin. "Why? What's going on?"

"Would you still love me if I was a Dreaming Telepath?"

"Of course. But you're not, are you?"

"I know I am part Coterie, Kipp. I know I have the capacity to be … to have telepathic powers, including the ability to have visions much like Dana." He hung his head.

I am the son of a monster. I do not believe that Kipp loves me like I love him. This feels like a dream. Or maybe Yace is manipulating him … manipulating me.

But he saw sincerity in Kipp's eyes.

"Maybe we go back to the animals," said Kipp. "You look like you could use some alcohol."

Irwin hugged his friend again. "Thank you."

"For what?" Kipp held Zamantha on his hip, bouncing her.

"For everything. You are the one person I need in my life. You are the only one I trust. I am thankful that you love me, accept me, even if I might have telepathic tendencies."

"I'm not afraid of you, Irwin. I mean, I've been scared of you in the past, but …. You've shown yourself to be true no matter the situation. Yace, on the other hand …." His look said it all. Yace terrified Kipp.

"Her devotion to you while you were unconscious was something else. It almost did not seem like her. Maybe, all this time, she has been someone else. Dephen perhaps. Or Emperor Somer. All I know is I do not trust her either."

"I'm not leaving you, Irwin. You've never left me. Your devotion to everything has always …. It's more than I can say about Yace's. She follows her own trail sometimes …."

"I will never leave you." Irwin grabbed Kipp's free hand.

"Good! Cause I don't wanna leave you either."

They smiled at each other. Irwin led them back to the quiet animals and their belongings—a lightness in his step. He was finally happy, contented to have found someone who appreciated him for who he was. But he couldn't help to be suspicious about Kipp's pledge of love.

Could Yace still be manipulating him, even after I've touched him? They did bond. But he is acting … like himself, albeit different … but so has Yace. I cannot tell any more. All these mind games. But Kipp is being true to himself. Genuine.

I want this to be real.

Irwin kept looking at Kipp, wondering if he had fallen asleep on the beach and this was just a dream.

Back at the beach, they relieved the horse and donkeys of saddle and packs. The animals roamed freely and found a grassy area to quietly munch. Kipp pulled out bread, cheese, a bag of plums and apples, and smoked meats. He placed a blanket down and tossed Irwin a flask of wine. He had his own flask of ale, pulled the cork off with his teeth, and took a swig. They sat together, allowing the child to run naked. She played in the sand and surf; the men enjoyed each other's company. They played tag, tiring Zamantha. After a wonderful feast, the child was fast asleep.

Kipp stayed close to Irwin that night, making sure to touch his hand or leg, but as they got increasingly drunk, the Clan-Duin became more forward. He kissed Irwin's neck, slowly seducing him onto his back. Irwin was not sure he wanted this to happen, but when Kipp's eyes held his—still golden—he gave into his passions and fulfilled all his fantasies.

47

WAS IT DEPHEN ALL ALONG?

Yace appeared before them the next morning; her belly bulge shaded their eyes from the morning sun. She kicked the Clan-Duin's feet. "Get up Kipp, it's time to go."

Irwin and Kipp were entwined in each other's arms, and Zamantha was asleep on top of them—mostly naked. Yace picked the baby off the men; they were slower than she to open their eyes and rise.

"Why the fuk are you all ...? Maybe I don't want to know." She took the child over to the small pile of baby clothes Kipp had brought. "I would've thought that you, Irwin, out of all people, would've kept the child clothed—I thought you were better than this. Instead, you're all running around like a pack of wild dogs."

"How did you find us, Yace?" Irwin quietly asked, but she must not have heard.

Kipp and Irwin were up, smelling of each other, but Yace had not yet noticed. She did, however, see, "Your eyes Kipp, they're golden. What'd you do?" She set Zamantha down and advanced toward Kipp. "You. You bonded with him?! What the fuk, Kipp. I told you he's leaving us. He doesn't want to be with us."

"That's wrong. Irwin doesn't want to be around you, with you. But he's always wanted to be with me."

"Oh, no you're not .... You're coming with me. Why the fuk would you—"

"Because I love him."

"No, you don't! You love me and only me."

"Your telepathy won't work on me anymore."

As they fought, Irwin recalled the few times Kipp's eyes had glowed golden; when he pledged to keep Irwin safe after only knowing each other a night; at the waterfalls talking about their future 'after delivering Yace to Dephen'; seeing Kipp post pig transformation; and twice during their night together in Arenu Village. He had also seen those golden eyes while Nuaki Village broke around the forge after believing that Irwin was dead; and after Jorge left him in their room at Illian's Inn in Daos City. And again, last night. Kipp had been jealous of Irwin several of those times, but other times he could tell that the Clan-Duin had missed him dearly—wouldn't trade any time they had together for anything. There was only a hand full of times he had seen Kipp's eyes glow golden, and now Irwin knew that Kipp had loved him all along.

Irwin stepped between Kipp and Yace. "What is your issue, Yace?"

"My issue? My issue is with you. You're a coward! Always have been. You left us, left all of Ozaroton vulnerable to your father's wrath. You didn't even stop to think about keeping everyone safe. You were scared, your tail fell between your legs, and you ran."

"Of course I ran! I was trying to draw him away. I told my cousins to do the same. There was no way I could have defended against his wrath, Yace. He would have stolen my metal. And any Erthin trick I tried, he would have snuffed out. I do not think you understand that I was of no help to anyone. Besides, it sounds like you were able to rid the world of him."

"Barely!"

"Is that why you are angry? Because I left? Or is it something else?"

"You knew what type of monster he was. He's killed dozens of people without a care. He murdered your whole family, Irwin! And you left Ozaroton susceptible to his wrath!"

"I know he is a murderer and a chauvinistic asshole, someone who would never back down from anything. He was rotten to the core. He never, ever, cared about anyone but himself. And yes, maybe that is why I ran. I was afraid."

"That's exactly why you ran. And you ..." She turned her venomous eyes on Kipp. "... I called for you to come back last night, but you didn't. And now I see that you've used him, touched him, grounding me out of you, and went on without a care."

Kipp stepped along Irwin's side and clasped the Metalist's hand. "I'm not your pawn anymore, Yace."

Yace's hands flew to her hips. "Who's trying to pawn whom, Kipp? Why did you bond with him? Was it to sever our link? Because I don't think you really love him. I think you're just using Irwin to get what you want!"

"Me?! Using people?" Kipp scoffed. "Oh, no. That's what you do, Yace. You've never asked me what I want, what I like. You've always assumed or made me do as you wish. You're the one that's weak—always using your telepathy to control me. Irwin's right. I should have my own choice. And I chose him. Every time." His golden eyes stared lovingly at Irwin.

"I should've never allowed you to come here."

"It's that shit right there! That's why I don't want to be with you. Allow me, what the fuk!"

Irwin puffed out his chest and placed himself again between Kipp and Yace. "I think your time here is done, Yace ... Dephen ... whoever you are. You can leave now. If Kipp wants to remain with me, he can. If he wants to go, he can. He can go anywhere he wants; I will not stop him—so long as he is not being telepathically coerced by someone like you."

Her lips twisted with amusement that quickly turned bitter. She reached down and picked up Zamantha as she toddled by. "I'll take her then."

"Why are you ...? Who are you trying to control? Is it me? Is it Kipp? That child? It will not work. Not while I am alive. Kipp is safe with me. And she will be returned to her family by tomorrow if I can."

"I'm not trying to control anyone. It's you who laced Kipp's mind with telepathic temptations. You're the one who's trying to gain all the control."

"You can go away Dephen." He said with a flick of his hand.

Yace didn't back down. "And I wouldn't give her back to anyone in your family, given your family's history with little girls?"

"I know she is better off with people who know about our powers than anyone else." He noticed her nose flaring more than before. "What are you angry about, Dephen?"

"I'm not Dephen."

"You are not Yace."

"I too am Yace."

Kipp piped up, "You don't act it."

Irwin continued to poke. "Is it because you cannot control me, yet you have always wanted to? Is that why you are acting this way towards me?"

She steamed, her blue eyes staring through him.

"Go, Yace ... Dephen ... whomever you really are. Just go. We do not need you—will be fine without you. Go to Daos. I know you will be an excellent ruler; it is what you have wanted all along—lord over the people. And you will have Turk. He can be your king and father to your child. Even Kipp believes the child is Turk's."

She hissed. "I'm Yace. And this baby is Kipp's. I'm sure of it! But if he doesn't want to be a father, doesn't want to help me raise *our* baby, then fine, I'll find a worthy father for our child—someone who will be there for me, who will dote upon me better than either of you ever have."

"If the child's mine, then I'll take it and raise it."

"You know nothing about child rearing, Kipp. You'd probably kill our baby trying to swaddle it."

Kipp squawked and Irwin cackled. "You sure like to pour on the guilt! Why do you enjoy making people feel guilty for your inadequacies?"

"My inadequacies?! I wouldn't trust Kipp to keep a child alive. And if anything, you're the inadequate one, Irwin!"

"That is right, Yace, use your words, your guilt to control." He couldn't stop chuckling at her. "Make everyone wrong for all they have done and be the one to show them the correct way to be. That is exactly what you should do for Daos; hold the men accountable for their actions; elevate the women's power and free them from their labors; and bring educational opportunities to the children—meanwhile reminding them that they owe it all to you. You might give them running water and full bellies, but there will be that tag of guilt. Does that sound right? To me it sounds like something Dephen would have implemented if he were still alive."

"There is no Dephen."

"Sure, whatever ...." He flicked his hand at her. "I would be happy to see you reverse all that abuse and neglect Daos's people have endured. But will you use your toxic words, or will you rise to the challenge and actually elevate the people? No matter ... it is the perfect role for you. And as an Ishik heir, it is your duty to facilitate that change—through your guilt—to accomplish such a task."

"Talk about guilt!" She laughed and stepped too close for his comfort. "You walk a slippery slope, Samuel Irwin Miner. I see what you're trying to do."

"I am not doing anything other than pointing out the truth."

"If Kipp only knew about you, what all you can do, he'd come to his senses right now and return to Ozaroton with me." She looked at Kipp. "I wouldn't trust his words, Kipp. Irwin's a Telepath too, you know. And he's had control over you for far too long. In fact, he's trying to work his powers against me right now, but I'm too smart for him."

"I am not the one bent on telepathically controlling everyone here."

She screamed and pointed, "Liar!"

"I am no liar, Yace. Kipp knows exactly what I am capable of. He has known it all along. He is not afraid of me—but he is afraid of you. I do not know what I did to make you so angry, but—"

"You're repugnant, just like your father." Her nostrils flared.

"What does my father have to do with any of this?"

"You're obstinate, full of yourself, just like him."

"Far from it. I have always taken charge of my actions and have been thoughtful of my words. And I have never led anyone astray." He was ready to cut through her emotional tapestry, but bit his tongue instead.

Kipp stood by, watching them argue, nodding with Irwin.

"You're still a naïve little cub, Samuel Irwin Miner. You haven't grown a bit since leaving that mountain top. Still a slave to your fear of your father. I wouldn't trust him, Kipp; he won't keep you safe. He can't even keep himself safe! Irwin's afraid of his own shadow. You should come with me, Kipp, and be my King. Then we can rule Daos together, forever."

There is no way this is Yace. So pokey. This must be Dephen. Or is it Somer? It is just like before when we were in the jungle, using their venomous words, trying to trigger me—to get me to react without thinking. I do not think Yace and Dephen or Somer, or whomever, can be separated. I think she gave herself to him, to them, accepted this fantastical offer to be the Empress of Daos—no questions.

He looked at their blonde friend, hands firm on her hips. The wind picked up her hair, flying it like a banner. She looked regal.

Kipp spat. "I don't want to be manipulated by you any longer, Yace. I'm done with it. I feel sorry for the baby you hold. Will you be like this to it too?"

She stared at him. "I will love our baby."

"Will you? Or will you be cruel to it like you're being to us right now?"

"I'm not being cruel, Kipp. I will love our baby. I'll love it more than you've ever loved me."

Kipp raised his voice and pointed at her. "Don't you ever say that! I've always loved you. You're the one who's had the change of heart a dozen times at least, if not more. I'm done being your toy. Like Irwin said, you can go, Yace."

"Are you fooling me? I can't believe you want this! Do you want us to be over, Kipp? You've wanted us to be together for so long. And we've a baby coming! I thought you loved me?!"

"I do love you, but I don't love how you treat me."

"Don't you care about our baby?"

"I do, if it's mine. But I'm not sure what's growing in you is mine."

"I know it is!" She rubbed her swollen belly. "This is your baby. You've always wanted a family, Kipp. We, you and I, can have that. But you can't have that with him. You can't make a family with someone of the same sex."

"That's horseshit, Yace, and you know it! Captain Hari and that one guy who died. I don't know why I can't ever remember his name."

Yace spoke over Kipp, "Lieutenant Rhomi."

"—but they adopted Fish. They were a family!" Kipp gazed at Irwin. "I won't leave, not without Irwin. He's been—"

"Fine. Then you two can come with me and we'll all live happily in Daos." She began nodding. "And if we're all there, we can make it a better place, together!"

"I refuse to return to Daos City, Yace," said Irwin. "There is too much metal for my mind to endure that place again."

"I can help you with that. There are telepathic spells that can dull ...." He kept shaking his head, and she sounded panicked. "But you've such vision for Daos, Irwin. You know what those people need. Someone like you can lead them. Your courage, your presence."

He laughed. "Your telepathy is dripping off you, Yace. Besides, I am not a ruler. That is what you are, what you want. I just want to live simply, quietly."

"But you're-you're Ishik too. We could rule side by side. You would be my king, and we could keep the masses satisfied."

Kipp barked, "Now Irwin's gonna be your King? You've no decency!"

Irwin waved her off. "Being a ruler is not what I want. But you, Yace, you would excel in that position. You love dictating how people's lives should go. And you enjoy manipulating people for your own benefit. Just like when Kipp was incapacitated, and you wanted me gone. Out of your life. Back then, you tried to get rid of me, but then conceded. You were like that all the way until the end, barely grateful of what I did for you."

"I was grateful."

"If you really were grateful, you should have told me. All I ever heard were complaints. Never once did you thank me. Except at the end when there were people around and you had to save face."

Both men stopped looking at her. Yace buried her face in her hands and cried, "I can't do this alone!"

"Are you asking for help? Or are you trying to command us?"

Kipp suggested, "I think she's trying to command us."

She seemed to quiver under their stares. "I'm just hoping you'll come with me."

"Hoping?" Irwin cackled.

Kipp barked, "Just ask us, Yace!"

"I love you Kipp," She moved closer to him. "I want you to be with me. And you too, Irwin." She said, extending her hand.

"I am done with this," said Irwin, wanting to walk away. "I cannot ... you-you are trying to run my mind in circles again."

"I love you too Yace, and I love our child, but I-I can't be with you either."

She attempted to grab Kipp, but he stepped closer to Irwin. "I don't want this to end, Kipp!"

Kipp snapped, "Then be nicer!"

"Yace will not stop. She is far to set in her ways." Irwin said, staring at Kipp. "Maybe we should leave."

Her face wrinkled with worry, and she moved around franticly. "Where? Where will you go? You can't return to Ozaroton."

"Yes. I heard. I would have liked to live in Ozaroton, but you made it so I can never return."

"It wasn't me! It was your family who made it so you can't return."

Kipp pointed at her. "That's a lie!"

"No, it's not. It's the truth. The Council said they'd refused Irwin's family before, and they'd do it now, if any of them were alive and seeking refuge."

"That is horseshit. Kipp said you were telling lies to Sunny and others, telling them I was dead."

"I did not!"

"Oh yes, you did!" Kipp pointed. "I heard you. You said he was one of the casualties. Why'd you do that? Irwin's not bad. Not like the rest of his family. He deserves a good place to live."

She looked at Kipp as if he were foolish for saying anything. Her attention returned to the Metalist.

"Just come with me to Daos, Irwin." She attempted to grab his hand. "If you do, we can make it home for you too. You don't have to be alone."

He pulled away. "No, Yace. Like I said, I cannot live in Daos. Not the Prime side or the other, nor the palace. I am not going with you. I will find my own way, my own place, as I have been." He glanced at Kipp. "Maybe—hopefully, we can find a place outside Minersville to call home. Maybe I get to know the rest of my family."

"I-I will make Daos into a place that accepts people like us. But if you two come with me now, it'll happen sooner."

His skepticism of her grew. "How would us being there help facilitate a quicker transition of power? We are not the all-powerful Telepath sent to save Daos. We are just friends, sex partners, minions of that Telepath. Besides, what you want to happen with Daos will only happen once you get there. Us being there has nothing to do with the outcome."

"I don't want to do this alone." Yace's focus was all on Kipp.

The Clan-Duin stared off. She shouted at him, "Kipp?!"

"I'm not going with you, Yace. I'm staying with Irwin. That's not to say that if you made Daos more hospitable for people like us, that we wouldn't visit. We'd do that, right, Irwin?" He glanced at Irwin for validation.

Yace balked. "Visit? No. I want you to .... I-I, a, I don't want this to end. What we have, it can't—we can't be done." Yace sounded desperate. "Maybe I come with you two. You know, maybe I help you find her family. And then ... and then afterwards we discuss our lives and how they should remain together."

"Why does it feel like you are trying to grasp us when we are but dusty sand grains in your dry hands? Why are you trying to control us? What do you want from us?"

"I'm not .... I don't want this to be ... us to be over."

Kipp cackled. "Seems like you're trying to manipulate us. Like Irwin said, you're dripping with telepathy ... 'er something like that."

Yace huffed, "No. I'm not doing that!" She glanced at both Kipp and Irwin. "I just don't want this to be over. I love both of you and want you to be a part of my life."

There was much deviousness behind those brilliant blue eyes. Irwin saw it and wanted to know her true intentions.

"Maybe we do not want to be part of your life anymore," said Irwin. "Why are you trying so hard to keep us when we have made it clear that we do not want to be with you?"

"Because I don't believe you. I think you want me around. You both searched high and low for me, did whatever it took to save me. You both took the journey of a lifetime. Why wouldn't you want to be with me after all of that?"

He was at a loss for words.

"So, then, we'll continue our journey. Take Zamantha up to her family and then ...." Yace waited for one of them to speak before filling the silence. "Of course, we must think of the what ifs. What if her family is dead? What if they're alive? Will they accept her? What'll you do if they don't want her? Or if they're dead?"

"Please, Yace, I do not want to think like that. Let us be positive, for Zamantha's sake. It is bad enough that her adoptive family is deceased. She deserves to live with her actual family. I am not a person to steal a child, but I will keep her safe until we find them." She exhausted him.

Kipp moved in close to Irwin and hugged him. "This is why I want to be with you. Your motives are always true," he shot a glare at her, "never ulterior."

"I don't have ulterior motives," gasped Yace.

Both Irwin and Kipp glanced at each other and snickered.

She squawked, "We all want the same thing here, happiness and love. I don't see why we can't try to get along."

They all stood there, feeling the day warming and smelling the sweet fragrances of flowers in bloom.

"We can get along just fine, so long as you do not use your powers on us," said Irwin.

Kipp asked, "Are we gonna take Zamantha home now?" Irwin nodded.

The Clan-Duin grasped his hand and smiled. They both notice Yace stiffen and quiet.

48

<u>RESOLUTION</u>

The men dressed and packed up what little belongings they had extracted from the bags. Yace remained in the shadows, holding Zamantha, possibly humbled by how well Irwin and Kipp were with each other. She might have seen them complimenting and offering help, as they did quite often for one another—although it had been a long time. There were many things about the two men's relationship that went beyond words alone. They had much respect and honor for one another. It was obvious by their interactions that they missed being together with each other—more so than being around Yace.

Soon the threesome, with the toddler in tow, led the horse and donkeys across the channel, walked down the straight avenue and through humid conditions. They diverted off the roadway far before arriving in Ozaroton and managed to climb around the settlement unseen.

It was long after dark when they emerged from an orchard on the east side of town, and far beyond the townsfolk's earshot. From there, they traveled up a switchback roadway for a brief time before stopping that night. They took from the pack of rations Kipp had acquired and shared the dried foods in solitude. Zamantha was the first to fall asleep.

Everything was different now—it was like they had all aged several years in a day. They were all ready for a change, reminiscing about old times while day-dreaming of future endeavors.

As they went along and up the gentle sloping roadway, Irwin noticed how much Kipp had transformed during those three moons of unconsciousness. He was like Yace had been after first recovering her memories, after regaining her powers. The things they all endured during their time traveling through Tropogagi land had solidified relationships and pointed out their flaws.

Irwin wondered if Yace's indiscretions were because of her changing body, her baby brain. Or if indeed she had been possessed by Dephen, or Somer, or some other telepath altogether.

We never had her checked by one of the local Telepaths.

I remember thinking about it. So much was at stake back then. We had just arrived. And I was tired. I should have though ... should have remembered. But then I forgot. Maybe that is how Yace/Dephen wanted it. They did touch me several times. Every time I have contact with her, she has access to me, my mind.

But she promised.

Dephen did not.

I really wish I had been there when she spoke to Nonbry and the council. But once again, maybe there was a reason I was not involved. Beyond me being marooned, she knows I would have questioned her and this plan to return to Daos. I would have asked all the Telepaths if indeed Dephen was manipulating Yace. But would they have been able to see it, or is it too late? Are Yace and Dephen so enmeshed that they are one, albeit hormonally charged, person? Does Dephen already have the council's minds too? Is that how she was gifted a return to Daos? Still so many unanswered questions.

Of course, it is possible that Yace has been of true mind this whole time. That indeed this has all been dramatized by horrible hormones ... baby brains.

It is all so hard to tell.

But it is obvious that Yace/Dephen has wound this mass manipulation the way they wanted it. Keeping everything controlled—contrived—attempting to keep everyone happy. I feel sorry for Kipp. Even in her absence, he is still tethered to her. And when that baby is born it will be worse. We must figure out a way for him to have access to his child, without Yace taking advantage of him ... of us.

And I must remember to remain two-arms' lengths away from her. I cannot let her touch me ever again.

Kipp stayed strong next to Irwin yet kept a hand hold on Yace. It was obvious that he wasn't ready to have her gone from his life. He confessed he wanted to be part of their child's upbringing but wasn't willing to commit to more than shared parenting with Yace—reminding her that he would remain with Irwin regardless of where she wanted to go after delivering Zamantha to her rightful family.

They arrived in Minersville by midday, after the bell tolled and the people had come into town for their lunchtime meal. The threesome stopped by the market and a stable yard to make a few purchases and ask questions. Irwin wanted to know about his family. Did anyone have knowledge of them and where they lived? To his surprise, several of the merchants had called him Jamie before realizing he wasn't. They guaranteed he would find his estranged family in the foothills—somewhere; no one seemed to know exactly where Irwin's cousin lived. That was until one of the locals had overheard the conversation and drew a crude map for them to follow.

Irwin led their hike late into the evening before making camp along a narrow roadway and on a hillside. There was no flat land for them to sleep on, not this night. They awoke early the next morning, still clothed, and ready to find Irwin and Zamantha's lost family.

As they went constantly up the long slope, Yace complained about rocks in her boots and forced them to stop several times so she could tear off her footwear and bang out the debris. By midday, they sat for a lunch break and devised a better way to locate Zamantha's family. Kipp took to the sky and used his Clan-Duin powers to smell for and locate the rest of the Metalists. Meanwhile, Irwin and Yace remained idle, letting Zamantha nap.

He stared at her. "Are you actually Yace, or are you Dephen?"

"I'm Yace. Why would you think I was Dephen?"

"Because you gave yourself to him, allowed him within your mind, and I am not sure he ever left. I think you two are one in the same now."

"Well, you're wrong. I'm Yace ... Empress Yace Ishik."

The shadow of a golden eagle flew across them. They looked up, watching it sail northward and over the forest.

Soon, his eyes fell back upon her. "You need to know that I will not follow you to Daos. And you cannot force me to."

"Oh, I know. I just want to be with you, and Kipp, a little while longer. I know I'll miss you two when I finally depart from here."

"How will you do it, get to Daos city from here?"

"Tresdahla has a giant port. That's where I would take a ship from. Maybe we can walk that road together. That is, if you two are going to return to the Gypsy. Of course, you do know that they're planning to arrive in Ozaroton when they can. But that'll be a while. Nonbry says they're taking the long route to Koumin.

But then from there they'll probably take a boat. It'll be at least a year, I imagine, before they arrive here."

He glanced to the east at the towering mountains. "I do not know what we will do after we return Zamantha to her family. But I think Minersville would be a suitable place to live and work and grow old. And once I meet my family ... it would be nice to be close to them too. I know Zamantha would probably be sad if I was not around in some capacity."

Yace stared at the baby girl who was making suckling sounds as she slept soundly between them. "Yeah, probably."

"Ideally, we find a place, a cave perhaps, or build ourselves a cabin, and live off the land as we have. But I do not want to make any plans without Kipp here."

"Well, if you live here, it'll make visiting Daos easier for the two of you. Kipp will want to see his child."

"If indeed it is his child."

She cocked her head menacingly. "It's Kipp's child. I know it!" Her glower continued, and she shook her head.

"What is that look for?"

"I'm not giving you a look."

"Oh yes, you are. It is almost like you want me to just shut up and accept what you say as truth."

"I don't give looks. You do!"

"Oh, Yace. Your manipulativeness knows no bounds. I do not know what you are trying to get me to do; what game you want me to play now? You need to understand that I will never be your pawn. I will never bow down to your haughty attitude."

"I'm not haughty!" He laughed. She continued to poke, "If anything, you're the one trying to manipulate this situation. You and that ego of yours."

"Manipulate! How, Yace, how?"

"With your Telepathy."

"I am no Telepath, Yace."

"Oh yes, you are. You've manipulated Kipp, and me. That little girl even!"

"Ha! She is the one who manipulated me. Not the other way around. This is all horseshit. You twist my mind, and his, tossing them against brick walls just to see the splatter. Do you even care, or is this all part of some grand plan?"

"I don't twist your mind."

"Oh, yes, you do." She scoffed louder than before, and he waved her off. "You know what? I take it all back."

"What do you take back?"

"Talking to you."

I am done playing Yace's mind games. I am done. Just stop engaging.

His attention drifted to the sky once more. He felt Kipp up there and flying toward their position. Slowly he got to his feet, wandered down the hill to relieve himself. By the time he came back to Yace and the sleeping child, the animals had perked up and Kipp had returned.

"I found them! They're that way." He pointed back to the way they had traveled. "We missed the trail. But don't worry, I know where to go."

After stuffing his body back into his clothes, Kipp led them. Irwin picked up the sleeping child and walked behind his friends, the donkeys and horse in tandem behind him. They paused when Zamantha awoke, and another time for food. The last time they stopped, Irwin was positive they were close to his family's home—he could feel their metal.

He left his friends at the base of a narrow and rocky trail that led up to a lit cave. Irwin could feel a large amount of metal within, and Kipp confessed he could smell the family downslope from the cave's opening. Zamantha was awake, but tired in Irwin's arms. After a short, steep hike, he delivered the child to the cave where her family lived. A Clan-Duin woman greeted him and took the little girl, although she was obviously wary of such interaction.

The young Clan-Duin woman said Jamie and his father Hurwin were gone, out hunting for a few days, but they would be back.

"They will wanna meet you," she told Irwin.

The idea of meeting his estranged family filled Irwin with glee. It was warm within the cozy cavern. He saw the similarities in Zamantha's twin brothers, Karl and Korwin; they were as tall, talkative, and wild on their feet as she was. Zamantha was quick to race over and be with her twin brothers. Irwin was happy the young girl was finally reunited with her biological family and felt safe in leaving her behind. But there was a sadness that lingered between their bond. He had a tough time discerning if it was his sadness or hers.

Irwin rushed back to be with his friends. He was relieved to be done with the energetic child. Now he knew it was alright to take time for himself and enjoy the world around him—be stationary for a while. After meeting his friends at the base of the cliff side, they followed the trail a little further and came across an amazingly large, pristine lake in the middle of the wilderness. It was there that they made camp. He pitched the large tent and made a raging fire. After sharing dried meats and juicy fruits and alcoholic drinks, they succumbed to sleep and bedded together, but with clothes on—Kipp slept between Yace and Irwin.

They slept through the sunrise and awoke by midmorning. Kipp went off to catch a meaty meal, and Irwin and Yace sat at the fireside. He was mending her boot for her. Silence lingered between them. A wind rippled the water's surface, softening the reflection of the deep blue sky.

"Hey Irwin, I want to say I'm sorry. I'm sorry about what I said the other day—about you not growing. You're nothing like your father. And I know you've grown, so do you. I think … I think I'm-I'm jealous … jealous of you. I might have been ever since we first met, before then actually—when Dana told me about you. I know I've been a bitch to you—a lot. I know what you've done for me. And you're right. I haven't always told you thank you—that I appreciate you."

He smiled. "Apology accepted."

"I'm not sure you've known, but Kipp's admired you for a long time." She caught his attention. "I've known it since …. It might have been that first time you two really sparred, you remember, after he had taught you a few of those kicking moves. I saw that golden sparkle in his eyes and was jealous of you then.

"Clan-Duins are funny like that. They're incredibly loyal. That's the best part about them, really. They always want to have a family—a clan; people to belong to. I know what I've done to Kipp in the past. How it's made him unstable toward me. I know he loves me, but he hates me too."

She reached for his hand, but he didn't let her touch him. Still, Yace stared deep into his eyes. "You're what Kipp's been searching for, a soul mate. Someone who will be with him until he dies. And you have … every time. I couldn't be that loyal. I've tried, but as you know, when I see things I like … well, I'm a Telepath. I'm not to be trusted."

"You can be trusted, Yace. You just have to work on not turning around and biting the person helping you."

How she looked at him made Irwin extremely uncomfortable. "If you had been different, maybe liked women, we could do so many things. We could rule Daos like the gods we are." He was ready to cut her off, but she added, "I'm glad you are you and that Kipp has decided to stay with you. He deserves to be happy—although I do want him to come to Daos with me. But if I did, I'd be forcing him to be with me.

"You're right, Irwin. If Kipp wants to be with me, I must give him that choice. If I made him, because of our child, he would resent me."

"What about your baby? If it is Kipp's, we both know he wants to be part of their life."

"She's not born yet. And we haven't gone our separate ways. Although ..." She looked to the southwest. "... I should get going soon. The Council has ... wants to know where I am. They want me to sail to Daos soon."

"You are still going through with it?"

"Daos needs a competent ruler. And you're right, I would be an amazing leader. Empress Yace Ishik has a nice ring to it."

"Empress Yace Ishik," He chuckled.

I think this is what Dephen wanted all along ... anyone but his former family residing, ruling over Daos. Maybe destroying the former Ishik Empire was a good thing.

"I would love some help." She stared at him. "But I understand why you might not want to return."

"If we were to come, it must be because we want to and not because you demand it. But there is no way I could ever remain indefinitely. There is too much metal, and those spaceships ... I could not do it for long."

Besides, I cannot handle how you hustle my mind.

She stood and dusted off her dress. "I should leave before Kipp returns."

"What? Why?" He stood with her.

"I really don't want fish for breakfast. But really, I don't want to ruin what you two have. I'm jealous of you. Isn't it obvious? And I-I don't want to be dramatic with him. He, and you, deserve the best—but especially you." She placed a kiss on his cheek. "Take care of Kipp, and he'll take care of you."

He thought he felt a spark of telepathy being laced across his mind, through that kiss, just like Dana had done to him when they first met over a year ago. But, unlike back then, he was now able to shrug off the spell.

There is still something ulterior about all this, about her. I must remain on guard.

"This is not goodbye, Yace. I know we will see each other again when the baby is born. Kipp will want to see it."

"Yes, you will. When she's born, everyone will know."

"How sure are you that your baby is a girl?"

Placing her hands on her fat belly, a smile stretched to her ears. "I'll name her Charlotte, after your mother."

"How do you know my mother's name?"

"I got it from your memories."

I would hate to think she now has complete access to me without me knowing. She said she would not touch my mind. But that was Yace. Not this person. They just tried something on me only a moment ago. I cannot allow her to touch me, to influence me any longer.

He gazed at Yace; they smiled at one another. He was happy and sad to have that memory, but glad to have shared it with her.

Having Yace in my life has been a blessing and a curse. I am glad she is leaving, but sharing a baby with Kipp keeps him ensnared in her telepathic agenda.

"What if it is a boy?"

"Charlie!"

She opened her arms, waiting to be hugged. He contemplated her and his next action. Their contact was brief. "Thank you Yace."

"For what?"

"Saving me. If I had not stayed the night in your camp so long ago, I would never have found what I was looking for."

"You're welcome, Irwin. Until we see each other again, take care of Kipp."

"I will. You take care of yourself and that baby."

He passed her the mended boot. She strapped it on and stood. It was obvious that she wanted to embrace him one last time, but Irwin folded his arms.

"Goodbye Yace."

"See you later, Irwin."

He watched her go, not sad to see her fade between the tree branches and up the narrow trail they had come down the night before. A sigh of relief parted his lips, and Irwin sat there, eagerly awaiting Kipp's return.

Epilogue

"I'm glad Yace's gone," said Kipp, after dressing—post falcon mutation. He nestled next to the fire and watched Irwin cook up the fish he had caught for breakfast.

"She said she was not hungry for fish. And that Ozaroton's Council was calling for her. I am glad she is finally gone too."

"Honestly, it's why I recommended fish for breakfast. I knew she wouldn't want any. Thanks for agreeing to it."

"After many moons of eating more than enough fruit, I now cherish every fish I get to eat."

Kipp drew in a winded breath. "Irwin, I wanna know your opinion. Do you think Yace is Yace? Or do you think Dephen is still with her?"

They stared at each other before Irwin replied, "Why do you ask that?"

"The things she's said and done these last few days just don't seem right. Don't seem like the Yace I know. But then again .... But I don't like this new different Yace. Acts like people owe her, not the other way around."

"KaryKaryn told me Yace has baby brain. That is why she cannot think linearly. But I have wondered about that, about her. If she and Dephen still share her body. It would explain her insistence that we go to Daos with her. She wants to keep us close, be able to use us, manipulate us whenever and for whatever reason."

"I noticed that too!"

"But even if that were the case, there is nothing I can do. If I was unable to ground that old ghost out of her, then she is doomed to host him for the rest of her life. Unless there is something mutual happening ... which would explain her moodiness and erratic behaviors while you were unconscious."

They both stared at the pan of frying food. The breeze had warmed, and the fir trees wrestled with the wind. A pinecone fell close to the fire and Kipp tossed it into the woodless blaze.

Irwin looked up from the now sizzling fish. "I need something from you, Kipp."

"Yeah, what is it?"

"I need to know if you meant it."

"Meant what?"

"Professing your love to me. Bonding with me. Did you mean it? Or were you using me to keep Yace from sinking her claws further into you?"

Kipp blinked. "I meant it, mean it. I love you, Irwin. And I've wanted to bond with you for a while. Well, ever since Jorge and you …. But then there was that time when Yace wanted to bond with me and you. She's wanted to do that with you since the beginning. But that's because she just likes to conquer things."

"As do you."

"But not like Yace. How she does it …. It hurts the soul. And I know how you feel about her."

Irwin nodded. "Yace is like a sister. An annoying older sister who wants things her way."

Kipp rubbed the back of his neck. "But yeah, maybe I used you to keep Yace from taking me away."

"So, everything you said was false?"

"No. No. That's not it. I don't want to live without you in my life, Irwin. I did for a time, and it was unbearable. But then I found out that it was all Yace's doing. Once again, she tried twisting my mind; tried to erase you. I couldn't let her." He grabbed Irwin's forearm. "I love you, Irwin. I don't want to live without you."

Irwin's heart swelled with emotion as he looked into Kipp's eyes, the sincerity of his words reflected in their depths. His touch was gentle yet firm, a physical manifestation of the unbreakable bond between them. The warmth of Kipp's skin beneath his fingers sent a surge of comfort and belonging through Irwin's entire being.

"I want you with me until the end of time," Kipp said, his voice barely above a whisper, yet filled with the weight of his love and devotion. The breeze carried his words, intertwining them with the rustling of the fir trees, as if nature itself was bearing witness to their declaration.

Irwin's gaze locked with Kipp's, a soft smile playing on his lips. In that moment, the world around them seemed to fade away, leaving only the two of them, hearts beating in unison. Irwin's hand moved to cover Kipp's, his touch a silent promise, a vow to stand by his side through every trial and triumph that lay ahead.

"Good," Irwin said, his voice low and filled with unwavering conviction. "Together until the end of time."

As they sat there, hands clasped, the crackling of the fire and the gentle sizzling of the fish seemed to create a symphony of their shared life, a melody that spoke of their unbreakable connection. The aroma of the cooking meal mingled with the fresh scent of the forest, creating an atmosphere of peace and contentment, a perfect backdrop for the love that had endured and grown despite the challenges they had faced.

In that precious, intimate moment, Kipp and Irwin knew that no matter what the future held, they would face it together, their love a guiding light that would never fade.

<u>If you're not ready for the story to be done, then I've got a treat for you….</u>
<u>A second epilogue!!!</u>
To continue the journey click HERE for the second epilogue
If you haven't yet read Book 0, the prequel … the backstory of all backstories … click HERE, or visit www.kdlumsden.com!
If you enjoyed Land of Cannibals, please leave a review.

Mind Games

Epilogue 2

Please forgive me for what I am about to do, Kipp, but I cannot let Yace have her way with you any longer. You are dying and I refuse to stand by and watch you both wither away.

I know if I heal you, in theory, I am healing Yace, too.

A ray of sunshine pierced through the canopy and warmed his eyelids. Kipp was slow to wake. His body felt heavy, hard to move, yet he forced himself to rise. He shifted and felt lighter. Leaves whispered to the breeze, and laughter from childish voices echoed close by. He shielded his sight from the sunlight and saw two youngsters splashing in a gentle, flowing creek just beyond his feet. They didn't look familiar, but screamed, "papa!" He rose carefully from his slumped position.

A young girl sat on his lap and dripped cool water. "How you sleep papa?" Her bright blue eyes gazed at him, and he tried to remember who she was.

"Do I know you?"

She giggled and then snuggled into his hairy chest. "Oh, papa! I love you."

None of this felt familiar, and he sat more erect. The older child, a young boy of maybe five years, plopped alongside.

"You were snoring papa."

A flock of crows flew haphazardly above them, drawing his eyes off the crooked, shady tree they sat beneath and upslope to a cottage partially hidden by the foliage of towering fir trees. The windows were closed, but the door opened revealing Yace. Her platinum-blonde hair flowed like a cape; her blue dress was snug against a belly bump. The sunlight shimmered off her hair. He blinked away sunspots.

"Supper's almost ready," she called to them.

The children bounded onto their spindly legs and raced for her. She spoke to them, and they darted for the homestead. Then Yace drew close to Kipp and watched as he stood. He wobbled and continued to study this unfamiliar landscape.

"You look tired." She stepped close, wanting to kiss him, but he didn't reciprocate. "Are you alright my love?"

"I had wild dreams." He still felt exhausted. "Dreams of Irwin."

She cocked her head, grabbed his hand, and pulled him along. "I made your favorite: chicken soup and sourdough bread."

The grass was warm, but the soil was cool against his enormous feet. Birds fluttered and called to one another, swooping to catch tiny bugs that flew out of the grass and into the blue sky. He continued to look around, trying to recall this place.

"I feel like I'm still dreaming. When did we ... how long have we lived here?"

Her teeth gleamed. "We've lived here forever, it seems."

They stopped. She touched his crown. He looked away, searching for something familiar. "I don't remember any of this."

"You must've slept deeply. Come along, my love." Her bright blue eyes tried to capture him, but Kipp's attention was everywhere else. He felt lucid, yet something was different ....

Like a songbird, her voice cut through his distracted mind. "Food is waiting. Once you're fed, you'll feel better."

Kipp forgot about his questions and his fears when his stomach's urges took over.

He glanced into the simple homestead, lit as bright as the sunny sky. At first, he thought it was barren of furniture. Stepping around Yace, Kipp pushed into the warm house. The brightness lifted like a fog, and he saw how cozy it was within. The main room was crowded with chairs, pillows, carpets, and many toys for their children. In a stone hearth, soup bubbled in a cauldron. The smell of fresh baked bread overwhelmed him and at once he realized he was hungry, almost starving.

Yace stepped alongside and grabbed his hand. "This is what you've always wanted." She drew him further inside. A ladder reached up to an open loft where the children's bedding and soft toys lay about. Aside the ladder, a thin tapestry—drawn halfway across a doorway—partially hid a large, cozy bed. His free hand landed on an old worn bearskin, draped across a rocking-chair. He felt the soft fur. Herbs hung drying from the rafters above a dining table, adding to the many scents in the room. Again, his stomach growled. A bowl of apples sat in the center of the single-slab wooden table. The children sat on a bench enjoying the fresh fruit. His nose and eyes fell on the hot sourdough bread still steaming on the stone hearth.

He felt weak and sat across from the children. "Why don't I remember any of this?"

"You said you weren't feeling well earlier, that your head hurt. Did you bump it?" Yace brought the bread with a knife stuck into its fresh crust. She turned softly and returned a moment later with a bowl full of soup crowded with chunks of vegetables and chicken and placed it before Kipp. "You'll feel better once you eat something." She sat next to him. Her warm hand rubbed his back.

Kipp sliced several pieces from the loaf and pushed them deep into the soup. He chewed and slurped. Although he was focused on the scrumptious meal, he remained confused by this place, and by Yace's behavior. He licked his lips dry and said, "Irwin wasn't a dream. He's real."

"It's okay. You don't have to prove anything to me. Just eat, replenish your energy."

He paused with the spoon mid-flight toward his open mouth. "How'd we come to be here? And where is here exactly?"

Yace folded her hands on the tabletop, her eyes bounded between the two children, and in a childlike voice she said, "Well. At one time, you and I were just friends, but then we became more than just friends, and decided not to follow the Gypsy anymore. We found a place outside a sanctuary city to call home. We've never regretted our decision. This place has everything we've ever wanted, a garden, kind people, and space to raise our children." She gazed at the little boy and girl who looked more like Yace than Kipp, blue eyes, light skin tone, and golden hair.

"That's not what happened." His spoon slapped the tabletop.

Kipp stared at her. His brow and cheeks hurt from concern.

"Yes, it is. What's gotten into you, Kipp?"

Glancing again at the children, their appearances seemed to waver, growing darker, appearing more Clan-Duin—more like him. His breath quickened, and the room spun before turning black.

I promised long ago that I would keep you safe. Now I know you do not believe I can save you, but I will. I must. I will break if I cannot. This is my pledge to you.

He was aware of the warmth before feeling a light shining on him.

Two youngsters were splashing in a peaceful, flowing creek just beyond his feet. This moment felt familiar, but the brown-skinned children did not. They called, "papa!" when he sat up.

The young girl sat on his lap, dripping water everywhere. "How you sleep papa?" Her bright brown eyes gazed at him.

"This is ...."

She snuggled into his hairy chest. "I love you, papa."

The five-year-old boy plopped alongside and said, "You were snoring papa."

A flock of crows flew haphazardly above, cawing for his attention, and drew his eyes upslope to a partially hidden cottage. It all looked familiar, especially when Yace stepped outside. Her platinum-blonde hair flowing, a baby-bump growing out of her snug blue dress.

"Supper's ready," she called to them.

The children jumped up and raced for her. She touched their crowns, speaking silently to them. They squealed when racing for the homestead.

Yace came to Kipp. Their eyes locked as he stood.

"You look tired." She stepped close to kiss him, but he stepped away while taking in this partially recognizable place. "Are you alright my love?"

"I had wild dreams. Dreamed of Irwin."

She grabbed his hand and summoned Kipp to follow. "I made your favorite: chicken soup and sourdough bread."

"You said that before." He pulled them to a stop and looked around at the flowing trees, puffy clouds, and vibrant blue sky. "When did we move here?"

Her teeth gleamed. "We've lived here forever, it seems."

His grasp on her tightened when he asked, "How long ago?"

"Ouch. Kipp! What's gotten into you?"

"We were just here, saying the same things .... What's going on, Yace?"

"I don't understand."

"Is this you? Are you doing this to me?"

"I'm not doing anything to you, Kipp. I made you supper. That's all I've done. You need to eat."

"Where's Irwin?"

"I don't know who you're talking about. Come on Kipp, you need to eat. To regain energy."

His mind was in a fog, his heart racing. But then his stomach growled."Maybe you're right."

He followed her into their house. It looked like it had before, with the bearskin draped across the rocking chair. Every part of that main room was crowded with chairs, pillows, carpets, and toys. The warmth and smell of soup emanated from the stone hearth. His mouth watered at the sight of the sourdough bread.

All at once, he felt weak and took a seat across from the children. They tore into their apples and smacked their lips as they chewed. He stared at Yace. "My mind is hazy. I feel like I'm in a daze."

She brought the bowl of soup and bread on a wooden tray. A cup of butter and a knife and spoon, two cloth napkins accompanied. As she placed the tray on the wide tabletop and said, "You mentioned you weren't feeling well earlier, that your head hurt. Maybe you bumped it." Her warm hand rubbed his back. "You'll feel better once you eat something."

He took in the meal presented and yet remained confused by this place. After eating half the bowl of soup, Kipp dried his lips and said, "How come you don't remember Irwin?"

"Don't worry about me. Just eat, replenish your energy."

He blinked. "I'm not worried about you. I wanna know where Irwin is."

"I don't know of anyone named Irwin."

"That's a lie, Yace, and you know it. Where is he?!"

"I-I don't know … honestly Kipp, you're starting to scare me."

"Horseshit! What'd you do to him?"

"Kipp, calm down. You've no reason to be angry."

He placed his hand on his chest; his breath had quickened. He looked at the children, trying to see himself in them. Even if they were dark like him, they still didn't look like a child born from his loins.

"Kipp."

He felt her hand on his, but his eyelashes blocked everything, and then the world went black once more.

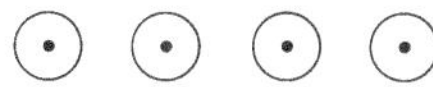

I have never told you this, but you are the one person I have always wanted in my life. A true best friend. Someone who will accept me with all my flaws. I cannot imagine my life without you in it, Kipp. Please live.

I love you.

A sunbeam warmed his body and at once he felt light enough to rise.

The babbling of a creek caught his attention before the eager sounds of happy children did.

Kipp sat up and scoured the landscape. This place was lovely. Trees swayed in the warm breeze, birds frolicked and sang, golden grass grew tall and waved back and forth like hanging velvet.

Two young children approached, dripping cool water on the ground and on him like before.

"Papa, you awake!"

"I'm not your papa," He snarled and jolted off the ground and away from these children who wanted to be with him, on him, in his arms.

They called after him, racing like it was a game. For Kipp, this was no game.

Once up the beaten path, he met Yace at the doorway, startling her. The happy children were only a few feet behind and thrust their wet selves agains this dry legs. They squealed and giggled. He tried to kick them off him.

"What have you done to me, Yace? What have you done?"

"I have done nothing. What's wrong Kipp?"

"That's horseshit." He grabbed her shoulders. "You've fuked with my mind again. I know it!"

"Why ... why would you say that?"

At once, his brow hurt. "Where is Irwin?"

"Irwin? I don't know who Irwin is, Kipp."

He pulled away from her. "Irwin. Our friend. He saved you, saved us. Where is he?!"

She appeared innocent, almost soft. "Kipp. I don't know who...who Irwin is, but maybe you dreamed of him. The children said you were snoring. You always have deep dreams when you snore."

He took another step backwards and snapped, "What'd you do? Where is he?"

"I didn't ... Kipp ... I've done nothing but make you food."

"And these aren't our children."

She gasped and grabbed him. "Don't you say that. These are our children, Walker and Odessa." Her eyes shot down to her protruding belly. "This one too. They're all your children, our children."

"I don't believe you." Again, another step separated them. "What'd you do to me?" Kipp snarled. "And where's Irwin?"

"I don't know what you're talking about. I don't know who Irwin is."

He began shaking, partially from rage, but mostly from fear. Then incoherent words stuttered from his dark lips. "I ... can't ... I .... I know he's real. Irwin's real."

"Kipp." He tried to yank away from her, but she was quicker. Yace pulled him in close. "Kipp, what's wrong with you? Are you alright?"

"You did something to me. Made me forget. Why? Where is he? What happened to Irwin?"

"I did nothing of the sort, Kipp. I think Irwin was a dream. It's all a dream. But now you're awake, Kipp. You're awake and with me now."

He felt her hands, her fingernails piercing his skin. He looked at them, then her blue eyes. "No! This is a telepathic trick. You've messed with my mind. You want me to forget him?"

"I truly don't know what you're talking about, Kipp. I've done nothing. No telepathy. Nothing!"

He tore out of her grasp and began running. He raced across the meadow, and the flowers, bugs, and butterflies scattered ahead of him. The breeze pushed at his back, pushing his hair into his eyes. He batted away stray strands—batted away tears. He raced into the dark forest that might have protected their quiet piece of prairie, his possible captivity. His lungs stung, and his heart beat intensely in his ears.

A used trail opened to him and he stumbled along. In no time, his body began to tire, and it suddenly became dark as death. His legs hurt, and his feet quivered as they ambled on and beat down the path. The sounds of nightlife, angered animals growling and frothing, grew louder, like a horrible migraine.

Kipp's eyesight blurred, and he collapsed against the wet ground.

I will do anything for you, Kipp. Always have, always will. You are everything to me.

The warmth from the sun was on him again.

He knew something was wrong the moment he became conscious.

None of this made any sense.

This time, instead of waiting for the children to drip water on him, he raced to find Yace. "Something's happening to me." He felt winded even though the run up from the babbling creek was an easy jog. "Something's wrong."

At once, she took his shaking hands and peered up at him. "What is it? What's wrong?"

"I keep hearing him. And I keep waking at the creek. This is a loop. None if this is real, Yace." Fear wrought her face, and she blinked while taking in his words. "It's Irwin. I hear him. But I'm stuck here. I can't ... I can't get to him."

"I don't know what you're talking about, Kipp. You're sounding confused."

"I am, Yace, I am. This isn't real. You're not real." He pointed at the children just now racing down the path towards them. "They're not real. None of this is real. What's happening to me?"

She looked as confused as he felt. "It's okay, Kipp. Everything will be alright. I promise."

"Why do I keep waking up at the stream? Why do I keep hearing him? What's going on, Yace? Did something happen to me? Am I injured? Am I dead?!" He was ready to cry, nearly hyperventilating.

"Calm down Kipp. Everything will be alright. You are alright. You know I would let nothing bad happen to you. Never. I will always protect you. I love you."

"Stop! You sound just like him. Right there. Those words. It's okay Yace, you can tell me what's going on. Tell me what's happened? To me? To him?"

She grabbed his hands, like she had before. Her flesh was cold, and he felt her fingernails pierce his skin. Her blue eyes were deep pools, swelling with tears. She moistened her lips and struggled to say, "I'm sorry. None of this makes sense. But I will help you figure it out. Don't worry. I'm here. We're together, as it's meant to be."

"All I want to know is where Irwin is. Has something happened to him? Tome? Or are you trying to cover something else?"

"I don't ...." She began to cry. "Oh, Kipp. We'll get through this, as we always have."

He pushed her away. "Don't coddle me!"

"Kipp, you don't have to be—"

"Just tell me where Irwin is!"

"If you want to name our next child that name, then we—"

"No. You're not listening; like always! All I want is Irwin. Bring him tome."

He frothed, and she cowered, "I don't know what to say, Kipp, I—"

"He's never manipulated me, unlike you. He's always let me be me and has never weighed me down with emotional baggage. I've known forever that he loves me. And you know what, I ... I love him too, and more than you. He's always been there for me. He's who I want in my life. Not you. He promised he'd never leave me. But he's not here. I know you're behind this fuked up dream, manipulating me as you've always done. Where is he, Yace!"

"I don't know what's going on with you, Kipp, but we will get through this together." Her hold on him was tight. He felt himself soften as his tears cascaded off his face and onto the shoulder of her dress.

"I just want Irwin. He will make everything better," Kipp sobbed. "He always has."

"I'm here for you," Yace kept repeating over and over. Slowly, Kipp succumbed to a tranquil slumber.

Everything I have done; I have done for you. Know that I will never leave you, Kipp. I promise.

Every time he awoke, it was with a surge of energy.

And every time, a white light seemed to blind his eyes as they fluttered open.

"Irwin!" He called out as this lucid consciousness found him once more.

The children came to his side and attempted to console Kipp as he howled for his lost friend. Yace heard the ruckus and rushed toward him.

"What's the matter?" She threw her arms around Kipp and their children.

"You took him away from me."

"I took no one away from you, Kipp. What's going on?"

"You did something to me, my mind. You're trying to make me forget him."

"Forget who? What are you talking about, Kipp? You're scaring me and the children!"

He shouted. "You've twisted me up. You've used your telepathy on me. You want me to forget him, but I won't. I can't!"

"Who? Who are you talking about?"

"Irwin. Irwin!"

"I don't know who—"

"That's horseshit Yace. You know who Irwin is. Why are you doing this tome? Why do you want me to forget him?"

"I've done nothing to you."

"That's utter horseshit, Yace." He pushed away and jumped to his feet." This is all you're doing—all your fault."

He looked to the forest that surrounded their piece of paradise and setoff at a vigorous pace. Yace called to him, begging for his return, but the shadowy forest swallowed his path. He took a trail that was worn at first, but then disintegrated after several hundred feet. His energy waned, his heart and head hurt.

Leaning against a thick oak, he felt the bark against his hand. Kipp then pulled both hands before his eyes, recalling a conversation he and Irwin had about dreams, and how to force yourself to wake from them.

"Look at your hands," Kipp muttered, raising his long fingers before his eyes. His palms and digits were line-less, wrinkleless. He then forced his eyes to open.

Bird calls murmured from all around; the clapping of oak leaves and rattling of branches and the thick scent of pine became overwhelming all-at-once. He tried to move—jerked—but realized he was bound.

A dog barked and came to investigate Kipp's state of awareness. A wet nose touched his nose and smelled his ears before moving down to his heart. The friendly canine then placed a fuzzy ear on Kipp's chest.

A moment later, Yace was there. Her blonde hair enveloped him like a veil and poked at his barely open eyes. He blinked profusely, and she howled, "Oh, Kipp! I'm so glad you're alive. You're alive!" She threw herself atop his chest, smothering his face in kisses. "I was worried that he'd hurt you worse than you already are." He saw those blue eyes staring at him. "You've thoughts. I can hear them. Hear you. I don't know how he … but you're better. I can see it. Too bad he gave his life for yours. Stupid asshole."

"Yace, be nice. Irwin do his best. He love Kipp. He did what he did for love."

"No!" She flew off Kipp and into KaryKaryn's face. "He did it because he's a selfish asshole who wanted to heal Kipp for his own reasons—his own way. It didn't matter to him what Shaman said about letting Kipp heal on his own—that it would take time. Shaman's a trained healer! No, oh no! For whatever reason, Irwin thought he'd learned how to heal every ailment ever and in one day. Ha! The audacity of that man—that asshole. I'm just happy that he didn't…" Her face sopped with big wet tears, Yace threw herself atop Kipp again. "I'm just happy he didn't hurt you worse. At least it doesn't look like it. And now I can hear your thoughts. And see into your eyes. He might have given himself to heal you, but you won't have to worry about him hurting you anymore." She grabbed him tight, nuzzled into his neck, inhaled his dirty scent, and pulled away coughing—nearly gagging.

He, too, knew he stank like he hadn't bathed in over a moon's time.

Yace ordered KaryKaryn and Turk to break down camp. Her eyes glared, and their blue became white. "Get the animals ready. We'll take all Irwin's stuff. He won't need it now. We'll leave his body for the Roha." She walked away from Kipp, to kick the lifeless body, returning a moment later. "Let's get you some water, my love. Are you hungry?"

He couldn't speak, tried to moisten his tongue, but managed to say, "Irwin. Where's Irwin?"

She snapped, "Get us some water, Kary! Now!" Her beaming love for him faltered when she replied, "Irwin's dead. He tried to heal you. But don't worry, he'll never ever hurt you again."

Kipp knew he had been harsh towards Irwin, even critical of the Metalist, many times during their long-winded journey together. Now he wished he hadn't been. Irwin had always acted from his heart—would never intentionally hurt Kipp. And Yace always acted from a place of power, of superiority—yearning for constant control.

Kipp wished he had been more supportive of his best friend. And patient. He knew Irwin always did his best, no matter what. Even when it came to healing people. Yes, Irwin had no training, but he understood how the body worked, regardless of his education. Kipp now understood that it was his undying loyalty to Yace that muddied the waters, made him doubt everyone's opinion but hers. He regretted not trusting Irwin, and so much more.

It was here, under the veil of Yace's hair, that Kipp realized how much he would miss the camaraderie he had with Irwin. Every moment spent with the quirky Metalist had been worth the pain and suffering Kipp now endured.

He coughed. His vision blurred. He sputtered, sobbed, and attempted to say Irwin's name again but only spit dribbled. He fought to get away from Yace, from her viciousness.

"Kipp. Kipp! No. No. Kipp! Stay with me!" Yace grabbed his shoulders. "Kip p!" Her long hair attempted to tickle his face, trying to keep him in this moment, but a dark energy summoned him into its heartless grasp.

Come back to me Kipp! You're mine, not his. Mine! He's trying to corrupt you. He wants to take you away from me. Don't let him. Remember, you surrendered your heart and soul to me, not him. You'll always be mine. That's how it's supposed to be!

The radiant warmth he had once felt wasn't as powerful, yet it pulled at his consciousness. This time, Kipp was afraid to open his eyes, but did.

White-washed walls surrounded them, two stories tall, and glowed amber from the afternoon sun. Coconut tree leaves clapped for his attention from the corners of the long courtyard. It was the children's excitement and the splashing of water that pulled his sight down from the blue sky above. A bright blue pool, three times as long as it was wide, filled most of the space before him.

There was a buzz of sound, but when he looked around, Kipp only saw two young children, like the two he had seen before. But here in this place it was all very different—yet it all felt familiar somehow.

In flowed Yace, a light blue silken robe sailing behind her. A child sat on her hip, in her arm, full head of brown hair. She looked pregnant again, but with child number four, he wasn't quite sure.

She floated to him, "Good morning, my love," and sat close to Kipp. "How are you feeling?"

He didn't respond, instead he continued to scour this new setting. They were in a wide, familiar courtyard. It took him a moment to recall, "This is the Ishik Palace." The words fell silently from his lips, yet Yace still heard him.

"Yes. This is where we'll live. And for the rest of our days together, this is where we'll be." She leaned in close to place a kiss on his forehead, but Kipp rolled off the bench he sat on.

"Don't touch me."

"What's wrong Kipp?"

"You know what's wrong! This is all you're doing."

"No. Not all of it. Come to find out, Irwin's placed a spell on yourmind. Beyond trying to heal you, he's been manipulating your thoughts."

"That's not true."

"Yes, it is. And I've created the best place I could for you, for us. His spells are powerful. Who would've thought he could do all of this? I've done all I can to keep you safe from him. Don't worry, he'll never touch you again."

He held his breath, stared at her. "What do you mean?"

"Irwin is a Telepath. And he used his powers to manipulate your mind. He made this place. Well, something like it. I thought he'd healed you ... but that asshole didn't. He placed you in some telepathic nightmare. He's trying to keep you from me." She sobbed. "Not only that, but you're still dying, Kipp. He didn't fix you at all. You're still dying and there's nothing anyone can do. Whatever Irwin did to you .... He fuked you up worse than you were. I told him not to touch you. That Shaman said you'd heal on your own."

"That's not true. None of it. Where is he? Where's Irwin?"

"Dead. We left him."

He fell to the stone floor. It wasn't hot nor cold. He grimaced, stretched his tired body. His deep brown eyes never left her blue eyes. "Why'd you leave him?

He's always been here for me, for us. I know he's got no formal training, but he would've healed me. You're the one manipulating everything. Not him."

"That's not true. I haven't telepathically touched you until now. No. Oh no. Everything you've been experiencing is all of Irwin's doing, his design. That asshole has a power over you. He's the one who did this to you. This spell. And I can't undo it, not fully."

Aghast, Kipp stuttered, "What? That's not true. He's not like you. He's not manipulative—not a Telepath."

"That's what he wants you to believe, Kipp, but it's all a lie. He's been trying to take you from me this whole time, but I won't allow that to happen. You're mine!"

He then thought about those previous dreams. The babbling brook with a crooked tree nearby—a perfect spot to sit and watch his children play and cleanup. The cozy hovel of a homestead, the bear's skin covered seat, the quaint bedrooms, and jubilant children—were all the things he had confided in Irwin that he dreamed of having when he and Yace were reunited. Back when they had been chasing after her, all he could think about was a cozy future where he was happy and with loved ones. But everything he told Irwin was in jest. Kipp didn't want any of that with Yace. Not then, not now. If anything, that was the life he wanted to live with Irwin, but he had been too afraid to speak about it—fearful that he would ruin their friendship.

Kipp's energy waned. He felt faint. He struggled against her power, attempting to pull away from her handhold on him.

"No Kipp, don't do that. Please, Kipp, I'm trying to save you." He felt her grasp tighten, but then everything went dark.

Don't pull away from me. Please Kipp, be receptive to me. I don't want to raise this child alone!

He wrestled against a soft blanket and turned onto his side. There was Yace, staring at him—face to face. The mystical warmth that usually surrounded was there, but it was cooling much like her saddened blue eyes.

"I love you, Kipp," she said and touched his face. "I've always loved you. I'm so sorry that I broke your heart, that I stole your mind, that I manipulated you to love only me."

"If you really loved me, Yace, you never would've done any of that. You would've allowed me to make my own choices. You wouldn't have forced me to devote my soul, my life, to you."

"Are you fooling me?! I've allowed you to make many choices. I let you go off and have the adventure of a lifetime with Irwin, Kipp. Sure, I could've taken you along with me, but you would've been made to do things ... things that.... I couldn't do that to you. And yes, I agree you deserve to be able to make important life decisions, and I let you. I allowed you to enjoy Irwin, to have a friend other than me. I know you've desired that for a long time; a close confidant—someone who wasn't me.

"I mean, you wanted more than that, but .... and you could've had it with him. You could've done anything with him. Anything! He's always been into you. You two could've gone off and .... You didn't have to follow me. But in the end, you did as I knew you would. You're bound by your loyalty to me. Always will be. Besides, we both know Irwin can't give you what I can give you. And that's how I know you'll always come back to me."

He scoffed. "Are you saying that it wasn't your father that manipulated us, that it was you?"

"You say you know me best. What do you think?" Her sinister side showed brightly for that moment.

"You're Dephen. Yace would never be this strategic." There was a moment, a look, a feeling. "Disgusting! Out of anyone, I didn't want to see you taken advantage of. I was afraid for you! We both were. We're afraid that your father would ... that bad things would happen. And now you're telling me you-you let it all happen?! That you let him into you. That all the torment was all by your combined design? All the cruelty and misleading trails? You both wanted me and Irwin to chase after you. That way, you could have him destroyed and break my heart. All-the-while hoping I'd come crawling back to you."

They stared at each other. Yace seemed to revel in the silence.

"This is why I wanted to leave you with your father in Onj Raha. I needed to escape you, escape this, your mind games. I wanted to be with someone who values me as a person. Not someone who will do what you've .... For so long, I've wanted to get over you, get beyond all this. You need to stop manipulating me, Yace! If you want me to still love you, you've gotta stop this madness."

"Ha! You'll never stop loving me."

"That's what's wrong with you, Yace. Ever since the beginning, since the Gypsy took you in, you sunk your claws into me and have used me time and time again. I can't believe that I feared the worst would happen to you, even though you've always been able to .... But this is the worst, and it's happening to me!I hate you."

"Oh, no you don't. You promised you'd love me forever."

"I also promised Dana and Nonbry that I'd keep you safe, but none of that made any difference to you. You took what you took, and you still take! I'm done. I refuse to be manipulated by you any longer."

"But I'm not manipulating you, Kipp. Irwin's telepathy is real. He's done all of this to you. This isn't me!"

He glanced up at the maroon tapestry strung across the ceiling of this foreign room. It fluttered in an unfelt breeze. "Yes, it is. Even now you are in my mind, taking me along the road you want me on. Let me go Yace. Just let me go."

"No! I can't, I won't."

"I don't love you anymore, Yace. I know I've pledged myself to you again and again, but I'm sure you made me say those words. I might've loved you when I was a naïve young boy, but my heart can't take the aches you've caused. And my mind can't handle the mental blows you've dealt. I'd rather die than have you in my life."

"Don't say that. No, please Kipp, you can't mean that."

"If you wanna keep lying to me, keep me in this place ... just don't. Just let me go."

He turned away from her, exhaled and the ever-present darkness shrouded him instantly

This is all Irwin's fault, Kipp. Please understand, I didn't do this to you. It's Irwin's fault, not mine, that you're dying!

The warm light welcomed him once more. Kipp didn't want to wake. He didn't want to feel. He was ready to go back to the heavy darkness that clung to him like thick mud.

Her voice jolted him awake. "How are you feeling?"

He slowly looked at her. Yace's face was vivid, but shadows hung closeby. "Leave me."

"You must understand this isn't my fault, Kipp, please understand."

"I don't want you here. You killed Irwin."

"He's not dead." A look of regret washed across her face.

"If that's true, I still don't wanna be with you. Either let me die or let me be with Irwin."

"No. He's not trust worthy. I won't let him touch you. Never again. He's not allowed to be anywhere near you. He hurt you. He used his powers on you when he promised he wouldn't. Tried to heal you against better judgement. And he's manipulated your mind and heart. No. He can't be trusted."

"I don't care what you think. I trust him. I trust him more than I trust you. I know he's not a snake in disguise, unlike you, Yace."

"You can't mean that, Kipp. Please, you must understand that I'm doing everything I can to keep you alive. He wants to kill you."

"If that is true, then let me see him."

"He can't be trusted. He's manipulated you, used his telepathy on you, taken you from me. I can't let him have you. You're mine!"

Kipp shook his head. "You just don't get it. That's not Irwin. It's never been him. He wouldn't take my mind and shake it up like you have. He wouldn't manipulate my heart to love only one person, unlike what you've done. I want him in my life, but you don't. Ever since he showed an interest in me, and not you, you've tried to shut him out of our lives. You said it before; you've never wanted me to get close to him."

She scoffed. "I allowed you to adventure with him!"

"Allowed. Huh. At what cost? The whole time I was with him, I couldn't stop thinking about you. But that's what you wanted. Even in your absence you kept me from my happiness, from my want of a companion who completes me. Yes,

I've had fun with him. And had there not been such urgency, things would've turned out different. But I think you've always known that. And that's why you don't want me with him now." He closed his eyes tight. "If this is how it's gonna be, then just let me die, Yace. Please, just let me die."

"No! Kipp, no! Stop being like this. You can't let him ruin you, ruin our life together."

"If I can't have Irwin in my life, then I don't wanna be with you."

"No!"

He felt himself vibrating; Yace was fuming. An all-to-familiar anger darkened her blue eyes. Again, he exhaled and turned away, but this time thought; *I want to hear from Irwin. Let him talk to me, please!*

Kipp. I regret to inform you that I have moved on. I am going to stay here in Daos with Jorge.

Although convincing, this voice didn't entirely sound like Irwin.

All the colors of the rainbow swirled when he jolted awake. Orange, red, violet, indigo, brilliant blue, vibrant green, and blindingly bright yellow swirled around, blending into a thick white fog that warmed him. He tried to orient himself, tried to find something familiar. There was nothing but bright white light. Kipp couldn't see his feet, nor could he spy the blue sky that was surely overhead—somewhere.

"LET ME GO!" He screamed. "Just let me go, Yace. Please! Let me go."

Silence enveloped.

He felt like he was crying, but his face was dry.

"Release me Yace, please!" He shouted, feeling defeated.

He awaited a response.

Kipp was unsure of how long he sat there in the fog. The haze floated before his eyes, coating his unstable mind.

"I just want to die. Let me die, please."

Again, silence shrouded him.

Kipp was beyond lost. And though he should have been fearful, he felt melancholy opposed to anything else.

"I don't want to exist without Irwin. Please Yace, let me go!"

Kipp realized he had been weightless. But in an instant, he felt his floating body turn heavy and descend quickly from the fog. Layers of cloudy masses wafted past him and gave way to a blinding warmth that felt like unconditional love. This feeling mimicked the first time when he awoke aside the creek with the children screaming and playing. But now he saw nothing except white light.

He tried to call out, "Irwin." Kipp believed he felt his arm lift, but couldn't see it, and continued to call Irwin's name.

Then, all at once, the bright light melted away and smelled his Metalist's friend before seeing those silvery eyes on him. "Irwin!"

"I am here Kipp."

"Where are we?"

"Ozaroton, my friend. We made it."

Kipp gasped, out of breath, bewildered by it all. "Is this real?"

"Yes, my friend," Irwin replied. "This is real. You are alive." Irwin's tears splashed onto Kipp's arm; each drop a testament to the truth of his words. In that moment, nothing else existed for Kipp—not the bustling medical staff surrounding them, not the sterile walls of the hospital room, not even the imposing figure of the Erthin Doctor at his side. His entire world had narrowed to the man before him—his best friend, his unwavering companion, the one person he now knew with absolute certainty that he could not bear to live without.

"I thought I'd lost you," Kipp choked out.

Irwin leaned closer. "I am here. I will always be here. Never will I let you go."

In the radiant light of Irwin's love, the darkness that had nearly claimed Kipp dissolved like mist beneath the morning sun. He was battered and bruised, but he was whole. He was home. And with Irwin by his side, he knew he could face anything the future held. Their journey was only beginning.

<u>Also By</u>

<u>The Metalist's Journey</u>
0.25 ~ The Last Metalist
0.5 ~ The Metalist's Journey Prologue
1 ~ Secrets of Urthis
2 ~ Elements of Power
3 ~ Sleeper Assassin
4 ~ Land of Cannibals
4.5 ~ Bound by Iron & Blood
(+2 more at least!)

If you liked this book please leave a review!

Want more information about Irwin and the world of Urthis?
Join KD Lumsden's newsletter at https://www.kdlumsden.com/

THE UNUSUAL CREATURES MENTIONED

ANCIENT DWELLERS

APPEARANCE: Unknown

UNIQUE TRAITS: Deities who created the universes. They wanted life to happen; to experience love, hate, melancholy, triumph, and sorrow. Everything exists because of them.

CLAN-DUIN

APPEARANCE: brown skinned, black hair, hairy bodies, eye colors can be gray/ green/ brown/ amber

UNIQUE TRAITS: shapeshifters, can be feline, canine, raptor, bear, ape, and/or marine mammals. Are very loyal companions, prefer to live in packs, but can be loners. Linear thinkers, they can be stubborn and foolhardy.

COTERIE

APPEARANCE: pale-skinned, white to blonde hair, white to blue eyes, but can take on darker appearances if bred with other creatures, such as Clan-Duins or Erthins.

UNIQUE TRAITS: Blended children of the Guru, infused with Mortal DNA. Their abilities are similar to Guru, but can be limited by Mortal blood. They are considered bastard children of the Guru and are impure. Often arrogant and egocentric, they live anywhere/anytime.

ELEMENTALIST

APPEARANCE: grey to olive-skin color, auburn-orange to red hair, green-hazel eyes

UNIQUE TRAITS: can harness every element known to exist. They can create elements from within themselves, or through interaction with organic and inorganic life. They are known to have the ability to live out in space without oxygen or nutrients, they can oxygen exist inside their lungs without taking a breath. It is said they were the first beings created by the Ancient Dwellers, that they were necessary for creating the known universes.

ERTHIN

<u>APPEARANCE</u>: grey to olive-skin color, auburn-orange red hair, green-hazel eyes

<u>UNIQUE TRAITS</u>: hybrid Elementalist and Mortal. They can harness the five most powerful natural elements: Air, water, fire, earth, and spirit. They can be pure-bred and have all abilities, or part-breed and have abilities specific to person (ie. the ability to harness only one element).

GURU

<u>APPEARANCE</u>: white skinned, white-ashen hair, white-blue eyes.

<u>UNIQUE TRAITS</u>: Direct descendants of Ancient Dwellers. They have can use any type of power (teleporting, telepathy, shapeshifting). Considered living gods, they hide in plain sight and across all the universes. They can live every-where/anywhere/anytime.

GYPSY

An enclave of like-minded people, usually Talented, who tour Urthis rescuing other Talented people. They often take the rescued to sanctuary cities.

HAKRA (Urthis's God)

<u>APPEARANCE</u>: black-skinned, blue-eyes, hairless.

<u>UNIQUE TRAITS</u>: considered a living god who resides in Akarah City, capitol of Urthis. Has lain the groundwork for Telepaths to shape Urthis into an interstellar hub; keeps the general population subdue through religion. Every few years produces a Tome for the people to follow, hypnotizes the masses through telepathic ideology; zealot followers are devout enough to turn in their brother or neighbor if they believe they are Talented. Every few years his followers take pilgrimages to Akarah to stand in Hakra's presence with hopes to be bestowed a gift.

ISHIK EMPIRE

Current rulers of Doas Territory, the Ishik Empire have been in control for the last thousand years. Believed to be the last full-blooded Coterie family, they claim to be purebred; to couple with someone outside the family brings dishonor. They tout their land to be free of Talented people, yet employ Talented people to work at the palace. They maltreat their subjects, taking boys away from their families at 9-10, to work iron mines, daughters are married off by 8-9, families live in small dome-huts, and when compared to the rest of Urthis, Doas Territory is at least one hundred years behind in technological advancements.

METALIST

<u>APPEARANCE</u>: ashen skin color, gray hair, silvery-gray eyes

<u>UNIQUE TRAITS</u>: can harness all types of metal including, but not limited to; gold, silver, aluminum, nickel, iron, zinc, mercury, cadmium, cobalt, chromium, platinum, lead, etc. They can hold up to eight pounds of any given substance within their own flesh, flushed it under the skin to specific places. Their ability to manipulate metal starts with extraction, turning the metal into its liquid form, and integrating it back into its hard form, and can form anything imaginable with any amount of metal. They are known to give off a deathly scent when holding metal within. Direct descendants to Elementalist.

MORTAL

<u>APPEARANCE</u>: always pale-skinned, brown-eyed, hair light brown to dark-brown/black

<u>UNIQUE TRAITS</u>: Bipeds with no superhuman powers. One of the five eldest beings created by the Ancient Dwellers. They have been exported from their home world, brought to foreign worlds to repopulate but often exploited as cheap labor.

PLANETAIRY CONSTIBLE PATROL (PCP)

Comprised only of people with Talents. Telepaths are given powerful positions (Admiral, Captain, Colonel, Corporal, Sargent), Erthins can hold powerful positions (Lieutenant, Sargent), Clan-Duins are considered working soldiers or minions, but can be demoted and placed in a "court-yard sitter" position. Also called "Population Control Patrol". They usually patrol in groups of four and are seen riding large "warhorses".

SANCTUARY CITY

Not necessarily a city, but a place where people with Talents are safe from the PCP and Hakran ideology. Most don't allow Mortals to reside. Most require those looking for permanent residency to prove they are a positive influence, that they will help protect others with Talents, regardless of abilities, and not cause issue within the community. There are rules within each community to adhere, and if someone breaks that main rule they can be banished from one, or all sanctuary cities. (*Note: All Sanctuary cities are interconnected by Telepaths.)

SHAYOT

A truly talented child, usually male, but sometimes are females brought through the ranks. They are usually multi-cultural (Telepath and Clan-Duin, or Erthin and Telepath, or any unique mixture) and are trained by the worst of the worse in order to understand how to think like murders and rapest, thieves and mercenaries. As an adult they are highly regarded and given positions of power within the Hakra regime.

TALENT, PEOPLE OF (aka TALENTED)

Any being who possess supernatural powers.

TELECAPRITIAN

<u>APPEARANCE</u>: pale skinned, white to blue eyed, white to blonde hair

<u>UNIQUE TRAITS</u>: can use telekinesis and telepathy, can shapeshift appearance but only into same gender roles. One of the five eldest beings created by the Ancient Dwellers.

TELEPATH

<u>APPEARANCE</u>: pale skinned, white to blue eyed, white to blonde hair

<u>UNIQUE TRAITS</u>: hybrid of TeleCapritian & Mortal, they cannot yield telekinesis. There are many types of telepaths; dreaming (they see visions future or past based), some can hear thoughts, some can manipulate beings though 'telepathic' brain waves, others can only do this through physical touch.

TELEKINESIS

The ability to move objects at a distance by mental power or other nonphysical means.

URTHIS

Fourth planet from the sun in the Oska'al solar system and one of the many places in the known universe that hosts supernatural and natural powered creatures. It is the planet on which Samuel Irwin Miner lives.

VOLATILE

A derogatory word used against people of Talent. (see: Talent, people of)

WARDEN

<u>APPEARANCE</u>: enigmatic. They have the ability to become anyone of the same sex

<u>UNIQUE TRAITS</u>: a Warden is a breed of person (can be male or female—usually male) that is of Telepathic, Clan-Duin, and Elementalist descent. They are considered greatest of warriors and hunters, usually former *Shayot*, and work directly for Hakra and his minions. The only way to kill a Warden is to cut off their head.

About KD Lumsden

KD Lumsden was raised on a small farm where her youth was spent running away from angry bulls, riding horses, fishing, camping, and daydreaming about fantastic worlds. Born dyslexic, she has learned to use her neurodivergent mind for the good of mankind—creatures on other planets are another story. Though she's not a fast reader or writer, her mind flies with many stories, eagerly waiting to be told. Better with numbers and art, KD became an architectural designer long before it was cool to work from home, and has always enjoyed drawing, creating maps, laying out and designing buildings, and of course other worldly planets with amazing settings and diverse people. She lives on a farm outside Eugene, Oregon, with her supportive husband, imaginative son, and their many two and four-legged animals.

Get to know KD more by visiting her socials ....

https://www.facebook.com/KDLumsden/
https://www.instagram.com/kdlumsden_author/
https://bsky.app/profile/authorkdlumsden.bsky.social
https://twitter.com/KDLumsdenAuthor
https://www.amazon.com/author/kdlumsden
https://www.bookbub.com/profile/kd-lumsden
https://cravebooks.com/author/author-kdlumsden
https://www.goodreads.com/author/show/22489719.K_D_Lumsden

BLURB

Secrets revealed. Loyalties tested. The Metalist's Journey continues.

In the heart of the Daos Territory, where cannibals lurk and danger lay in wait, three friends must navigate the treacherous path of self-discovery and survival. Irwin, a powerful Metalist, Yace, a Telepath with a mysterious past, and Kipp, a shapeshifting Clan-Duin, have already faced countless challenges on their journey. But nothing could have prepared them for the trials that await in the land of the Tropogagi.

As Yace's memories slowly resurface and her powers grow stronger, the trio seeks refuge with Shaman, an enigmatic healer who may hold the key to unlocking Irwin's true potential. But tensions rise between the friends as secrets are revealed and loyalties are tested. In the hidden city of Ozaroton, Yace's pregnancy takes a dangerous turn, forcing Irwin to make tough decisions that will shape the future of their journey.

With the sudden arrival of Irwin's abusive father, Albert, and the shocking discovery of a young Metalist girl named Zamantha, the stakes have never been higher. Irwin must confront his past, protect those he loves, and uncover the dark legacy of his family before it's too late. As the friends navigate the complexities of their relationships and the dangers of the jungle, they will discover the true meaning of sacrifice, love, and the power that lies within.

www.ingramcontent.com/pod-product-compliance
Lightning Source LLC
Chambersburg PA
CBHW062114290726
48975CB00001B/221